Critical Praise

"I devoured this book. The dual storylines captivated me and the characters stayed with me even when the novel wasn't in my hands. I loved learning more about Guatemala, and that Jessica O'Dwyer didn't shy away from some horrid parts of humanity that many children—and their first parents—must face as part of their own history."

— Lori Holden, author of *The Open-Hearted Way to Open Adoption*, honored by the Congressional Coalition of Adoption Institute in 2018 as an Angel in Adoption®

"Multi-layered and suspenseful, Mother Mother is sure to provoke discussion among readers. As an adoptive mother to three young adults from Central and South America, I couldn't put it down."

— Leceta Chisholm Guibault, Founder and Director of *OUR Guatemala: Travel with Purpose*

"Pain, loss, and love are showcased side-by-side, highlighting how motherly love goes beyond social status, country, and family background."

—Rossana Pérez, editor of *Flight to Freedom: The Story of Central American Refugees*

"Jessica gives a very clear and knowledgeable panorama of Guatemala, from its colonial roots to today's society pervaded with racism, classism, and an inoperative government. At the same time, she describes the sublime, real, and extremely hard truth of adoption. I could relate to each line as a Guatemalan and as an adoptive mom."

—Cynthia M. Guerra, National Director of Education at the Ombudsman Office in Guatemala 2014–2017; human rights activist and educator

"At its heart, *Mother Mother* is a story of family, relationships, the bonds of blood and beyond. As O'Dwyer herself writes, 'Love is an action, not a concept.'"

—Janine Kovac, author of *Spinning: Choreography for Coming Home*

"*Mother Mother* was such a moving story that I couldn't put it down. The book is one I'd recommend to readers who want a novel that will draw you in, blurring the lines between reality and fiction."

—Carlie-Rae London, *Hey It's CarlyRae!* book blog

"*Mother Mother* is realistic and different, gripping and tragic. Novels don't often take you to Guatemala. This one does, showing in a raw way how hard life is in that largely unknown country."

—Marjolein Balm, *Marjolein Reads* book blog

"Wow is such a minuscule word to describe this book, but I can't think of a better one."

—Sheryl Smith, Co-Founder of East Bay Guatemalan Adoptive Families

MOTHER MOTHER

MOTHER MOTHER

A Novel

Jessica O'Dwyer

First Edition

Casebound ISBN: 978-1-62720-314-2
Paperback ISBN: 978-1-62720-315-9
Ebook ISBN: 978-1-62720-316-6

Printed in the United States of America

Design by Katherine Kiklis
Editorial development by Lauren Battista
Promotion plan by Lauren Battista
Cover artwork by Hugo González Ayala (Guatemalan, b. 1954) *Nahualá* (detail), courtesy of La Antigua Galería de Arte; cover design by Bryn Kristi and Kathryn Kiklis

Apprentice House Press
Loyola University Maryland
4501 N. Charles Street
Baltimore, MD 21210
410.617.5265
www.ApprenticeHouse.com
info@ApprenticeHouse.com

For Mateo, Olivia, and Tim
And in memory of my parents

ONE

SAN FRANCISCO, CALIFORNIA

FEBRUARY 2002

Julie Cowan was halfway to her car on the second level of the museum parking garage when the third contraction hit. Bracing herself against a steel pillar, she squeezed her legs together. Sweat drenched the backs of her knees. If she stayed still, she could keep time from moving forward. If she stayed still, she could keep the baby inside.

She'd left work early, panic mounting at the first cramping twinge. Her boss told her, *Go. Whatever you need.* Her husband was on a flight to Florida. No one was around.

She reached into her purse for her cell phone. Her OB's receptionist answered on the second ring.

"I need help," Julie said. "I've miscarried twice."

"On a scale of one to ten, how would you describe the pain?" the receptionist asked.

"Eleven?"

"Hang tight. Doc will meet you at Emergency."

The doctors couldn't figure out what was wrong with her, why Julie couldn't take a pregnancy to term. Just that she couldn't.

They'd named this baby Rowan. She was at seventeen weeks, three days.

I can't lose you, Julie thought. *We won't survive it. We love you. We need you. Stay with me.*

Hanging up, she punched in 911. Rowan couldn't come yet, she tried to tell the operator. It was too soon. Julie needed an ambulance.

"Can you count the seconds between contractions?" the operator asked.

"I'm sorry. I need to lie down. I'm in a garage."

"A parking garage? What's your exact location?"

"1202 Belmont. The Orrin Clay Museum."

"Is there a floor or section number?" The operator's voice sounded far away.

Julie pushed herself off from the steel pillar and lurched toward her car. She was so close.

Above and around her, a yellow light appeared, glimmering and radiant. It came from nowhere, turning the air golden. Julie reached for it, and her hand went straight through. She couldn't catch it. Nothing was there.

Warm liquid flowed out between her legs, soaking her pants. She looked down, her vision a white blur.

She was empty. Rowan was gone.

SIX MONTHS LATER

REDWOOD GLEN, CALIFORNIA

AUGUST 2002

Julie sat with her laptop in the Cowan kitchen and gaped at the digital photo of a chubby infant with a tuft of curly black hair. Propped against a giant teddy bear and dressed in a blue onesie, Felix Fernando smiled enough to show two deep dimples and sparkling eyes. Julie's heart raced. Without a doubt, Felix was the cutest boy who had ever been born.

"Eight pounds of bouncing energy at birth," the email from Kate Hodges-Blair at Loving Hands Adoptions read. "Two-month-old Felix Fernando is yours if you want him."

Eyes on the computer screen, Julie called out, "Mark, we got a baby." Her voice broke on the last word. When her husband didn't arrive in seconds, she ran down the hallway toward their bedroom to get him. His gray-flecked brown hair was still damp from his morning run; he hadn't yet cooled down. Julie grabbed his hand and led him to the kitchen. "Can you believe how adorable this child is?" Julie said. "How did we get so lucky?"

Mark squinted for a closer inspection, while Julie stared harder at the screen, as if to memorize every pixel. "It all makes sense now," she said. "The infertility, the treatments. Everything led us to here."

They drank in Felix's marvelousness, too overwhelmed to speak. He was a beautiful boy, healthy and robust. "Is this how it happens?" Julie finally whispered.

They both laughed quietly. The air felt sacred.

Julie scrolled through Kate's email seeking more details. There weren't many. Only that one day a man rang the orphanage doorbell holding Felix. "This belongs to my daughter. She can't keep him," the man said. He handed Felix to the housekeeper, jumped back into an idling car, and drove away. Tucked in a fold of the baby's blanket was a note with a phone number and the name of the man's daughter, Felix's birth mother, Ida Manuela.

Julie skimmed the lines of the email. "They found the mother. She lives in Guatemala City. Kate's lawyer went to her house to get her to sign off with permission." Julie stared at Felix's photo, trying to picture Ida Manuela holding him, and Ida Manuela's father, Felix's grandfather, giving the baby away.

"What do you think?" Mark asked, his expression neutral as if not wanting to sway Julie either way. "Is this our son?"

To see a digital image of a baby and believe him to be hers would have seemed preposterous to Julie even five minutes earlier. Yet deep inside her, something stirred. The connection she felt to Felix transcended logic. It felt magic. Out of the thousands of babies abandoned in the world, this little boy was meant for her. Felix's face went blurry as Julie's eyes filled with tears. She stood up, wrapping her arms around Mark.

"Hello, Mommy," he said.

*

Julie created lists of activities to pass the time required for Felix to become their son. Friday night she cleared out the art supplies she'd stored for years in the spare bedroom closet—dull charcoal pencils, used drawing pads, and dried paints she couldn't resurrect but for some reason held onto—and filled a bag for Goodwill. The hundreds of postcards publicizing exhibitions at cafés and galleries: into the recycling bin those went. Saturday, she did laundry and she and Mark hiked six miles. In between, they spackled and sanded and primed, and applied the first coat of paint in Felix's new room. Still, she wanted it all to move faster.

Sunday morning, they drove down the 99 freeway to Fresno from their home in Redwood Glen to visit Julie's sister, Claire. Out the window, the rolling hills of California's Central Valley glowed like spun gold. As Mark drove, Julie glanced at the legal pad on her lap, listing the items they needed to buy. "A stroller costs almost as much as my first car," she said.

Mark grunted. He hated spending money. They lived in a bungalow they'd bought from Mark's parents before moving them into assisted living, a year before they both died. Real estate in their neighborhood had since been bought up by tech zillionaires so rich they felt poor by comparison. This, despite the fact that Mark worked as a pathologist at San Francisco General and Julie was a curator.

Mark held the steering wheel with one finger. This stretch of road was so flat and straight, the car almost drove itself. The cruise control was set to eighty. Acres of lettuce beds spread in every direction. Those stooped figures picking could be from Guatemala, Julie realized.

"Did Claire like the picture?" Mark asked.

"She didn't say." Julie's sister usually responded to email instantly, efficient as she was. After Julie sent the picture? Silence.

"Maybe she didn't see it yet," Mark said.

Julie doubted that. She knew Claire wasn't off at church on Sunday morning. And that computer of hers could open anything. No, it was more likely the usual: Claire being Claire. Withholding and, dare Julie say it, aloof.

"She's young," Julie said, as usual giving her sister the benefit of the doubt. "She hasn't started the baby chase."

Claire was six years younger than Julie, only thirty. Mark clicked on his blinker and swerved to the right lane to exit at downtown Fresno. "Once they realize how cute this little guy is, they'll fall in love," he said.

A few minutes later, Julie and Mark stood in the front hallway of Claire's sprawling faux Tudor, Julie's purse still on her shoulder, front door not yet closed. After a round of air kisses, Claire squinted at the printout of Felix's photo. "Is he really that brown?" Claire said. "Oh Jeez. What I meant to say is, 'I love his color!'"

Julie grabbed back the picture as Claire's husband Ethan appeared from the kitchen down the hall.

"Shut the door, Claire, you're air conditioning the neighborhood." Ethan skirted around Mark and Julie, pulling the door shut himself. "He's Mexican, right?"

"Guatemalan," Mark said.

"Indigenous Guatemalans invented the concept of zero," Julie said. "They used it when they built the pyramids at Tikal. The indigenous are called Mayans, in case you're interested."

Claire reached out to pat Julie's head as if her older sister were a puppy panting for a treat. "I love how you come up with these arbitrary facts." Claire turned toward her husband. "Isn't the groundskeeper at the club Guatemalan?"

"A bunch of the guys are." Ethan clapped Mark on the shoulder. "Big news, bro. You didn't want to go American?"

"Not a lot of babies are available." Mark shrugged. "You have to compete for them. Make photo binders. Write up a story."

"You're an MD-PhD for Chrissake. You guys aren't top of the list?"

"Birth mothers here often want religious parents," Mark said. "And in domestic adoption, the mother can get them back. That happened to one of our nurses."

"How awful." Claire's hand flew to her mouth as she frowned at Julie.

"You got a picture?" Ethan asked.

Julie handed Ethan the printout and he stared at the photo, tipping his head from side to side as though weighing two options. "What's his name?"

"Felix," Julie said.

Ethan leaned into Mark and spoke in a stage whisper. "You might want to change that, buddy. Guaranteed, first day on the playground, he'll be Felix the Cat. Don't do that to a kid."

Ethan passed the photo to Claire. "One of our drywallers has a kid looks like that. Miguel. No, José."

Claire looked at the photo again, then returned it to Julie. "What about adopting from foster care?"

"We liked Guatemala," Julie said. "I studied Spanish in high school, in case you forgot. Plus, the country is kind of in chaos. A lot of kids need families."

"Aww. Our resident bleeding heart saving the world," Claire said.

"Why do I come here?" Julie said to no one, to the room. "That's what I ask myself every time we get in the car to drive to Fresno. Why?"

"Joking, Julie," Claire said.

"Ladies, ladies." Ethan stepped between them. "We menfolk are hungry. Let's eat."

Julie stalked down the hall after her sister. In the kitchen, bright copper pots hung from a rack over a central island and the mahogany cabinet fronts gleamed. Fans with blades like oars scissored in the white cottage cheese ceiling. Cheerful yellow curtains framed the windows. Condensed steam dripped down the glass, making it look molten. The house was an ice box, frigid. Whatever the season, Fresno was twenty degrees hotter or colder than Northern California, and Claire and Ethan burned fossil fuel summer and winter. *Carbon footprint be damned,* thought Julie.

The huge farmhouse table was set with hand-painted Italian plates and linen napkins. Claire bustled between the table and the giant fridge, setting out plates of artfully arranged cheeses and olives.

"I made Thai coleslaw," Claire said. "Knowing how much you like foreign foods. Here. Taste." She placed the bowl of coleslaw on the central island while Julie grabbed a fork from the drawer. A splash of rice wine vinegar and some chow mein noodles and now coleslaw's foreign? Julie wasn't sure how they grew up in the same family. Claire was a great cook, though. Julie had to give her that. With their mom sick so long with emphysema, and their father gone, Claire had practically raised herself. They both had.

Dropping the fork in the sink, Julie moved the bowl to the table while Claire sliced a loaf of olive bread on a cutting board. As she returned to the island to ferry the bread, Claire put out a hand to stop her. "The last thing I want to do is offend you."

"Noted," Julie said, uncertain where the conversation was headed.

"You've got blonde hair and blue eyes. Everyone will know Felix is adopted."

"Certainly, everyone will know. It'll be obvious." Julie crossed her arms, frowning. "Can you please be happy for us?"

A cloud passed over her sister's face. "I am happy. I'm just worried you don't understand what you're getting into."

"We know exactly what we're getting into. Felix needs a mother and father. Mark and I want to be parents. Why is that complicated?"

"Because you're white and he's Guatemalan?"

Julie threw up her hands. "Listen. I want to be a mother. Just like you, just like untold numbers of women since the beginning of time. I don't care what color his skin is." She picked up the bread to set on the table, but Claire wouldn't let her go.

"This probably isn't the time to tell you." She laced her fingers across her belly, her smile sheepish. "We're pregnant."

The copper pots hanging from the dish rack seemed to sway and Julie held the counter to steady herself, as she might in an earthquake. Then she put down the bread and hugged Claire, careful not to press too closely. She wanted to stay positive for her sister.

Claire's voice drifted to Julie's ears as the sisters pulled apart. "We're at twelve weeks. We'll become mothers together."

Julie clamped her mouth shut. She wanted to remind Claire that two of Julie's three miscarried pregnancies went to seventeen weeks. Claire wasn't out of the woods. But let Claire do things her way. She always did.

Ethan and Claire must have timed it to break the news together because Mark's congratulations echoed in the kitchen. "Good deal. Outstanding."

"Once you relax, maybe it'll happen for you," Claire was saying.

"Well, now we have Felix."

"I mean if you want your own."

It was at that moment that Julie decided to stop talking about Felix until after he arrived. She couldn't bear to be told what she was doing wrong, or that her son wouldn't really be theirs. True, he'd look nothing like them, but so what? They lived in liberal Marin County, close to San Francisco. Julie was proud they'd create their own rainbow coalition.

Felix would grow up the big boy to his younger cousin, the way she was big sister to Claire. He *would* be their own.

*

With her three lost pregnancies, Julie had felt changes in her body, kicks and turns, her belly getting bigger with new life. With adoption, she felt nothing physical. No moving, no kicking, no tightening of the waistband to announce, *Hey, Mom! Here I am, don't forget me!*

What she fixated on, instead, were her copies of their one photograph of their son. One copy hung on the refrigerator door, where it greeted her every morning. Another lived in a Ziploc bag in her purse. A dozen times a day in her office at the Orrin Clay Museum she peeked at the Ziploc to study the details—his curly black hair, his round cheeks. *What was Felix doing now?* she wondered. Newborns slept and they ate and they slept and ate some more. A co-worker just back from maternity leave informed everyone who would listen about her breast milk: pumping it, banking it, its vitamin and mineral content. How much healthier breast milk was for babies than God-forbid-formula. Julie had to walk away whenever the conversation started or else she'd hyperventilate. With no breast for Felix to nurse, did he get enough nutrition? Did one particular nanny give him his bottle, or did the task rotate? Julie struggled to forget the image from Kate's presentation of an assembly line of babies with bottles propped beside them. Were infants even strong enough to hold onto a bottle and suck?

Daily, Julie emailed for updates. "He's thriving," Kate wrote. "Don't worry!"

But Julie did worry and couldn't wait to visit so she could hold him herself and never put him down. Kate forbade the first meeting until after the test to ensure a DNA match. That was when birth mother and relinquished child were reunited in an office in Guatemala City, a photo was taken of the pair, and the inside of their cheeks were swabbed for tissue samples. Kate guaranteed DNA within one month. But a month was so far away.

After DNA, everything was simple. The social work report, the review by the Guatemalan attorney general's office, the rubber stamp by the U.S. Embassy—none of it was going to present a problem. Until they got a positive DNA match, Julie should hold off booking any flights.

*

Fifteen days later, Mark stood at the kitchen counter in front of two bowls of homemade granola. "Bananas, strawberries, or blueberries?" he asked.

"Blueberries," Julie mumbled from her chair at the table, opening her laptop screen as she waited for messages to appear. "Interview and DNA," read the subject line from Kate. "About time she got it done," Julie said.

"That's why we pay her the big bucks." Mark set down Julie's bowl of granola and walked over to the sink while she skimmed the page.

"This is impossible." She sat up straighter.

"What is it?" Mark was beside her, reading over her shoulder. *A red flag by the U.S. Embassy. Based on the agent's observations during an interview, DNA was not done. The agent believed the woman was not Felix's birth mother.*

"Not Ida Manuela?" Julie said. She read the sentences over and over, but the words didn't change. "Now what do we do?"

Mark looked resigned. "We walk away. It's over, Julie."

"It's not over. Felix is our son."

"He's not our son. He's a baby we saw in a jpeg. We never even held him. For all we know, he's not even real."

"Felix is real, Mark. Trust me, Felix is real."

She turned back to Kate's email. *This sometimes happened,* Kate explained. *Rarely, but it happened. They tried to be careful, but people occasionally slipped through.* Blah blah blah blah. Excuses. Kate ended by saying they'd returned Felix to the lawyer, hoping caring relatives would raise him.

"The relatives are the ones who gave him away in the first place," Julie almost screamed. "He's going to wind up in an orphanage."

"Maybe they'll give him back to his birth mother. The real one."

How could he just walk away? Julie knew she'd never forget Felix, or the way, for a few weeks, he had been her son. She grazed a finger over the print-out of Felix's photo on the refrigerator door, a wave of sadness rising. "What are we supposed to do with this? Tear it up like he never existed?"

Mark walked over, removed the magnet, and took down the picture. He stared at the likeness for a long moment before folding it into quarters and slipping it into his shirt pocket. "I'll put it somewhere." His voice caught. "For the record, I thought Felix was a fine name."

Julie bit her lip, grateful for this small acknowledgement. If Felix wasn't real, why did it feel like somebody died? Why did her heart feel empty? She dreaded opening her purse to find his photo in the Ziploc, which she'd placed with such optimism. She asked Mark to fish it out and hide it with the other one. There was no ceremony to mourn a child who was never theirs in the first place.

Hours after losing their referral for Felix, they got a follow-up email from Kate. *Forget Felix,* she wrote. *Focus on finding the child meant for you.* Julie hoped they gave him back to Ida Manuela, or whoever his mother was. She hoped Ida Manuela loved and cared for him, always, the way Julie would have loved and cared for him, if she'd been given a chance.

That night Mark and Julie lay in bed with the windows open. They had debated whether to switch agencies and countries and start the process over again from the beginning. Everything about that plan exhausted Julie. Another country might be worse.

Mark folded his hands behind the pillow and sighed. "We never seriously considered an egg donor and surrogate. We know Claire can get pregnant. She might be willing."

Julie sat up, wide awake. "My husband and my sister making a baby together. I'm not sure I'm that evolved."

"An anonymous donor, then. We can pick traits. Athletic. High I.Q."

"Egg donor is a little too engineered for me. At least this process is a hell we know."

Julie flopped back on her pillow. She loved Mark and her job at the Clay and their life together, but it no longer felt like enough. She longed to be a mother, to shower a child with her love. To give her child the kind of life she never had.

She stared at the ceiling. "I can't believe we're at square one. Do you think this is a sign?"

"Only a sign of how screwed-up the system is."

Mark unfolded his hands and slid his body closer, melding into Julie. "Time to focus on something else."

*

It was late Friday afternoon when Julie called Kate from the Clay conference room for extra privacy. Kate spoke briskly over the phone. "I don't advise waiting to start a second adoption. Guatemala could close any minute."

"Don't they always say that?" Julie asked.

"This time it's real. You saw the article. The U.S. government doesn't like looking bad."

An Associated Press article claimed professional "finders" called *jaladoras* were combing the Guatemalan countryside in search of pregnant women, and that adoption fees paid by Americans were given to birth mothers to relinquish their babies, after *jaladoras* took their cut. Yet Kate had told them their $30,000 went to attorneys, U.S. and Guatemalan, and covered the cost of foster care and doctor visits until the baby was picked up by adoptive parents.

Julie asked Kate point blank: "Is it true they're paying birth mothers?"

"Nobody needs to go looking for birth mothers. Not when so many women are willing to give their babies away."

Julie tried to visualize a place where mothers willingly gave away their babies. Where they presented themselves to *jaladoras*, saying *Here's my baby. Take him.*

Kate's voice pulled her back. She said the U.S. wasn't fooling around. They were signing the Hague Treaty, which imposed strict limits on inter-country adoption. The Hague would require Guatemala to seek placements for children in-country first, as well as to adhere to a strict level of transparency. There was no way Guatemala could comply. The U.S. had set the closure date for adoptions. December 31, 2002.

That date was less than four months away. "You're telling us this now?" Julie said.

Kate said if they held tight, she'd put them at the head of the line. The $30,000 would be carried over to the next referral. Julie's shoulders shook, from excitement or fear. Maybe both.

"We'll only agree if you promise you'll get us a baby."

"Done," Kate agreed.

"Because we can't go through that again."

Kate clucked in sympathy. "You won't have to, Julie. Trust me."

Although no baby could replace Felix, a new dream child began to take shape. Probably another boy—most adoptive parents preferred girls, so boys were easier to get—handsome like Felix, but in his own unique way. A boy somewhere who maybe wasn't yet born, who was waiting to come into this world. Wherever he was, whoever he was, when he finally presented himself, Julie and Mark would be ready.

The message from Kate appeared three weeks later. "Referral," the subject line read, and although Julie trembled with anticipation, she didn't open the photo attachment. She waited until nighttime, when Mark got home from the lab, so they could meet the boy who might be their son together. They stood at the kitchen counter in front of Julie's open laptop.

His name was Juan Rolando Garcia Flores. Born on August 1, 2002, to a birth mother named Karla Inez Garcia Flores in a city named Escuintla. Five pounds three ounces at birth. Black hair and brown eyes, sitting up against a blue blanket, hands clenched at his sides.

Julie stared at the picture and tried to stop her heart from racing. Did she dare believe this time would be different? She'd already fallen in love with Felix and the three babies she'd miscarried. Juan was an infant alone in the world, and he needed her.

The baby's Apgar scores were good, his vaccines up to date, and he showed no evidence of HIV. Was it true? Was Juan Rolando their son?

And just like that, they decided.

TWO

BAY AREA, CALIFORNIA

SEPTEMBER 2002

Monday morning, Julie walked from the parking garage through the Clay Museum's front garden, where a special events crew was taking down tables from the wedding held in the courtyard the Saturday before. The museum's bottom line depended on renting out its space. The sculpture garden, with its beds of calla lilies and abstract sculptures, including a prized Alexander Calder mobile, was a favorite bridal venue. The garden was also where they hosted evening exhibition openings in warm weather. Artists who made it to the Clay had good reason to celebrate, and champagne and wine flowed freely.

Julie pulled open the front door and threaded her way through the warren of offices past colleagues bent over their keyboards, until she reached hers at the end of the row. Shoving her purse into the bottom desk drawer, she opened her computer.

"Hey, Jules. Have you heard the news?"

Eames, from the office across from hers, rolled toward her on his desk chair. He was the Clay's head of publications. "Talbot got tapped for the Lochnivar gig. He's moving to New York."

"As assistant director?" Talbot Jones was director of the Clay, the big boss. Technically, an assistant directorship was a step down, but the Lochnivar Museum was three times the size of the Clay and New York the most respected and vibrant art market in the world.

"It's his foot in the door," Eames said.

Julie scrolled through her emails to scan the announcement. The board of directors thanked Talbot, enumerated his many accomplishments during his fifteen-year tenure, and wished him well. As soon as possible, they'd conduct a nationwide search for a suitable replacement. "I wonder who we'll get," Julie said.

"One of the usual suspects. We'll be fine, as long as New Person doesn't want to shake things up with New Team."

Why hadn't Talbot told her about the new job himself? He'd hired Julie as a curatorial intern twelve years earlier, plucking her resume from the hundreds submitted by hungry art grads, and kept her on after graduation, molding her into the curator she'd become. More than that, Talbot had always defended her artistic vision, no small feat in a museum where everyone from the president of the board to the receptionist voiced an opinion on the appearance of everything from typeface to the color painted on gallery walls.

Julie was more than a little miffed. The museum was their obsession—Talbot's and hers. Together, they'd grown it from an assortment of paintings, lithographs, sculptures, and drawings donated by the fabulously wealthy, art-loving philanthropist Orrin Clay, into a significant collection of work by ground-breaking, emerging artists.

She just hoped the new director didn't mess things up.

*

The search had been underway for two weeks when Talbot's assistant, Doni, asked Julie to come to the office. Talbot wanted to speak with her.

Julie ticked off deadlines in her mind, artist studios she was scheduled to visit, sure she hadn't missed any. Nevertheless, her heart thrummed loudly as she walked to Talbot's office, pausing at Doni's desk while the assistant buzzed him to let him know Julie was waiting. An air of formality clung to the director, despite his urban hipster uniform of fitted black suit, striped socks, and narrow purple tie. Julie paused again at his doorway until he signaled her to come in and sit down. Talbot's last day was in three months, but already the shelves in his office were bare and the floor filled with taped boxes.

"How's the adoption coming?" he asked, and Julie thought of Juan Rolando somewhere in Guatemala, out of her reach.

"Fairly well," Julie said. "Thank you for asking."

Talbot nodded. "I've put your name forward for the director position. The search committee should be contacting you soon."

"Me? Are you kidding?"

"You know the Clay from the bottom up. A director needs that."

Julie almost laughed with shock. True, she'd dedicated years of her life to the Clay. True, Talbot had been her consistent champion. But she never dreamed he'd advocate for her this way.

"I've worked hard to establish the Clay and want to leave it in the best hands," Talbot said. "That means you."

"I'm honored. Thank you."

Talbot passed her a yellow legal tablet so she could take notes on ways to maximize her chances to land the position: what to say, how to behave during interviews, pitfalls to avoid. He asked her not to tell anyone until the board contacted her for an interview, which he promised would happen very soon. They shook hands and she left his office, nodding to Doni on her way out, almost floating through the labyrinth of offices, back to her desk. Eames lifted his head with a quizzical raised eyebrow, but Julie gave nothing away.

That night, she drove home in a daze, inching her car forward in heavy, early evening traffic over the Golden Gate Bridge toward Redwood Glen. Achieving the position of director would justify her career choice of giving up trying to make it as an artist and moving to curatorial. Her destiny was to support the masters, not become one herself. She viewed herself as if from above, leading a tour of high-end donors through the galleries, lauding this artist or that, dropping hints about who was bound to be the next art star, whose work was the best investment. Because that's what it was about for many collectors. Art as investment. Julie could talk investment. With the right buyer, the value of an artwork could skyrocket overnight. The art market was very impressionable. Which is why Talbot dedicated most of his energy to developing relationships with museum patrons. That, and fund-raising. About which Julie knew nothing. But she could learn. Couldn't she?

She drove up the hill to their house and turned into the driveway, past the garden bed outside the kitchen window where yellow chrysanthemums blazed. Mark kept that square plot planted so Julie always had something lovely to look at as she stood at the sink. She clicked open the garage door and unlocked the door to their kitchen. Life would be different as a director. Julie might not be the one who made dinner every night, for example. She might not be the one who collected the mail and paid the bills while waiting for her husband to come home. Julie might not be the one who was primary caregiver to their son, if their son ever arrived, if his adoption was ever completed. She measured out brown rice to steam and cut up vegetables and tofu for stir-fry. Actually, even if she got home late, she'd probably remain the one who did those things. Julie was so eager for a stable home life she sometimes overcompensated.

"Hard work pays off," Mark said later, practically leaping from his chair with enthusiasm as he congratulated her. "What else have you been slaving toward all these years? Did he discuss a salary increase?"

Julie had forgotten to ask about money, but Mark was right, an increase in salary must be a given. She didn't know exactly how much Talbot was paid, but Eames often complained it was twice the amount they made. Not that Eames should care: he lived on his trust fund, as did most of Julie's colleagues, she'd discovered. She was one of the few employees who depended on her salary to pay bills.

"More than what I'm making now. We can pay off the line of credit we took to pay Kate."

"First thing," Mark said.

"I can't believe he asked me. I mean, most directors have PhDs and I just have a master's." They'd talked about her returning to school at some point, but she'd gotten the internship at the Clay, and the day never came.

"Those are just letters after somebody's name," Mark said.

"Said the pathologist with a medical degree and post-doctorate."

"We're talking about ink on paper, not analyzing cells for cancer."

Julie smiled grimly. In his own way, Mark was defending her, protecting her from critics who might question her qualifications or ability. In his eyes, she was more than capable of handling any position. But after all their years together, he didn't quite understand that the art world had a hierarchy, the same as any profession, and people got promoted based on degrees, internships, resumes, and connections. She watched as he leaned over his plate and shoveled the first forkful of broccoli and rice into his mouth.

"Remind me who else is in the running?" he asked.

"Everyone from everywhere."

He rubbed his hands together conspiratorially. "That'll put you on your best game."

"Ha. Says you."

After dinner, Julie went out to the garage and climbed onto the workbench, careful not to disturb the hooks where Mark hung his hammers and wrenches. She wanted to look at her old portfolio. Go back to the beginning. She clambered onto a chair to access the crawl space above their cars and pulled out the large black sleeve. She carried it to the dining room table.

Here were the artist's proofs of her *Birds, Nesting* series, the one that won the Senior Artist Award at Davis. Here were the dozens of sketch books she'd carried since adolescence, pages of fluid and quick lines that captured the essence of things seen: street lights, hub caps, an array of ceramic plates on a table, the hands of old people, entire studies of cobs of corn and another of crinkled paper bags. And here were early drawings from when she was a girl: cheap paper torn from spiral-bound notebooks, drawings of their kitchen cabinets, the placemats like maps, the back of her mother dressed in a short bathrobe and standing at the sink with a glass of gin.

She remembered seeing a poster in the public library of a mother and child painting by Mary Cassatt, and the effect was like a current of electricity passing through her. The picture was beautiful, but it was more than beautiful. Cassatt had used paint to make emotions visible.

Julie saw pure love as solid as the baby's fleshy legs and chubby little hands.

Julie felt Mark's arms around her waist and tilted her head back into the notch of his shoulder. "What made you start drawing?" he asked, although he knew the answer.

Nobody told her to draw. She'd simply picked up a pencil and started drawing, all the time, on any flat surface. It was like a compulsion, her need to express herself.

She gathered the drawings from her childhood into a pile. She was good. The work was good. Tomorrow, she'd delve into the Clay storage closet to assemble a portfolio of artists she'd discovered, their exhibition catalogues and press releases, their folders of press clippings. That's who the committee wanted, the person she had become. And Julie would give her to them.

The next morning, she sifted through museum storage crates with the eagerness of a prospector panning for gold. So much had happened in her twelve years at the Clay. The capital campaign to raise funds for the expansion. Two years of construction dust and the staff pounding away at computers in hard hats. The debut of the emerging artists gallery and launch of the sculpture garden. The years had blurred into one another, not stopping or slowing down.

But Julie's greatest contribution was the artists. The ones she spotted during open studio nights, not only in San Francisco because that was obvious, but Vallejo, Richmond, Oakland. Unknown painters and sculptors working diligently in obscurity until Julie walked into their studio, basement, or converted closet. She'd chat with them a few minutes, artist to artist, to make them comfortable, before inspecting whatever was on the wall or table or floor. And within one second, she knew. She knew if the work held.

Discovering Patricia Westerman had been like that. Patricia was selling her ceramics at a crafts fair when Julie stopped short to inspect the tabletop display of horse heads and necks—graceful and arresting, rendered in metal, only eight inches tall yet amazingly evocative of the larger animal. Julie told Talbot, who eventually granted Patricia a solo exhibition. Confidence boosted, Patricia expanded her vision from parts of the animal to the whole horse. She conceptualized on a grander scale, constructing larger-than-life sculptures from steel, iron mesh, copper, slate, and sticks. Now, Patricia Westerman was on the pages of every art magazine, her sculptures collected worldwide.

Julie had thought Talbot was exaggerating when he said she knew the museum from bottom to top. But examining her contributions this way, objectively, she saw he was right. Her efforts to support the Clay had been relentless.

She'd compete for the director job. Because she deserved it.

THREE

BAY AREA, CALIFORNIA

OCTOBER 2002

Until they got DNA approval, they weren't telling anyone about Juan Rolando. They'd learned their lesson. They'd even debated whether they should hang his picture on the fridge, agreeing to wait until after DNA. Kate promised to have the test done by late summer, early fall. Halloween at the latest.

Despite her caution, Julie couldn't stop herself from prowling the aisles at Babies "R" Us after work, comparing cribs and bedding, car seats and bottles, making notes on what she planned to buy when they were sure Juan was theirs, when she wouldn't have to hide or donate painful reminders of what might have been, in case they lost him.

On weekends, she and Mark hiked the trails around their house and biked the path at the Cove, the waterfront park with views of the Golden Gate Bridge. Julie dug out her high school Spanish CDs and enrolled in a three-night-a-week Adult Ed class in intermediate conversation. At Kate's suggestion, they joined an online group of waiting families from around the United States who used Kate's agency. The group was called Guate Parents. Members signed their posts with timelines, stacking up dates.

Paper ready 2/14/2002
Got DNA 2/28/2002
Moved into Family Court 3/16/2002
PGN 4/12/2002
PINK ??????????
—Sandra, mom to three homegrown, one Guatemalan princesa

PGN stood for *Procuraduría General de la Nacíon*, the bureaucracy that bestowed final Guatemalan approval on a case before passing it to the U.S. Embassy. And PINK, Julie learned, was the color of the paper on which the U.S. Embassy printed its final approval, the green light to get the baby's medical exam and temporary Guatemalan passport necessary for travel.

At night over dinner, Julie kept Mark up to date with what she'd learned from the group by reading from the yellow legal tablet that now never left her side. "Sandra moved from DNA to PGN in two months. If we get DNA by Halloween, Juan'll be home by Christmas."

Mark nodded while Julie pondered the logistics. The new director would need to hit the ground running after Talbot left. Some of the work was doable from home, but much would need the director's on-site attention. There'd be meetings with the board to discuss long-range goals, finances, and acquisitions, in addition to ideas meetings with staff, gallery personnel, conservators, maintenance people. Plus, many more evening and weekend events—cocktail parties at donors' homes, speaking engagements, dinners with artists. And those were just the expected responsibilities. Talbot was wonderful, but he never reached out to community leaders the way he could have, the way Julie did. Julie believed everyone deserved access to art, just as she believed artists thrived in every neighborhood.

Luckily, she'd be the boss, and bosses made their own schedules. Either way, she'd need daycare. A dependable provider for Juan. She jotted a new note: Find nanny.

And if she didn't get the job? If that happened, she'd take advantage of the Clay's family leave policy—eight weeks. Then again, they might not be finished as quickly as Sandra, mom to three homegrown, one princesa. *Amber, waiting on Ella*, for example, had been in and out of PGN three times.

Submitted PGN 6/14/2001
Kicked out PGN 8/12/2001
Submitted PGN 9/3/2001

Kicked out PGN 10/2/2001
Submitted PGN 1/16/2002
STILL IN PGN
—*Amber, waiting on Ella*

The smallest clerical error—a misspelling or typo—got a file ejected from wherever it was in the process, leading to weeks or months of delay before a Guatemalan attorney corrected the error and put it back in the queue.

"No clerical error will trip us up," Julie told Mark emphatically. With her color-coded schedules and flow charts that tracked future exhibitions three years in advance, Julie was a master of organization.

Mark smiled indulgently. "You got that right."

Babies were what Guate Parents wanted, the younger the better. Not because of their own narcissistic need—*we must have a baby!*—but because the younger an infant, the more chance he had of forming a healthy attachment. Attachment meant touch and snuggles and hugs. Lack of attachment meant the opposite.

Charla T., MSW, a behavioral therapist in the group, sounded alarms in her posts.

> All: This is not your mother/sister/best friend's toddler experience. Don't compare! Think about it. Before our kids come to us, they're born and separated from their natural mothers, and cared for by strangers for months or years. Then they come to us and the real fun begins. New language, food, smells, sounds. I'd scream, too, people!
> —*Charla T., MSW, Mom to a Guate kiddo in process, two foster-adopts*

"I thought my life was hard," Julie said often to Mark. "Not anymore." After her father left, Julie's mother kept Claire and Julie with her, even while drinking, even while suffering from lung pain, up until the very end when she died when Julie was fifteen and Claire only nine. Their aunt may have been chilly and reserved, but she respected her sister's wishes and saved the girls from being thrown into the foster care system by taking them in herself.

Adoption from Guatemala felt to Julie like a roulette wheel, with an outcome unpredictable. For all the Guate Parents, the deadline of December 31, 2002 loomed like a chasm, ready to swallow their children whole. Panic reigned in the tone of every post:

> The back of Taylor's head is flat from lying in the crib. Anyone else see this? He needs to come home!
>
> Trying to get a medical visa for our Doris, with club feet. Who was the attorney someone used that was good?
>
> Gilma's legs are covered with flea bites. Our girlie can't stop itching. Foster family great except too many cats!
>
> Agency promised we're in PGN. Seven months later!
>
> WE MUST GET OUT BEFORE THE SHUTDOWN!!!

For Julie, December 31 may as well have been doomsday. Adoptions would close, possibly leaving Juan in a legal limbo. She'd either be the new director, or not. Both outcomes were out of her control. She managed to stay composed in the office because she had to—people were watching—but at home, she let out her pent-up steam. She slammed the dishes Mark had left in the sink into the dishwasher and plucked up the dirty clothes he'd dropped on the floor and hurled them into the hamper that sat inches away.

"How many times do I have to ask you?" she said.

Mark raised his hands as if shielding himself from a projectile. His natural sloppiness never seemed to bother her before. She'd tolerated his untidiness for years. He demonstrated the way she should breathe, intensely with lungs filled, while Julie glowered, not trusting herself to speak.

"We might not even get him," she said finally.

"We'll get him." Mark opened his arms toward her. "We'll get him."

"How do you know?"

He kissed her neck and moved downward. "You need to stop reading this Guate Parent stuff. It's like poison."

But Julie couldn't stop reading. The other Guate Parents were the only people who understood what it felt like to be a mother, yet not a mother. An almost mother. Mothers in name only.

*

An envelope from the DNA testing company arrived in their mailbox on Monday, October 28, a few days before Halloween. Two points for Kate. Julie carried the legal-sized envelope with the Labcorp return address into the house and picked up the phone to dial Mark. "We got DNA!" she said to his voicemail. "Call me!"

She wanted to open the letter, but dreaded opening the letter. Instead, she opened the refrigerator and poured herself a glass of white wine. Normally she didn't drink during the week, if only because her mother did, and Julie tried in every way to live her life differently from her mother. Tonight, though, belonged to her alone. To her and to Mark, and, fingers crossed, to her and to Mark and Juan. This was it.

She took her glass and the letter into the living room and parked herself on the couch. Setting down her drink on the coffee table, she took a deep breath, blew it out, and carefully unsealed the envelope with an index finger. "Labcorp," the masthead read. Finally.

Official stamps crowded the margins. A bold-faced line said the lab results indicated 99.9 percent accuracy, the highest number possible, proof that Karla Inez Garcia Flores gave birth to Juan Rolando.

They'd passed the first legal hurdle.

Julie skipped the rest of the paragraph and jumped directly to a color copy of a Polaroid in the middle of the page. The image showed Juan cradled on Karla's lap, both facing the camera.

Juan was dressed in a yellow onesie and white socks, too small to sit up without help. Karla supported him with her arms around his belly, so they formed almost a single being, and for a second, Julie imagined her son floating in the other woman's womb, his body tightly curled, safe and protected.

The last thing Julie wanted to imagine was her son in another woman's womb. She preferred not to think of her son in utero at all. Nobody had warned her, the impact of seeing her son with his mother. The image was physical evidence of Juan's origins, a beginning that didn't include Julie. He was only a baby, but in Karla's face, Julie could see the man he would become. Karla was gamine and slight, enchanting. Adidas hoodie, hair parted down the middle and tied in a ponytail. Perfect except for one small flaw: her left eye drooped slightly. This Kate had not mentioned. Juan's eyes were half-closed, as if his tummy were filled with warm, delicious milk, and he was ready for a nap.

Julie stood and walked to the kitchen. She needed to move, to shake off the mental picture of her baby with the woman who gave birth to him, their connection and closeness, their identicalness. She opened the fridge and stared at the contents, then closed it empty-handed.

She returned to the front window. Orange jack-o-lanterns glowed on the steps of the house across the street. On Halloween, like always, their doorbell would ring nonstop with trick-or-treaters. Next year would be different: she'd buy Juan a duckie costume and a basket shaped like a pumpkin. They'd go out early, down the hill to a few houses, then come home to open the door and give out candy.

At least he was only two months old. Too young to remember the cradle of his mother's arms, the soft cushion of her body. Infants didn't have memories from that age. Julie certainly didn't.

The room had turned dark. Julie turned on the floor lamp. Squaring her shoulders, she picked up the letter from the couch and studied it again. At the bottom of the page, Karla had signed her name. Hers was a rounded, precise signature, the careful penmanship of a girl just learning cursive. Karla was eighteen, but maybe never had much reason to write. Kate said girls like her didn't study past third grade.

So much to do. They'd just taken a giant step forward and must keep the momentum going to get grandfathered in before the shutdown. Julie grabbed her legal tablet and made a list.

- *Email Kate to bug lawyer.*
- *Family Court. PGN. ASAP.*
- *Book flights. Reserve hotel.*

The list was short, and she couldn't focus on it. She picked up the letter to study the picture again. Her son. He was exquisite. So small and so exquisite. Kate had said they'd be allowed to visit after DNA. Soon, Julie would hold Juan, her son, in her arms. She felt a pang of longing.

Her cell phone chimed. "Did we pass?" Mark asked.

"The DNA matched!" She read him the results, the 99.9% certainty, the irrefutable proof that Karla was Juan's biological mother. "Her left eye slants on the side."

"Probably a birth injury. Nothing genetic to pass on to Juan."

"She's young. Pretty."

"As are you," her husband said.

Julie pressed her lips together, silent. Before, Karla was a name in an email, an anonymous giver of life. Now, she had a face, a signature, a distinctive eye. Julie felt as if she were drowning in a swell of emotions: joy, sadness, gratitude, guilt, love. All from seeing Karla holding Juan.

After they hung up, Julie folded the letter into thirds and inserted it back into the envelope. In the family room, she opened the black metal file cabinet and stuffed the envelope in the manila folder labeled JUAN ROLANDO. The cold metal drawer clicked shut.

She'd tell Mark where to look if he wanted to read the report himself. She couldn't bear to see the image ever again.

FOUR

SAN ROLANDO, GUATEMALA

SEVENTEEN YEARS EARLIER—JANUARY 1985

Three trucks carried the soldiers up the dark mountain road to San Rolando, a village in Guatemala's western highlands. They rolled past corn and bean fields, past grazing pastures for goats and sheep, past rows of adobe houses with thatched roofs. The trucks lurched to a stop in the central plaza next to a stand of pine trees beside the white-washed church. The tailgates clanked open and soldiers jumped out, fingers on the triggers of Galil rifles. The soldiers wore the maroon beret of Guatemala's elite commandos, the Kaibiles. Their polished black boots were silent on the packed dirt.

They were there for revenge: Two weeks earlier, a band of guerrillas had come down from their camp and ambushed an army convoy. They'd killed twenty-one soldiers and stolen nineteen rifles. Somebody needed to pay.

The commanding officer stood in front of the troops. He was light-skinned and tall, Ladino to the village's indigenous Maya. "I want every one of these traitors out here. Men in the plaza. Women and children in the church."

Dogs barked as the units fanned out. Cold mist hung in the air.

A sergeant kicked in the door of the first adobe house. It fell to the floor with a thud. In two steps, the sergeant was beside a small cot covered with a gray woolen blanket. A farmer jumped up, his eyes darting to the doorway, where his machete hung on a nail.

"Where are the rifles?" the sergeant yelled.

The farmer's voice was quiet, submissive. "*Señor*," he said, "we have no rifles."

The sergeant slapped the farmer's face. "Where are the rifles?"

The farmer's eyes shifted to the lumpy form of the gray woolen blanket. "*Señor*, we have no rifles," he said again.

"Indio shit." The sergeant jammed his rifle into the farmer's stomach, bending him in two. Reaching down, the sergeant pulled off the blanket to reveal the farmer's wife hunched over a baby, with a small boy and a girl curled up on either side. The sergeant yanked the farmer's wife's thick black braid and pulled her to her feet; her white cotton sleeping dress bulged over her pregnant belly. She swaddled the baby into a sling, tying on the bundle. The boy and the girl pulled on clothes.

The sergeant unhooked the farmer's machete from the nail on the wall. "What's your name?"

"Juan Jorge Piox Oxlaj."

"Bring your identity card. We have a list."

The sergeant herded the family outside. Neighbors from all over the village began walking together down the gulley toward the plaza, their movements stiff and deliberate. Their bare feet scuffed the still-damp dirt. Dawn broke with a pink sky. Squawking chickens, bleating sheep, and bellowing cows added to the cacophony of howling dogs. The sergeant pushed the wife and her children toward the church's side door and continued with the farmer to the plaza where the men were being gathered.

The commander stood on the church steps with his feet splayed. Mirrored sunglasses shielded his eyes. He lifted a megaphone. "Hear this, you communist sons of whores. Traitors to Guatemala. We have a plan to help you remember the location of the stolen rifles. First, you dig a ditch. Then you will fill it."

Soldiers who spoke the local language, Ixil, translated the commander's words for any who didn't understand. Soldiers were of the villages, too. A boy might be on a bus to town to sell his family's corn, get stopped at a checkpoint, and find himself enlisted. But once they wore the uniform, the maroon beret, these boys forgot their dark skin, their straight hair, their village roots.

The sergeant shoved the farmer Juan Jorge toward a line of a dozen men tied together by a rope looped around their necks and fastened him to the end of the line. Without a word, the men crammed their shovels into the packed dirt and turned over soil. A large mound grew behind them as sweat glistened on their faces.

Inside the church, the women and children huddled in the wooden pews, holding hands and praying. A soldier fingered a silver candlestick from the altar and slipped it into a sack. Two other soldiers picked up the carved santos of San José and the town's patron, San Rolando, and punted them like soccer balls. A third man stood at the altar smoking a cigarette, and, when ashes fell onto the sacred white cloth, brushed off the small sparks with his pinkie.

Babies first, that was the order. Two soldiers patrolled through the aisles. The wife of Juan Jorge pushed her baby deeper into the sling. A soldier pointed straight at her. The boy and the girl grabbed her arms. "Mamá," they whimpered.

"Shut up!" the soldier commanded. He aimed his rifle at the girl's face and jerked his head toward a corner where the young girls and teenagers were corralled. Next, he swung his weapon at the boy and gestured toward a circle of boys in another corner. The separation process continued until the pews were emptied. A soldier led Juan Jorge's wife and her baby out the church's side door.

The wife squinted against the morning sun, eyes straining past the soldiers and trucks toward the pine trees. Two dozen men now stood roped together next to their shovels, faces and clothing flecked with dirt. The ditch they dug was finished: fifteen feet long, four feet wide, and eight deep.

The rest of the mothers with babies filed out of the church behind the wife, and one, whose infant had been baptized on Sunday, lifted her blouse to let him nurse.

The commander strode down the church steps, fingers flicking over a pistol holstered on his right hip. A young boy in uniform carried the megaphone. The commander waited while the soldiers gathered the mothers with babies into a group. The newly baptized infant sucked on his mother's breast.

"Now you will see the fate of people who betray our great country," the commander said. "We kill their seed."

He nodded at a soldier who then reached over to the nursing infant and pulled him from his mother's breast. A strangled gasp rose from the throats of the captive parents. The soldier carried the infant to a pine tree, and with one swift motion, swung him against the rough trunk. The infant's soft skull cracked open, seeping a mass of clear fluid. The soldier tossed the body into the trench.

The infant's father surged forward, dragging the other men to the ground. With one shot, the commander dispatched the infant's father. The wailing mothers torqued their bodies toward the gunshot. The soldier loosened the noose around the dead man's neck and kicked the corpse until it also fell into the ditch.

The infant's mother collapsed to her knees, weeping. The commander walked in a circle around her. "You smell too bad for me to take you," the commander said. "I'll wait for your daughter to be brought from the church. Fresh and sweet." As the infant's mother lifted her hands to cover her ears, the commander aimed his pistol at her sternum and pulled the trigger.

Juan Jorge's wife's legs felt weak. Her baby would be murdered and she would die, too. She closed her eyes and murmured the words of the Ave Maria, asking the Blessed Mother to spare her boy and her girl. She begged the Virgin, "Let my children live." She clutched more tightly to her baby in the sling.

The commander holstered his pistol and adjusted his sunglasses. Licking his bottom lip, he said, "You traitors killed twenty-one of my boys. I want to see you suffer."

He gave a signal and the sergeant who had taken Juan Jorge's machete walked in front of the line of mothers and their babies, brandishing the knife. The mothers stared at the ground. The sergeant with the machete stopped in front of the wife.

"Give me the baby," he said. Tears ran down the wife's face as she fumbled to untie the knot at her neck that secured the sling. The sergeant waited. One second, two seconds. He wrenched the full sling off her body, throwing it onto the hard-packed dirt.

The farmer's wife shrieked. In a second, the sergeant raised the machete shoulder-height and with one strike, sliced across her neck. Her body crumpled, twitching on top of sling and baby. The air filled with moans of the mothers, the babies, and the captive men. Using shovels, soldiers pushed the bodies into the ditch.

The commander lifted the megaphone to his mouth. "Any of you bastards remember where those rifles are now? Because it's not over until you do."

He lifted his free hand as though tipping a bottle. "We found their stash of guaro liquor. You soldiers got work to do first. Finish the women and let the Indios bury them. The men eliminate each other with machetes. You get to watch."

Later, when night came, the soldiers set fire to the thatched roofs of the adobe houses. They burned the plots of corn and beans and torched the town hall.

They searched every hiding place in the village and found no stolen rifles.

Two days later, three brave men from the nearby hamlet of San Lorenzo Chal walked over local trails to investigate. In the trench by the church, they discovered a pile of the dead, and as they offered prayers, heard a faint cry. They burrowed through the pile, and at the bottom, found a bloodied sling with a baby wrapped inside, skin puckered from dehydration and left eye swollen and bruised.

But the baby was alive.

FIVE

SAN FRANCISCO AND GUATEMALA

NOVEMBER 2002—ONE MONTH BEFORE THE SHUTDOWN

Candidates for the Clay directorship marched through the gallery like a black-clad parade. Curators from Kansas City, Fort Wayne, and Houston; assistant directors from Portland, Minneapolis, and Detroit. Julie recognized some from profiles in *ArtNews*, *Art Forum*, and the *New York Times*, but others were unknown, untested associates on her level, yearning to cross the yawning professional divide from mid-management to stratosphere. As they filed in, she lurked behind a sculpture or installation to scope them out, creative types like her but from someplace else and therefore more desirable: one sporting green-tinged bangs, another exotic leather oxfords, a third an emaciated body—her self-deprivation an implied statement of purpose.

Never before had Julie allowed herself to dream so big, but once she'd opened her mind to the idea of *yes*, she was seized by desire. She reminded herself she was worthy, deserving, and more than competent. She wrote affirmations on sticky notes and stuck them beside her computer, repeating the phrases, absorbing them into her subconscious. *Wonderful things unfold before me. Everything works out for my highest good. I am enough.*

She hoped Talbot might drop a hint about her chances, but he didn't offer a morsel. He seemed to be avoiding her and everyone else, coming in late and going home early, leaving his office vacant for board members to conduct interviews. Was she even in the running? She was afraid to ask. Arranging their travel plans to Guatemala distracted her. Kate had said they needed to visit Juan right after DNA and Kate knew the system. "The Guatemalan government keeps track of who visits and who doesn't," she insisted. Julie was able to book two seats on a red-eye the Saturday before Thanksgiving, the last available anywhere because of the busy holiday.

The second week in November, Julie was at her desk when she felt a hand on her shoulder. She turned to behold the face of Talbot's assistant Doni.

"There's a small, intimate dinner party at Talbot's Sunday evening. The board president and his wife and two major donors. You're invited."

"Is it possible to reschedule? We leave for Guatemala Saturday."

Doni raised her eyebrows. "Let me know by end of day today," she said, withdrawing to return to the administrative offices.

Talbot, the board president, major donors. These important people wouldn't be able to reschedule because the date was inconvenient. These important people were busy. Julie and Mark could go to Guatemala another time. Deal with it.

Pushing back her desk chair, she grabbed her yellow legal tablet and paper calendar and hurried to the conference room, carefully closing the door, not bothering to move to the table to sit down. She dialed Kate and explained her dilemma. "Are you out of your mind?" Kate asked.

"We'd fly first week of December," Julie said. "Before the Christmas crush."

"What's to say they don't jerk you around then? You reschedule and some other meeting comes up. You've worked there how long?"

"Twelve years."

"And they don't know what you can do by now?"

Julie didn't answer. She wasn't sure they did.

"If you want to risk losing Juan, be my guest," Kate said.

Julie was dumbstruck. Of course, she didn't want to risk losing Juan. How could Kate even say that? She didn't want to sabotage the directorship, either.

"Listen, Julie. If the job is meant for you, you'll get it."

"Can't the same be said for Juan? We'll get him if we're supposed to?"

Kate laughed cynically. "We're talking about Guatemala. There are no guarantees."

After hanging up, Julie paced the conference room floor for only a minute before dialing Mark's number. In a rush, she told him about the invitation and Kate's response. "We're going," he said without hesitation. "Screw the museum."

"Really? Because I want to. Juan needs us."

"The flights are booked. Period."

The Saturday before Thanksgiving, they flew the red-eye to La Aurora Airport, Guatemala City as planned. Julie worried she hadn't groveled enough in her apologetic email to the board president and his wife, but Mark waved away her fears. Tired from late nights over the microscope, he was fading as they boarded the aircraft and snoring before the end of the safety presentation.

Julie couldn't sleep. In less than twelve hours, she'd meet her son. In less than twelve hours, she'd get to hold him in her arms and be his mother. They'd spent months pushing toward this moment, years if counting the fertility treatments. She could barely contain her excitement.

Mark, on the other hand? Julie almost laughed to see his head falling forward while he kept jerking it up, not waking. The poor man. She extricated one of the airline blankets from its plastic bag and placed it in a roll around his neck for support.

She opened the book she'd brought about Guatemalan politics. It focused on the history of an American corporate giant, United Fruit, in Guatemala, and the legacy of President Jacobo Arbenz in the 1950s. United Fruit exported bananas and seized acres of land to grow them. The socially progressive Arbenz planned to take back fallow land owned and unused by United Fruit and give it to landless Mayan peasants. Arbenz also threatened to raise United Fruit's taxes, slashing company profits. The Eisenhower White House smelled communism. In 1954, Arbenz was deposed in a military coup orchestrated by Guatemalan conservatives and the CIA.

A period photo showed the disgraced former president stripped to white boxer shorts and presented to international photographers before being exiled from the country. A reign of dictators followed, with a policy called scorched earth. Civil war raged between the Guatemalan army and guerrillas for thirty-six years. Two hundred thousand people were killed: innocent farmers, women, children. Six hundred villages were destroyed. Peace Accords finally were signed in 1996.

There was so much to take in. Too much. Julie closed her book as a flight attendant moved down the aisle selling refreshments. Julie swiped her credit card and purchased tapas. Tearing open a bag of crackers, she dipped into a wedge of packaged cheese and munched on black olives. She couldn't believe the power a private corporation was able to wield over Guatemala. United Fruit's corporate greed led to political decisions by the United States that damaged Guatemala irrevocably. The civil war ended, but the country continued to struggle with its legacy. At that time, Guatemala had one of the highest murder rates in the world, consistently among the top five, and one of the highest rates of femicide, also among the top five, with women crushed into submission by abusive systems and partners. Drug traffickers and gangs ruled urban neighborhoods as well as remote areas, where they controlled roadways and airstrips. Impunity was the rule, not the exception. Crimes rarely were prosecuted.

Julie stuffed the snack packaging into the box and pushed up her window shade. They were getting closer. Below was a large lake, surrounded by mountains she knew were volcanoes. Guatemala had an impressive number of them. She'd seen numbers ranging from thirty to almost forty. The densest concentration of volcanoes in Central America.

The captain's voice crackled over the speaker and announced they were beginning their descent into Guatemala City. Mark stretched and yawned. "Catch any sleep?"

She held up the book to show the cover. "Brushing up on my Guatemalan history."

They'd passed over the lake and trees gave way to low buildings sprawling for miles, condensing into a core of high rises clustered in the city center. The capital was the largest urban area in Central America, home to some two million of Guatemala's fifteen million inhabitants. Julie pointed her camera out the window, shaking off thoughts of the museum dinner party she was missing. She'd made her decision and needed to live with it.

They followed the crowd through the terminal toward passport control, and although Julie should have been worn out from no sleep, she felt energized. Nearly everyone around her was Guatemalan. Young, old, male, female: these were Juan's countrymen, his people. She felt pulled toward them and wanted to proclaim their purpose: *We're meeting our son! Everyone! Today's the day.*

Occasionally Julie glimpsed other white faces, heads of light-colored hair—missionaries in scripture-bearing t-shirts, a high school girls' soccer team—but they felt oddly separate, visitors to the country. Julie and Mark would forever have a connection.

La Aurora Airport was due for an upgrade, shabby and a little cramped, with kiosks to change money and buy phone cards. Julie had been expecting it, especially after spending the past few hours reading about the country's bleak history. After passing through passport control, they went to the luggage carousel to claim their three enormous suitcases packed with diapers, formula, vitamins, and clothes. Kate had given them a long list of supplies to bring for Juan's *niñera* or nanny to use while she cared for Juan. He'd stay with her until the adoption was final.

Outside, the terminal smelled like diesel fuel and gasoline, car exhaust without emission controls. Crowds of people pressed against barricades, with families calling out, private drivers holding signs, and children selling baskets of chewing gum and hacky sacks. Mark spotted the shuttle with the Marriott logo and the driver loaded them in.

"The book said seventy percent of Guatemalans live below the poverty line," Julie told Mark as the shuttle made its way through the city streets.

Mark looked out the window. "Doesn't seem too bad," he said, and it was true. Expensive cars driving on the tree-lined boulevard of the Zona Viva, joggers dressed in chic gear, office towers sheathed in glass. And the hotel itself was magnificent, with a sweeping central staircase and smartly attired staff.

They arrived at eleven; Berta, the *niñera* assigned to Juan, was due to arrive with him in an hour. The nursery, called an *hogar*, housed twenty children being adopted by Americans, who paid Kate a monthly fee for food and care. Mark and Julie were allowed to keep the baby for five days after they promised not to leave the hotel with him under any circumstances. "We can't go to a restaurant?" Julie had asked.

"The food's safer at the hotel," Kate said. Besides, Juan wasn't legally theirs. They shouldn't take any risks.

While Mark checked in, Julie surveyed the lobby. On every couch was the same tableau: white people cuddling brown babies, flanked with children of varying shades. For a second, she wondered what Guatemalans thought of the scene, but her emotions squashed the thought. She wanted to be there too, cuddling her baby, never letting him go. Soon. Soon. In less than an hour. Juan was three months old now. She didn't want to miss another minute.

They were so fortunate. In a few weeks, adoptions would close completely. Julie visualized a door slamming and dust flying underneath, the pathway to adoption sealed off.

After freshening up, they commandeered a small mauve couch tucked under the sweeping staircase beside a potted palm tree and kept their eyes on the revolving front door. Taxis drove up, shuttles unloaded, telephones rang, a group of men in dark suits passed. Finally, a middle-aged woman in a blue uniform dress and white apron appeared, holding a bundle of blue blankets.

"That's them," Julie exclaimed, recognizing Berta from the photo Kate had sent. Julie stood up. Everything around her evaporated. Berta placed Juan in her arms. Julie was one with her son, their own universe. Finally. She was a mother.

For someone so small, he felt heavy, substantial. Maybe twelve pounds? His hair was black and thick, his eyes wide open with long straight lashes, looking past Julie and Mark beside her, searching for Berta, sitting on a chair. Julie breathed in the smell of a soap she didn't recognize, touched his smooth forehead. His fingers were curved, nearly transparent, heartbreaking in their perfection. He was breathtakingly gorgeous.

"Is he hungry?" Julie asked in Spanish, sitting beside Berta.

"Always." Berta handed her a bottle and Julie shifted Juan to one side and pressed it gently into his mouth. He turned his head away and wailed. "Except when I'm feeding him," Julie said self-consciously.

Mark patted Juan through the blue blanket, then swiped at his own cheek with the back of his hand.

"You're crying," Julie said.

"You, too," he said.

Berta told them Juan's schedule: naps morning and afternoon, bedtime at seven. He slept through the night in his own crib. He took bottles of regular formula, nothing solid yet. Of the twenty children in the *hogar*, she added, Juan was the baby most calm and sweet.

Julie and Mark had read horror stories from other Guate Parents about first visits: screaming babies, sleepless nights, miles logged pacing up and down the hotel hallways.

But it turned out Berta was right. Juan was a calm and sweet baby. He slept between them in their king-sized bed, and Julie marveled at the feeling of that warm, solid little being beside her, his quick breath. She was overwhelmed by him, the fact of him, his being her son. When he was awake, she never put him down. He preferred to be carried in the Snugli, close enough that their hearts beat together. Mothering was more physical than Julie had imagined: up and down, in and out, lifting and carrying him. Good thing her arms were strong from shuttling artists' portfolios, paintings, and framed prints.

They spent their days by the pool, meeting and talking with other waiting adoptive parents whose cases would be grandfathered in after the shutdown. Everybody was on Guate Parents and they recognized one another's names and stories. "How old is your daughter?" and "You're the one with three other kiddos," and "Has anyone met Charla T., MSW, in person?"

They ate sandwiches together and drank lemonade in lounge chairs, cheered when paperwork advanced a step or someone got positive news. They heated infant formula in the restaurant microwave, changed diapers in the lobby restroom, and splashed in the pool. They told their babies their adoption stories, as simply as possible. "You were born in another lady's tummy. You're our forever child now." They snapped a thousand photos. The other babies were cute, too, lovable in their own ways. But they weren't Juan.

*

At 8:30 on Monday morning, Julie stood in front of the mirror in the Clay staff ladies' room, stealthily dripping eye drops into her bloodshot eyes. Their flight home had sat on the tarmac for four unexplained hours in Guatemala City, causing them to miss their connection in Houston. They landed in San Francisco with just enough time for Julie to catch a taxi downtown and brush her teeth and change into her pleated black Issey Miyake dress before her interview with the board. Thank God she'd thought ahead to potential snafus and left her resume in her office.

"I am enough," she said to the mirror as she wiped an errant eye drop from her cheek and clasped a necklace made from a chunk of blue resin around her neck. Statement necklaces were her signature, functioning both as wearable art and failsafe conversation starter. That, and her stylish short haircut. "Wonderful things unfold before me," she said. "Everything works out for my highest good."

She gathered her travel clothes into her duffel and walked to her desk. Eames was slouched in his seat, hair gelled into spikes, checking his email. "How was the trip?"

"Fabulous. Juan is a gem. A really sweet boy." Her voice softened and she re-squared her shoulders. "It's good we went."

"Word is you're in the running."

Julie startled, as if just remembering her nine o'clock interview appointment. She picked up her portfolio. "We're rooting for you, Jules," Eames said.

She hurried to the administration area. Doni was at her post, at the ready to screen visitors. She barely glanced up as Julie arrived, waving her into Talbot's office. The board president sat in Talbot's chair behind Talbot's desk, with Talbot on one side and two board members—a man and a woman—on the other. The men rose slightly when Julie walked in. "Good morning," the president said, settling back into his chair and gesturing toward the lone empty seat after everyone had shaken hands.

Julie's throat went dry. The woman wore a lime-green, raw silk jacket over a black pencil skirt; Talbot his uniform black suit and purple tie; the other man a blue cashmere blazer and narrow loafers. Julie measured herself against the visual information, relieved she'd chosen the black Issey Miyake.

The president started in by asking her about vision. She talked about her loyalty to the Clay, the way she viewed the museum as something to be nurtured and tended. She'd dedicated herself to that mission for twelve years. Since she began, attendance numbers at openings had tripled, and museum membership was steady and climbing. She was careful to address each of them, shifting her gaze from one to the other. She sensed their understanding and felt her confidence rise.

The man in the blue cashmere blazer wanted to talk future expansion. Talbot had been brilliant in getting them this far, but they needed to go bigger. Technology had exploded in the Bay Area, and with the boom came young people with money, unprecedented amounts of money. The Clay needed to grab that audience and their pocketbooks.

Julie was startled. The paint was barely dry on the first expansion. A second expansion felt like a curveball.

"How do you sell these tech people on the Clay?" the man asked.

"No sales pitch is more effective than passion." Julie hesitated, hoping she didn't sound too woo-woo. "Share our vision. Show them the budget and a specific way they can help. Give them something to be part of."

The board members bent their heads in unison and made marks on their notepads. The woman in the raw silk said there was something she'd been curious about for a long time: she wanted to know how someone judged an artwork as exceptional.

Technical merit was part of it, Julie said. Composition and where it fit historically.

But more than anything, she looked for the essence of the artist within the work. There were thousands of exquisite Renaissance paintings hanging in museums. So why did everyone cross the room to study only one, the *Mona Lisa*? Because inside the painting was a piece of Leonardo da Vinci.

The board members murmured and nodded. Julie had helped them see. The president thanked her for her time and promised to be in touch.

Just over half an hour, and her interview was finished.

*

The second week in December, Doni called Julie to tell her to come to Talbot's office immediately. Julie jumped out of her chair, not bothering to close her open files. She'd heard nothing since her interview and the suspense had almost crushed her.

Talbot's shirt collar was uncharacteristically unbuttoned—on his last day, he must have allowed himself one concession to casual dress—and without his purple tie he looked like a younger, more callow version of himself. The moving boxes were gone and the desk empty. Any trace of Talbot had been scoured. "I have bad news," he said.

He wasn't at liberty to disclose who they'd chosen, but Talbot was confident Julie would be pleased with their decision and helpful during the transition. The golf-ball-sized lump in Julie's throat made it difficult for her to talk. It was a few seconds before she choked out, "I appreciate your going to bat for me."

"You're terrific," Talbot said. "That much is true. Also true is we fielded some outstanding candidates. Tops in their field."

She waited for him to say something else—about her dedication or talent, or how much he'd enjoyed their time together—but Talbot looked as dismayed as she felt. "We'll introduce the new director at tonight's reception. You and Mark will be there?"

"Wouldn't miss it."

Talbot stood and stepped around the desk, opening his arms for a hug. Their relationship had always been one of handshakes and distance, but in this case, an embrace seemed appropriate. She wrapped her arms loosely around him and squeezed.

"Count on me for anything," he said. "I'm an email away."

She walked past Doni's desk with the golf-ball-sized lump still lodged in her throat and toward the office maze. Eames leaned out, his face a question mark. Julie shook her head.

"Idiots," Eames said.

Dropping into her chair, she swiveled toward the office's back wall. She'd never aspired to be a director of anything so not being one shouldn't devastate her. It was a job, not life or death. She swiveled her chair to her bottom drawer for her purse with its packet of tissues. Inside was the Ziploc bag with its photo of Juan. She pulled it out gently and pressed him against her heart.

A few hours later, both of them showered and polished, Mark stopped the car a block from the Clay. He never valeted, always parked in the public lot three blocks away. Julie didn't complain; she was grateful he came. Mark cringed at crowds and hated small talk. He attended because it made her happy. That, and the free food and drink.

"Chin up," he reminded Julie. "You're the best at what you do, and everyone knows it."

She flipped down the lighted visor mirror over the passenger seat and plucked a speck of mascara from underneath her bottom lashes. "They can't forgive me for going to Guatemala," she said. "How could we not meet Juan?"

"It was the right decision. End of story."

She flipped up the visor. "I know."

"It's done. Don't second-guess yourself."

"How does it feel to always be right? You make these pronouncements and never back down."

"Better than punishing myself."

Julie sighed. "True." She pecked him on the lips and put her hand on the door handle. "Meet you at the coat check."

"You're a champ," he called after her as she stepped onto the curb. She merged into the stream of donors and artists alighting from taxis, limousines, and cars, the donors red-carpet ready in cocktail dresses and suits, the artists dressed down in immaculately clean, expensive tennis shoes and artfully disheveled hair.

Two searchlights set up on the Clay's roof criss-crossed white beams in the night sky, and buoyant riffs of jazz saxophone wafted out from the lobby. Julie stepped into the dazzle inside. White-clothed tables topped with carved platters laden with shrimp and beef en brochette, vegetables arranged by color into modernist decoration, bouquets of white peonies blooming from vases shaped like Picasso-esque figures. White was the favorite color of a donor they'd been soliciting. Flowers this quarter were decreed white. She moved through snippets of conversation like turning a dial: vacations to Europe and studio visits and new restaurants and divorces and children off to university.

Her name being called broke through the static and she veered toward Talbot. Talbot with a woman wearing enormous, red-framed, circular glasses and a fitted black pantsuit. She was built like a runway model and towered over Julie.

"May I present our new director, Dr. Amelie Conrad," he said. "From the Kentridge in New York." The new director's black hair was chopped into bangs like a thirties film star. The shade of her matte red lipstick matched her eyeglass frames. Her skin was as white as paper.

"Julie's our ace curator," Talbot said.

Dr. Conrad's eyes behind gigantic red glasses appraised Julie, and even though Julie was dressed in her best— little black cocktail dress, statement silver and onyx necklace, and Stuart Weitzman high heels— that one glance reduced her to the category of a rube who'd crashed the party.

"Charmed," the new director said.

"Would you mind escorting Dr. Conrad out for a bit of air? We'll begin the introduction in ten." Talbot was tightening up the knot on his purple tie, practically sweating. Julie had never seen him so nervous.

She led the way through the throngs in the Atrium and out the side door to the sculpture garden. The night was dry and chilly. She walked over to the Calder, the large, sheet metal sculpture protected by a low concrete wall. Its flat orange and blue paddles lifted and fell on invisible winds, like small sailboats on a lake. Usually when Julie directed guests to the Calder, they were impressed. But the new director came from the Kentridge, with ten times the status of the Clay. She didn't glance at the Calder.

The new director grasped the lapels of her black suit jacket and pulled them tight. "Brrr. They said California was warm."

"That's SoCal," Julie said.

The jazz combo was playing "I Left My Heart in San Francisco," a standard at Clay events. Most major donors were over sixty, and bands chose a songbook they would recognize. Later, when the oldsters had gone home, a techno band would take the stage and the artists would dance.

"Smoke?" Dr. Conrad asked.

"Cigarettes?"

"Out here, you must think marijuana." Dr. Conrad reached into a pocket and produced a pack of red Marlboros, along with her first smile. She inserted a cigarette between her red, matte lips and flipped open a lighter.

"No. No, thank you," Julie said. Dr. Conrad lit up, her eyes opening widely behind her red glasses as she took a long draw. Julie hadn't smelled cigarette smoke up close in years.

"Interesting necklace," Dr. Conrad said. "Who makes it?"

Julie told her the artist's name.

"You do what?" Dr. Conrad asked.

"Curator of emerging art."

"For how long?"

Dr. Conrad exhaled a curl of smoke like a genie released from a bottle, and Julie had a sinking feeling she'd wasted the past twelve years of her life.

The party was under way and they'd turned off the searchlights out front. Years ago, when the Clay first started using searchlights—they were popular at Los Angeles openings, the influence of Hollywood—neighbors signed a petition complaining. The compromise was the lights stayed on only during arrivals. Julie remembered the entire back and forth. The moon remained bright, though. A white spotlight. She turned toward the museum, hoping to see Mark.

The band started playing "New York, New York," the cue that Talbot would soon take the podium to make his introduction. The new director took her cigarette from her mouth and ground it into the low cement fence surrounding the Calder. "What should I do with this?" She held up the mashed butt.

There were no ash receptacles outside, not even a nearby trash can. Julie couldn't allow the new director to throw the butt on the ground. That was a fire hazard, plus littering. Julie stretched out her palm and the new director pinched the butt between two fingers and deposited it.

Julie followed her toward the music, carrying the cigarette in her flat palm like a footman holding a pillow with Cinderella's glass slipper. She lifted a shoulder and sniffed discreetly. Her skin smelled dusky, like cigarettes.

*

The door to adoption between the United States and Guatemala slammed shut on December 31, 2002. January 2003 passed. Juan remained in Guatemala. He was five months old. Guate Parents lit up:

> The only correspondence we've had is sending two Cashier's Checks for $15,000 each. Not a single receipt. Praise Jesus for tracking numbers and photocopies so we have proof.
> —*Hannah R.*

> We filed our Power of Attorney YESTERDAY. Agency lied about the Hague. Why wasn't this information publicized????
> —*Amber, waiting on Ella*

> Very black depression. Like I'm watching a crystal vase about to fall off the edge of a table, knowing it will shatter.
> —*Julie C.*

Julie thought about Juan while sitting in her office at the Clay, his warm body against hers, his soft breath when he was sleeping. She thought about him in the weekly ideas meetings, when she was required to present three new ways to increase audiences and improve outreach. She pictured him in orange floaties and a swim diaper at the baby pool at the Marriott, slapping down his hands on the water and grinning at the splash. Did Juan remember her? Was Berta still his special *niñera*? Julie called Kate every Friday during lunch, eating a sandwich at her desk while Eames and their co-workers went to one of the neighborhood cafés—"Where are we? What's happening?"—and over the phone line, she could practically hear Kate shrug.

"Their country, their rules," Kate said. "You can't rush them."

After hanging up, Julie logged onto Guate Parents to see if anyone else's case had progressed:

Paying $150 a month for foster care! I'm a single mom and not made of money. In PGN since June 2002, now we're at the back of the line??? Has anyone heard of Adoption Supervisors? Someone said they check on cases.

Adoption Supervisors good, but expensive. We paid $1K to find out no DNA.

We'd still be stuck if they didn't harass our Guatemalan attorney. Worth it.

Nobody seemed to have hit on the right strategy, nobody had unlocked the secret to unraveling the system. Nobody had figured out how to finalize their adoption and get their baby out. It was maddening. Before Eames and the others returned, Julie power-walked around the block to get her heart rate up and improve her mood. She wasn't going to lose Juan by not paying attention.

On March 3, Claire was scheduled to give birth to her first son, a boy they'd named Gunther. She'd invited Julie to be present, along with Mark, if not in the delivery room itself, then right outside, close by. Julie had never witnessed a birth and wanted to go, planned to leave after work on Friday. But as she was unlocking her car in the parking garage—the same parking garage where she'd lost Rowan—Julie shook uncontrollably and couldn't stop. She slid onto the front seat and placed her head on the steering wheel, gasping.

She called Ethan with an excuse about a sudden onset of a virus she was afraid she might spread. She could barely hear Ethan's reply because of party noises in the background. Gunther would be the first grandchild, and Ethan's extended family had gathered in Fresno to celebrate.

"No problem," Ethan said. "You can watch the video."

She hung up, sadness weighing her down. Not for herself, for what she couldn't do and didn't have, because Juan had made her forget that. No, it was sadness for her son. There was no family celebration. No video. Had his birth mother even counted his fingers and toes? Julie imagined Karla had to distance herself from Juan, remain stoic to survive their separation. Had Karla even kissed him good-bye?

Julie rummaged in her purse for the Ziploc with photos from their visit. She stared at the images: Juan nestled in a Snugli against her chest. Juan on her lap by the pool. Juan and Mark on the couch in the hotel lobby.

"Somebody loves you now," Julie whispered to her son's photos. "Somebody loves you forever."

SIX

SAN LORENZO CHAL

WESTERN HIGHLANDS, GUATEMALA

NOVEMBER 2010

My name is Rosalba Puzul Tuc. I am twenty-five years old. My Testimonial tells of my life and the lives of other *indígena* mothers. Our country robs us of power. Our country silences our voices.

They said you are a group of mothers and fathers from the United States. They said you have children born in Guatemala. My father, Chelo, lives in your country and I think it's a good place. I hope that it is. This is why I tell you my story. I trust you will understand.

My translator is a missionary sister who lives here and knows me well, for many years. She speaks Spanish and English. My languages are Ixil and Spanish. I will speak slowly for her to translate. Thank you to her.

I was nine years old when I discovered my mother was not my real mother. Or that Rosalba wasn't my real name. This is how my story begins.

In our family, everyone worked hard at many things. Carrying water, preparing tortillas, tending to animals, washing and cleaning. We were Maya Ixil, from the village of San Lorenzo Chal. Like most children in Chal, my little brother, Daniel, and I worked every day in the corn field. At this time, I was a girl of nine years and Daniel two years younger.

One afternoon, we came in from the field as usual, when the sun was finishing its trip across the sky. We got to our house, where Mamá sat on the edge of the bed with baby Isabel hugged tight. On this day, Mamá's face looked different. Swollen and red. When she saw me, she wiped her eyes with Isabel's sling and put down her head. I walked past them to the stove in the corner to stoke the fire and pat out the evening tortillas. Seeing Mamá's face like that scared me and I didn't like it. I was used to her being brave.

Papi came in after us with my older sisters, Marta and Yanira. When Papi moved, it was like wind blowing, strong and forceful. Behind him, Marta and Yanira were like breezes. Their faces were lighter than mine and their hair thinner. Papi hung his machete by the door and picked up baby Isabel to kiss her. Mamá didn't lift her head.

I dished up the rice and beans and tortillas and we sat on our heels on the floor eating in silence. We never lit candles because the army might be watching. We stayed close in the blackness, like mice being hunted. Our eyes became good at seeing in the dark and the light.

After the meal was finished, I gathered the metal plates and put them in the pan. Papi waited until I knelt again before he started talking. "I'm going to los Estados," he said.

Even without candles, I saw Mamá's face was blank, the same way as when my older brothers Josué and Marcos died by the fever. As though she felt nothing.

We heard about los Estados by the radio. They always told stories of men from Chal sending money for their families. When Josué and Marcos had been sick, we couldn't afford to buy medicine. Sometimes to buy rice was too much.

"In los Estados, everyone is rich," Papi said.

Many men in our village had gone. They lived in towns called Arizona, Arkansas, and Texas. They called on the telephone at Doña Yoly's *tienda* and made their families rich. In Arizona, Arkansas, and Texas, children attended school. Hospitals accepted the sick without money. Everybody wore shoes.

In Chal, Papi tended the corn with Daniel and me and served as a civil patroller for the army. All the men did. They guarded against subversives who came from the mountain to buy food or steal a cow. The men resented the duty because the army didn't pay them. But they did it, or they got hung by a tree like Gaspar Xic or shot like Pablo Chocoj.

My oldest sister Marta asked Papi when he was coming back from los Estados.

Papi said when he earned enough for me and Daniel to continue school. And to pay for Marta and Yanira to get married. That was when he'd come back.

But that didn't happen. At first, he wired money to help pay the smuggler who helped him in the journey. He called once a month on Sunday afternoon and we talked to him on the telephone at Doña Yoly's *tienda*. The last call came from California, when he was gone for two years. Everything seemed the same. He talked about work and money he was earning, how he was able to help his family. But the next Sunday, we heard nothing. Or the Sunday after that. We didn't know if he was alive or dead. If he forgot about us or was in trouble. We became like an unplanted hillside in heavy rain, slipping down, down, with no roots to hold us.

Life was difficult with no father to help. Our village was high up in the Cuchumatanes Mountains with only one dirt road to the next village. The capital city of Guatemala was a twenty-hour bus trip. There was only the one telephone, in Doña Yoly's *tienda*. Everyone waited in line to talk. We walked to the public well to collect water. We had no electricity in our homes.

I tell you this so you understand how it was.

After Papi left, a man started helping Mamá with repairs to our house. We called him Tío Eldon. Tío Eldon walked with a cane due to one leg being shorter than the other, and his breath smelled sour. But he always gave my brother Daniel and me a Chiclet, so we didn't mind having him around.

Tío Eldon asked Mamá what project she needed to have done and she said, "Nothing." Then she looked around and saw things. He brought wood to build Mamá a table and six chairs so we didn't need to kneel to eat. Five for us and the baby, and one for him. He put in a metal faucet and running water came into our yard.

"Why does he help us?" my sister Marta asked Mamá the first night we ate dinner at the new table. It felt strange to sit on a chair, as if we were eating from a pew at church. "Does he expect you to pay?"

Mamá didn't have money to pay Tío Eldon. Sometimes she invited him to eat with us and he did. Mamá was grateful jobs needing to be done were finished. She chopped firewood and sold it to pay for food. Marta and Yanira worked for Doña Yoly, in her house and her *tienda*. Daniel and I worked in the corn field. Even so, Daniel and I didn't have shoes so we couldn't go to school. I practiced reading and numbers at home, with books Padre Andrés from the church gave us. I kept the house neat and tidy.

Usually the oldest girl made the tortillas, but in our family, the job belonged to me. Every morning, I took the prepared corn to the tortilla mill to have it ground into masa for the day's tortillas. On the Feast of Candelaria, I climbed out of bed carefully, so as not to disturb Marta and Yanira. My feet found the straw mat that covered the floor next to our bed. Mamá splashed water on her face from the pan near the stove while I lit the match for the morning fire. Smoke curled up to the blackened thatched roof. Ears of last year's harvest hung from the rafters.

I walked down the lane to the tortilla mill. The thumping sound of the mill's engine welcomed me as I opened the door. The *señora* poured the lime-soaked kernels into a chute at the top of the mill and the machine crunched and sputtered, kneading the kernels into soft masa. I paid the *señora* as the machine squeezed the masa through a tube and into my plastic bowl. Balancing the bowl on my head, I closed the door.

I didn't see the man standing under the tree down the path until he stepped in front of me. I jumped enough from surprise that the bowl of masa tipped off my head and bounced to the ground.

I bent to scoop the masa back into the bowl and placed it back on my head, standing still to let it balance. "Do you always come here this early?" Tío Eldon asked. I nodded with care not to upset the masa. He put his head closer to mine. "Isn't it dangerous? With guerrillas in the mountains?"

We never said the word guerrilla out loud. Papi taught us that. "The civil defense patrol will protect us," I said.

"I'm a patroller," Tío Eldon said. "I can protect you."

He was talking to me like I was a grown-up, instead of nine years old. Maybe he got confused between Marta and Yanira and me.

We walked towards home, with Tío Eldon rocking left to right when he stepped on his bad leg. Chal was waking up. Today on the Feast of Candelaria, we would go to church. Men passed wearing good white shirts, and women with shawls covering their heads for early mass. Our house came into view, not far. Wood smoke rose from our chimney and swirled in the brightening sky. Isabel and the girls and Daniel would be awake, hungry for tortillas.

Our house was less than twenty steps away when Tío Eldon stopped, dug the tip of his cane into the dirt, and leaned into it. "You know, Rosalba. I've been thinking. You don't look like your older sisters or Daniel or Isabel. You don't look like your Papi or Mamá." He tapped his stick three times into the dirt and chuckled as if remembering something. "You look like girls from the hamlet of San Rolando."

I had never been to San Rolando because the army burned it to the ground.

"San Rolando is where your Papí found you," Tio Eldon explained. "Wrapped in a sling like a little *tamalito*. In a deep ditch. That's why your eye is funny." He pulled down one of his eyes with a finger and my face got hot. No one was supposed to tease me for my eye that drooped, but they did.

"Your Papi, Chelo, brought you around to each house asking if they wanted a baby. Nobody wanted a girl baby because they're not strong enough to harvest corn or cut sugar cane. Besides, everyone had enough babies. So Chelo took you home to Mamá Delma."

I was confused. Papi found me in a ditch?

"Delma, your mamá, didn't want you at first. She said, 'Only a witch could survive what the army did to San Rolando.' Killing everyone and burning it to the ground. But Chelo insisted. 'This girl is not a witch. She's a miracle. If we don't take her, she'll die.'"

The outline of his face became wavy like someone was holding my head down in a bucket of water. My ears started to ring. I took the bowl of masa from my head and held it in front of me with two hands like a wall. The ringing in my ears became louder. "I wasn't born in Chal?"

Tío Eldon cleared his throat. "Delma wanted to tell you. Oh, how she wanted to tell you. Chelo didn't want you to feel different."

The ringing in my ears became louder. "What do you mean 'in a ditch?'"

Tío Eldon looked off toward where the village of San Rolando used to be, where the only thing left was ruins of the church. "Chelo knew your father, Juan Jorge. It was the bad time everywhere. Worse than now." Tío Eldon shrugged. "Delma treats you like her own. You shouldn't complain."

I wasn't complaining, although I felt I might be dying. My soul seemed to be floating to the sky, away from my body.

The door to the house opened and Mamá came out. She was dressed in her same *corte* and *hüipil*, her hair tied in a long braid. But she wasn't my mother. She was someone else. Delma. How could I be nine years old and not know?

She called out for me to come quickly. They were hungry for tortillas. I answered that I was coming. The word "Mamá" stuck in my throat.

Tío Eldon put one finger to his lips. "Not a word to anyone. Our secret."

Not long after, I stood at the stove patting out tortillas, my wrists turning over and under, over and under. Pat, pat, pat. I flattened out the small balls of masa and placed them on the clay cooker over the fire. The room became warmer. My eyes stung from the flames.

My name wasn't Rosalba. Mamá wasn't my real mother. Everyone knew. They had to. In our hamlet of Chal, everyone knew everything about everyone, as soon as it happened. Wherever people gathered—at the river washing clothes, drawing water at the public well, at church, in the plaza—news traveled fast. Why didn't anyone tell me? Tío Eldon said they didn't want me to feel different, but I had always felt different, anyway.

Sometimes I thought Mamá was angry at me for reasons I didn't understand, or for no reason. She blamed me if the fire went out, or if we didn't have enough tortillas. Maybe the reason was that I hadn't come out from her. I wasn't the same.

I tossed my finished tortillas into a neat stack in the basket and covered them with a clean cloth. Mamá brought Isabel to the table and as they brushed by me, I felt myself pull back. I couldn't help it. Who was she, if she wasn't my mother?

The girls and Daniel joined us at the table and pulled out chairs. We lowered our heads and thanked God for His blessings.

The next morning, I returned from the tortilla mill and found Tío Eldon on the path again, leaning on his cane. We were halfway between the mill and home, with trees and no people around us.

"You're a smart girl, Rosalba," he said. "Do you know what the word 'collaborate' means?"

I shook my head.

"It means when people work together. It means you can earn money to help your Mamá." His hand was in his pocket and then in front of me. A Chiclet sat in the middle of his palm.

"Someone in Chal is aiding the guerrillas," he said. "Selling them loaves of bread. We're paying four hundred quetzales to whoever tells us his name."

Who had that much money? I glanced down to Eldon's palm. Against it, the Chiclet looked bright white. "Nobody talks to guerrillas," I said.

"Somebody does." He shook his palm. The Chiclet jumped. "Take it."

If I took the Chiclet, he might think I agreed to do what he said. To collaborate. If I didn't take it, I might appear disrespectful. Pinching together two fingertips, I picked up the Chiclet, without touching any part of his hand. I slipped it into the pocket of my apron to save for later.

"Thank you," I said.

I didn't know why he asked these questions. Whichever was closest to Chal was in charge at that moment, the army or the guerrillas. We were caught between both.

SEVEN

SAN FRANCISCO, CALIFORNIA

APRIL 2004—SIXTEEN MONTHS AFTER THE SHUTDOWN

Only three people sat around the conference table for the weekly ideas meeting: Julie, with her pen and yellow legal tablet; Dr. Conrad, sheathed with her odor of cigarette smoke; and Eames. Doni brought in the tray of coffee and pastries that was delivered every Monday from the French patisserie around the corner and set it on one end of the table. The curtains on the large window were opened to the gray morning light, and in the sculpture garden, three men from the maintenance crew were breaking down tables and stacking chairs from the wedding the night before.

"Did you bring the magazine?" Dr. Conrad asked Doni as her assistant set a cup and saucer in front of the director, poured her coffee, and stirred in half-and-half and two sugars.

Doni nodded, laying out a linen napkin before holding up the latest issue of *ArtNews*. The cover featured a photo of the Bilbray Institute in La Jolla, an oceanfront gallery about the size of the Clay, located smack in the middle of San Diego's exploding biotech corridor.

Dr. Conrad snatched the magazine from Doni and threw it down in front of Julie and Eames. "San Diego's a cultural backwater. Explain to me how the Bilbray has expanded."

Julie and Eames squirmed uneasily. Newcomers to California often underestimated the cultural landscape of San Diego, overlooking its vibrancy. They saw beach, they saw palm trees, and could only conclude backwater.

Julie reached for the magazine and flipped through the pages. It was a twelve-page spread in the middle of the book, with before-and-after construction photos, aerial shots, and details from the galleries: customized niches for sculptures and yards and yards of wall space for monumental paintings. An entire page was dedicated to a Q and A with the Bilbray director.

The Clay's expansion had been featured in a similar spread several years earlier, and the magazine ran an in-depth profile of Dr. Conrad when she was named director. Julie didn't point out any of that as she passed the magazine to Eames.

"I was hired to make rain," Dr. Conrad said. "That's who I am. The president's going to read this"—she grabbed the magazine back from Eames and shook it again—"and he's going to ask me what we're doing to keep up."

The low buzz from the recessed lighting was the only sound. Doni picked up the coffee pot to top off Dr. Conrad's cup, but the director hadn't yet taken a sip. Nobody had. Doni set down the pot and rearranged the cream and sugar on the tray. The room was getting brighter, the sun peeking out from a pile of cushioned clouds and sending a ray over the Calder and into the conference room.

"The endowment's getting a good return," Eames said. The endowment was the stockpile of cash that generated interest dollars to pay for daily operations. Dr. Conrad's eyes bulged behind her red eyeglass frames. "That's your trust fund mentality talking. Think again, Eames."

Eames closed the magazine. "Are we brainstorming ways to raise money?" Julie asked.

"We're always brainstorming ways to raise money," Dr. Conrad said.

Julie muttered something and Dr. Conrad leaned toward her. "Excuse me? I couldn't hear what you said."

"I said, I thought we brainstormed ways to show good art."

Dr. Conrad sat back with deliberation, sipped from her coffee cup, sputtered and set it down. "This is cold. Take it away and get me a fresh cup."

Doni appeared at the director's elbow and whisked away the offending cup and saucer. Julie doodled hatch marks on her legal tablet, creating an abstract design that grew into the shape of the Clay.

Doni returned with a steaming cup of coffee, set it before Dr. Conrad, and stirred in cream and sugar. Eames sat with his chin in his hand. "The Bilbray had oodles of land to expand into," he said. "We've maxed out our footprint."

Julie sketched the façade of the building, the low, elegant, glass box structure amid tall condo towers. Eames was right. They'd built out to every available inch. Unless they bulldozed the sculpture garden, the Clay had nowhere to go.

"If we want more space, we'll have to move," Julie said. "South of Market. It's the hip new place."

"The new ballpark is there," Eames said.

"Aren't we obligated to this site?" Dr. Conrad asked.

"The terms of the gift were about keeping the collection intact," Julie said. "The terms don't specify where."

Dr. Conrad pulled the tray of pastries toward her and broke off a piece of croissant. She dipped it in her coffee and chewed silently. "And this is paid for how? To circle back to our original question."

Eames pulled on his bottom lip. "If we moved, we could lease our space to another non-profit."

Dr. Conrad groaned, breaking off another piece of croissant. Most non-profits were as cash-poor as the Clay. Julie drew the museum from another perspective and sketched in the Calder. She remembered the day the crane rolled in to install it. Television crews everywhere and Talbot all over the evening news. They'd sacrificed so much to get through the expansion, and the Clay's location was prime. Julie hated to throw that away. She moved her pen and drew a shelf-like structure above the museum, and over that, layered horizontal stacks. There was more than one way to expand.

"What about up?" Julie pointed her pen toward the ceiling. "Vertical."

"The Landmarks Commission will never allow it," Eames said. "It destroys the building's integrity. You know that."

"What if we sell our air rights? A developer buys the rights and builds a condo tower on top of us."

Eames raised his eyebrows, nodding slowly. Doni hovered with a tea towel behind him, also nodding. Dr. Conrad picked up her coffee cup, sipped, and set it down carefully into the saucer, wiping off a red lipstick print with her napkin. "Go on."

"We expand up into the lower floors and build an escalator to connect the two spaces. The condo tenants upstairs pay our mortgage."

Dr. Conrad pushed her cup and saucer away and folded her napkin onto the table. She turned Julie's yellow legal tablet toward herself and studied it for a moment. "May I take this?"

Julie tore the sheet from her tablet and handed it to the director. And with that brief and simple exchange of paper, selling the air rights became Dr. Conrad's idea.

*

> GUATE PARENTS
> Call, write letters to your Senator. Harass, harass, harass.
>
> Anyone get PINK this week? Where are we?
>
> Amber waiting on Ella asked me to tell everyone she lost her referral, is starting adoption in Uganda. Blessings to all.

Nobody understood the unique agony of waiting for a child except other parents who were waiting. They banded together on Guate Parents and updated one another obsessively.

The old days of timelines that stretched to ten months seemed ludicrous, enviable. Their infants developed into toddlers, their toddlers to little boys and girls. They became experts at finding cheap flights and prided themselves on quoting inter-country adoption law chapter and verse. When they returned to Guatemala to visit, they buttered up nannies and foster mothers with gifts of blue jeans and Nikes and prayed their kids recognized them.

When Julie overheard Doni talking about her to a cluster of artists at an opening, saying Julie should give up, it was hopeless, Julie didn't acknowledge Doni for two weeks. Walked right by her into Dr. Conrad's office or at the sink in the restroom without saying hello.

When Claire called and said, "Gunther's walking, he's babbling, and by the way, when are you getting that kid?" Julie didn't return her sister's calls or emails for a month. It was too painful. As much as Julie wanted to be a good sister and even better auntie, she couldn't. Claire doted on Gunther, lived for that boy, as she should, just as Julie lived for Juan. Julie didn't want to drag her sister down. And with her long hours at the Clay, Julie had no energy to drive to Fresno to visit. She felt terrible that Gunther was two and she'd only seen him once, on his first birthday.

If only Juan weren't so far away. If only the adoption would get finished. No adoptions were getting finished. Every case was stalled. No explanation was given by the Guatemalan government. The process simply stopped. The parents whose children's cases remained in the pipeline dubbed themselves "The 600." Even the U.S. Embassy couldn't give the group an exact number of how many cases were stalled. The number six hundred covered all possibilities. Only one impulse drove them: to get their children out.

Over the next year, Julie and Mark flew to Guatemala three times, suitcases stuffed with gifts for Berta and clothes for Juan in bigger sizes. They spent a long weekend over Easter, Juan's August second birthday week, and the week between Christmas and New Year's, when the Clay's offices and Mark's lab were shuttered. Their private joke was they'd accumulated premier status on United and seen nothing except the inside of the airport and the hotel. Only from watching the news were they aware that narcos controlled the country and gangs infested Guatemala City, three hundred bus drivers were assassinated every year for failure to pay kickbacks, and ninety-nine percent of crimes went unprosecuted.

Juan often arrived with a minor ailment: a cough or slight fever, a mild case of pink eye. Nothing that two Tylenol and a tube of ointment couldn't clear. Mark attributed the bugs to *hogar* living, reassuring Julie their son would be fine once they got him home.

Their visits followed a pattern. Breakfast in the Marriott restaurant with Juan and any other American families in residence. Juan's morning nap, while Mark answered emails and Julie socialized with the other mothers, catching up on the latest shutdown updates. Who was in, who was out, did anyone get pink? Lunch, delivered to the hotel by Domino's or Little Caesar's, and Juan's afternoon nap. Dinner, again, in the Marriott restaurant. The best was when Emily and Jake were there with Gabriela, or Rachel and Matthew with Carmen, or Kayla with Mia or Grace with Argelia. The presence of so many other Guate Parents meant no one was getting out. At least Julie wasn't falling behind.

She was tempted to move to Guatemala permanently—several women in the hotel had stayed for months and told her of others who rented apartments in the small city of Antigua—but they couldn't afford that. Although life with Dr. Conrad as boss became more challenging by the day, she needed to keep her job to pay for Juan's *hogar* care, vaccinations, medical check-ups, plus airplane flights, hotel, and meals.

Julie didn't care how much it cost. To watch Juan toddle on stiff legs, reach for her nose, splash in the baby pool, she'd spend their last dollar. He liked polenta and papaya, mashed up champurrada cookies served at the hotel's Sunday buffet, and watching Plaza Sésamo. The hotel's only acknowledgement of the Christmas season was a wooden Nativity scene by the concierge desk in the lobby. Juan liked a Wise

Man and the Baby Jesus, and they took pictures of him playing with both.

On day six, they had to return him to Berta, and afterward, Julie's arms felt useless, the hotel room unnaturally quiet. She posted on Guate Parents:

> At the Marriott, again. Missing him already.
> —*Julie C.*
>
> Be grateful you're there. Too expensive for us to travel. :-(
>
> A gift he's in good hands with a loving nanny.
>
> Eight trips for us. Second mortgage LOL. Got permission for our son's eye test. Now understand why he kept bumping into furniture!
>
> Just missed you guys. Tears to leave her, and we've got two others at home. Remember this time is not wasted, you're building a bank account of trust with your child.
> — *Charla T., MSW. Mom to a Guate kiddo in process, two foster-adopts*

The Guatemalan government released the children in spurts. Nothing happened for months and then half a dozen cases finished. There was no pattern. Nothing moved, until a chunk of it did. The chat boards lit up with announcements from relieved and ecstatic parents. "God is Good!" "Persistence Pays Off!" "Oh, Happy Day!" Local TV stations in Minnesota or Kansas or Massachusetts broadcast the homecomings at the end of the evening news and proud moms and dads circulated the links.

Rachel and Matthew, with Carmen, posted from Albuquerque. Julie sat at her desk and replayed the footage until she had it memorized: The weary yet triumphant parents emerging from the airport gate to baggage claim. The adorable, baffled Carmen clutching their hands, blinking at the camera crew and lights and soaring airport ceiling. The aunts and uncles and neighborhood kids who, upon spotting the returning heroes, waved their balloon bouquets and American flags and shook hand-lettered signs that cheered "Welcome Home!" "You Made It!" and "USA!"

The opening shots dissolved to B-roll of cute referral pictures, birthday cakes glowing with progressively more candles, the Marriott pool with Carmen in funny sunglasses and water wings, and overhead shots of grim Guatemalan neighborhoods far from the hotel, with razor wire fences and police officers armed with automatic weapons. Finally, the perky reporter traded quips with the anchorman as she wiped away a single tear, peppering her comments with words like "Third World," "corruption," and "Forever Families."

Although Julie's insides churned with a bitter stew of solidarity and envy, she couldn't turn away. What did Rachel and Matthew know that she didn't? What magic did they possess and how could she get some? Was there someone she needed to pay off?

Sometimes after watching one of the newscasts, Julie took out a calculator and estimated the number of bureaucratic work hours that had transpired since the shutdown began. She tried to imagine how it was possible to drag out a process so long. Say a Guatemalan social worker logged thirty hours a week, for forty weeks per year, factoring in generous vacation and legal holidays. That was twelve hundred hours annually. For one employee. And surely many more than one was assigned to handle adoptions. The process trapped them like a never-ending loop of changing rules and regulations. She wondered if this was the Guatemalan government's way of getting back at the United States for its political meddling, beginning with Jacobo Arbenz humiliated in his boxers back in 1954. The children stuck in the pipeline were collateral damage.

Julie sent off volleys of emails to California's two senators and her district representative, following up with phone calls and more emails. She signed petitions to the presidents of Guatemala and the U.S. One of The 600 solicited funds for a documentary he was making about the abysmal state of international adoption. She mailed a check.

Juan Rolando turned three. They flew down for his birthday and celebrated at the Marriott. He was able to run and say more words, in Spanish and a sprinkling of English. He called them *Mommy* and *Daddy*. When he put his little hand in Julie's to motor to the restaurant or pool, her heart melted. He had two rows of square little teeth. He still liked papaya and champurradas, but not as much as the tres leches birthday cake they served for his birthday.

Kate assured her the lawyer was doing everything possible and that Juan was in the best *hogar*, cared for by Berta, the best *niñera*. Kate reminded her it could be so much worse. He could be in a state-run orphanage with no staff, peeling paint on the walls, and swill for meals. A place straight out of Oliver Twist instead of his beautiful *hogar* with a *niñera* who doted on him.

Sometimes Julie stood in the doorway of the room they'd finally felt brave enough to prepare and imagined him playing with the mobile of a crescent moon and yellow stars. She saw herself sitting in the rocking chair and serenading him. She'd arranged a montage of photos from their visits on the wall and in each one she noticed slight changes and the progression of time. He'd been so tiny when they first met and was getting to be a bigger boy.

*

Julie learned of the Guatemalan government's latest stumbling block the way she learned everything important about adoption: on Guate Parents.

"Listen to this," she said to Mark, reading to him from her laptop after a late dinner at home on a Thursday night.

JUNE 2006

The new buzzword is REUNIFICATION. As in, reuniting baby with family.

Nobody wanted Toño before. Why now?

Heysel's three years old and (finally) recognizes us.

They had their chance!

Suddenly, the family situation is stable?

Birth mothers were being questioned to determine if they'd decided to keep their baby, or if anyone in the extended family was able to take custody. Charla T. heard the government was paying birth mothers to say they changed their minds.

"They keep moving the finish line," Mark said.

Julie kept reading. "The 600 are sponsoring a vigil in D.C., at the Guatemalan Embassy. We should go."

"When is it? I can't take more time off."

"They're calling it a Stroller Brigade." Julie ignored Mark's protests. "Everyone pushes an empty stroller to symbolize a child who's waiting."

Two Fridays later, Julie and Mark strode through a nearly deserted SFO at four -thirty in the morning, Julie pushing Juan's empty stroller to gate check. "You forget something?" an astonishing number of people asked—in the security line, ordering breakfast, while waiting for the aircraft.

Julie usually made a joke, except when she made the mistake of explaining the shutdown to a man sitting beside her at the breakfast counter.

"You know governments hate to be told what to do," the man said.

"Ours or theirs?"

"Both," the man said. "You push, they push harder."

Julie shifted uneasily, wishing she could trade seats with Mark.

"Fight the good fight," the man said, raising a fist as he left for his flight. Julie raised a fist in return.

They'd never participated in an organized protest. Nothing had meant so much to them before. Adoption wasn't something they'd spent their lives planning to do, but they were committed now. Juan was their son. There was no turning back.

They emerged from the Metro onto a sidewalk lined with a canopy of trees. The air was warm, almost balmy. The early evening sun cast long shadows of lace. Ahead of them, two other couples also pushed empty strollers.

They walked toward the Guatemalan Embassy, toothbrushes and pajamas stuffed in a single backpack, stroller wheels rumbling over the sidewalk. The street in front of the embassy was cordoned off, and from the corner a block away, they saw the glow of hundreds of candles, heard the chanting of hundreds of voices in call and response.

"What do we want?"

"Justice for children."

"When do we want it?"

"Now!"

"What will we do?"

"We won't give up, we'll never give up. We won't give up, we'll never give up," the voices cried.

Julie got goosebumps. She'd never been a person to raise her voice—she didn't even sing along to the radio—yet found herself pushing her stroller to the rhythm and joining in: "We won't give up, we'll never give up," she yelled, with Mark chanting beside her.

They crossed the street. From the edge of the crowd, she stood on tiptoe to see the embassy steps. Framed baby pictures were leaned against the lower steps, reminding Julie of a disaster scene with photos of the missing. Empty strollers filled the top steps like a row of gravestones, each empty seat a forlorn memorial. Candles set in candelabras flickered, each a tribute to a child, alone and afraid. The steps were an altar and a monument, a reminder of families kept apart. And the gathered parents were their people, the ones who understood. If Julie and Mark could have hugged and consoled each one of them, they would have.

"Julie from the Marriott? Mark, is that you?" A woman touched Julie on the shoulder. It was Emily, of Emily and Jake, and with her, Kayla and Grace. "You came all the way from California? How's Juan? Any news?"

"You need a candle," Emily said, giving one to Julie. Julie grasped it tenderly, as though it were Juan himself, cupping her hand around the wick, protecting the flame from the movement of people around her.

She watched the smoke unfurl into the sky as a black cloud and sent up a silent wish. *Keep Juan safe. Let him know we love him.*

The leader of The 600 spoke into a microphone. "Please tell the person beside you the name of your child and how old they are. Please share with the person beside you how many years you've been waiting."

The parents turned to one another, eager to tell stories of their children. No matter how long it took, or what paper the government demanded, what obstacle they invented, the parents would never ever stop fighting.

"We won't give up. We'll never give up. We won't give up. We'll never give up."

As Julie talked about Juan, she suddenly remembered Felix, dropped back into the system. They said he was being returned to family, but who knew where he ended up? She imagined Felix in a crib, crying and crying, finally falling silent because nobody heard him.

She would never abandon Juan to the same fate.

*

The museum still hadn't found a tenant willing to lease airspace atop the Clay. The Landmarks Commission had threatened to pass a bill outlawing any construction that lacked a solid foundation, citing earthquake concerns. Worse than that, the economy was smack in the middle of a full-on recession. Never one to admit defeat, Dr. Conrad initiated a capital campaign and continued to fundraise for the second expansion. Easier to ask for forgiveness than permission, she said. The first bulldozer would roll in before Landmarks had a chance to say no. But the museum wasn't close to meeting the goal.

The board was concerned enough to call a special meeting. Two banquet tables were set in the atrium for luncheon to be served. Everyone was there, even members who were seldom seen: the oldest of old money, the fifth-generation developers whose surnames graced signs on San Francisco streets, the gold rush heirs and land barons. Dr. Conrad stood at the head of one table and tapped a silver teaspoon against the rim of her Limoges coffee cup. The room quieted as board members scraped their chairs in the direction of the podium while waiters circumnavigated the tables, removing luncheon plates to make space for dessert. Julie and Eames stood in the back of the room, Eames with a camera to document the event for the society pages and Julie with her yellow legal notepad.

"We've raised six million dollars, no small feat on the Left Coast," Dr. Conrad said. Her scorn for the West Coast's reputed lack of *noblesse oblige* was one of Dr. Conrad's repeated themes. "But allow me to say how impressed I am with those in this room. Your pockets are deep and I'm grateful."

Julie took a step closer to Eames and whispered, "Smooth."

"Finishing school polish," Eames whispered back.

On the screen behind Dr. Conrad, a slide of the proposed remodel materialized, the cantilevered tower hovering over the gallery like a Damocles sword ready to lacerate the Clay roof at the first tremor. It wasn't one of Julie's best ideas, and she frankly never expected it to take hold. But life was like that. A thing started small and gained momentum and grew into something else.

A hand was raised and Julie recognized the elderly yet surprisingly well-preserved Orrin Clay, the man who'd deeded the property to the museum in the 1980s and whose private collection formed the core of the museum's holdings. "With all due respect, Dr. Conrad, I think we should consider tabling the second expansion plan, at least temporarily. This isn't the climate."

A murmur rose from the other board members. Dr. Conrad cleared her throat, a muddy, gurgling sound. "I think you're right, Orrin. I thought so from the start, when Julie Cowan suggested the idea."

Julie snapped to attention. *Julie Cowan?* Dr. Conrad continued. "What did I know? I was the new kid on the block." Her voice, joking.

The board members turned to one another and started talking at once. Then, a few rotated to glance toward Julie, a piece of driftwood cast onto shore from a turning tide.

"What the hell?" Eames said.

Julie plastered on a grin and kept it in place. Should she wave to acknowledge the attention? She nodded as if accepting accolades, still grinning. She wanted only to flee from her humiliation.

Dr. Conrad took more questions while Julie ducked out of the room and rushed through the galleries to her desk. She called Mark, fuming. "Conrad threw me under the bus. Everyone hates the expansion idea. Now she's saying it was my idea all along."

Silence from Mark. "Wasn't it?"

"Yes. Yes, it was. One of my many ideas. I never thought it would fly. She's blaming me."

"Can we discuss this tonight? I've got an intern here with a question."

"An intern with a question. By all means."

She hung up, pushing her yellow legal pad against her office wall, resting her head against it. Mark hadn't even noticed her sarcasm. Sometimes he was so out of touch. She couldn't worry about Mark and his shortcomings now. She needed to focus on salvaging her reputation and keeping her job so she could get Juan out of Guatemala.

Except she couldn't focus. Not now. She dashed off a note explaining her absence and taped it to her computer screen. She ran to the street and jumped on a bus to Mark's office, not sure what to say to him except "I need you." *I need you to listen to me, I need you to hold me, I need you to understand how hard it is for me to get through my days without our baby*. Maybe she hadn't made that clear. Maybe Mark was also suffering. Juan was his baby, too. Maybe she'd been too obsessed with the adoption to see it.

She stared out the window as restaurants and storefronts whizzed by. She remembered a day she'd won a certificate at school for "Best Artist" and was sitting on stage with other award-winners. She kept scanning the audience, expecting to see her mother, but never did. Nobody clapped extra loudly, just for her, when she walked across the stage to shake the principal's hand. After school, she'd gone home and found her mother in bed asleep, a cigarette smoldering in the ashtray on the night table beside her. When Julie picked it up to snuff it out, the long ash broke off like a dried twig.

Her mother never protected them. Julie was going to be different.

She hurried through the lobby of the lab. Stations of hand sanitizer were fixed to the wall every few yards. As she waited for the elevator, she rubbed the recommended pea-size glob between her two hands. A young man in a lab coat appeared beside her and rubbed sanitizer up to his elbows.

"Are you here to see someone?" he asked.

"Mark Cowan."

"He's in my lab, on seven. And you are?"

"Julie Cowan. His wife."

"Mark's married?" The man moved his forearms through the air to evaporate the sanitizer. "Dang. I didn't know."

For the second time in less than an hour, Julie plastered on a grin while the man held open the elevator with his foot.

She and Mark met sixteen years ago, in May of Julie's junior year at UC Davis. Groggy from a late night finishing a drawing project, ten minutes before the start of her morning shift as tray girl in the dining hall kitchen, Julie was parking her bicycle in the rack outside the building. Everyone rode bikes on the bucolic Davis campus, and the rack was crowded with students vying for space. Mark had ridden up and skidded to a stop, swinging his leg over the bar and nosing his wheel into the rack.

"I'm sorry. Did I take your spot?" Mark asked, instead of edging out her wheel like so many people did when in a hurry.

"Not at all," Julie said, flustered. She was about to re-set her bicycle wheel when Mark reached for the rack to stop her. A spider had spun a web in a corner of the slot Julie was aiming for. Droplets of moisture clung to the delicate threads and shone like mirrors.

"Nature's perfect design," Mark said, as Julie shifted her wheel over to another spot.

"Are you in the design department?" Julie asked. She'd transferred to Davis that fall from a two-year junior college and between school, dining hall shifts, and her duties as a teaching assistant, hadn't met many people.

"I wish I were that creative. I'm in the medical school. Pathology. I stare through a microscope."

"So you're a visual person."

"I guess I am." His face brightened, and in that split second, Julie saw his blue eyes were kind. He had a softness. Julie wasn't used to that. Most people she'd met at Davis were competitive and hard-edged, with eyes to match.

Julie unsnapped the strap on her helmet and clipped it onto her handlebars. "I once saw a leaf under a microscope. All the little cells moving. It was like cars on a racetrack."

"Exactly. What about you?"

"Studio Art. Drawing and Painting."

"That explains the outfit," Mark said.

Julie was wearing one of her thrift store purchases, a black cotton kimono embroidered with large colorful birds. She'd never seen another one like it anywhere on anyone. They secured their bikes to the rack and walked together toward the dining hall.

Mark held open the door. The smell of freshly baked bread and cheese omelets enveloped them. Free meals were the perk of her work-study scholarship Julie most cherished. She ate well at Davis. She reached into her backpack for her apron while Mark pulled out his meal card. Groups of students straggled in behind them. Julie heard her name being called from across the room, saw her manager waving a hand to get her attention.

Mark leaned toward her, not much taller than she was. "Weren't you in the Medical Illustration class in the Science Building? Last semester."

"I was," Julie said. "How did you know?"

He touched the sleeve of her kimono, his hand lingering a second more than necessary. "I recognized the birds. And your hair. It's shorter than most."

Julie didn't want the conversation to end, but her shift was about to begin.

"To be continued?" Mark said, and Julie agreed.

A few nights later, they sat in Mark's studio apartment sharing take-out and drinking beers by candlelight. The place looked like the quintessential bachelor pad, or maybe just the home of a distracted scientist: unwashed frying pan on the counter and a glob of toothpaste in the bathroom sink. Still, he'd tried: a dozen red roses sat in a vase on the kitchen table.

Every few minutes the building's intercom buzzed, followed by a tromping of footsteps in the hall. Music blared from somewhere close by. Mark's long-time girlfriend had recently broken up with him, he told Julie. "She hated my long hours," he said. "It wasn't meant to be."

Which Julie was glad to hear, because Mark had those alluring blue eyes and was the most normal, stable guy she'd ever met. She'd never had a relationship that didn't go down in flames.

"My last boyfriend accused me of being too sensitive," she confessed. "He referred to me as 'the raw nerve.'"

Mark pushed the take-out boxes to one side of the table. Candlelight flickered across his face as he traced a thumb across her mouth. "What did he expect? You're an artist."

Julie snapped out of her reverie and stepped into the elevator. The man pressed the button for the seventh floor.

"Mark is absolutely married," she said. "Happily so."

EIGHT

GUATEMALA/CALIFORNIA

AUGUST 2006

Julie and Mark loved the pool and restaurant at the Marriott, but for Juan's fourth birthday on August 1, they wanted the day to be extra special. Kate said they would be permitted to spend a morning at the Guatemala City Zoo, provided they hired a taxi driver recommended by the Marriott. The zoo was less than a mile away, near La Aurora Airport and close enough to walk, but Kate refused to take chances by letting the Cowans loose in the city.

One of the other families joined them—Emily and Jake, and their daughter, Gabriela. They'd just gotten pink, and tomorrow would get Gabriela's Guatemalan passport to travel. Emily kept reassuring Julie they'd get pink soon, and Julie kept agreeing, if only to make Emily feel less uncomfortable for being finished.

Like the airport, the zoo had been updated recently and was modern and clean. The animals roamed freely in large, enclosed environments that were secured by plates of thick glass. No cages for them. Juan and Gabriela ran from savanna to bog to rain forest and pressed their faces against the glass. The giraffe's long tongue, the hippos' enormous toenails, the tigers' shoulder muscles like rippling waves. Even the turnstile that led into the aviary was a marvel to behold.

"Wowee," Juan said over and over, making Gabriela laugh as he imitated the phrase Julie used often when teaching him English.

"They're just like regular kids," Julie said, and the two mothers embraced at the simple gift. When they pulled apart, Emily asked, only half-facetiously, "Do you believe in arranged marriages? Because I do."

They wondered how they got so lucky, out of all the children in the world, to get two who were so smart, so handsome and pretty, so engaging and happy. And this was without years of Gymboree and Baby Mozart, near-birthrights for kids born in the United States. They counted their blessings.

Around noon, it was time for pizza and Juan's birthday cake. The moms settled the kids at a table in the food court while the dads went to Domino's to order a few pies. The taxi driver sprinted out to the van to bring in the cooler with the tres leches cake, a requirement for Guatemalan birthdays according to him. After the pizza was finished, Julie put in four candles and led them in "Happy Birthday." The taxi driver started in with the Spanish version, *Feliz Cumpleaños*. When they got to the final lines—*we want cake*—the driver followed Guatemalan tradition and sped up and applauded. Mark stood behind Julie and wrapped her in his arms as they witnessed it: their son joyful, celebrating with friends and family, blowing out candles on his fourth birthday.

*

Juan was four years and four months old when Kate's phone number flashed on caller ID. Mark and Julie were sprawled on the family room couch watching *It's a Wonderful Life*. Their Christmas tree was decorated with ornaments, including the limited-edition one depicting a multi-hued family and stamped *Formed in our Hearts.*

"Is he out?" Julie asked without preamble, pressing the button for speaker phone.

"I won't leave you hanging." Kate went silent, as if rooting around for the right words.

"Hello? Are you there?" If Kate wasn't going to leave them hanging, why was she leaving them hanging? "Is Juan okay?" Julie and Mark asked in unison.

"Juan's fine." Kate stopped. "But he's not out. In fact." She cleared her throat and started over. "For reasons I don't understand, a judge has ruled that Juan be put in what the court calls protective custody. Meaning, on Monday they will transfer him from the private group home to a state-run orphanage, Love the Child."

"What? Why?"

"Reunification. You've heard of it? Returning kids to their biological families. Even though Juan's mother, Karla Inez, has submitted the required signatures saying she wants him adopted. The judge is ignoring that."

Juan was hurtling away from them, unprotected, into a black hole. Why were the courts moving children from a stable *hogar* with familiar nannies to institutionalized care? Not because it was cheaper. The families paid for everything. Julie was seized with dread. "Why are they moving him anywhere except here?"

"They never give reasons. They just act."

Mark interrupted. "Do they think the birth mother might change her mind?"

Julie stared at Mark, stricken. Change her mind? After four years? And they'd take him away? Not again, not Juan. Please no. There had to be a mistake. Juan was theirs. This was impossible.

"Can we at least visit?" Mark asked.

Once a month, Love the Child orphanage had a designated Family Day. Kate promised to email the address.

As soon as they hung up, Julie logged onto Guate Parents to ask if anyone else's child had been moved to Love the Child. Only Miriam from South Carolina responded:

> My son's in House of Angels. For a year. Kids are
> under ten there, not as bad as when there's teenagers.
> Praying for you.

Love the Child didn't allow visitors until February, two months away. Mark was flooded with cases at the lab, so Julie told Dr. Conrad she had a family emergency and booked a flight alone.

Eight weeks later, Kate's taxi driver, Carlos, picked Julie up at the Marriott in a white SUV with windows tinted a dense black. The orphanage was in a bad neighborhood, Kate said. She also told Julie that Carlos would be armed—this was a good thing—and as Carlos helped Julie into the passenger seat and closed the door, his black leather bomber jacket fell open, confirming that he was. His dyed hair was slicked back, and he wore steel-toed combat boots. His green aviator glasses were as opaque as the dark windows. His skin was Ladino light, clean-shaven. He looked like a Hollywood version of Special Ops.

Julie expected he would be the silent type but discovered the opposite. As they drove through the capital, he pointed out places of historic interest and locations of shops and shared his plan to introduce hot salted pretzels to Guatemala by opening an Auntie Anne's franchise. He told Julie his three children were enrolled in the city's international school and spoke English, and seven of his twelve siblings lived in the United States. "Near Kate," he said. "San Francisco Bay Area." His green aviators turned. "You know it?"

"The Golden Gate Bridge. Cable cars. Chinatown. I live there, too."

They passed through blocks of cement row houses with roll-down aluminum doors and streets full of dusty cars and packs of roaming dogs. They were deep in the Guatemala they saw on the news but had never experienced in the Marriott neighborhood. "Almost there," Carlos said.

A few blocks later, he yanked the steering wheel to the left and pulled up to a driveway in front of a cement wall with a massive steel door. Leaping out of the driver's seat with the engine running, he spoke into a keypad and the gate creaked open. A guard in an orange vest waved them in, and Julie turned to see the gate creak shut and the orange-vested man secure it with a steel bar.

A two-story concrete-block building stood at the end of a dirt driveway. Every window was barred. Although the orphanage housed sixty children, there was no physical evidence of children. No scattered toys, no bicycles laid on their sides waiting for a girl or boy to jump on and pedal. Aside from the dirt itself, the dirt courtyard was spotless.

Along the edge of the driveway, ten to fifteen teenage boys and girls sat on a low wall, leaning into each other and chatting, tossing pebbles at the ground, or simply staring at Julie as the car drove by. They were waiting for family to visit, Carlos explained with a gruff snicker. Except they never did. Not once had Carlos ever seen a relative visit the orphanage.

"Do you think they'll let me give him the cake and photo album?" Julie asked as they pulled into a parking spot. Juan loved tres leches cake. She'd brought another cake, along with a photo album of Mark and her on a hiking trail, in their garden, cooking at their kitchen stove.

Carlos dug the tip of one steel-toed boot into the dirt of the courtyard. "You can ask."

Orange Vest walked over and met them at the front door. "No photographs, no cell phone, no notebooks," he announced.

Julie lifted the cake box with the photo album on top of it. "Okay?"

The guard didn't say yes and he didn't say no. Instead, he held out his hand for her camera and cell phone and slid each one into a pocket of his orange vest. He held out his hand again and she gave him the photo album, wondering if she'd ever see any of those things again. He led them to the front door and selected a key from a ring clipped to his belt.

Inside smelled strongly of bleach. They skirted past three teenage girls with buckets, on their knees, silently washing the linoleum floor with wire brushes. Close by, an older woman stood and watched them, her expression critical. In the middle of the hallway, swinging doors were propped open with two bricks to show a large room filled with long industrial tables and benches. On the wall was a blackboard chalked with the Menú del Día: Lunes, Martes, Miércoles, Jueves, Viernes, Sábado: Arroz con Frijoles. It seemed like a nasty joke: beans and rice every day except Sunday when the word "pollo" appeared.

Where was the polenta and papaya, the scrambled eggs, the champurradas? Julie's hands tightened around the cake box. She knew Juan would like it.

The guard led them further down the hallway and unlocked another door. The waiting room was bare, the only furniture a couch covered in brown corduroy, flattened and shiny, and a scuffed wooden end table. Three narrow windows were closed and barred.

"Juan Rolando Garcia Flores, *claro?*" the guard said to Carlos, and when Carlos nodded, the guard spoke into a crackling walkie-talkie.

"I'll wait outside," Carlos said, and he and the guard left. Julie placed the cake on the end table and stood next to the corduroy couch. Years ago, she and Mark had visited Alcatraz and a Park Service warden locked them into a cell to simulate the experience of jail. When Julie heard that door slam shut, she had almost hyperventilated, banging on the metal and begging him to let her out; she had thought she was going to faint. She had the same feeling of light-headedness now, in the waiting room, of being locked in with no escape.

She forced herself to inhale, then exhale slowly on three long counts. She couldn't crumble. She needed to stay strong for her son.

A few seconds later, a stout woman in a blue apron appeared, leading Juan by the elbow. A shapeless gray jogging suit hung on the boy's frame. His head was shaved and his cheeks hollow. He saw Julie and stopped short.

"Mommy." He burst into tears. Julie reached for him, craving him, her hand just grazing his shirt before the caregiver jerked on his elbow and shushed him. Juan stopped crying, instantly. A shudder shot through Julie's body as Juan instantly obeyed, as if anticipating severe punishment if he didn't. Julie's instinct was to ask the woman, to tell her, to stop jerking and shushing Juan, but Julie sensed she'd only make her son's life more miserable if she did.

The caregiver left and Julie smiled bravely. She didn't want to scare him by being afraid. She hugged him close, and his backbones were like spines on a cactus.

"Tres leches?" she asked, slicing him a piece with the plastic knife she'd bought. She handed him a small square. He stuffed the entire piece into his mouth.

"*Más?*" Julie asked, but before he could answer, the caregiver returned, grabbing the box as though seizing illegal contraband.

"No food from outside," she said in Spanish, scowling. Was she spying on them? Had she seen Juan eating cake? Julie was outraged to realize the caregiver had been standing by to punish any infraction.

"*Para más tarde?*" Juan asked after the caregiver left. "For later?"

Julie couldn't bear to tell him what she suspected, that he would never see that cake again. That cake was as good as eaten, by people who weren't him. Julie just hoped Juan wouldn't be made to pay in other ways for her mistake.

They hadn't even sat down. Julie lowered herself to one end of the couch and Juan sat on the other. "How's the food?" she asked in Spanish.

Juan stuck four fingers in his mouth and licked off cake crumbs, then wiped his hands on the leg of his baggy pants. He shrugged.

"What is your room like?" At the *hogar*, he'd shared a room with five other kids, each in his own bed. A palace compared to this prison. He didn't answer.

"Are the other kids nice?" The orphanage housed kids from infants to teenagers. The kids in front looked like full-grown adults. Juan looked at the floor.

"Are you safe?" Julie's voice broke.

Juan's right index finger drifted to the tip of his nose, and he tapped himself over and over, his eyes vacant.

"Juan. Juan." Julie extended her hand across the middle couch cushion, and instead of reaching for it, Juan tucked his hands underneath himself and sat on them.

He was so vulnerable. There was no one here to protect him. Whoever was responsible for moving him here, Julie wanted to strangle with her bare hands. "Daddy says hello, and the house in California says hello, too," she whispered, wiping her eyes. She continued slowly, translating to Spanish in her head. "We have a nice garden. Hummingbirds fly from flower to flower." She flapped her arms fast to demonstrate. "Do you know about crows? The crows are very naughty." She opened her eyes wide. "You know about the fruit named cherry? Small, round, red fruit, very sweet. The crows eat them. And the gophers eat our strawberries and tomatoes. All our strawberries and tomatoes."

She called into the ground, chewing noisily. "Hey, guys, leave some for us." She winked. "These guys have gotten *tan gordito*, very chubby."

"Are there bunnies?" he asked with a shy smile. Julie hopped her palms around the couch like little rabbits. "*Muchos. Muchos*!" One of Juan's hands crept out from under his legs and he reached for Julie. As soon as he did, the caregiver reappeared carrying Julie's cell phone, camera, and photo album, informing Julie their time was up.

*

Julie fell into her husband's arms at SFO, unleashing the torrent of tears she'd suppressed during the entire flight home. Leading her out of the traffic flow of passengers to a corner near the luggage carousel, Mark pulled out his phone to call Kate. Julie heard him repeat, "I understand, I understand." But Julie didn't understand. She didn't understand. Who decided to put him there and how could they get him out? She'd left her son in a harsh, abusive environment, with people who might do bad things to him, evil things. She grabbed Mark's arm. "Tell her. Tell her she must get him out of there. Tell her." Mark nodded, made a soothing expression with his face. Julie gaped at him, wild-eyed. She couldn't live with herself if she and Mark didn't do everything possible.

But it was *their system*, Kate said. *Their rules*. There was nothing to be done.

Kate emailed every few days to say she had no new information. On two weekends, Julie and Mark drove to Fresno, to see Claire and Ethan, and to hug Gunther. He was an active, curious, lively boy.

Julie wanted to develop a relationship with him, for herself, and to lay groundwork for a relationship between him and Juan. Claire and Ethan didn't ask questions. They were subdued around Julie, respectful, almost as if Juan had died. Julie distracted herself by working long days, partly to impress Dr. Conrad enough to not be fired and partly to fill the hours before bedtime. Anything to crowd out the memory of her son, stuffing cake into his mouth and stifling tears.

*

The Friday before Labor Day weekend, Julie was at her desk when Kate called. Julie heard only one word—"pink"— when a sound like she'd never made before rose up from within her, an animal-like keening. She felt hysterical, out of control, unable to rein herself in. She jumped up and down in place, not caring how unprofessional she appeared. Juan was five years and one month old.

Julie called Mark, who screamed with triumph. "We did it!" they congratulated each other. "Unbelievable!" She called Doni to leave a message for Dr. Conrad and sent an email to staff announcing the news. "OUT!" she wrote and became giddy whenever anyone offered their congratulations. The tremendous weight she'd carried for five years was lifted.

Childcare needed to be figured out. She'd take the full eight weeks the museum gave. Juan needed to be with her. Julie whipped out her yellow legal pad to write notes. She was ready for their life together to begin.

*

Conflicting emotions battled inside Julie as their airplane broke through the clouds and bumped down onto the short runway of La Aurora Airport. Excitement to be back to claim their son and bring him home. And loathing for the country that had punished him, and them, for years, and for what? As she said to Mark in the back seat of the Marriott shuttle, Julie hoped never again to set foot in this godforsaken nation. Even never would be too soon.

It still felt good to be recognized by the Marriott staff, who greeted the Cowans by name, asked about Juan, and filled them in on the status of other adoptive parents. Adoptions, new adoptions, had stopped years ago; adoptive families no longer overflowed downtown hotels. The only Americans were hangers-on like them who visited their children as often as they were able or permitted, until they got out.

The Cowans were required to meet their attorney on Wednesday morning in the judge's chambers in Courtroom Two of the Judicial Building in downtown Guatemala City. Another family had hired their driver, Carlos, so they hailed a taxi outside the Marriott during a break in one of the late rainy season's worst storms. There was no car seat, but what could they do? While traffic crawled through the city streets, water rushed past like a fast river. Storm drains either didn't exist or weren't functioning. Cars stalled and tires spun. People waited for buses in ankle-deep water.

The driver knew the way. Over the years, he'd driven many Americans to the courtrooms downtown. The gray stone Judicial Building was large and imposing, tiered like a pyramid. They passed through the metal detector and an officer patted them down.

The elevator whisked them upstairs and opened on a dark hallway. After Julie's eyes adjusted, she saw a row of closed doors, and in front of one of them, two figures, tall and short, a woman and a boy.

"Juan!" Julie's heart thumped as she raced down the hallway. Crouching, she pulled her son close. He felt thin and small, as if he'd eaten little in the months since she'd seen him. She leaned back to examine his face, so dear to her, so solemn and serious, and then Mark was crouching beside her, holding Juan's hands. "We missed you, we love you. You're our son forever," they said.

"You must be the Cowans. I'm Raquel."

Their lawyer was a woman, wearing stiletto heels and a turquoise-colored suit, wavy-haired and impeccably turned out. Julie and Mark stood to shake Raquel's hand. They'd never met their

Guatemalan lawyer, had never known a name. Kate was cagey about releasing specific information. Too many other Americans had contacted their lawyers directly, demanding answers and making threats. Kate refused to let her clients mess up their own cases by interfering.

"Thank you for everything," Mark said.

"The pleasure is mine." Raquel looked down at Juan, now clinging to Julie. "He's a good boy. He deserves a family."

Julie sucked air through her teeth, squashing her impulse to rant about the unfairness of it, the length of the process, the government's refusal to let them visit. Raquel looked up and down the hallway, past the Cowans, and over her shoulders. She leaned in confidentially. "Most Guatemalans won't adopt a stranger's child. If they do, they treat them like servants."

Julie blinked, not knowing how to respond. Mark nodded.

"Come," Raquel said. She patted Juan's head. "You're lucky, little ducky."

After everything he'd been through? Julie and Mark followed Raquel into the door marked Sala II.

The judge's chambers were small, empty of people except for a uniformed officer who stood by a door at the front of the room. A few feet away were a wooden desk with a gavel and a large rubber stamp on it, two plastic folding tables, and eight plastic folding chairs. Raquel directed the Cowans to sit in the chairs with Juan between them. Julie held Juan's hand, a part of her afraid he might bolt.

Soon after they were seated, the officer spoke. "Ladies and gentlemen. Please rise for the judge."

The judge emerged from the doorway, slipped behind the desk, and sat down, gesturing for them to do the same. His olive skin was as pale as Raquel's. After plucking a pair of wire-rimmed glasses from a pocket, he tapped the gavel and called the session to order.

He peered over his glasses before lowering his head to read from a thick printed document. The gist, as Julie understood it, was that although he, the judge, believed children should stay in Guatemala with blood relatives, Juan's case was different. Juan's mother had signed the necessary consents, and no relatives had stepped forward to claim him.

The judge addressed Juan. "Do you want Mark and Julie Cowan to be your parents?"

Julie turned to Raquel, rattled. The lawyer hadn't said anything about the judge asking Juan's permission. Juan nodded vigorously and in a clear voice said his first words of the day. That he wanted to go with them right this minute, *ahorrita*.

The judge pounded the rubber stamp across the front of every page of the document. He read out their names as Juan's legal parents, and passed the stack of documents to the officer, who slipped them into an envelope which he handed to Raquel. The judge tapped the gavel again, and it was finished. They were done.

Julie and Mark sat frozen, too choked with emotion to react. Was this really it? The officer instructed them to stand and the judge exited through the same door through which he had appeared. As the door closed, Julie and Mark hugged each other, still too overwhelmed to speak. They bent to hug Juan, their first hug as a legal family.

"Let's go, my friends," Raquel said. "Before he might change his mind."

She hustled them out of the chambers, down the hallway and elevator, and straight to the curb. The taxi driver, who had waited for them and was talking on his cell phone, clicked it off and motioned them in. Raquel gave Mark the envelope with the documents while the couple thanked her one last time. Mark jumped over the rain water at the curb, pooled like a shallow pond, and slid into the front seat while Julie opened the door to the back. She fumbled to buckle Juan with a seatbelt.

"Looks like you got what you came for," the driver said into the rearview mirror.

"We did," Mark said, pointing to Juan's seat-belted chest and holding up the envelope. Julie had brought Juan a stuffed gray rat which she didn't want to give him until they were safely underway. Claire's son Gunther had one and loved it. The rat was dressed in a vest and bowtie and sunglasses and carried a violin case.

Julie drew the rat out of her purse slowly, revealing his ears, his forehead, and finally his pointy face. "*Para mi*?" Juan said, touching his chest.

Julie pressed the rat's stomach. "You dirty rat," it said in a voice like an old-time mobster.

"Ratón talks," Juan said, incredulously. Julie turned to look out the window so he wouldn't see her crying.

"How about you adopt me next?" the driver said. "Take me to United States."

Julie pretended to laugh. She wanted to tell him adoption was harder than it looked. Then again, struggle was a natural part of the driver's life. Guatemalans had a word, *tramites*, which translated as paperwork, but sounded to Julie like "trauma." Citizens in Guatemala seemed used to it. Only Americans expected it to be otherwise.

The shoulders of the road remained flooded, with only two of four lanes opened. The cab moved slowly, as though through a flume. Julie felt claustrophobic. They still had to schedule a medical exam for Juan and get him his Guatemalan passport to travel. Their flight home was scheduled in four days. Juan twisted in his seat and held Ratón up to the back window so it could observe the puddles.

Suddenly, a policeman on a motorcycle drove alongside the driver's window, signaling him to pull over past the right lane.

"Is this about not having a car seat?" Julie said, worriedly. The cab drifted to a stop and the driver opened his window.

The policeman asked questions and the driver explained the hotel was up ahead two blocks. The policeman nodded toward Juan. "*Papeles? Pasaportes?*"

God, no. Julie was filled with alarm. They needed to present the documents to the U.S. Embassy to show they'd been approved by a Guatemalan judge. Mark passed the envelope to the driver who handed it to the policeman. He turned around in the seat and instructed Julie to give the officer what he'd asked for.

Julie dug in her purse for their passports, her hands shaking. She wanted Mark to say something, anything, to fix the situation, to argue, but naturally he couldn't. He didn't speak Spanish. Or the driver. The driver should say something.

She explained to the officer that Juan didn't have a passport yet, but here were passports for her and her husband. As she handed the blue passports through the window, she felt like she might throw up. The policeman dismounted from his motorcycle and kicked down the kickstand, passports and papers in hand. In his knee-high leather boots, he waded easily through the puddles to the curb, talking into his cell phone.

The rain was receding, and cars and buses drove past a little faster, with waves from their tires sloshing against the parked motorcycle and taxi. Pedestrians splashing past on the sidewalk stared into the windows. Fifteen minutes passed with no information and the policeman still on the phone. Juan sat quietly with his toy, not pressing him to make a sound, which impressed Julie. Kids she knew from the United States would be climbing over the seats and out the window, pressing Ratón until his battery ran out.

"Do you think he'd mind if I grabbed us a snack?" Mark asked the driver. "There's a Fast Gas up ahead with a *tienda*. Juan's probably hungry."

"Better if you give money to the policeman instead," the driver said, staring straight ahead.

"How much?" Mark asked.

"How much do you have?" Mark handed over his emergency stash of two hundred dollars in clean, new twenty-dollar bills, and the driver signaled the policeman. The envelope and passports were exchanged for the bills.

Later, in the hotel room, as Juan slept between them, they reviewed the scene. Mark reminded Julie the driver had been on the phone as they'd gotten settled and she buckled in Juan. The driver could have tipped the police then. "It's our fault for being trusting innocents," Julie whispered, not wanting to wake Juan. She reached across her son for her husband's hand. "Let's not let this ruin the happiest day of our lives."

NINE

SAN LORENZO CHAL, GUATEMALA

NOVEMBER 2010

Now I will tell you the story of my oldest sister, Marta, when she became a mother. My Testimonial continues.

When Marta was fifteen, she wanted to live in the house with her boyfriend, Jaime. At first, Mamá didn't accept this because Jaime's family lived in a house smaller than ours on the edge of Chal and were known to be poor. Jaime had four younger brothers and sisters. His father was a drunk. But Doña Yoly, who owned the *tienda,* told Mamá that Jaime worked hard milking Yoly's cows and keeping the chickens fed and the yard clean and Mamá began to think Jaime wasn't so bad.

Jaime was the same height as Marta, with strong arms and a sturdy back. When he came with his mother to discuss the arrangement, he reminded me of a bull because of his thick neck. His mother was thin like thread. Jaime said his papa didn't come because he was sleeping off guaro liquor from a celebration; for what, I didn't know.

Marta was not herself around her boyfriend, or was a different self. The Marta who belonged to us was a second mother when Mamá was too tired to pay attention. Every morning, the Marta who belonged to us reported for work with Doña Yoly and cared for Doña's children. She talked a lot. At month's end, she brought home quetzales to help pay the smuggler's debt for Papi Chelo. Not many quetzales, but enough to contribute.

This other Marta, the Marta around her boyfriend, didn't talk. This other Marta laid her head against Jaime's shoulder and held onto his arm. Not in front of his mother and Mamá, but outside where they couldn't see, or inside when they weren't looking. This other Marta covered her mouth with her hand to hide her words or her laugh.

The agreement was made and Marta and Jaime would become husband and wife.

All of Marta's belongings fit into one black plastic bag. Her woven wraparound *corte* and sash and two *hüipiles*, one for every day and one for holy feasts. Three pairs of underpants, enough so one pair could always be clean. Doña Yoly had bought for Marta one pair of brown sandals with low heels, to wear when going to the market or to drop off Doña's children at school. Those, Marta brought, too.

The tradition is for the *suegra*, or mother-in-law, to make for her new daughter-in-law a fresh apron, fancy with frills. Once she becomes a wife, a daughter-in-law's duties are in her new home. Soak the corn in lime and pat out the tortillas. Clean and cut up the chicken and boil the bones. Sweep the floor and carry in the firewood. Take care of the new husband. Make many children.

The apron Marta's *suegra* presented was frayed at the edges. I wondered if this was because the *suegra* was poor, or if it was a sign she didn't believe Marta would be a good wife. Marta tied on the apron as though it contained the finest needlework and thanked the *suegra* for the generous gift.

Another custom is for the girl to make a special meal for the family of her boyfriend before they're married. Most girls can cook and make tortillas. Marta cannot. This is because I cooked and made the tortillas. What was normal for our family was not normal in others. Before this day, the *suegra* never asked Marta to make her a meal. Maybe because the *suegra*'s husband was a drunk or maybe because the *suegra* preferred to cook herself. I don't know why Marta never made the meal, but she didn't.

We left before dark to take Marta to her *suegra's* house. Daniel ran ahead with a stick and I followed close to watch him. Far behind were Marta and Jaime, Yanira, Mamá with Isabel and the *suegra*.

Daniel had almost reached Jaime's house when he skipped back to me. "Puppies," he said in a singing way.

From far behind us, Mamá picked up a rock to throw, which is what we did when we saw a wild dog. "Sha," she called to Daniel. "It's dangerous."

I picked up a rock, too, and lifted my arm to throw until I got closer and saw that the puppies were spread across the path and not moving. Some of their eyes were closed, some of their eyes were half-opened. Around the edges of their pink mouths, some had a line of white coating. Their flesh seemed too big. The puppies that weren't dead would be, soon. Someone had left them to die.

Daniel leaned down. "Don't touch," I warned.

He straightened up, his face sad. "We should have come before."

Even if we wanted to, we couldn't feed starving puppies.

Mamá and the *suegra* came up behind us, breathing hard from walking fast. With a big toe, Mamá pushed the smallest puppies out of the way of the path. "Keep walking," she said. "It's better."

"How is it better?" Daniel asked. Mamá ignored him. "How Mamá?" Daniel asked again.

Mamá's arm reached out like a crow diving and twisted Daniel's ear. Daniel pulled away, his ear bright red.

"Good," said the *suegra*, nodding to show she approved. Mamá smoothed the front of her *corte* and pushed back her shoulders to look proud. Never before had Mamá twisted anyone's ear. She didn't want to be crossed in front of the *suegra*.

I stepped around the puppies and stood outside the *suegra's* door waiting for her to invite us inside. Four little children hid behind the pine trees nearby. The *suegra* opened the door and first Jaime entered, and then the rest of us. It felt strange to go into a place knowing we would leave behind Marta. Especially a place like this. There was only one room, with one wooden bed, so I wasn't sure where everyone slept. The bed didn't have a fabric mattress like ours, just a pile of straw across the bed slats. Maybe Marta was to share a bed with her new husband and her new *suegra*. Maybe the children slept on the floor. The room smelled like wet animal.

A rabbit with dirty fur hopped across the room. A rooster walked through.

They didn't have a brick stove. In the corner was a pile of sticks for cooking. Something moved near the pile of sticks. We shuffled our feet, fearing a rat. Only then did we see the hammock with the old woman curled inside, her bones like another pile of sticks. Daniel nudged me. I nudged back to show I saw.

"Good afternoon, *Abuelita*," the *suegra* said.

The old woman turned a little.

"I present my new daughter," the *suegra* said.

Marta stepped forward. The rest of us didn't move. Marta took another step and bowed. "Nice to meet you," she said.

Abuelita's cheeks were sunken. Her feet sticking out from under the edge of her *corte* looked like dried brown leather. A soft rattle came from *Abuelita's* chest, like pebbles being tossed in a gourd. "Her breathing is bad," the *suegra* said.

The rabbit hopped back across the room. Daniel reached down as if trying to touch its fur. "Sha," Mamá said. "Leave it."

Daniel stood up, holding his hands together.

The *suegra* turned from *Abuelita* to Marta and pointed at the sticks. "Here's the fire. And the *comal* for tortillas." The large griddle made of clay was split almost through with a crack. Next to it was a grinding stone. "Marta's tortillas are very good," Mamá said. "The best."

How would Marta fool her *suegra* to believe this was so? Lifting my eyebrows, I gave Marta a sign she could meet me at the tortilla mill and I would help her.

"I made boxbol," the *suegra* said. She reached for a plate on a shelf, and as she lifted it, a swarm of black bugs flew off. She presented a pile of corn meal rolled-up into green slimy squash leaves. The dish is usually served with boiled tomato salsa and toasted squash seeds, which the *suegra* didn't offer. I always accept food someone presents, yet hoped Mamá wouldn't make me. When the *suegra* held out the plate and Mamá took one, I knew I must, too. We didn't kneel on our heels. There were no chairs or straw mats. We ate standing up.

Mamá put her hand to her throat and swallowed. "Delicious. Thank you."

The rabbit edged close. Jaime tore off a bit of squash leaf and let it fall. The rabbit gobbled it up and moved away.

The door opened and the husband of the *suegra* stood with the light behind him, the outline of his straw hat like a bird on a post. The smell of corn alcohol and old clothes came in like a second person. Jaime's four younger brothers and sisters crowded behind their father.

"We should leave before it gets dark," Mamá said. She wiped her hands and mouth on her apron, then put her arms around Marta and patted her back. It was hard to believe we were going to walk out of that house and leave my sister behind. But we did.

The next Sunday, we didn't see Marta at church. As Padre Andrés recited the prayers during the Celebration of the Word, Daniel, Isabel, and I kept turning to look for her. After mass, we decided to walk to Marta's new house. As we approached, we saw Marta carrying a large plastic basket filled with wet clothes, a trail of four children behind her. When she saw us, Marta dropped the basket and came forward. She threw her arms around Mamá and started to cry.

"What is it?" Mamá asked.

Marta wiped her eyes with her fist. "I'm happy to see you."

I looked down and saw the heads of the two children closest to me were crawling with lice. I couldn't help it, but I stepped away.

"How is it?" Yanira asked. Marta looked toward the house.

"Where's Jaime?" Mamá asked.

"Inside," Marta said. "Maybe asleep."

"Let me help you." Yanira took up the basket of wet clothes.

"I can do it." Marta picked up a heavy wet *corte* and lifted it to the clothesline. As she did, she swayed backwards, almost falling.

"What is it?" Yanira said.

Marta pushed up the sleeve of the sweater she wore over her *hüipil.* The top part of her arm was purple and black. Yanira drew in air between her teeth. "Don't tell Mamá," Marta hissed. "I make the tortillas too slow. I need to learn to make them faster."

The front door opened and Jaime walked out. Marta stretched out a *corte* to pin along the clothesline.

"Can't the little girls help?" Yanira whispered.

"The girls are my responsibility. The boys too." Marta talked very fast. "I can't leave the house to go to the tortilla mill. I must use the stone and grind the corn by hand. It's slow. My palms start bleeding." She pulled the *corte* tight to hang straight on the line. Yanira reached for one of Marta's palms and Marta pulled it back. "Don't make it worse," she said. She stepped toward the house, calling, "Jaime. I am here."

Marta and Jaime were married. We saw Marta rarely after that. Sometimes at the market or the washing place, never at church. Mamá said Marta was part of Jaime's family now, just as Mamá had become a member of Papi's family. This we understood, yet we still worried about Marta.

Yanira and I believed Marta was under a spell and had no power to leave. Mamá believed living with Jaime was Marta's destiny. She needed to have a baby. We respected Mamá and what she said. Only God knew.

In a few months, Marta was expecting her first baby. When Mamá found out, she brought Aracely, the midwife, to the *suegra's* house to make sure the baby was in the right position. The *suegra* shook her fist at the midwife and told her to leave, she didn't have money to pay for another birth. Mamá told the *suegra* not to worry, she would take care of it and Aracely said she helped everyone, no matter if they could pay or not. The *suegra* refused. Mamá would not be stopped. She whispered to Marta that when the baby was close to coming, she should come home. Mamá and Aracely would help.

Aracely had helped Mamá with the birth of each of her six children. Marta, Yanira, Daniel, Isabel, and Josué and Marcos, the brothers who died from fever while working on the new road. I used to think seven children, but I changed that number to six after Tío Eldon said Mamá didn't birth me. I never asked Mamá myself. I think I didn't want to know.

Aracely carried special tools in a *morral*, the crocheted bag like the men wore—white thread to tie around the cord, scissors to cut it, matches and a candle to burn the cord's end. She gave Mamá a set of tools for herself. Everyone respected Aracely.

One day a few months later, I returned from the tortilla mill to find Yanira in our yard filling a large bucket from the spigot. "It's time. Daniel left to fetch Aracely." My heart jumped to think of Marta with a new baby. I grabbed one side of the full bucket and Yanira and I carried it in to Mamá, the water sloshing between us.

Mamá was at the stove, tending the fire. Marta stood close by, holding onto the back of a chair with two hands. The back of her *hüipil* was soaked and her face covered with beads of sweat. The floor around her was stained dark with water.

"I have to get back," Marta was saying. "There's no one to make the tortillas."

"After," Mamá said from the stove.

Marta moaned, the sound like a tree being split down the middle from a lightning strike. Her hands twisted on the chair and she leaned over in half. Mamá moved toward Marta and pushed back Marta's hair, stuck to her sweaty face. "Aracely will be here soon."

"When?" Marta said. Her knees bent and she lowered herself to the floor. Mamá dropped to her knees beside her.

"Help me, girls," she called to me and Yanira. Help her how? I stood stuck to the spot. Isabel was hunched on the bed with the blanket over her, her eyes wide.

Mamá and Yanira loosened Marta's skirt and lifted it above her hips. I stood not knowing what to do. "Kneel behind her, hold her hand," Mamá said to Yanira, and Yanira did as she said. "Get the scissors and candle," she said to me. "The thread."

Mamá knelt lower in front of Marta. Something dark and wet appeared between Marta's legs. "It's coming, it's coming," Isabel said from the bed.

I didn't think Mamá wanted Isabel in the room, but I couldn't move to make her leave. The dark, wet head disappeared and appeared again. "Push," Mamá said. The head slipped out again and stayed out, followed by narrow shoulders covered in blood. Then two legs and more blood, spilling out onto the straw mat on the floor. The baby wriggled in her hands and kicked. She swatted it on the back and the baby howled.

"Give me the thread." Mamá measured four fingers away from the baby's belly and tied the cord. I passed her the candle and she cut the cord with scissors and burned the end with the flame. The ends shriveled and dried.

She handed me the baby. It was a boy. Wet and bloody. His mouth opened and closed.

"There's another one," Mamá said. She bent under Marta while a second black head appeared and slid out. "A girl," Mamá said.

When Mamá said *a girl*, Marta leaned against Yanira and moaned, causing Yanira to almost fall over. Twins were bad luck. An extra mouth to feed. The girl baby was silent and Mamá tapped her on the backside. Girl baby began to cough and sputter. She didn't howl or kick.

Once again, Mamá took the thread and scissors and candle to cut the cord. She pressed on Marta's belly and a large smooth ball of what looked like bloody meat came out. I set the cords I had cut and the ball of meat on the edge of the stove. Anything done to these things would affect Marta and the twins, so they deserved respect.

The door opened and Aracely rushed in with Daniel behind her. "Twins," she said when she saw the two babies. She took the boy baby from me. "A strong healthy boy," she said, and carried him to the bucket to clean and put on a cloth. Mamá brought her the girl baby to clean. "The girl is smaller," Aracely said.

Yanira and I hooked our arms under Marta's elbows and helped her into bed. Birthing two babies required much effort. After the babies were clean, Aracely brought them to Marta to suckle. Marta turned her head toward the wall, not looking at either baby. Aracely pushed aside Marta's *hüipil* and lifted each to a breast so they could latch on. The boy began sucking noisily. The girl seemed too weak to hold on.

"We must make the herbal tea," Aracely said. I moved from the bed and poured water from the drinking jug into a pan to heat and added three pieces of wood to the fire. As the room grew warmer, I watched to see if girl baby would latch on.

"We must put a pinch of salt on their tongues," Aracely said. This was our custom so babies would not grow up to say unkind words. Yanira brought the dish of salt while I carried over a cup of herbal tea. Marta's cheeks were streaked with white from the salt of her sweat. I put the cup to her mouth and warm tea dribbled out of the sides.

"She's tired," Aracely said. Marta wiped her mouth with the back of one hand. "I'm cursed," she said.

Mamá dabbed at Marta's face with a damp cloth. "Who would curse you? We have no quarrel with anyone." Marta didn't answer.

Perhaps the *suegra* was jealous of Marta and gave her the evil eye, although the babies were the *suegra's* own grandchildren. Or a neighbor had a quarrel with Papi for leaving for los Estados or some other reason. Someone might envy Marta because we owned our corn field. People gave the evil eye for many reasons.

We still needed to give Marta and the babies their baths, which was the most important custom. Daniel and I went outside to make the fire in the adobe temascal and set rocks to heat. After Marta rested a while, Aracely wrapped a blanket around her shoulders, and everyone walked outside with her to the temascal and ducked inside. Marta sat on a chair with slats on the bottom and Aracely used her hands to direct the steam to the area where the babies came out, to help Marta heal. Aracely placed the cord on the fire and as it burned, Marta closed her eyes and said she felt the heat go into her womb. After that,

Aracely used a special black soap to give the babies their massages and tied Marta's sash tightly around her hips to pull in her bones.

After the ceremony, we walked back into our house, with Yanira and me helping Marta.

Later, Aracely left, and Marta fell asleep in bed with the babies, waking many times to suckle. The next morning, Yanira left for her work helping Doña Yoly and I left for the tortilla mill. No one had slept very much because of the babies. On the way home from the tortilla mill, I passed several people who asked after Marta and the twins. The news had spread fast. Jaime and the *suegra* were sure to arrive soon.

I barely finished patting out the tortillas when the wife from the house next door knocked on our front door with a loaf of wheat bread and a jar of honey. She wanted to see the babies. Daniel stood with her at the front door while I crossed the room to the bed. Marta's right hand was pressed against the boy baby, holding him close. Her left hand had drifted from the girl baby, who was sliding down Marta's side, into the space between the wall and Marta's body.

Marta opened her eyes and her hand pressed more tightly against her son. He moved a bit and opened and closed his mouth, hungry. I reached around Marta's body to the edge of the bed to pick up the girl baby. She felt as light as an empty cup. Her hair was thin and her skin so fair I could almost see through it.

Carefully I set the girl baby on Marta's chest, beside her brother. "The girl," I whispered. We didn't name our babies for eight days, when the parents were sure the baby was healthy. The new mother stayed in bed with her baby until then.

I picked up Marta's hand and pressed it against the girl baby's back. "Hold on," I said. She left her hand in the position where I put it. But there was no energy behind her action. Mamá stood at the stove over a pot of boiling water for more tea, not looking in the direction of Marta and her babies.

Tío Eldon had said families didn't want girl babies because they weren't strong. I wasn't sure if Marta felt this way, but she didn't touch or hold the girl the same way she touched and held the boy.

Raising my voice so it would reach across the room, I told the wife from next door, "Marta's not feeling well. The birth was difficult. I'm sorry."

The wife made a little sound of displeasure. For a second it seemed she might take back her bread and jar of honey. She was sure to be on her way to spread gossip.

Marta lifted her head from the bed to watch our neighbor leave. "Maybe she's the one who cursed me." She turned roughly onto her side, causing both babies to slip off dangerously.

The boy baby wailed. The girl baby stayed silent. I picked up the boy to comfort him, and he nuzzled against my *hüipil* as if seeking more milk. I felt sorry for the girl baby who was left, so I picked her up, too.

"Why does she look like that?" Daniel asked.

"Like what?" Mamá's voice from the stove came fast. Daniel tipped over his head to his shoulder and closed his eyes. "Like she's asleep when she's awake."

Mamá picked up the pot of boiled water to make another cup of herbal tea. "Girl baby's not strong," she said.

"Why not?" asked Daniel. The boy baby was still biting at my *hüipil* with his mouth, now with a lot of force.

"He's hungry," I said to Marta. She raised her arms to reach for him and arranged him on her *chiche* to suckle.

Mamá carried over the cup of herbal tea. "Drink this. You'll feel better."

A small smile came to Marta's mouth as she watched boy baby suckle. "I feel fine."

Girl baby nuzzled against me, but I had no milk in my *chiches* to feed her.

The next day, girl baby never woke. Mamá found her squeezed next to the wall. Marta must have rolled over and covered her during the night so baby couldn't breathe.

Mamá couldn't pay for a box or a funeral or for Padre Andrés to say prayers so we wrapped baby girl in a clean cloth and buried her behind the house. Mamá covered her little body with the earth and Daniel marked the spot with a cross made from two pieces of pine. Gone before we named her.

For a few days, her twin brother lifted his head from nursing and looked around as if to say "Where is she? What happened to the girl who shared my food?"

For the rest of us, we never talked about her. It was as if girl baby had not been born.

TEN

REDWOOD GLEN, CALIFORNIA

SEPTEMBER 2007

The night he came home, Juan put on the pajamas decorated with red fire trucks, brushed his teeth with his new Elmo toothbrush, and climbed into the single bed under the mobile of moon and stars that had been hanging from his ceiling for more than four years. Mark sat at the foot of the bed. Julie settled into the rocking chair they'd bought at the resale store and reached over to the bookcase for *Guess How Much I Love You?*, one of the dozens of board books she'd collected in anticipation of her son's arrival. She read it in Spanish and English. In both languages, she had to stop to collect herself when she reached the final line, "I love you up to the moon, and back."

Juan's face peeked out at her from under his new blue quilt and seeing his brown eyes and black eyelashes, his soft cheeks, she thought she might explode from love. She remembered a phrase of Walt Whitman's: "I contain multitudes." Her love felt that vast.

It had been a long day of travel and Juan behaved like a trouper, wheeling his own carry-on and not whining when they sat for six extra hours in La Aurora Airport due to flight delays. At first, he thought the airport was somehow connected to the Marriott Hotel, but soon figured out it was someplace different altogether. Everything fascinated him: the conveyer belt, the x-ray machine, the food court with McDonald's and Taco Bell. The only time he'd complained was when they picked up their minivan in the long-term lot in San Francisco and attempted to strap him into his car seat. He wailed so loud and long a parking attendant scooted up in a golf cart to investigate. They explained their son wasn't used to being restrained with belts and straps because he was adopted from Guatemala and had only just arrived.

"Welcome home, son," the attendant said before scooting off, and Julie and Mark marveled at the arc of their day, of being in Guatemala in the morning and that night coming home to California with a son.

After finishing the book, Julie touched Juan's leg through the covers and blew him a kiss. Mark patted Juan's shoulder. "Nighty-night, sweet dreams," Julie said. She turned off the light. The room was shrouded in darkness.

The covers rustled as Juan sat up. *"No te vayas, Mommy."* "Don't leave."

"I'll be down the hallway, close."

"No, Mommy," he said, his voice rising. *"No te vayas."*

She sat back down. Mark stuck in his head. "You coming?"

"Soon," she said.

In the *hogar*, Juan had shared a crib with another baby, and then his own bed in a room with five other children. Julie hadn't seen the orphanage dormitory—they didn't let her—but was aware of the many beds with many children, a background chorus of steady breathing. He probably had never slept in a room alone. She wished she knew a Spanish lullaby, or even one in English. Her mother wasn't the type who sang. Maybe a poem. "Four score and seven years ago" popped into her head, so she lulled her tired son to sleep by reciting the Gettysburg Address.

In a few minutes, she fell asleep herself, startling awake when her head fell forward. She shifted from one hip to another. Juan sat up. "Mommy?"

"I'm still here. Go to sleep."

She slid down sideways, resting her head on one arm of the rocker. Thoughts crowded her brain, reminders of what not to do, of mistakes she'd already made. In the airport long-term lot, had she really referred to Juan as an *adopted child*? The preferred language was that she was *an adoptive mother;* they were *an adoptive family*. The Guate Parents had taught her this and so many other facts. She and Mark had created the artificial construct of adoption. Juan was a passive player. And she needed to stop saying *came home*. Juan had never been to California. It wasn't possible for him to *come home* to a place he'd never been.

So many ways to screw up. Julie dozed off vowing to do better.

The next morning, Mark came into Juan's room with a cup of steaming coffee and grasped Julie's shoulder to wake her. He put a finger to his lips and pointed at Juan. Today was the day they woke up with their son in the house. Which made them, at last, parents. They turned to each other with goofy expressions. Astounding.

She followed Mark into the kitchen. "Once he fell asleep, he was fine."

"He'll settle in." Mark opened the refrigerator. "After my run, I stopped by the grocery."

"My hero," she said.

Although Mark hadn't been able to take time off, Julie had her eight weeks of family leave, fifty-six days to devote to bonding with her son. As they kissed good-bye, she promised she'd bond enough for the two of them.

A minute later, Juan was in the kitchen, clutching Ratón. He hopped up on a chair as she scrambled eggs and fried bacon. The legs of his fire truck pajamas pooled on the seat. They were size five, which was for his age, but they were huge on him. Dark shadows hung under his eyes.

"*Huevos*, eggs," Julie said. "*Tocino,* bacon."

Por supuesto, of course, they wanted him to keep his Spanish, but he needed to regain the English he'd lost living in the orphanage. Conversation was the easiest way, so Julie kept up a nonstop monologue: "Refrigerator. Microwave. Stove. Don't touch. Hot. Window. Flowers. Rose bush, outside."

Juan kept his eyes on her mouth as her lips moved, not trying any words yet, listening. Kids learned languages *rápido.* She knew this from the experience of other families on Guate Parents. Set a child among other children and one day soon he'll start talking. Most kids were fluent in less than a year.

After they ate breakfast and got dressed, Julie coaxed Juan through the sliding glass door in the dining room out to the backyard. In September, their strawberries and raspberries were past full bloom, but the tomatoes would grow until Thanksgiving. The Meyer lemons would last year-round.

They had bought a trampoline. Everyone said trampolines were great for kids, especially kids who were adopted. Charla T., MSW, on Guate Parents recommended daily jumping. The up and down helped their systems regulate.

Julie kicked off her shoes and climbed through the net doorway, bouncing tentatively to show Juan.

"*Saltar,*" she said. "To jump."

Juan stared at her through the netting, one finger drifting up to touch his nose. Neither the *hogar* nor the orphanage had had a trampoline. She was certain he'd never seen anything like it.

Julie held open the netted entrance. "*Pase, pase.* Come on in. The water's fine."

He studied her face as if to gauge her reaction, not understanding her joke. He so wanted to please her.

She walked around the perimeter with long, springy strides. Juan stepped after her, as if dipping a toe into quicksand. She picked up her pace, faster and faster in a circle, until she was running, with Juan close behind. She counted out loud: One, two, three, all the way to ten. Over and over, like it was one word: onetwothreefourfive.

Then without warning, after what felt like the hundredth repetition, she pivoted to run the other way. Surprised, Juan kept moving in the same direction, and crashed into the backs of her legs. Julie fell down on impact, taking him with her. Juan was silent, uncomplaining.

"I don't know the word," she said, gasping. "*Reverso? Cambiar?* Other way."

Juan rolled and they lay on their backs. The morning fog hadn't yet burned off. The sky was as gray as pencil lead. Although Julie's hand was close enough to Juan's that they were almost touching, she didn't touch him. She didn't want to overwhelm him. They lay there like that for a long time.

On the third day, Saturday, Claire and Gunther drove up from Fresno to meet Juan. Claire insisted on coming, even though she hated to drive, and even though Julie told her she didn't have to. "What kind of sister doesn't come to meet her nephew?" Claire said. Julie didn't answer. She didn't say, *the kind who never once came to Guatemala with me during the five-year adoption process*. She only wanted her sister to meet her son and drink in his amazingness.

After his long Saturday run and shower, Mark drove off on weekend errands. Claire and Gunther arrived at ten, bearing shopping bags filled with outgrown toys and hand-me-down clothes. Gunther was growing fast, already wearing size 6X.

"I'm so happy for you," Claire said, hugging her sister. "Where is he?"

Juan was in the living room, lying on his stomach in a patch of sunlight on the area rug on the floor. He was coloring in a Dora coloring book, a blue crayon gripped in one hand, Ratón gripped in the other.

"Look who's here," Julie said. "*Mi hermana y su hijo. Clara y Gunther.*"

Juan dropped his crayon and stood up immediately. Claire nudged Gunther forward, who extended a hand to his cousin. Gunther towered over Juan like a husky older uncle. Beside him, Juan appeared wispy, almost ethereal. "Hi," Gunther said. "Nice to meet you."

"Nice to meet you," Juan repeated slowly.

Claire leaned toward Julie. "He's a peanut, huh?"

"Good nutrition, vitamins. He'll catch up."

Claire asked what he ate and Julie said anything they put in front of him. Eggs and bacon for breakfast. Grilled cheese for lunch. Spaghetti and a meatball for dinner. On Juan's second day, she had made tortillas. She'd researched Guatemalan tortillas and learned about soaking corn kernels in lime water overnight and grinding them in a hand-cranked mill to produce a paste. Locating a hand mill to grind corn kernels seemed above and beyond, even for her, so she used the bag of masa harina they'd had for ages in the pantry and watched a YouTube video on rolling and patting the dough.

Claire looked impressed. "How'd they turn out?"

"Like hockey pucks, except with less flavor. Even Juan rejected them."

"There's got to be someone around here who can teach you." Claire said this as if expecting a tortilla maker to materialize any minute.

"I'll add it to the list."

Gunther ran outside to jump on the new trampoline while Juan examined the bag of toys. Board puzzles, Lego bricks, stuffie friends for Ratón. Juan pulled out each item with a look of disbelief that the entire treasure trove was intended for him. When Julie confirmed that it was, Juan carefully selected a stuffed squirrel and placed it facing Ratón, as though the two were in conversation.

Julie and Claire packed snacks and juice boxes. Gunther had been given a list of supplies he needed for kindergarten, and Claire suggested a trip to Target. After three days, Julie was happy to get out of the house, even just to Target.

"Okay, boys," Claire announced as Julie loaded the minivan. "Up and at 'em."

Juan submitted to the car seat better than he had on his first ride from the airport. It helped that Gunther jumped in the back right away, carrying his own booster. "Excellent work showing your cousin how it's done," Claire said.

Gunther had taught himself to read at age four. From his booster, he read off a checklist of items: Pencils, crayons, scissors, glue sticks, backpack. "You want pencils with the good erasers," he said to Juan.

"Not sure he understands you," Claire said from the front seat.

"He's not in school yet, but thank you," Julie said to Gunther.

Juan's eyes shone as they approached the vast emporium marked with a giant red bull's-eye. As far as Julie knew, he'd never been inside a mall or megastore in Guatemala, or a *tienda* for that matter. Aside from airport shops, this would be his maiden retail experience.

After parking, she and Claire snagged a shopping cart apiece. Gunther hopped up onto one side of Claire's cart and Juan followed suit on Julie's, her cart wobbling until Julie righted it by gripping more tightly on the handle. Finally, they were being mothers together. The sun had broken through the fog and the sky was as bold as Juan's blue crayon. The day matched her sunny mood.

They passed by the food court with its smells of popcorn and pizza, through the clothes for women and juniors, around the jewelry and shoes. School started on Monday for most of the state, and packs of middle-schoolers and elementary-age kids roved the aisles with their harried parents. School supplies were displayed in their own section in the back, three dedicated aisles. Juan's eyes opened wide.

Julie paused her cart at the end of the first aisle, the better to survey the goods. Gunther hopped off Claire's cart and held up a package of mechanical pencils. "See these? You don't have to sharpen them." He tossed the pack into his mother's cart, before moving down the aisle and picking up a tester pen and scribbling circles on the piece of paper provided for samples.

"Gel pens from Japan are awesome," he raved, grabbing a selection and throwing them on top of the pencils. Juan gawked at the bounty.

Gunther was like a small adult; he was so competent and self-assured, so physically large. And his English was outstanding. Julie knew he'd been accepted into a school program for the gifted and talented, but really, his intelligence seemed off the charts. In ten years, he'd be in AP English and Math, destined for the Ivy League.

Juan got down from Julie's cart in front of the wall of pens. Erasable, retractable, fine point, roller ball. Felt tip, fountain, Comfort Stick, Sharpie. He reached out and picked one up, a purple gel, and hovered over the sample paper.

"Try it," Julie said.

He drew a tentative line on the page, his eyes as filled with wonder and delight as if he'd just tasted sugar. At the other end of the aisle, Gunther held up a blister pack of markers. "These glow in the dark. They're neon."

Juan seemed not to hear his cousin, focused as he was on drawing purple lines and purple circles.

"Aunt Julie," Gunther said. "Tell Juan."

Julie pressed on Juan's shoulder. "*Mira.*"

Juan glanced at the neon, then set down his purple gel to investigate. Claire wandered over, picked up the purple pen and put it in its proper place.

"Juan's looking a little fuzzy," she said. "You think it's snack time?"

Julie checked her cell phone clock and reported he was fine. They'd just finished breakfast.

They turned the corner to the next aisle where Gunther filled his cart with erasers, construction paper, hand sanitizer, and glue sticks. Juan trailed a few steps behind, pausing to examine the cover of a black marble notebook and run a finger over the raised markings on a plastic ruler. Julie took the black marble notebook and tossed it into her cart, along with a pack of neon markers and box of sixty-four crayons.

"When do you go back to work?" Claire asked.

Julie told her.

"You think you should? Juan doesn't even speak English yet."

Julie debated how to answer. Her job was demanding, but it energized her. Besides, they needed the money. Not going back was out of the question. On the other hand, her son needed her, maybe more than the typical child. Claire stayed home with Gunther and he was thriving. Although, truth be told, Gunther would thrive anywhere.

Julie was about to say she wasn't prepared to think about this today when a frenzied woman and her daughter shoved past her in the aisle.

"You have a backpack, the pink camouflage," the woman was saying. "Pink's for babies!" the girl cried. A pod of giggling middle-school girls pushed past, cart overflowing with locker supplies, leggings, and jeans.

"That reminds me, Gunther needs cargo shorts," Claire said.

"And I need to buy Juan clothes," Julie said, grateful for the subject change. In her gut, she agreed with Claire: Juan might need more time to adjust than they'd anticipated. She and Mark were so focused on finalizing the adoption, they hadn't thought of a future beyond that.

She turned to ask Juan if he wanted anything else. He was wedged against a display of planners midway down the aisle, clutching a calculator, almost panting. His black bangs were plastered to his forehead. Julie hurried over and dropped to one knee in front of him. Beads of sweat glistened on his nose.

"What's the matter?" she asked, taking the calculator.

He lifted his arms to hide his face, moving his elbows as if to shake her off.

She repeated the question, and when he shook his head, she pulled down his hands gently to lock eyes. "Please tell me."

He reached into the pocket of his shorts and pulled out Ratón. His hand with the toy drifted to his face, and he pressed Ratón against the tip of his nose, over and over. Juan seemed almost mesmerized.

Julie felt her stomach curdle. Seeing Juan press the rat against his nose was like watching a demonstration of anxiety played out. Lots of kids had stuffies, but she'd never seen a child press one against his face rhythmically, the way Juan did. It unnerved her.

"*Es desmasiado*," he said finally.

"Too much? What's too much?"

He buried his head in Julie's shoulder and tears dampened her neck.

"What's wrong with him?" Gunther asked.

"I told you he was hungry." Claire spoke from behind Julie.

Julie pressed Juan against her body, rocking them side to side. How could she have been so dense? To take him from nothing and drop him here. The children Juan had left behind in the orphanage had nothing, while Juan, suddenly was confronted by this. Target was too much, too big, too crowded, too loud. She needed to slow down.

*

They got take-out from the In-and-Out Burger near a playground in Redwood Glen. Claire wanted Gunther to burn off energy at the playground before they turned around to drive back to Fresno. Julie hesitated—one big activity a day might be enough?—but the idea made sense and she made a note to remember it. They ordered at the drive-through, and Julie pulled into a shady spot in the corner of the parking lot.

She and Claire took their burgers and French fries from the bag, then passed it to the back seat. Juan unwrapped a burger and smashed half of it into his mouth before swallowing. Gunther stared at his cousin with his own mouth gaping open.

"Does he know how to chew?" Gunther asked. Julie didn't answer. Although she didn't want Juan to choke, coaching him on table manners wasn't a priority. Helping him gain weight was the goal. Finishing her own lunch, she collected the trash, threw the car into reverse, and headed for the playground.

Julie and Mark had driven by the playground countless times, but had never stopped in. The acres of groomed, green lawns seemed somehow off-limits, to belong solely to moms and dads, kids and babies, nannies and grandparents. And now, here she was, a mother with her son, on her first foray of many. In no time, she planned to know the other parents and their kids, arranging play dates and birthday parties. She hoped to become a regular.

"That play structure is ginormous," Gunther said.

"Our tax dollars at work," Julie said.

Claire turned in her seat and motioned two fingers from her eyes to Gunther's. "Play safely or we leave. Understood?"

"Understood," Gunther said, unbuckling his booster and bounding out. Juan remained strapped in, licking ketchup off his fingers and gazing out the window: Climbing walls, ladders, look-out towers, a sand box. Swings, slides, soccer nets. He almost seemed to be in shock at the magnificence. Julie wondered when that would stop happening.

Claire said she worried about the rigor of Gunther's kindergarten curriculum, whether it was gifted and talented enough to challenge her son. Trying not to sigh, Julie said it was hard to predict. Claire would have to wait and see.

Julie turned to the back seat. "We could stay in the car," she said to Juan.

"No," he said. "I want to."

Juan moved toward the play structure with the tentative steps of someone traversing a pond of cracked ice. One hesitant foot, then another. Kids swarmed all over the structure—up, down, in, out—and the air vibrated with their voices. Moms, and a few dads, sat on park benches—administering juice boxes, chatting, changing diapers, talking on cell phones. Mostly white parents, Julie noticed, with white children. The only faces of color belonged to one or two Asian and Indian families and the obvious nannies. No other parent-child combination resembled hers and Juan's. It was a jarring realization, their difference.

Julie urged Juan forward to join the hubbub. He stood tapping his nose for a moment before taking a few steps toward the ladder for the slide.

Relieved he was giving it a try, she claimed the end of a bench with Claire. A woman in a tennis dress and visor had claimed the other end, slouched with long, tanned legs outstretched. Julie nodded hello, but kept her eyes on Juan.

Redwood trees provided cool shelter and, banks of purple lantana, bright color. Julie caught the fragrance of white roses withering after their late-summer blooming.

Fresh air and exercise were what Juan needed, what every child deserved, especially after being trapped for months in that orphanage. Those days were over, she reminded herself with relief. Across the green lawn, Juan scrambled up the ladder to the slide as though he'd been doing only that his entire life. He slid down fast, and even from a distance she saw his face was open and carefree. She stood up, heart swelling with love, and raised a hand, calling out "*Good job, Juan!*" then perched back on her edge of the bench.

The woman in the tennis dress smiled. "Is that your son?"

Julie nodded, a little embarrassed by her outburst.

"What a cutie pie," the woman said. "Is he adopted?"

The question stopped Julie short. Naturally she'd expected the question, maybe just not their first day out. She recovered, and said he was, and the woman nodded, as if she'd gotten the right answer on a quiz.

"We thought we might have to adopt," she said. "Then we got pregnant with twins." She gestured across the playground toward a man with a double jogging stroller.

Julie's face reddened. "How nice for you. Congratulations."

The vibration of kids' voices wafted over the warm air, and from the cacophony, one familiar voice singled itself out. Her son's. Where was Juan? Alarms went off in her body. She heard but couldn't see him. "Excuse me," she said and dashed over to the play structure.

Juan stood at the top of the ladder of the play structure look-out tower, his legs open, his arms stretched out to the handrails, like a conqueror tasked with blocking anyone else from coming up. "Mine," he declared loudly, staring down at the line of kids waiting on the ground as if he were king and they his minions. "Mine! Mine! Mine!" he repeated.

Julie felt her insides liquefy. *Oh my God*, she thought. Juan's body was rigid, his face like stone. She needed to lure him down, but how, with what? He wasn't going to respond to reason, that much she sensed. A clutch of parents had gathered, calling to Juan about the necessity of taking turns, while their kids yelled *get down* and *move it*.

Claire appeared beside Julie brandishing a snack bag. "Bribery works," Claire said, handing her sister a Ziploc of low-sugar gummy worms.

Julie approached the group of parents and waiting kids and in her desperate expression they must have recognized a mother because they moved aside to give her space at the base of the slide. Above her, Juan stood firm, his stick-figure arms grasping the handrails. She jiggled the bag of gummy worms, beseeching him to get down. "Come, *mi amor*," she said. "Gummy worms. Down here."

"Mine, mine, mine," he said, stamping a foot for emphasis.

"Well, he knows one word of English," Claire said.

As Julie moved to climb the look-out tower ladder, a man broke ranks from the parent group and scaled the tower's side like an acrobat from Cirque de Soleil. Landing on the tower platform, he lifted Juan from under the armpits and set him feet first on the slide. "Hey buddy, you can do it," the man said, pushing Juan gently down as cheers erupted from the assembled kids.

Julie darted to the end of the slide repeating "*You did it! Great job,*" Claire behind her. Juan was already on the ground, hands on his waist. When he saw Julie, he crouched over, and, as she got close, stood upright and kicked her, hard, in the shin, before running back to the ladder.

Julie stood paralyzed, stunned. He'd kicked her, and it hurt. Did anyone else see? She rubbed her shin briefly before taking off to follow him as he zigzagged around the playground. He skidded to a halt and fell, wrapping his arms defensively across his face. Heart galloping, Julie scooped him up, half-carrying, half-dragging him to the bench where she'd sat moments earlier, thinking she would give him a time-in, per the counsel of Charla T. of Guate Parents, who advised adoptive parents to discipline with a close holding. Juan didn't want time-in. He pressed his thumbs into Julie's forearms to release himself, the backs of his heels an eggbeater against her lower legs.

Julie let go, and Juan dashed away. She ran after him, shins throbbing, gasping. Who was this kid? What happened to her loving son? How would she survive until he was eighteen?

Juan ran back to the slide, but the gaggle of kids prevented him from climbing up. Julie grabbed a corner of his t-shirt. Claire and Gunther appeared, and the three of them joined hands and formed a circle around him. Moving as a unit, they got him into the car.

They exchanged few words on the drive home. Julie was too shaken to form coherent sentences. What just happened? Could she have prevented it? Claire had years of practice as a mother, but Julie was a rank beginner. She felt like a fraud.

When they got home, Juan ran down the hallway to his room and slammed the door.

Claire sent Gunther for a quick jump on the trampoline and closed the door to the kitchen. "You need to stop coddling him. He kicked you in the shins. He slammed the door." She hit the side of her head with one palm as though to demonstrate the emptiness of Julie's skull.

Julie worked on keeping her expression blank, her gaze unfocused. Did Claire forget the past five years, what Juan had been through? If Gunther had endured the same situation, he might behave the same way. Any of them would. "He's been here less than a week," Julie said.

"It's not him I'm worried about. It's you. You need to take control of your son."

Julie's body went cold. She did what she was supposed to; she'd tried time-in. She thought she was in control.

"Take it off," Claire said.

"The door?"

"Yes, the door. You're the mother."

Julie felt too defeated to respond. She still wasn't convinced that she was.

Claire said she needed to get home in front of traffic and went out to the trampoline to collect Gunther. Julie crept down the hallway to Juan's room. After knocking lightly, she found him huddled in his closet, Ráton smashed against his face. She sat on the floor at his eye level and spoke in basic Spanish.

"Can we talk? I know you're sad. Everything is different."

Juan ignored her. She tried again, pantomiming her simple words.

"In our family, we use words. In our family, we don't hit with feet. We have hugs. We love."

Juan smashed Ráton against his face harder.

"Sweetheart. Juan. When you're angry, tell me. When you're sad, tell me. I promise I am going to listen."

Juan squeezed his eyes shut. Claire called to Julie from the kitchen. "We're taking off. I'll call you."

"Thanks for coming," Julie called back.

Juan kept his eyes shut. Julie stood up, sighing. "We'll get through this," she said in English, as much to herself as to her son, then went to the front door to say goodbye to her sister.

In late afternoon, Mark returned from running errands. After unloading the car, he prepared to make dinner. Weekends, Mark cooked, always something grilled. As he laid out salmon steaks and asparagus on a platter on the kitchen counter, Julie rolled up her pant leg to show him her purple bruise. "Juan freaked out," she said.

"Ouch," Mark said. "Hate when that happens."

Julie almost wished the purple was a deeper shade so he would understand how serious it seemed. "We did Target and the playground."

"In one day?"

"An amateur's mistake," Julie admitted, rolling down her pant leg. "It was a nightmare."

"Cut yourself some slack," Mark said. "We're both learning."

"He's hurting so much," Julie said.

Mark took the food outside to grill, while Julie went to Juan's room to bring him to the kitchen. He'd moved to his bed, where he lay staring at the ceiling, clutching Ráton. "Time to eat," Julie said, in English and Spanish, as if the playground incident hadn't happened. Mark returned to the kitchen with the platter and the three of them ate together at the kitchen table. Juan was quiet, carefully using his knife and fork to cut his food, eating only one piece at a time, chewing with his mouth closed. Julie compensated by being overly cheerful, remarking on the tastiness of the salmon and the firmness of the asparagus until Mark motioned that she needed to lower the effusive quotient.

Later, Mark and Juan picked the last of the tomatoes from their garden, while Julie sat on a deck chair to relax. She liked looking over the deck rail to see her husband and son in the garden, plucking tomatoes from the vines and placing them in baskets. Julie wanted nothing more than to have a happy family. She comforted herself by remembering the wisdom of one of Charla T.'s recent posts:

> Our kids come with a long, slow on-ramp. Nothing happens quickly. You'll lose friends and be alienated from family. Hang in there.

Julie was too far away to hear their conversation, but as Mark held up different types of tomatoes one by one, she knew he must be educating Juan on their differences. Mark was born to be a father. He'd teach his son everything he knew—how to ride a bike, camp, tend a garden. She imagined the two of them playing baseball or soccer, Juan maybe joining Boy Scouts. The adventures they'd go on together.

Juan came running up the steps of the deck for a drink of water, looking flushed. His body temperature always ran a little hot, a vestige of institutional care, Julie guessed. She went inside to fill a bottle with water and ice to take back outside. He stepped inside the sliding glass door to wait for her in the dining room.

As she handed him the bottle, he asked when the *visitante* was leaving.

She looked around the dining room, but no one was in the house except the two of them. "Visitor?" she asked.

"*El hombre.*"

"The man? What man?"

Juan pointed outside.

"You mean, Mark? Mark lives here, too. He's your dad." She paused to let the information sink in, then pointed to herself. "I'm your mom. Mommy."

Juan glanced around the dining room as though noticing his surroundings for the first time. Early evening sun streaming in tall narrow windows, sheer linen curtains, chunky wooden dining table with six chairs, credenza topped with photos of them rimmed in silver frames.

"*No voy a volver?*"

"No, you don't go back. This is home. We're your family."

She reached for both his hands and held them. Juan gnawed on his bottom lip as though debating the meaning of her announcement. How she wished she knew enough words in Spanish to make him understand, to know what actions to take to make him believe this place was forever. His brown eyes looked solemn. "*Primera vez,*" he said.

First time. Home.

ELEVEN

REDWOOD GLEN, CALIFORNIA

NOVEMBER 2007

Five mornings a week on the way to work, Julie or Mark dropped Juan at a private kindergarten called The Cabin in the Woods. It cost a fortune, but what could they do? Juan needed a small setting to feel secure and comfortable. And in a town where eager parents subscribed kids to school waiting lists while still in utero, The Cabin was the only one with a slot available. Juan was five years and three months old. He'd been with them for two months.

Juan liked the routine of hanging his jacket on a hook with his name on it and placing his Mario Brothers lunch box in his own cubby. Every night before bed, he laid out the next morning's ensemble—a clean pair of miniature blue jeans and a red polo shirt—and took great care to cut up an orange into precise sections and remove the crusts from his cheese sandwich. In the morning, he fluffed his pillow and tidied his room.

His preparations delighted Julie. Driving into work, she called Claire. "You can bounce the proverbial quarter off his bed. He could be a Marine."

"He makes his bed?" Claire said.

"I can't take credit. He came this way."

One slight concern was Juan's lack of interaction with other kids. When Julie went inside early to sign him out, before the goodbye circle, during free play, he always seemed to be sitting by himself at a table in the corner, drawing or building something with Legos. He didn't have any special pals.

Julie accepted Juan's holding back as a natural response to his developing language skills and new situation. The students at the Cabin were basically all white though, and one day on the drive home, she asked him how he felt about that.

"They're peach, really," he said. "I like peach people. I live with them."

Julie hadn't known whether to laugh or cry.

And he still had trouble sleeping. After Claire's warm milk suggestion didn't solve the problem, Julie reached out to the crowd-think on Guate Parents, and when someone went on about a background noise machine, ordered one on the spot. At night, after she finished reading Juan a book, she'd flip the switch, and a dull roar filled the room—chirping crickets, falling water, ocean waves. The cacophony was far from soothing to her, but the racket seemed to produce the desired effect for Juan. Sometimes, as he drifted off, he'd roll over to one side and Julie would sneak a hand under the covers and press against his back through his pajama top, a brief massage. On Mark's nights in Juan's room, he did the same. Unlike when he was a baby, Juan didn't like being held on their laps, so the bedtime ritual was the best way for them to get physically close to their son, and they were grateful for it.

Afterward, the on-duty parent would stumble back to their shared bedroom where the other one slept. Occasionally, Mark would make noise and wake Julie and she'd stay awake long enough to make love. Mostly, though, he slipped under the covers and didn't cross his side of the bed for weeks at a stretch. Their sex life had always been good, and if Julie had had more energy, she would have initiated sex herself. She reminded herself marriages went through peaks and valleys, and they were in a dry spell.

Besides, she had enough on her plate getting herself to show up at the Clay every day. Dr. Conrad had made her life hell, publicly scorning Julie's expansion idea from two years before as a "debacle" at every ideas or board meeting and taking total credit when Patricia

Westerman, the artist Julie had discovered five years earlier (*at a craft fair!*), was accepted to participate in the prestigious Venice Biennale. Julie's humble background didn't help. Dr. Conrad's first question about anyone was "If they're so smart, why aren't they rich?" and Julie kicked herself for letting slip that her mother drank and her father had abandoned her and Claire, because weakness was what Dr. Conrad most despised. Julie became skilled at steeling herself against the criticism. She couldn't lose her job because they were still paying off their line of credit that had financed the adoption and related costs.

Julie reminded herself often of all she'd overcome. She had gotten Juan out of Guatemala, and she'd get through this.

*

One year passed.

When Juan was six, Julie enrolled him in first grade in the public elementary school down the hill from their house. After she and Mark dropped him off at the classroom the first day and walked back to their cars, Julie said, "More white kids."

"What are we supposed to do?" Mark asked. "Move?"

Julie shrugged.

"Juan seemed to take it in stride."

"He's used to it. For better or worse."

The second week of school, Juan announced his name wasn't Juan. His name was Jack. Two other boys in first grade were named Jack and the kids knew how to pronounce it, unlike his name, which kids pronounced *One* or *Wand*. Juan's birth name of Juan Rolando Garcia Flores had morphed into Jack Cowan, a shift in identity so grand Julie didn't know how to absorb it.

Julie announced the change on Guate Parents, asking for reactions. The group assured her the name change marked a new confidence in Juan-now-Jack, an assertiveness of how he wished to be known. Julie worried the change went along with her son's growing anxiety. He'd insisted on learning how to use an iron so he could iron his bed sheets because he didn't like "ripples." He Windexed smudges from his tennis shoes so "they don't look used." Juan seemed obsessed with being flawless.

Charla T., MSW, told Julie not to over-think either issue. Being tidy was one thing. Changing one's name was another. Charla T. shifted the discussion to something larger:

> SEPTEMBER 8, 2008
> Your child is Guatemalan, from Guatemala. What are you doing to incorporate elements of your child's heritage into his or her life? Discuss.
> — *Charla T., MSW*
>
> Took Heritage Trip last summer. RECOMMEND! Ten days in Antigua with families like ours—kids loved the Choco Museo, donkey ride at Finca Azotea, cooking class at *El Frijol Feliz*. Daughter age 12 said "I belong here."
>
> Latin American Culture Camp in Lake Tahoe. Workshops for parents and kids. Teens kayak and zip line. Fiesta Saturday night with DJ. Fun!
>
> Struggling to teach our kids Spanish. Duolingo app, classes at school. But they resist! Anyone?
>
> Bilingual school. Spanish/English. Son, 12, on soccer team, best friends with kid from Mexico.
>
> Bilingual schools here are French or Cantonese. Go figure!

Julie vowed to start cooking Guatemalan food, find a Guatemalan restaurant, research Latin American culture camps, and re-start speaking Spanish. As soon as she could find a minute for all of it.

A few nights later, Jack sat at the kitchen table with a math worksheet while Julie microwaved a plate of chicken nuggets and boiled corn on the cob. Mark was working late as usual, a crisis in the lab or a report to finish. It was impossible to complain about a man who researched ways to cure deadly diseases, although, internally, sometimes Julie did. Not because she blamed him. She just wanted him home more, for Jack and for her. She missed him.

Today had been a good day. Threatening clouds had gathered in late afternoon, and rain was beginning to fall against the skylight in a cadenced patter. Julie and Jack were in jeans and t-shirts, padding around the kitchen in bare feet. The kitchen felt cozy.

The bell dinged on the microwave and Julie pulled out the chicken nuggets. She turned off the stove and drained the steamed corn. Washing her hands and drying them on a dish towel, she arranged the food on two plates. Jack was bent over his math worksheet, a pencil gripped in his hand. He pushed back his chair. They were learning number lines, an abstract concept a step beyond addition and subtraction. First grade math was so much tougher than Julie remembered.

"I hate this," he said, and threw his pencil across the room.

"What do you hate, Jackie?"

"Math. It's stupid."

"Guatemalans are great mathematicians," Julie said, ignoring Jack's scowl. She repeated the one morsel of math history she knew, that the ancient Mayans created the concept of zero, and used it to build the pyramids at Tikal. Humming, she remembered a Guate Parent pearl of wisdom. She didn't have to attend every fight to which she was invited. She continued to hum, folding the dish towel and putting it in a drawer.

Jack picked up a piece of paper and crumpled it. "You wish I had blue eyes."

Hands on hips, she shook her head at his ridiculousness. "If I'd wanted a kid with blue eyes, would I have adopted from Guatemala?"

"You're not my real mother," he said. *Then what am I doing here?* she thought, but before she could respond or react, he leapt from his chair and lunged for her, dragging his fingernails down her face.

Julie's mind went blank. Cupping a hand over her eye, she inched toward the sink and turned on the faucet, grabbing the dish towel to dampen it. She bent to inspect her eye in the reflective surface of the toaster. There was a slight scratch, hardly bleeding. From behind her, she heard the door to the garage open, and Jack go down the two steps from the kitchen.

A dull thumping sound echoed from the garage. Pressing the damp dish towel to the scratch, Julie went to the kitchen door. Jack was jumping on the hood of her minivan, brandishing one of Mark's hammers. "Please get off the car and give me the hammer," she said, edging into the garage.

"Make me."

"Jack, please," she said, counting backward from ten. What would Mark say if he saw dents? "You need to get down now."

The hood's sloped angle made it difficult for Jack to keep jumping and he slid off, hammer in hand, and lurched toward her. As she pitched forward to catch him, he lifted his arm with the hammer. *He's going to hit me*, she thought, as she reached to catch his wrists.

"I can't breathe," he howled, twisting, although she held only his wrists. "You're hurting me."

Gasping from the struggle, Julie let go and Jack broke away, hammer in hand. He ran back to the minivan. "I hate you," he screamed. He lifted the hammer and banged a huge dent right into the middle of the hood.

"Stop. Jack. Please." *Why was he acting like this? Was he crazy?* Mark would know what to do. She stumbled into the kitchen, grabbed the phone. "I'm calling Dad," she said. Jack rushed toward her, swinging the hammer.

Dropping the phone, Julie stepped backwards, cowering against the wall, then grabbed for the hammer in Jack's hand. He twisted away from her, his arms flailing. He found the button to open the garage door and pressed it. The door slid open. Still clutching the hammer, Jack dashed through the garage and outside. Julie ran after him.

Rain pounded down in a solid wall. The cement of the driveway felt cold and jagged under her bare feet. Reaching the sidewalk, she turned left down the hill after Jack. Already, he was half a block away, a black shape moving. A shard of something stuck in her foot and she hopped to favor that side, not stopping. She rushed down the hill, lopsided.

The bottom of her wet jeans dragged like chains. *There was a reason she wasn't able to have children,* she thought: *she didn't deserve to be a mother.* Someone else could handle him better. Maybe she should give him to them.

The black shape stopped and turned. "Leave me alone!" Jack shrieked.

"Your feet will get cut. You're getting all wet."

"Go away."

"Give me the hammer."

She was two feet away from him now. She felt as if she'd run miles, shaking and breathless. The hammer hung low against Jack's knee and, as she reached for it, he hurled himself against her body, wrapping his arms around her waist. "Don't leave me, Mom. Don't leave me."

"I'm not leaving you. I'll never leave you."

She held the hammer above his head as he clung to her with both hands.

A car climbed the hill slowly, its high beams sweeping over the two of them like a searchlight. *Please let this be Mark. Let the car stop and be Mark and not one of our neighbors.* What would a neighbor think of her, of Jack, if they saw them there in the rain? The car kept up its slow climb. Stiffly, Julie shaded her eyes and waved to let the driver know they were fine, to keep moving, they were just another mother and son out for an evening stroll. She hoped that whoever was behind the wheel didn't recognize them, although how could anyone not, they looked like no one else in the neighborhood.

She leaned over to shelter Jack from the rain. He clutched her free hand with both of his and didn't let go.

They trudged up the hill and into the garage, where she hung up the hammer on the proper hook and patted the handle as if to assure it that was where tools belonged. She climbed the steps into the kitchen and Jack followed, sidestepping the puddle they dripped. Opening a drawer, Julie handed Jack a clean dish towel to dry his feet and another to press against her cut foot.

"You're bleeding," Jack said as she inspected the dish towel.

"Just a little."

"You need a band-aid."

Julie hopped over to the junk drawer and rooted around for one.

"We'll tackle homework later," she said, trying to sound off-handed as she dried her foot and applied a few band-aids. "Let's change into pajamas."

Jack went down the hall with no protest and Julie went into her room to change, favoring her cut foot. She peeled off her clothes like a robot and threw them into the hamper. She put on a fleece sweater, sweatpants, and thick socks. She felt as if she wouldn't ever get warm.

When Jack returned to the kitchen in his red pajamas, wet black hair slicked straight up, Julie carried the two plates of food into the family room on a tray, setting them on an ottoman. He snuggled under a blanket on the couch and Julie sat on another ottoman, close but safely distant, cutting the nuggets into even smaller bite-sized pieces.

She left the TV off. The only sound was the rain pounding outside. "Did something happen in school today?" she asked. Jack picked up a piece of chicken with his fingers and stuffed it in his mouth.

She lowered her head to make eye contact. "Jack. Did something happen?"

"One of the kids laughed and said, 'You're adopted,' like it was a bad thing."

"Jesus Christ," she said. "Who?"

"One of the other Jacks. With blond hair."

"Those other Jacks don't know anything about it," Julie said. *Didn't the parents around here talk to their kids about adoption? Or do I need to educate every single person in our universe, one by one?* It was impossible to protect her son from hurt that came at him from everywhere.

Jack pushed away his plate and pulled the blanket over his head. "I wish I was in your tummy."

Julie couldn't answer. There was no answer. Another question from beneath the blanket. "What was that other lady's name again?"

Julie ignored the stab of jealousy that cleaved her in two. "Your birth mom? Karla Inez Garcia Flores."

Jack flattened himself under the blanket and stayed there. Julie picked at her corn but had lost her appetite. She popped a Scooby Doo DVD into the player and Jack peeked out from under the blanket, his eyes trained on the flickering images of Scooby and Shaggy and friends. Neither said anything. Their food turned cold.

The garage door opened an hour later, signaling Mark's arrival.

Julie kissed her fingertips, turning them toward Jack, and padded through the hallway to the kitchen where Mark stood, incredulous. "What happened to your car?"

"Jack."

"Why didn't you stop him?"

"I tried."

"It'll cost a thousand dollars to fix the dents. More."

The air in Julie's lungs drained. "You don't know what it's like for him. Sometimes I wonder what we were thinking, bringing him to the most competitive place in the universe, to live with a bunch of white kids." She opened the silverware drawer, then slammed it shut, as if this would emphasize her words.

"Julie." Mark's voice softened. "None of this is your fault."

"Whose fault is it? I'm the mother."

"He's testing you."

"I know he's testing me. And I'm failing the test."

"I'm sorry about what I said about the car. We'll get it fixed. No big deal."

"He scratched my face," Julie said. "I cut my foot."

Mark put a finger under her chin to inspect her cheek and watched as she unfurled her sock to show him her band-aids. "You didn't know you signed up for combat duty," he said. She fell into his body, her cheek against his beating heart.

The sound of something in the dining room made them both turn to look. Silhouetted in the darkness, Jack was crouched in the doorway, wrapped in a blanket.

"Everything's fine, Jack," Julie called over. "Mom and Dad are here. We love you."

*

Julie didn't know if she was supposed to incorporate more Guatemala into their lives, or less, but since less wasn't working, she opted for more. She googled "Guatemalan restaurants" in her zip code and found only one in the zip code one town over—"El Chapín"—with a signature dish, shucos. Chapín was a nickname for Guatemalan people used throughout Central America, referring to leather sandals worn by Guatemalans in the old days. Shucos was a cross-cultural amalgamation of hot dog with guacamole, cabbage, and green sauce.

On a Friday night, the family drove out of Redwood Glen and crossed the freeway to El Chapín for dinner. The restaurant sat back on a frontage road, between a car wash and used tire dealer. The parking lot was filled with pick-up trucks.

"Looks promising," Julie said as Mark found a spot. She opened her door to unbuckle Jack from the back seat and gripped his hand as he jumped out.

They walked single file to the restaurant and Mark held open the door. Light blue and white crepe paper hung from the ceiling. A free-standing refrigerator was filled with bottles of Jarritos, Mirinda, and A&W Root Beer. Two large-screen TVs broadcast two different international soccer games. Every head in the place seemed to turn when they walked in.

Not since Jack's pick-up trip had Julie been among so many Central Americans. *This must be how Jack feels every day of his life,* she realized. Like an outsider. Of everyone assembled, she looked the least likely to be her son's mother. Never in a million years would anyone put the two of them together.

"Are you wondering if anyone here is related to Jack?" she whispered to Mark as the hostess led them to a booth in the back.

"No. Never. Why would I?" Mark slid into one side of the booth and Julie and Jack into another. They opened their menus.

"The shucos sound good," Julie said to Jack. Mark closed his menu and stared up at the TV screen.

A young woman approached their table, semi-circle earrings bordered with rays of the sun dangling almost to her shoulders. Her name tag read Esther. She placed a water glass with ice in front of each of them.

"Some appetizer to start? Guacamole, *queso fundido*, spicy carrot?"

They gave their orders, and when Esther finished writing, she looked from Jack to Julie and Mark to Jack. "Is he your son?" she asked Julie.

"He is," Julie said.

"From Guatemala?"

"*Sí.* Yes."

"From where he is?"

"Escuintla."

"The coast? He doesn't look. His color's like mine." Esther held out an arm, comparing.

Julie returned the menus. "Well, that's what the paperwork says. *Tramites?* Escuintla."

"You speak Spanish good. *Tramites.*" Esther looked at Jack. "He speak?"

Jack was ripping open small packets of sugar, pouring them into his palms and licking up the granules. "Please," Julie said, swiping the wrappers off the table and stuffing them into her pants' pocket. "Jack? You speak Spanish?"

"*Poquito.*"

"*Poquito?*" Esther said merrily. "*Cómo te llamas?*"

"Jack." He reached for another sugar packet. "Juan."

"He's fluent," Julie said. "It's his best subject at school."

Esther smiled down at him with fondness and said it was important to remember. Julie asked her if she were from Guatemala herself.

"*El Altiplano.* The highlands. Nebaj." Esther accented on the second syllable and pronounced the final "j" a guttural, German sound.

Julie had heard of Nebaj, one of the remote, northern sections where women dressed in embroidered blouses and woven skirts, referred to as *traje*, and people spoke a local language. She asked if Esther spoke a language besides Spanish.

"Ixil," Esther said. *Ee-sheel.* She returned her order pad to her pocket. "I place your order."

"She's from Guatemala," Mark said to Jack as Esther headed for the kitchen.

"She speaks Ixil," Julie added. "That's so cool."

Jack tucked his legs underneath him and surveyed the restaurant's crowd. "All these people speak Spanish. They're gardeners and landscapers and stuff like that."

It was true. Most of the other diners were men dressed in outdoor work clothes and wore heavy shoes caked in dirt and mud. "They're Guatemalan," Mark said, and Julie wondered if that was a positive or negative thing to note. "They came here to work. They probably didn't get to go to school back home. Their families didn't have money."

Jack inhaled water into his straw and capped the top with his finger to retain it for a second before removing his finger and letting the water drip back into the glass.

Someone on TV must have scored a goal because everyone in the room started cheering. The cheers faded, replaced by bursts of laughter. Julie felt a part of something large, as well as separate from it.

"Do they get to keep their kids?" Jack asked.

"Who?" Julie said.

"The gardeners. If they're poor. Or do they give them to someone?"

"Probably keep them," Julie said. "Or if they're too poor, maybe give them to relatives." She glanced toward Mark, who made a slicing gesture that meant she should change the subject. Jack pulled several napkins from the dispenser and began to rub circles on the table in front of him. "It's not fair," he said, buffing the tabletop. "You clean and it just gets dirty."

"That's true for a lot of things in life. You have to keep at stuff, or it falls apart," Julie said.

"Well, I hate it." He crumpled the napkins and threw them to the middle of the table. Inching a millimeter closer to Julie, he fluttered his eyelashes. "Do you love me?"

"What kind of question is that?" Mark interjected. "She's your mother."

Julie covered her heart with both hands and stared directly into Jack's eyes. They'd had this conversation before, probably a hundred times, including on the way to school that morning. "I do, I do, Jack. I love you. I love you. Dad loves you."

"Will you ever give me away?"

"Never. Never, ever," Julie said. "We will never give you away, no matter what. You're our son, Jack. Forever."

"Did my birth mother love me?"

Mark made a "tsk" sound. "Yes, your birth mother loved you. That's why she did what was best for you."

Julie gave him a warning look. It wasn't that simple. The issue wasn't that easily put to rest. Her impulse, too, was to say yes, to reassure Jack his relinquishment was an action based on careful decision, motivated by love. But Charla T., MSW, and the Guate Parents insisted they answer Jack's questions only with what they knew to be true, which was a social worker's report that didn't use words like love or any other emotion.

"We have just one photo of your birth mom," Julie said. "The DNA photo. She held you so tight. Like she was giving you a great big hug." Julie gave Jack a sideways hug of the same great bigness, to recreate the feeling of his mother's embrace. "To me, that sure feels like love."

Jack fidgeted before pulling out from under her arm. "If she loved me, why did she give me away? Those gardeners kept their kids."

Julie reached to hug him again and he batted at her arm. Mark made a sad face at Julie, frowning. Even if they got through this moment, others like it were waiting to advance and fill in, cratering out the hole of loss at the center of Jack's being. The loss felt like a wound Julie could never heal.

"Your birth mother must be special," she said. "Because you are."

"Sometimes people make hard choices," Mark said.

Jack cupped his fingers around the base of his glass. "When I lived with her, I had a pet hamster named Norman."

Mark took a deep breath. "You never lived with her, Jackie. Berta took care of you. And the people in the orphanage. You're confusing Norman with Ratón."

"No. I remember," Jack said.

Julie knew the emotions were too big, too hard to fit into reality. She'd told Mark before. "Jack, my love. You might have had a hamster named Norman. We don't know for sure. It's possible." She directed her last sentence at Mark.

Mark lifted his palms, surrendering.

Who was to say? Jack could be the nephew of a president, the brother of an inventor, the great-grandson of a Mayan king. He could be anybody or nobody, nobleman or serf. Because deep at Jack's core, where the family tree with roots and limbs was supposed to be planted, a swirling, bottomless abyss resided, his origins a mystery.

TWELVE

A FEW HOURS LATER AFTER DINNER

Julie set Jack's background noise machine to summer night and a chorus of chirping crickets filled his bedroom. A Spiderman night light cast a rosy glow. Julie snuggled down against a bank of pillows on the bed beside him, to read aloud from a chapter book about the childhood of Walt Disney. Lately, Jack's favorite books were biographies of famous people when they were kids. When she paused between chapters, he touched her elbow, asking if they could stop. "I'm tired," he said.

He turned his cheek against the pillow and closed his eyes, not answering when she spoke his name. Jack was never tired at bedtime. She pushed back his thick black hair, placing a palm against his forehead. He didn't seem to have a fever. She hoped he wasn't reacting to something he ate at El Chapín. He hadn't complained of a stomachache and hers felt fine. After hearing his steady breath of sleep, she slipped out of the room and headed for her own bedroom.

"You're here early," Mark said, as she slid in beside him.

"Jack's out of sorts," Julie said. "He's super tired."

"The poor kid's worn out," Mark said. "We might have gone overboard on the Guatemalan thing."

"One dinner. That's hardly overboard. Could it be food poisoning? He never falls asleep that fast."

Mark yawned. "He's in overwhelm mode."

They would return to El Chapín. Before Julie could try to convince him, they were both asleep.

The next morning, Mark sprang from bed for his usual six a.m. run. Julie stood in the kitchen and drank a cup of coffee while staring out the window over the sink. In the garden bed below, a few of Mark's hardy camellias were in full bloom, taking their turn in the rotation of color.

"My throat hurts." She turned to see Jack, his cheeks crimson.

"When you swallow?"

"All the time." Jack coughed a cough that sounded like a bark. His eyes looked murky.

The lock in the door turned and Mark bounded into the kitchen, glistening with sweat. Julie lifted her cheek for a kiss. "Jack's throat hurts," she said.

Mark knelt beside Jack, staring into his eyes and feeling his forehead as Julie poked in a thermometer. "Ninety-nine," Mark said. "Not too high." He asked his son to open wide and say *ah.* Jack leaned forward to cough his bark cough before opening his mouth.

"You think he should go to school?" Julie asked. Mark patted Jack on the shoulder and stood up. "Give him two ibuprofen. He's fine."

Julie poured Jack a glass of orange juice, sticking in a straw for him to sip through, and after he finished, sent him down the hall to get dressed.

Shortly before noon, Julie's cell phone vibrated on her desk. The school nurse was calling, saying she'd taken Jack's temperature. It was 100. When was Julie able to pick him up?

Right away, she answered, feeling mortified about the 100. Mark had underestimated the danger of 99. Jack was spiking a fever. She should have let him stay home. At work, she resented colleagues who taped themselves together well enough to come in, only to get everybody else sick. She'd turned into one of those people herself.

Julie walked into Jack's school to find him slouched in a chair by the admin's desk, backpack by his feet. As she signed him out, he asked for a tissue. He coughed into it and showed her a wad of green gunk. His murky eyes looked murkier.

At home, Jack went back to his room to put on pajamas while Julie got out two more ibuprofen and heated chicken noodle soup. When the soup was ready, she poured him a bowlful and set it on a tray to bring to him in bed. She found him underneath the covers, in his school clothes, asleep. She lay on her side next to him, watching his chest rise and fall. Every few minutes he coughed, his closed eyes squinting with the effort. Jack was never this lethargic. His breathing sounded wet.

Julie must have fallen asleep because she startled awake. Beside her, Jack's body radiated heat like a furnace. She jumped up and ran to the kitchen for the thermometer, poked it into his mouth. 104.

She speed-dialed Mark. She told him about the barking cough getting worse and the temperature of 104. "Why did we send him to school?" she almost screamed.

"Call the pediatrician," Mark said. "If she can't see you right away, and his temperature stays high, take him to the ER."

Nobody answered in the pediatrician's office, but someone called back five minutes later to ask the name of their local pharmacy. The doctor was prescribing Tamiflu, which Julie could pick up. She stood by Jack's bed with the phone in her hand. He was piled under layers of covers, shaking. Tamiflu wasn't going to fix this. She gave the nurse the pharmacy information she requested, hung up, and called Mark.

"He's shaking with a raspy gunky cough. He looks terrible. I'm taking him to the ER."

Mark said he would meet her there.

She bundled Jack in a blanket and buckled him into the back seat of the minivan. The hospital was only three miles away, but the route was under construction so the trip seemed endless. Every few seconds Julie glanced over her shoulder to see Jack's head dropped to the side, nearly strangling in the seat belt. She should have brought a pillow.

The Emergency lot was half-full. She unbuckled Jack, carefully helping him out of the back seat, draping the blanket around his shoulders like a cape. They plodded across the parking lot and through the automatic doors.

The receptionist at the ER, a young woman with a gold ring through her upper lip, handed Julie a clipboard and asked for Jack's insurance card. "My husband's a physician pathologist in San Francisco," Julie said. Normally she would never drop Mark's name. "Dr. Mark Cowan." The receptionist gazed at Julie coolly as she took back the clipboard. "I have no idea who that is," she said.

Fifteen minutes later, a gray-haired nurse in green scrubs led Jack and Julie to a small exam room, where she took Jack's vital signs and entered them into the computer. In an upbeat voice, the nurse told Jack to change into a paper gown and left while he did. Julie helped Jack stretch out on the exam table, tucking the blanket closely around him, trying not to feel frantic. Pressing her body down against his to keep him warm, she dialed Mark again and got his voice mail.

A man in a white coat rushed in with the gray-haired nurse behind him.

"Hi Jack, I'm Dr. Tanner," he said, ignoring Julie and staring at Jack's face. Julie moved to a small stool on wheels and rolled to the corner. Tanner pressed a stethoscope up under Jack's gown and ordered him to take a deep breath.

Jack inhaled deeply. He barked his cough, wincing with the effort. Dr. Tanner smiled at Julie. "You haven't been waiting long, have you?" Not pausing for an answer, he moved his stethoscope over Jack's chest, systematically listening to each area.

"What are the vital signs?" he said to the nurse.

"Pulse 140. Respiratory rate 32. Blood pressure 90 over 70. Temperature 105."

A hundred and five. That was impossible. A few hours ago, he was drinking orange juice, and everything was fine. Mark said to give him ibuprofen and send him to school. Julie dropped him off like everything was normal.

Dr. Tanner told the nurse to order a complete blood count and chest x-ray, then pressed a hand on Julie's shoulder with a sympathetic frown and rushed off. The nurse clamped a rubber tourniquet around Jack's upper arm for the blood draw, and Julie winced as the tourniquet tightened. Before Jack could protest, the nurse jabbed the needle in his forearm, covering the spot with a band-aid. Strapping him onto a gurney, she whisked him out for a chest x-ray.

Julie trotted behind, standing back from a metal wall as they lay a lead apron on her son's small body, and trotted again as they returned to the exam room. The nurse typed notes into a computer, shutting the door as she left.

Jack sat up on the table, hunched over and struggling to catch his breath. Was this the flu, or what was happening? Anxiety twisted Julie's stomach. She dialed Mark's number again and just as she was leaving a message he walked in, passing her and going straight to Jack.

"They did a bunch of tests," she said, standing beside Mark, hysterical. "What's going on?"

Dr. Tanner and the nurse hurried in. The room felt crowded with the adult bodies, warmer. Mark introduced himself to Dr. Tanner as a physician pathologist at San Francisco General and the two men shook hands. Tanner motioned to Julie to sit on the small stool on wheels. She rolled back into the corner, her heart pounding. The nurse stood in front of the computer and navigated the mouse. Dr. Tanner pointed to the screen with a pen. "The x-ray reveals consolidation on one side of the lung." The image switched and Dr. Tanner pointed his pen to numbers on a chart. "Here's his white blood cell count." He and Mark glanced at each other without speaking.

"It could be due to pneumonia," Dr. Tanner said to Mark. "I think he ought to be admitted. Don't you agree?"

*

Mark and Julie sat on two chairs in a corner of the family waiting room on the pediatric ICU ward upstairs. Two people waited in the other corner, a man doing crosswords and a woman working a

Rosary through her fingers. They had left Jack down the hall propped up asleep in a bed, shivering under two blankets, on oxygen.

Mark grasped Julie's hands between both of his and explained in a steady voice that Jack's white blood cell count was very high, a condition that could just be due to pneumonia. Or something more serious.

"What's more serious than pneumonia?" she asked.

He pressed one of her hands between his. "Possibly leukemia."

His words hit her like a truck, and she recoiled from the impact, the air knocked out of her. She was speechless, reeling. Mark said they would rule out possibilities with more tests. The elevated white count was very worrisome. If it was leukemia, they should anticipate possible chemo and radiation. Down the road, it would be critical to know genetic family in Guatemala, for history and possible bone marrow donors.

"Bone marrow donors? Leukemia?" Julie felt she'd been lifted into a tornado, the ground below her swirling, indistinct.

Mark's eyes watered and he brushed away his tears before reaching to brush away hers. He put his arms around Julie, gasping once with a sob. "We get through this," he said. "We're not going to lose him. Whatever it takes."

*

Julie and Mark stood beside Jack's bed, staring at his face, listening to him breathe. A nest of tubes ran from a machine on the wall into their son's arm, pumping a river of antibiotics. Every few minutes, Mark picked up his son's forearm and timed his pulse. He seemed to need to feel useful. Nurses spoke in hushed voices, a murmur of buzzing bees, constant and steady. Julie wasn't a person who prayed, but she began praying, bargaining with whatever higher power may be listening. *Please let him be fine. Please let him not have leukemia. I promise to be a better mother. Please make him better.*

Dr. Tanner came in with a team of young doctors in white coats and asked them to return to the waiting area. More people sat there, rustling bags of ham sandwiches and potato chips that smelled like mustard and grease.

Mark called Julie's sister and, after describing Jack's condition, handed the phone to his wife. Claire's voice broke as she said she was sorry. "I'll come if you need me. Tell me what I can do."

"Claire, he was fine. Then out of nowhere."

"It's terrible," Claire said.

"I know," Julie said and handed the phone back to Mark.

They dozed in the chairs, alternating getting up to pace the hallway. Six hours in, Dr. Tanner returned to say Jack's blood count was dropping. His temperature stabilized. 102, 101, 100. They were allowed back into Jack's room. Their son opened his eyes and when he saw them said, "Did I miss school?" Mark and Julie bumped heads as they rushed over to kiss him.

The elevated white blood count was a leukemoid reaction, Dr. Tanner said. It was the body's immune response to pneumonia, which presented in a way like leukemia, but was not leukemia.

"He won't need chemo or radiation? No bone marrow transplant?" Julie's kneecaps quivered as her body absorbed the new diagnosis.

"Bed rest and monitor his temperature," Dr. Tanner said.

Mark and Julie hugged. She felt like they were survivors on a life raft.

Three nights later, finally back home, they stood in Jack's room beside his bed gazing on his sleeping face. An occasional car drove up the hill, its headlights illuminating Jack's window in a sweeping flash. The crickets on his white noise machine chirped. The Spiderman night light glowed. How small, how cherished, how vulnerable he was.

Mark whispered that they still needed to find Jack's mother and Julie knew he didn't mean her. Not only for possible donors, which God forbid they wouldn't need, but for medical history. Mark was right, but Julie didn't want to hear it. She didn't want to consider Jack's life before he came to them. She didn't want to think of anyone else connected to her son. She wanted to be his only mother.

Mark urged her to call Kate Hodges-Blair tomorrow. "We don't have to meet her in person. When Jack's eighteen, he can decide. We just need to know where she is."

He put his arm around Julie's shoulder. "I understand it's painful. But if something worse happens, we'll never forgive ourselves."

The next morning after Mark went to work and Jack slept, Julie paced up and down in the kitchen and dialed the number she'd never forget. Kate answered on the first ring.

"Sorry about your boy," Kate said. "But I wouldn't do this if I were you." She launched into a list of reasons why searching for Jack's birth mother was a bad idea: Karla Inez might barrage Julie and Mark with requests for money, for herself and extended family. Jack might become confused, split by his allegiance to two mothers. The birth mother might have a new partner, who doesn't know about the other man's baby. By inserting themselves into the birth mother's life, Julie and Mark might upset the natural order of things.

"She's his biological mother," Julie said. "It doesn't get more natural."

"Let me tell you a story about an adoptive mom who tried to help out. Birth mother calls, asking for money to buy her boyfriend a new power saw. Boyfriend's a carpenter. Adoptive mom wires money, boyfriend buys the power saw. Fine and dandy, help the guy out. Problem is, boyfriend has no idea how to operate a power saw. Or any high-octane tool. First day, he saws off his own hand, effectively ending his carpentry career."

"Oh my God," Julie said.

"Right?"

"That's an extreme example. Jack's situation is different," Julie said, although she knew nothing about Jack's situation except his birth mother's name and what she looked like.

"You heard what's going on with that adoption in Kansas, with the birth mother demanding her kid back? Google it."

Julie wasn't going to back down. "This is more a courtesy call," she said.

Kate said she wished them luck.

Julie opened her laptop and typed in Kansas + adoption + Guatemala. Article after article came up. A birth mother in Guatemala, Leidy Ortiz, claimed her three-year-old daughter, Veronica, was snatched from her front yard while Leidy's back was turned. Unknown and unidentified figures had stuffed Veronica into a taxi and whisked her away. The girl was delivered to an adoption attorney with the claim she'd been abandoned. Supported by international human rights advocates, Leidy Ortíz joined other Guatemalan women who claimed their children were stolen. The women staged a hunger strike in front of the Guatemalan president's residence, holding signs that read "We Will Not Yield."

Julie stopped reading. This was why Mark and she had hired Kate, the good agency director, who worked with Raquel, the good attorney. So they wouldn't be mixed up with corrupt attorneys who kidnapped babies and laundered their identities.

She logged onto the Guate Parents site and scanned the archives for Reunions.

> To see Mayson with her birth mother. Like a circle being closed.
>
> They're essentially identical, down to the shape of their fingernails.
>
> Malvy thrilled because her birth mother's favorite color is also periwinkle.
>
> His four brothers play soccer. He's six inches taller than his mother.
>
> His two youngest sisters were adopted. Anyone with a birth mother initials CMVB?

Since adoptions closed, searching had become the new industry. Secrecy about birth family was said to be harmful to children, and more Americans wanted their kids to know their whole story. Posts cautioned against searching yourself. First, Guatemala could be dangerous. Second, you didn't understand the culture.

Julie was starting to be convinced that finding Jack's birth mother was the necessary next step. She needed to hire a professional. Guate Parents recommended a dozen—all women, except for one man. The most trusted searcher seemed to be a Guatemalan social worker named Candi. She spoke and wrote English fluently, and was said to respond to requests to search within a few hours. She'd need the social worker and court reports, the DNA photo, and a copy of Karla Inez's official Guatemalan identification card known as a *cédula*.

Julie dialed Mark's number. She'd found a searcher, she said breathlessly, recommended by everyone. Candi. Eighteen hundred bucks.

"Go for it," Mark said.

Clicking open her email tab, she wrote:

> *"Dear Candi,*
> *We are the parents of a precious boy born in Escuintla, born in 2002 and now six years old. We call him Jack (his request), but his birth name is Juan Rolando. We would like to find his biological mother, Karla Inez Garcia Flores. Can you help us?"*

Julie pressed Send.

THIRTEEN

SAN LORENZO CHAL, GUATEMALA

NOVEMBER 2010

Excuse me while I take a drink of water. My Testimonial takes a long time.

Soon after my sister Marta gave birth, our priest, Padre Andrés, told us he was leaving. He told us this during a Sunday mass. The country of Belgium had sent him to us, and the country of Belgium was calling him back.

Why, why? we asked. Padre Andrés baptized every child in Chal. He gave us first holy communion. My books that taught me Spanish, he gave me. He helped repair our houses and shared vegetables from his garden. Who would do those things now?

Padre told us stories about priests who had been killed. One was flying in a small plane that was shot down over the jungle. Another was riding a horse. One priest was machine-gunned in his own bedroom in Santiago.

Padre said no priest was safe in Guatemala.

Padre didn't carry a gun. He traveled from hamlet to hamlet on horseback. He carried communion wafers and the daily missal.

When mass ended, Padre said good-bye at the door to the church. He touched fingertips with the adults, which is our traditional way. He tapped the heads and shoulders of the little ones. He told us to be responsible. To make sure our children went to school. For us to help them gain a better life.

Padre Andrés was with us, until he wasn't. The next Sunday, one of the catechists, Luis, who had studied the bible with Padre, said the mass. When we reached the part of the consecration, Luis stopped, because only a priest could transform the wafer and wine to the body and blood of Our Lord. All the same, we knelt at the communion rail. Luis gave us wafers Padre had blessed.

Our lives continued. Even without Padre, or Papi, and the other men who had left. But without the men and without a priest, our lives were different.

Violence was everywhere in Guatemala. People were found hanging from trees with their tongues cut out, or sliced into pieces and thrown over bridges.

We lived far up in the mountains, and still received information. We had transistor radios in Chal. That's how we heard news. One day, we started hearing about a "Rally for Peace." This was a gathering to be held at the National Palace in Guatemala City. We heard the announcement many times. Rally for Peace, Rally for Peace, over and over again. The announcer said any Guatemalan who loved democracy and freedom was invited.

Daniel asked Mamá what freedom and democracy meant. She said they were ideas for rich Ladinos and not poor *indígenas* like us. They were a promise for land, a promise for equality. In truth, nothing ever changed.

A few weeks after the announcements for the rally began, we were at church again. Luis was leading the liturgy. He said he wanted to introduce someone. And from the curtain behind the altar, a military officer stepped out. He wore a military uniform with many medals and ribbons pinned to the front. On his belt was hanging a gun. He had a thick mustache and curly brown hair.

The military officer called us "my fellow Guatemalans." He called himself our "compatriot." He kept saying, "We must show the world a united Guatemala. The guerrillas will not win. We cannot allow the guerrillas to win."

No one expected a military officer at church on Sunday morning. If we did what the officer said, we could stay safe. If we didn't, we knew what would happen.

Two days later, a bus loaded up the men for the rally. Tío Eldon went, with all the civil patrollers. After the rally, Mamá and Tío Eldon began to spend more time together. She was relieved he came back.

Daniel and I came home from the field to find them sitting on the low wall outside our house, with Isabel playing with the ball made from rags and string that Tío Eldon brought. They looked like a regular family. Daniel didn't seem to mind, but I worried Isabel might forget Papi and think Eldon was her father. Soon she might call him "Papi."

If Mamá were a widow, people would understand. Neighbors help widows who are left with children to support. Since Papi went to los Estados, people said it wasn't right for Mamá to receive visitors. Only women of low character did that. Also, Tío Eldon remained married to his wife, Tía Paty, and had children who were grown. Mamá acted foolish with Eldon there, too, wrapping good ribbons through her braids and tying her sash embroidered with flowers around her waist.

I understood Mamá was grateful to Eldon for helping us, but I wished he would go away and not come back.

At harvest, Tío Eldon offered to help Daniel and me bring in the corn. We agreed, because sometimes corn was stolen—by hungry neighbors, or the army, or subversives—so it needed to be harvested and brought in fast, carried down in nets before nightfall. Tío Eldon set out with us in early morning to climb the mountain to our plot.

We picked together through morning and afternoon, stopping only to eat tortillas Mamá sent with us. Because the day became hot and we were three in number, we drank the supply of water we brought before we finished. Tío Eldon asked me to go to the river to refill the clay jugs. I agreed at once.

Although the sun was high, the path to the river was thick with trees, and as I lost sight of our field, I could hardly see. Swarms of mosquitoes fed on my ankles and feet. They must have been hungry because every one of them found a piece of my skin to bite. I knew better than to scratch although it was hard not to. To help, I focused on the call of the birds, every one of them different. Horned guans, mountain trogons, and blue-throated motmots. This was the hour of their afternoon call—higher and slower than the morning call, louder than the call closer to night.

A short distance from the river, sun broke through the tops of the trees, and fell onto the ground in an intricate pattern. I was studying the pattern when the sound of leaves rustling disturbed me. An animal? I shifted my eyes left and right in search of it. Nothing.

I walked north along the riverbank to the place there is a spring where we collect clean water. As I got closer, I heard what sounded like voices. I put up my ear and listened. Then I crouched low and walked a few more steps.

On the riverbank beside the spring, the trees had been cleared. Inside the clearing were five green tents, each with their flaps closed and tied. Was it the army? Or guerrillas? I didn't see any men. I saw only that the encampment looked as if it had been in that place for days. There was stacked wood and a charred black fire circle. Beside the circle sat a transistor radio, its antenna reaching toward the sky.

I knew I should run, but my feet wouldn't move. I had to get back to Tío Eldon and Daniel to tell them what I saw. I turned and crept along the river's edge. My heart thudded.

Every tree felt like it was hiding an enemy. I wanted to throw the jug down to move faster. But that would tell them someone had walked this path. They could follow and track me. The forest felt so quiet. I just moved forward, without making any sound.

When I saw the border of our field, I rushed through the corn stalks. It would be easy to get lost among them. But I didn't dare travel outside the boundary in case whoever owned the tents saw me.

"Daniel," I said quietly. "Tío Eldon."

No one answered. I elbowed through the stalks. "Daniel. Tío Eldon," I said louder. Mosquitos flew into my mouth and I swatted at them. Where were they?

From inside the tall stalks, I heard Daniel, crying. I stopped and called for him.

"Run!" Tío Eldon's voice shouted. "Run, Rosalba!"

Without thinking, I turned and ran back through the corn. Get to the river. Get to the river. Don't stop. Don't stop. At the river's edge, I turned away from the direction of the encampment and ran as fast as I could.

One shot rang out, and another. I jumped sideways into the river, my *corte* soaking through and pulling me down. Mud clouded the water. The river flowed fast.

On the shore I heard men's voices, urgent.

A few feet down the river, low branches from a tree created a small shelter. I struggled to wade over to the first branch, caught hold of it, and ducked under the bower. I kept my nose out of the water and snuffled some down from breathing so hard. I tried not to cough, but it overcame me. Once, twice. I couldn't risk coughing again. I held on to the lowest branch and the higher ones kept me hidden.

Above me, the men's voices got closer. My whole body shook with fear. I was afraid the men would see the ripples I was creating. I hid under the tree branches and heard their voices above me.

What did we do? What did they want? I couldn't be sure, but I thought I heard one say Tío's name. *Eldon*. I prayed over and over, *Make me disappear*.

The voices faded and went in the direction of their camp. I stayed where I was, clinging to the low branch, praying. I remained in the water until the moon rose in the sky. Only then did I emerge from the river and creep home.

We never discovered if it was the army or guerrillas. Some people in Chal said one, some said the other. It didn't matter who was responsible because in the end Daniel was dead, and Tío Eldon, too. I told Mamá about Tío Eldon shouting *Run*. She didn't blame me. Tía Paty and Mamá worked together to arrange for the funerals. Tía Paty and Mamá had to be satisfied with a mass said by catechist Luis, and so they were. Although satisfied may not be the right word. More like acceptance of a thing they couldn't change. A shouldering of a burden that was. We buried Eldon with Tía Paty's family and Daniel with ours. Their caskets were light. They contained only bones. Dogs had gotten to the bodies first.

For many mornings, Mamá didn't get out of bed. She lay with her arm across her eyes, as though the world was too ugly to look at. Isabel remembered Daniel the way she never remembered Papi. She kept looking for him under the table and behind the latrine. Watching her was terrible. Yanira worked more at Doña Yoly's, leaving after morning tortillas and returning at sunset. Marta was even sadder at the home of her husband.

That harvest, the corn was stolen, and without Daniel, tending the field was difficult. At night, I dreamed of food.

FOURTEEN

CALIFORNIA

DECEMBER 2008

Claire talked Julie into a trip to Disneyland a few days before Christmas. Julie had her doubts—the park was loud and crowded, a breeding ground for meltdowns—but Claire convinced her. "Meltdowns are the norm at Disney," she said. "Nobody will notice." Both Mark and Ethan begged off, claiming important meetings, which didn't surprise the sisters. They'd developed workarounds for their busy husbands. And although Claire and Julie didn't have a model relationship, they looked forward to Disney. They'd visited once when they were young, before their mother's emphysema had debilitated her, and neither had been back since.

On the morning of the trip, Julie crept into Jack's room to wake him. Ever since his fever episode the year before, she approached him with trepidation. She probably would forever. Jack's face was turned to the side on his red fire engine pillow. One brown eye opened.

"Is today Disneyland?" he asked. Without waiting for an answer, he rolled onto his side and jumped out of bed, falling to a squat. He hopped to his closet like a frog and picked up the jeans and t-shirt he'd ironed and laid out the night before, tucked them under an arm, and hopped back to bed, diving under the covers to change from his pajamas.

"Did you know rats burp?" he said. "Did you know if you peel a grape it looks like an eyeball?"

"I didn't know that."

He sprang back up from the mattress and skipped in a circle. He skipped over to his small suitcase, packed and ready, and rolled it to the middle of the room. He skipped around it, glancing up to make sure Julie was watching before throwing her a kiss. She pressed her hand against her cheek, pretending to catch it.

My God, how she loved him. Always, but especially during rare moments of closeness like this one.

They loaded the car and started on the long drive.

The entrance to Disneyland was brilliant with dozens of lighted Christmas trees and the petals of a thousand poinsettias sparkling with gold glitter. A real-live Santa greeted guests from his mount on a life-sized sleigh outfitted with nine robotic reindeer, but Jack was so distracted by Rudolph's glowing red nose he didn't seem to notice. His Ratón with its own big nose was securely stashed in Jack's front pocket. Julie had made sure of that.

"Walt Disney adopted a child," Julie told Claire as their admission tickets were scanned and they pushed through the turnstile. "His second daughter, Sharon. Nobody knew because back then adoption was hush-hush."

"And somehow you found out," Claire said.

"Adoption was Walt's favorite theme. Bambi, Cinderella, Dumbo, Pinocchio. Every movie, orphaned children and absent mothers."

"You know you're obsessed."

Julie didn't expect her sister to understand. Until they adopted Jack, she didn't understand herself, the way adoption would change her world view.

They rode the Matterhorn Bobsled and the aptly named roller coaster, California Screaming. Flew through the air in flying elephants and spun in cars at Mater's Junkyard Jamboree. Jack trotted after Gunther from one attraction to the next, humming along to "It's a Small World" and yowling with ecstatic terror at Pirates of the Caribbean. Julie was thrilled to see them operate as a team, rocking to the rhythms of the Tiki Room's warbling parakeets and downing goblets of pink lemonade in the Rainforest Café, although only

Jack noticed how clean the streets were, remarking on the crews with brooms and dustpans.

The one blip was at a food kiosk where they stopped for afternoon snacks. Claire and Gunther stepped aside after getting their dippin' dots, but when it was Jack's turn, the vendor said he'd run out of the mint chip ice cream Jack had ordered.

Julie acted fast. "Try moose tracks. The chocolate's in ribbons instead of chips."

"No," Jack said.

"Or mint jubilee, just plain mint." She ran through other flavors: mocha, pistachio, raspberry sherbet. Or an ice cream sandwich.

"No!" Jack screamed. He grabbed Julie's forearm and twisted until it turned red, his face contorting.

Claire rushed up and pushed him backwards. "Stop negotiating with this terrorist," she snarled.

"Don't touch him," Julie snapped. Her forearm stinging, she spoke directly to Jack, keeping her voice steady and quiet. "We can get moose tracks here. Or look for another kiosk that might have mint chip."

His face scrunched as he started to wail, big tears dripping.

Julie apologized to the vendor, bought a cone of moose tracks, and moved out of line with Jack to a bench under a tree. After handing him his cone, she sat down, angry at her sister, at the vendor for running out of Jack's flavor, angry mostly at herself. She should have anticipated he'd be hungry. Lunch was four hours earlier and they'd been walking since then.

Jack moved with Gunther under the shade of the tree while Claire lowered herself to the bench beside Julie. "I don't know how you do it," Claire said finally.

"What choice do I have?"

"You could send him back."

Everyone had heard about the adoptive mother in Tennessee who'd stuck her son on a plane back to Romania with a note pinned to his shirt. "I no longer wish to parent this child," the mother had written, calling her son "mentally unstable" and "violent." Two new words on Guate Parents were *disruption* and *re-home*.

Julie stared straight ahead at the passing crowds, controlling her fury at her sister. "Ain't gonna happen," she said.

They ate dinner, and afterwards, the families returned to their adjoining rooms and Jack dropped into bed with his clothes on, asleep within a minute. Julie made a cup of tea in the room's coffeemaker and carried it and her laptop onto the balcony. On the ground below, people wearing Mickey Mouse ears and Goofy hats streamed by. Disneyland was like Las Vegas: There was no day or night.

As she scrolled through her inbox, the searcher Candi's name appeared with the subject heading: Juan Rolando Update. Finally! Julie had almost given up hope. Her pulse quickened as she opened the message. "After many dead ends, an answer," Candi wrote. "Please call me."

She must have found Karla Inez. *Stay strong,* Julie told herself. *I'm Jack's mom, too. That doesn't change.*

Candi's voice was as clear as if she were in the same room. "I'm sorry to inform you. My news is distressing."

Julie's body went into high alert. "Distressing how?" she said.

Candi explained that Karla Inez Garcia Flores lived in a barrio in Escuintla, a city on the coast, southwest of the capital. Escuintla was the city to which many Guatemalans traveled to cut sugar cane during the harvest. Many called it ugly and dangerous.

"Yes," Julie interrupted. She knew of Escuintla's reputation.

Candi found the correct barrio and, following her method, knocked on doors with a DHL envelope in hand, pretending to be delivering a message from the United States. "Many Guatemaltecos have family who send money, so this envelope is not surprising."

"Yes," Julie said again, dreading the distressing news but impatient to hear it.

An old woman directed Candi to a house in the middle of the block, saying it was the home of the family Garcia Flores. Candi reached the house to discover a young woman in her twenties sitting outside in the yard with a baby in her arms. Candi asked the young woman if she belonged to the family Garcia Flores. The young woman confirmed she did. Next, Candi asked if her name was Karla Inez.

Here, Candi said, the young woman's expression changed. "Karla Inez is dead," she said. "She died fifteen years ago."

Karla Inez couldn't have died fifteen years ago because Karla Inez was the mother of Julie's son who was sleeping five feet away and was six years old.

"She identified herself as Karla Inez's older sister, Hortensia," Candi said. Karla Inez had died from measles when she was three. Hortensia remembered Karla's age because the day she died was the same day Hortensia was supposed to receive her first holy communion. Hortensia's mother had bought Hortensia a brand-new communion dress, and Hortensia was more upset about not getting to wear the brand-new communion dress than she was about her sister dying.

"Hortensia remembers her sister's death with clarity," Candi said. "To this day, she feels guilty about regretting the dress."

No, no, no, no. Julie refused to believe it. "Maybe when she said *dead,* she meant *dead to us*, because Karla did something terrible. Or maybe Hortensia was lying."

Candi snorted. "Hortensia would have to be a magnificent actress to make her story so believable."

Hortensia went inside the house and brought out her own *cédula* to prove her family name. The *cédula* read "Garcia Flores."

Julie felt a jab of hope. "Where's the problem? The *cédula* says Garcia Flores."

"The *cédula* is real. It's Juan's paperwork that was faked."

"You keep saying faked. What do you mean, faked? I don't get it."

Candi said someone probably sold the *cédula* of the dead Karla Inez to a player in the adoption chain: *jaladora,* attorney, doctor, orphanage owner. Or to the mother herself who gave birth to Juan Rolando.

"Why would she do that? Why couldn't she use her own *cédula?*"

"Perhaps she didn't have one." Or, Candi speculated, perhaps the mother was under eighteen and her parents didn't know. Or, if the mother was married, she needed the identity of someone who wasn't. The government of the United States didn't allow married Guatemalans to relinquish their babies. Candi hesitated. "Or possibly someone took the baby without permission and invented a new identity to cover."

"Took the baby. You mean kidnapped?"

Candi sighed.

Julie was stunned. Kidnapped. Her son, kidnapped. "Are you saying the girl in the photo isn't his mother? They look exactly alike."

"She might be his mother. But she's not Karla Inez Garcia Flores."

In her years of searching, Candi had come across only three such cases of laundered identity. Those families were forever unable to connect with birth mothers. Candi said Juan Rolando's case was closed.

Over the edge of the balcony, an explosion of fireworks burst in the dark sky. Music drifted up, with faint echoes of a crowd ooh-ing and ah-ing. Jack's papers were faked. Julie was furious. "You knocked on one door. You followed one lead. There has to be another way."

"There is no other way. I'm sorry."

Why had no one caught this deception sooner? The U.S. Embassy, the Guatemalan court, the judge who ruled on Jack's case. Somebody created a false *cédula* with a picture of Jack's mother. Didn't anyone notice it look doctored?

Fireworks continued to explode in the sky. Huge bursts shattered into a thousand fragments of colors. From far away, a band played "ZippidiDooDa" and "Chim Chim Cheree" mixed with "Carol of the Bells" and "Let It Snow."

Julie felt guilty and ashamed. She peered into the dark as though she were being watched.

Fake papers happened everywhere, every day, she told herself. Migrant workers in California carried fake drivers' licenses, fake social security cards, fake passports. The birth mother who took the name Karla Inez must have had a reason.

Who was that family in Kansas? The Wengers. The birth mother, Leidy Ortiz, claimed the baby was snatched from her arms. A victims' organization in Guatemala protested to the U.S. State Department. Was the baby really kidnapped? Were the Wengers forced to give her back?

Julie frantically typed in *Wenger adoption.* Pages of articles came up. The Guatemalan protesters had raised the stakes with hunger strikes. The case was spread over the front pages of Guatemala's newspaper *La Prensa*, with birth mother Leidy Ortiz portrayed as a victim of the corrupt adoption trade. She demanded a DNA test and the Wengers refused. They held onto the baby, and the U.S. government backed them up. The case would be argued for years.

Julie and Mark had entered the U.S. with a Guatemalan passport for someone whose identity was manufactured. Jack's California birth certificate listed a city where he may not have been born. His legal middle name was Flores, connecting him to a family who wasn't his. The DNA photograph that proved a genetic link showed a woman who may or may not be his mother.

Nobody must know. Especially Claire, Ethan, and Gunther. Especially Jack, who couldn't be trusted not to tell people. Nobody at school. Not anyone, anywhere. Only Mark.

Unable to sleep, and too upset to talk coherently to her husband, she lay awake in bed, hatching plans. She could fly to Guatemala and go to the *La Prensa* office with the DNA photo. Or to the main Guatemala City TV news station. Guatemala was a small country. Somebody somewhere would recognize the birth mother who presented herself as Karla Inez. And then what? The woman steps forward and demands her son back?

In the bed beside her, her son's breath rose and fell. No matter what happened, Julie would never give him back. Ever.

The next morning, Julie's hands shook as she drank coffee in a lounge chair beside Claire on the hotel pool deck. Jack grasped the wall in the shallow part, watching water lap in and out of the drain while Gunther did cannonball after cannonball off the diving board in the deep end, each entry causing a gigantic splash.

"You should sign him up for lessons at the Y," Claire said, and Julie nodded, too distracted to be offended by her sister's insistent need to give her advice. "Swimmers are the best students," Claire added. "They've done studies."

Across the pool, Jack scrambled out of the shallow end and, shivering with his hands clasped in front of his chest, tiptoed toward the baby pool. Julie sat back and closed her eyes. She knew she should do a lot of things. She couldn't worry about swimming lessons today.

The families showered and checked out at noon, with Julie declining Claire's offer for a final late brunch at the Chip n' Dale Café. They'd stop at a drive-through. She needed to get home.

Julie took the 5, straight up the middle of California. Jack watched DVDs the entire trip, sitting in the back seat with a snack tray on his lap and headphones clamped onto his ears. Every half hour or so, Julie glanced in the rearview mirror, grateful he was content and distracted. Jack didn't notice how tightly his mother clutched the steering wheel, how often her mouth twitched as she ground her jaw. Julie couldn't believe she and Mark followed every rule and this happened. The entire international adoption business was bullshit. Did they think no one would notice? She wished they'd never searched.

The glare from the setting sun blinded her as they crested the rolling hills of the Central Valley and dropped into the East Bay, where spinning turbines harnessed wind to provide power. Julie flipped down the visor and shielded her eyes with a piece of paper she found on the car floor. Maybe this explained why Kate backed off when Julie asked for her assistance in finding Karla Inez. Kate had claimed everything was above-board, but she must have had suspicions.

Julie hadn't yet told Mark, or even forwarded the email, fearful someone in his department might read it. This was news she needed to share in person. Mark was rational and logical and would be able to calm her down. Gripping the steering wheel, Julie squinted at the dotted white line, struggling to stay straight. Out of nowhere, a pick-up truck swerved into her lane from the left. She slammed on the brakes, hard enough for Jack to lift his headphones and call out, "Mom, slow down."

They drove up their hill at seven o'clock at night, the lone streetlight guiding Julie toward their driveway and into the garage. She guided Jack down the hallway and helped him get ready for bed, placing his Mickey Mouse ears beside him on the pillow before settling in the rocker as he fell asleep.

This boy, she thought as she rocked back and forth. *Where was he born? Who was he, really? If he asked, how would she tell him she didn't know?*

Mark was due home soon. Julie boiled water for pasta and pulled out a Ziploc of pesto she had made from their basil plants and frozen. As the water simmered, the garage door opened and a minute later, Mark appeared.

"How was it?" He hugged Julie tight, stepping aside as she drained the noodles and mixed them with pesto. She arranged the food on plates while reporting Jack did great, with only a few minor tantrums, entirely understandable. Disneyland was superb, the kids got along famously.

She leaned against the kitchen counter, crossing her arms. "We got news from Candi. Not good."

She sketched the outlines of Candi's search report—the false name, the death of the real Karla Inez, and Candi's assertion that there was nothing else to be done. "Which is ludicrous," Julie said. "She followed one freaking lead."

Mark picked up the two plates and carried them to the table. "Would you mind grabbing the parmesan?" he asked.

Julie jerked open the refrigerator, grabbed the bowl of parmesan, and almost threw it on the table. He twirled spaghetti onto a fork. "We did the best we could," he said around a mouthful of food.

Julie's throat constricted. *How could he give up so easily? It was his idea to search.* "I don't think you understand. Our son might be kidnapped. Somebody might come looking for him. We don't know where this could lead. Somebody might take him away."

Chewing with deliberation, Mark held up one finger. His swallowing seemed to take an inordinate amount of time. "None of this is our fault, Julie."

"Nobody cares whose fault it is, Mark!"

Their kitchen was a shrine to Jack. His stick figure drawings on the fridge, his tennis shoes neatly arranged by the door, his returned school assignments piled in a box. On the morning they'd left for Disneyland, he'd draped his Spiderman bathrobe over the back of his kitchen chair where it remained because he'd uncharacteristically forgotten to hang it in his closet. Tenderly, Julie pressed it to her cheek as though it were a talisman. Jack was her world. Life without him was unthinkable.

"The best predictor of future behavior is past behavior," Mark said. "No one's looked for him yet."

"The kid's mother's name is wrong on his birth certificate. His place of birth says Escuintla. Don't we have some moral obligation to tell somebody?" She felt like they were speaking two different languages.

"Tell somebody, why?"

A feeling of hope pulsated in her chest. Could they do that? Not say anything. Pretend everything was normal. As infuriating as Mark could be, he was also reasonable. "What do we tell Jack?"

"The truth. The searcher couldn't find her. We hope someday she surfaces and they're able to meet."

Julie nodded, the throb of hope growing. "Do you think he'll believe us?"

"That's what we know."

She hoped what they knew, what Kate had told them, was the truth. She tamped down the image of Jack nestled in the arms of Karla Inez, a tableau as beautiful as any Piéta. And from nowhere, a stranger appears and peeks inside the blanket to admire the boy's handsome face, before snatching him from Karla's arms. The stranger evaporates into an alleyway, ducking into the back seat of a waiting car as Karla screams for help. A chain of unethical people manufactures a fraudulent identity to cover the crime.

"Jack doesn't deserve this," she said.

Mark dug out another spoonful of parmesan and sprinkled it on his remaining pasta, stirring it to incorporate the cheese. "Every day I analyze cells from people who are sick. They're good people, hard-working, innocent. A lot of them suffer. A lot of them die. Not one of them deserves it."

Mark had laid down his trump card.

"Are you upset with me about something?" she asked. "Because I would have expected you to be more—I don't know—sympathetic to your son. What this might mean for him."

An expression Julie couldn't read flickered across Mark's face. Frustration? Annoyance?

"It just gets crazier and crazier," he said.

"What does? The search? The adoption?"

"Everything," Mark said. "Our life."

They stared at each other. Julie shrugged, her expression a peace offering. "It does get crazy. At least we're stuck in this deception together?"

Mark reached for her hand. "I won't tell if you won't."

FIFTEEN

REDWOOD GLEN, CALIFORNIA

FEBRUARY 2009

Julie left the Clay early and rushed over the bridge to Jack's school for her shift of yard duty, every third Wednesday of the month. She breezed through the office to sign in and get a name badge, nodding hello to the school admins and assistants. February was cool in Redwood Glen, but the staff dressed as if prepared for the Arctic: fleece vests and hats, scarves and gloves, and this was indoors. Julie was just as guilty, in her down vest and lambswool-lined boots. They were spoiled in California, didn't know what it was to be cold. She clipped on her badge and headed to the playground.

The blacktop was alive with moving children: kids playing hopscotch, tetherball, double Dutch. Zooming down slides, scaling play structures, improvising dances. Kids in pairs and trios and packs. Strolling, bending, dashing, leaping. *Red Rover. Mother May I? Tag, You're It.* Their bodies zinged back and forth across the playground like pinballs.

Julie scanned the mostly blond crowd for Jack's dark hair. He ate during this shift and must have been somewhere else on the playground. It was then she noticed a girl in the double Dutch jump-ropers. Her skin was dark, and her hair closely cropped. Dainty and slim, she wore a fitted white ski jacket and black ski pants, looking as if she'd just finished a downhill run.

Why had Julie never noticed her before? She was always careful to spot the one or two kids who stood out as different. She scanned the playground for another volunteer who might be the girl's mother, or someone else who clearly belonged to her—that is, someone with the same color skin—before realizing she was doing exactly what people did to her son, assuming he only belonged to people whose DNA link was obvious. Once resemblance was removed from the equation, a child's parent could be anyone.

But there was no one. Just the other white yard duties wearing name tags, each loitering in her own area, keeping order.

"Am I late?" A large-boned woman in her mid-forties and wearing a flowing wool poncho over bell-bottomed blue jeans rushed to Julie's side under the overhang. PIPER, her name badge read. "This is my first day."

"Nobody's keeping track." Julie pointed to her own name badge. "Welcome."

Gray roots showed through Piper's blonde ponytail, a rare sight in their land of expensive highlights, and a map of wrinkles creased her face, also unusual. She pulled out the elastic band from her ponytail and re-did it, tighter. "We just registered. I've been homeschooling. Which I don't recommend."

"You're brave."

"Insane's more like it." Piper plucked out a pair of glasses and surveyed the playground. "Oh good. She found the double Dutch. She's excellent at that."

"Which one is she?"

"The very short hair. I don't think I'll say hi. Looks like she's having fun."

Piper didn't mention her daughter's dark skin, Julie noticed, which on this playground of white kids was her most defining feature. Julie knew why. Piper wanted to present herself as a person who didn't notice color. Yet, how could she not? Everyone else did, including Jack. White, peach, tan, brown, dark brown, black. He noticed everybody's color.

Julie didn't care because finally, here, on the playground, was another adoptive mom. Julie was so thrilled that her mind leapt to planning their first playdate, lunch, and dinner together. Suddenly, Jack came crashing into her, with such force she almost lost her footing.

"Hi, Mom. Bye, Mom." He ran off.

"Was that your son?" Piper asked.

"That's Jack. First grade. From Guatemala," Julie said.

"We thought about adopting from there, but by the time we got our act together, it was closed. Too corrupt, I guess."

"He's a legal citizen," Julie said. "Somebody approved his paperwork." That was her story and she was sticking to it. Besides, Piper's daughter was obviously adopted, either privately from the U.S. or foster care or a nation like Ethiopia, since that was the latest hotspot, possibly Uganda, maybe Haiti. Did Piper think any nation involved in adoption was exempt from corruption?

"Mexico's like that," Piper said. "My husband's family owns a home in Cabo. You can't park at a curb without paying someone. They call it a tip."

"What's your daughter's name?" Julie asked.

"Farah. From Haiti."

Bingo. "She's gorgeous," Julie said.

"Thank you." The women knew they couldn't take credit for their children's attractiveness or any other quality that came to them naturally. What else to say, though, when told one's child was gorgeous, except thank you?

"She came home five months ago. P.S. After two years of waiting. We have Farah and her sister, Beti."

"How's it going?"

"The truth? Challenging."

Julie wasn't sure she'd hid her shock. She would never be frank with a stranger or even other yard duties. If someone asked for details of their current life, which they never did, she'd claim everything was marvelous.

"We have two teenage sons of our own," Piper said. "I got greedy and wanted girls."

Two teenage sons of our own. Piper said the words the way biological parents did, as if adopted children were something other than that, as if they didn't belong to their adoptive parents, not really. Something inside Julie bristled, the way it bristled when Claire talked about Gunther's delivery in a minute-by-minute account.

"How old are they?" Julie asked.

"Farah's nine now, allegedly. Closer to twelve or thirteen."

Thirteen or fourteen was more like it. Not a chance the girl doing double Dutch was nine.

"The agency said Beti was five when we finished, but when we took her to the dentist, he said six or seven."

Typical adoption agency behavior. Young was good, younger even better. Everyone wanted a baby.

"The worst part? They're not even sisters. The girls dropped that bombshell the first week."

"They're sisters now."

"You know what I mean. It's not the same."

Julie bit her tongue. Was *not the same* code for *not as good*? As she considered ways to pose the question politely, shouts erupted on the playground near the tetherball area.

"Duty calls," Piper said. Julie put on sunglasses and they headed into the glare. As they passed the double Dutch, Piper gave Farah a wave. Her daughter promptly dropped the one end of the jump rope she was turning.

"Momma!" she said, rushing to throw her arms around Piper. A silence fell over the other girls, and Julie imagined the questions Farah would face later: "Is that your mother?" "Who was that?" "She doesn't look like you."

Julie pushed the sunglasses onto her head as Piper made the introductions.

"Nice to meet you," Farah said, her eyes not meeting Julie's. Then she looked in Julie's direction, and her smile was dazzling.

"Julie has a son who's adopted, too. From Guatemala."

"I am born in Haiti, near the capital city of Port au Prince," Farah said. She spoke with a lilting accent that sounded French.

Julie gestured toward the playground. "My son is over there somewhere. Name's Jack."

"Farah!" a girl cried. "Turn the rope, Farah!"

Piper gave Farah a squeeze. "Math tutor after school today."

The two women made their way to the tetherball poles, where whatever had erupted earlier seemed to have died down. The four other yard duties were clustered near the play structure, so they lingered near the tetherball.

"Farah's English is terrific," Julie said.

"Better than my Haitian Creole," Piper said. "I don't know what it was like in Guatemala. Haiti's the Wild West." She leaned in. "They claimed the girls were AIDS orphans. That's how they hook you. True, the mother died, or one of their mothers died. The dad was very much alive. Or the uncle, the brother, whoever he was, with six or seven other kids."

"You met him?" Julie asked.

"You can, in Haiti. We finalized after the earthquake. The system was bedlam."

Julie remembered the Guatemalan courtroom where the judge granted them permission to adopt Jack from Karla Inez. Or not Karla Inez. Whoever she was. If she'd truly relinquished her child.

Julie searched the playground for the reassurance of Jack's black hair. That's what adoption was about. Loving her son. Not dwelling on what may or may not have happened, or how they got to where they were. What purpose did that serve?

Jack must have felt Julie's eyes on him because he looked up from where he was eating at a lunch table and waved. Julie waved back. She hoped he and Piper's girls could become friends. At least the younger girl. What a treat to be around a family like theirs. Julie's other adoptive friends existed only online, and Jack didn't have any.

"Is he your only child?" Piper said.

"He is."

"We've got the issue with the hair," Piper said. She'd found a salon forty miles away in Oakland that specialized in hair of people of color and the girls spent five hours each with a stylist who shampooed, combed, and braided. Within a week, the braids had loosened, and their hair was unmanageable again.

"Who has time for that?" Piper asked. Her husband, Nick, took them to his barber in San Francisco and twenty minutes later, the girls walked out with cropped heads.

"How'd the girls react?" Julie asked.

Piper shrugged. "Honestly, everything is so foreign for them. Hair was just one more thing."

Piper said her boys, her biological sons, Spencer and Beckett, were near-clones of Nick—excellent at math; musically gifted enough to play trumpet, his instrument; and athletic enough to compete on varsity teams. Spencer, the older boy, captained the track team; Beckett, the younger, played golf. The girls, the adopted ones, not so much, although whenever they heard music, they started to dance.

"They said they danced a lot at home. They tried to teach my sons." Piper did an imitation of an uncoordinated person on a dance floor, throwing out arms and legs. "Besides the white man overbite thing, my sons were decent."

For the first month, Farah was plagued with a rare stomach bug and placed on an antibiotic drip. Beti, on the other hand, ate constantly, fearful food would disappear. "The kid can scarf down a meal," Piper said. "I'm afraid she'll choke to death. Not having food really screws up a person."

"Amen to that," Julie said.

They stood beside each other in companionable silence, surveying the yard. It was safe to say most of the children in front of them had never suffered deprivation of any kind. A part of Julie wanted to shake them and their parents, demanding if they knew how lucky they were. For them, a fenced playground with abundant food and clean drinking water was normal life. Every one of them, Julie included, was privileged.

"How old was Jack when you got him?" Piper asked.

"Four months when we started. Five years when we finished. Long story."

Piper drew in a breath. "I thought it would be easy. We'd bring the girls home and they'd fit right in." She stood taller and swiveled her neck to take in the vista of the playground. "Bring it on. I'm an experienced mother. I got this."

The bell that signaled the end of first lunch rang, increasing the energy on the playground three-fold. The four other yard duties at the play structure bent over their phones, no doubt synchronizing schedules.

"You're the only other adoptive mom I've met," Julie said.

Piper swept one arm wide to encompass the other mothers. "Likewise. No way these alpha moms are going to take on somebody else's kid."

Somebody else's kid. That's not the way Julie thought of Jack, not when it sounded so negative. But she knew it was the way he was viewed by others.

*

At the end of April, Julie invited Piper and the girls over to play. Jack spent half an hour in the bathroom getting ready, gelling back his hair and filing his fingernails. He emerged immaculate in white tennis shoes and a Madras shirt buttoned up to the top button. Watching him spin in front of the hall mirror to inspect his every angle made Julie realize that except for Claire, she and Mark never entertained, adults or children. Most of their time was spent working.

At the sound of the doorbell, Jack ducked into the hall closet and hid.

"Get out here, please," Julie said, sighing in exasperation before giving up to answer the front door. As she greeted Piper, Farah and

Beti scampered past her to the sliding glass door to gaze at the trampoline. They were dressed identically in neat denim shorts and matching denim jackets, Farah a head taller than Beti. Giggling behind their hands, they spoke to each other in what Julie assumed was Haitian Creole. Jack emerged from the closet with an impish grin. Without a word, the three of them dashed outside and across the deck, down to the trampoline.

Julie and Piper followed, sitting side by side on deck chairs, admiring the view from their vantage point: the Meyer lemon tree laden with yellow fruit, a carpet of early-blooming poppies, the cherry tree not yet blossomed and covered with black netting to protect the buds from hungry birds. Within minutes, the girls had peeled off their jackets and were jumping as high as pole vaulters. Jack called out questions, timing his words to every footfall—"What's ten times two?" "How do you spell 'fire engine?'" "What's the capital of California?"—and the girls shouted out numbers and words and sounded out syllables.

"Did the girls come with religion?" Julie asked. She'd noticed Farah wore a cross necklace.

"Christian."

"Are you guys anything?"

"The family's nothing. I do yoga."

"I wonder if Jack went to church at the orphanage," Julie said. Until she saw Farah's necklace, she hadn't thought of religion.

"We can't tailor ourselves to them," Piper said. "They become part of our family unit, not the other way around."

"Huh," Julie said. "It's the opposite for us. Our lives revolve around Jack."

"The difference between having one kid and four," Piper said. "Just saying."

The two women looked over the deck railing to the trampoline. Farah was lying in a fetal position while Jack and Beti jumped high, their downbeats bouncing Farah across the trampoline surface like a sack of potatoes. With every landing came peals of laughter.

"He hasn't had his growth spurt yet," Piper said.

"A few years before that."

"Buckle up. A different ballgame when they go hormonal."

Julie realized she'd never considered puberty. Somehow, she never thought beyond the next day with Jack, the next week. In a few months, he'd be seven.

Piper's voice caught. "I've gone from being the only female in the house to being the old lady." She smoothed under her eyelids and pressed the flesh on her cheeks as though to iron it. "Farah came fully formed. It's not like she grew up with us."

Julie glanced back to the trampoline. The roles had switched, and Jack and Beti were lying down, and Farah was jumping. Julie regarded Farah through Piper's lens and saw that Farah's denim shorts showed off slender legs while her cute, polka-dotted crop top called attention to her dainty figure.

"She is quite stunning," Julie said. "Not that you aren't."

"Oh please. Look at me." Piper grabbed the end of her ponytail and pulled it over one shoulder. The lank hair lay there like the tail of a squirrel. "I got the fat genes from my father and never lost the baby weight from the boys. I'm a hausfrau." She slid down farther in her chair. Piper had such an appealing face, Julie thought. Mark probably would call her Rubenesque.

"It's hard not to compare adopted kids to bio ones," Piper said. "My boys were so much easier."

"You got them as babies. You gave birth to them. Think of the times you gazed in their eyes, kissed and hugged them, made them feel safe and protected and loved. Now think of the years our kids lived in who-knows-what group home where nobody did any of that." Julie shifted in her chair and rolled her shoulders, trying to throw off the load of her son's past. A familiar feeling of claustrophobia descended, the one that materialized whenever she allowed herself to remember the cement-block building and steel gate, or the week's menu posted on a chalkboard, Monday through Sunday rice and beans. The smell of soiled diapers and bleach. The boys and girls in their tattered hand-me-downs, the older ones rumbling on a dusty patch of dirt. "My recent realization is that every adopted kid has special needs," she said. "How can they not?"

"You think so? Every one of them?" The prospect of mothering two girls with special needs wasn't an image Piper seemed to have considered. She frowned.

Sounds of commotion came up from the trampoline. Piper sat forward and stretched an arm over the railing. Jack and Farah had gotten off the trampoline and were standing on two sides of the cherry tree that Mark had netted, their hands up in front of them, as though grasping at something. Beti was on the trampoline, her face pressed against the safety net, looking out.

"What's going on down there?" Julie called.

Jack put his finger to his lips. "Be quiet, Mom. A bird is trapped."

A small bird—a chickadee? A sparrow? Not a crow, something smaller—had flown in through what must have been a hole in the netting over the cherry tree and couldn't find its way out. As it flapped its wings frantically trying to escape, the black net punched out in spots like two characters rolling around in a cartoon fight.

"It's going to die," Jack said dramatically.

"Do you want scissors?" Julie asked.

"We need a ladder."

Through the commotion, Farah remained standing on one side of the cherry tree, her hands now by her side. She stepped close to the netting, making a sound like trilling. A bird call of some kind, that Julie had never heard and would have no idea how to make.

"Eeeeeeeee-Laaaaaa. Eeeeeeeee-Laaaaaaaa." A silence fell over the rest of them. "Eeeeeee-Laaaaaaa," Farah called again.

From where Julie stood on the deck, she saw a clear silhouette of Farah's close-cropped hair, her petite physique. Slowly Farah pressed her hands together and lifted them up, like someone making an offering. Carefully and gently, she inserted them inside the tear in the netting. "Eeeeeeeee-Laaaaaaaaa," she trilled. "EEE-Laaa."

She pulled her hands back through the tear, with the bird cradled inside. Sitting. Not flapping, not flying, not anxious. Just sitting, contentedly, as though on a throne. Still holding the bird, Farah strode toward the women and climbed up the steps with the bird tented in her hands.

"Is a wing broken? Is it hurt?" Piper asked.

Farah moved her head from side to side with deliberation. No. A luminous smile creased her face and she lifted her hands to the height of Piper's collarbone and opened them wide. In a swift, smooth motion, the bird flapped its wings once and flew off.

Julie couldn't believe her eyes. "How'd you do that?"

Farah dropped her head and shook it. The other kids came running up the stairs.

"That was awesome," Jack said.

Piper reached out an arm and squeezed Farah's shoulder.

"Did you see that, Mom?" said Jack. "That bird liked her."

Julie glanced again at Farah, not believing what she'd seen. Who were these children from other lands who spoke the language of birds and held tiny beating hearts in their bare hands? She turned to Piper. "Not to go all rainbows and unicorns on you. But look at us. Look at our children. The rewards outweigh the challenges."

SIXTEEN

SAN FRANCISCO, CALIFORNIA

MAY 2009

Julie and Eames sat in the conference room brainstorming ideas before the weekly ideas meeting. Since the debacle of her high-flying expansion idea, Julie had been reluctant to offer any input to the ideas meeting, but Dr. Conrad would never allow that. Staff were required to demonstrate they were thinking, at a minimum.

"How about we raise another million to expand the parking garage?" Julie said. "Easy parking's a draw."

"Rooftop sculpture garden?" Eames offered.

"Not bad. Except for the cost," Julie said. She tried to think like Dr. Conrad. The director was about making money, not spending it. Julie longed for the old days with Talbot as director, when ideas meetings focused on the exhibition schedule and not get-rich-quick schemes.

"How about we sell the Calder to one of the tech companies," Julie suggested, half-kidding. "Plunk it down in the middle of their campus. Instant coolness."

Eames wagged a finger. "No de-accessioning. Stipulation of the endowment contract."

"More art classes for rich people."

"We've saturated the market."

"Art tours. To expensive countries. They'll need tour guides." Julie motioned between Eames and herself. "Road trip."

The door opened and Dr. Conrad swept in with her usual fragrant cloud of rose perfume. Doni followed behind, hoisting the silver tea tray with pots, cups, and pastries. Julie and Eames sat at attention.

Dr. Conrad waited while Doni poured the director's coffee and placed a scone on a plate in front of her. "Who do you have for me today?" Dr. Conrad asked.

With spring breaks and holidays, attendance had been slightly down, which was normal. People were focused on travel and late-season skiing. The good news was that items in the museum shop were selling well, thanks to the steep twenty percent discount Eames had suggested at a previous ideas meeting. They'd raised the prices first, so the twenty percent took a smaller bite from the bottom line. Eames was a shopper. He knew retail.

Julie's ideas, that moments before felt clever and original, seemed old and shopworn. She wondered if Eames felt the same about his. But he seemed to be riding high on his museum shop success. Julie twisted her hands in her lap. With home life so demanding, she needed to stay on Dr. Conrad's good side and keep her job stable.

Dr. Conrad turned to Julie.

"I went on a studio visit," Julie said. "Gilberto Cruz. He sketches people. Random people. Ones that he sees, who are often unseen."

She described Gilberto's process of sketching a figure, taking a slide of his drawing, and then enlarging the image to life-size by casting it on a blank wall. He traced the now life-size image on a large piece of paper he'd taped to the blank wall, cut out the outline, and laid it on thick cardboard. Using a matte knife, he cut a second figure from cardboard, this one like a giant paper-doll.

"He places the figures in nature. They function like temporary sculpture. You must see it."

Dr. Conrad rolled one hand, inviting further explanation. "A comment on?"

"The ephemeral quality of life," Julie said. "How fragile and brief."

The room was silent. "Also, seeing the invisible," Julie added.

"Intriguing," Dr. Conrad said at last. "Where are they? Can we see any?"

"At his studio. Nothing's been installed. He just moved here from San Diego."

"Has the Bilbray shown him?"

"No one else has seen this work."

Dr. Conrad tucked a thumb under her two front teeth, her eyebrows drawn in a straight line. "Put together photos for me to present to the board," she said.

"Paper dolls," Eames piped up. "It will become a thing."

Dr. Conrad stared into space, as if visualizing who might be rendered in three dimensions. "I like it," she said.

*

Julie rented a deluxe van to take board members to Gilberto Cruz's studio in the Mission. Gilberto's grandparents had emigrated from Brazil, and, to set the mood, Julie played samba music over the loudspeaker and gave commentary on the buildings they passed. The walls with political murals, the district's namesake Mission Dolores, a hall for salsa classes, the restaurant that boasted the city's most renowned *feijoada*. She felt connected to the neighborhood because of her Latino son, more than she would have if she wasn't an adoptive mother, although she didn't let on. This tour was not about her. During work hours, it was as if her existence was owned by the Clay, and nothing else mattered.

Gilberto greeted each board member with a penetrating gaze, as if he detected a secret inside each of them. Dr. Conrad stood beside him, chin up, pleased to the point of elation. The board members and their significant others pumped the artist's hand as though honored to be in the presence of such intensity. Julie hovered at the doorway like a proud, anxious parent, crossing her fingers that her proposal to show Gilberto's work would sail through the approval process.

Gilberto led his guests to his studio's large back room, and Julie shuffled behind them, hanging back to observe the installation's impact. Life-size temporary sculptures studded the space and the figures Gilberto had chosen to represent were people who ordinarily blended into the background: a middle-aged woman carrying a bucket of cleaning supplies, another pushing a vacuum cleaner. A young man in overalls with a rake over his shoulder, and a stooped, older man wielding a leaf blower. The figures were rendered mid-movement, as if trapped in a lava flow. The effect was almost like watching a stage play where minor characters stepped out from the shadows to center stage, and thus revealed their intrinsic humanity and majesty.

Dr. Conrad sidled up beside Julie. "Gilberto's work is new and innovative. You did well."

Julie was so astonished to hear a compliment from the director she couldn't respond.

"They said you had a gift and they were right."

"That's very kind."

"Not kindness. Truth. We're lucky to have you."

Dr. Conrad moved away from Julie and drifted toward one of the board members. Julie fixed her gaze on the arrangement of figures, trying to sort through her boss's comments. Eames wandered over, asking what was up.

"Dr. Conrad paid me a compliment," Julie said.

Eames shivered. "I just felt hell freeze over."

*

The dishwasher was purring through its cycles when Julie greeted Mark at the kitchen door by pushing her body against his and pressing her hands against his hips.

"Am I in the wrong house?" Mark asked.

"Funny." Julie waited while he hung up his keys on the peg board over the calendar and slipped off his shoes. "Dr. Conrad loved Gilberto

Cruz's work. Totally got it." She spun in a circle, head thrown back and arms outstretched.

Mark skirted around her and opened the refrigerator, placing left-over containers on the counter. "I'm glad for you."

She waited while he loaded food onto his plate and slid it into the microwave before she put the leftover containers away.

"Jack asleep?" Mark asked.

"For two hours." Julie clapped gleefully, her eyes shining. "Finally, Conrad gives me credit for something."

Mark sat at the table and Julie handed him a napkin. He placed it on his lap and dug into his food. Within a minute and a half, the plate was empty. He wiped his mouth and set the napkin beside his plate. "Although I'm a little surprised by how much you care."

"Dr. Conrad's the one who signs the paychecks," she said, stung. "Remember?"

Mark placed his fork and knife in an X across his plate. "And I thought I married an artist."

Julie felt stung again. "Are you serious? You're not serious. I was never going to make it as an artist. First, I wasn't good enough. Second, we needed money."

"Artists make money."

"Successful ones make money. I was never going to be successful."

"Not with that attitude." Mark stood, picking up his plate. He touched the handle of the dishwasher. "This on?"

When Julie didn't answer, he set his dish in the sink. "When I met you, you were an artist. Now you're…."

"What? What am I?" Julie asked.

Mark rubbed a hand over both eyes and massaged the bridge of his nose. "I'd rather not say, Julie. Let's go to bed."

She stood up in front of him, toe to toe. "No. Tell me what I am. Tell me what I am besides the mother of your son. Some people can do everything. Be great artists, work full-time, be great moms. I can do two of those things. I'm sorry."

Mark wrapped his arms around her hips and brushed his lips across her cheek, suddenly conciliatory. "What about amazing wife? You didn't mention that."

"Amazing wife," Julie repeated. "That, too."

She received Mark's kiss and didn't return it.

SEVENTEEN

REDWOOD GLEN, CALIFORNIA

MAY 2009

On a May morning in the Cowan kitchen, Jack leaned over Julie's shoulder as she re-read the Evite from Piper. The party was in honor of Piper's eldest son, Spencer, who recently got his acceptance letter to Stanford and was graduating high school. He had a 4.8 GPA, with the maximum AP classes junior and senior year. Nobody was surprised. Multi-tasker that she was, Piper had folded in a Haitian theme, and even hired a chef from Haiti she found on Craigslist.

"Piper said we should arrive hungry," Julie said. "She's serving pork *griot* and *pain patate*."

"What's that?" Jack asked.

"Don't know, kiddo. We'll find out."

Julie and Mark were delighted to be invited to Piper's house. Julie was particularly pleased that Mark would finally meet her one adoptive-mom friend. The day was unseasonably warm for May. Julie packed swimsuits and towels.

Piper lived on the other side of the hill, in a sprawling ranch house that fronted a deep canyon and sat behind a tall bamboo fence. Julie opened the gate like she was entering Oz. Paths of river-smooth rocks meandered through clusters of red camellias and pink azaleas. A gingko tree with fan-shaped leaves led to a display of bonsais set on green moss. Water trickled in a niche beside a pond, where a Buddha with long earlobes sat crossed-legged, his expression wise and serene. Pagoda lights twinkled.

"Look at this tree," Mark said, petting a cascade of yellow-red leaves on a Japanese maple. He bent to a bed of fiery orange flowers, his fingers grazing a blossom. "These are Lilies of the Nile on steroids." At any minute, Julie expected a spa attendant to appear carrying waffle-weave, organic cotton robes and pairs of vegan leather slippers. Now, this was living.

Piper emerged from the front door, dressed in a blue-checkered, off-the-shoulder dress cinched at the waist and down to her feet. Gold sandals showed off her matching blue toenails. "You're here!" Piper air kissed Julie first and then Mark. "Dr. Cowan," she said. Although she hadn't met him before, Piper always referred to Mark as "the esteemed pathologist," which amused Julie. Piper's husband, Nick, was a partner in a Silicon Valley investment firm that made fortunes for its partners, and Julie had never met him in person, either.

The Cowans followed Piper into a great room half the size of a football field, with a ceiling as high as a hotel atrium. The space felt familiar, and Julie realized she'd seen either this home, or one exactly like it, in a hundred design magazines: A large L-shaped leather couch with a chrome light fixture arched behind it and a chunky square marble coffee table topped with peonies in a silver vase. Abstract, monochromatic paintings that would seem monumental and outsized anywhere else lined the walls.

They stopped at the edge of the area rug, so fluffy and clean they weren't sure if they should walk over or around it. A dozen guests holding champagne flutes and wineglasses milled around. The cavernous space accommodated everyone, and still appeared empty.

"Let me find the girls," Piper said to Jack. "We'll introduce you to Spencer and Beckett."

"The man of the hour, and his brother," Mark said. "You must be proud."

Tossing out little finger waves to her guests as she passed, Piper led them through the great room to the kitchen where slow, pulsing music played through unseen speakers. As they drew closer, the air smelled of garlic, peppers, chile, and other spices Julie didn't recognize—exotic and enticing. Food from Haiti, Julie guessed, and her stomach growled.

A woman wearing a chef's apron, an off-the-shoulder dress similar to Piper's, and about ten beaded necklaces stood in front of the stove, a wooden spoon in one hand. Six burners were flaming. "Josette, have you seen the girls?" Piper asked.

"Outside with the boys."

Piper peered over the stove. "Can you tell our guests what you're making?"

"*Griot*. What you might call fried pork." She pointed with her spoon. "This is pork we've marinated in many spices. And this over here"—she indicated fritters on a flat skillet— "is our *pain patate*, with sweet potatoes and banana."

Her voice sounded French, with accents placed on unexpected syllables, just like Piper's daughters. Piper excused herself and disappeared through a sliding glass door.

Josette watched as Julie inhaled the spicy aromas and seemed satisfied with the obvious appreciation of her cooking skills. "Is this your boy?" she asked. Julie curled a hand around Jack, pulling him closer. "He is."

"You're not from America," she said, addressing him.

Jack shook his head. "Guatemala."

"Adopted?"

"Yeah," Jack said.

Josette turned back to Julie. "In Port-au-Prince, I've seen many Americans adopting children from Haiti. Now you and Mrs. Piper. Why do so many white people want dark-skinned babies?"

Julie felt Jack's body stiffen against hers and she pulled him in closer. It was noteworthy how people from other countries felt more comfortable asking personal questions about adoption than Americans did. Or maybe, instead of asking Julie to her face, Americans discussed her behind her back. Had Josette already asked Piper the same question?

Julie felt Mark's arm slip around her waist, his voice at her ear. "Jack is our son. His skin happens to be brown. No mystery to it."

Josette aimed the spoon at Mark. "Good answer."

A young woman server came up beside Julie with a small round tray of drinks. Julie selected a red wine, as did Mark. Jack took sparkling apple cider. "What do you say?" Julie prompted.

Another server appeared on the other side with a tray of hors d'oeuvres. "What are these?" Jack asked, his fingers hovering over the selection. "Fried goat and spicy beef kebobs," said the server.

Jack pulled back his fingers.

"No, thank you," Julie corrected him, before taking one for herself. They headed outside to join Piper.

The pool seemed Olympic-sized, its water agitated with the flailing bodies of young men, their shoulders massive, broad, twice the size of a regular person's. Piper stayed back a yard from the pool's edge to avoid getting splashed, but water still sloshed on the cement deck, dampening her dress to her knees. "They get in the zone and it's hard to break the spell," she explained, pulling the soggy fabric out from her legs. She scanned the bodies in the water. "There's Beckett. Not seeing Spence."

Spiky hair, bleached chlorine-yellow, and eyes like iridescent cornflowers. Tall, fit, healthy. Boys like that grew up to run the world, or at least run the country and every business in it.

Julie skimmed the crowd on dry land. A group of blonde-haired girls lounged in chairs on the pool deck in teeny bikinis that showed off ripped abs and formidable biceps, specimens of young womanhood so fine they seemed otherworldly. Occasionally one would glance at the boys in the pool and let out a whoo-hoo or deign to smile, but mostly they stared at their phones. They were the female counterparts to Piper's sons. *A den of Amazons,* Julie thought. *When Jack was a young man, is this who he would date?*

Piper bent toward Jack. "Do you want to go in the hot tub? Are you wearing a swimsuit?"

"We brought one," Julie said, patting her tote bag. Piper pointed them inside, toward the powder room down the hallway where Jack could change.

As Julie waited for Jack outside the powder room door, she noticed the hallway walls were covered with framed photographs. She walked slowly to inspect them: a young Piper and Nick at their wedding—a thin Piper, drop-dead gorgeous with hair blonde and not gray, and Nick, trim and bearded. Baby pictures of the boys: young towheads on bicycles, on top of mountains, on racing blocks with medals around their necks. The family posed in front of the Eiffel Tower, Buckingham Palace, on the Great Wall, and the Hollywood Walk of Fame. This family traveled. No photographs of the girls.

Julie heard Farah giggle, then her lilting voice asking, "Why are you doing that?"

A few feet away, a door was half-open. Another eruption of giggles. "That's my party dress."

"You're wearing a swimsuit under," said a young man. "Pink."

"Momma got it for me."

"I like the color." Something in the young man's voice had changed. It was deeper, more raw, a near growl.

"That's nice." Farah's voice, sweet and soft, open.

Another few seconds. Nothing. Julie realized she was dreading the sound of bed springs, but she heard only her own blood rushing. The hallway was empty. Farah's voice again, breathy and light. "What is that?"

No response.

Why did they stop talking? Why was Farah alone with a boy?

Julie tapped open the door three inches. A young man in red nylon running shorts was lying on the bed, Farah pinned underneath, arched against the mattress, a frill of white dress bunched around her hips. Was this what it looked like?

"Hello?"

The young man jumped up, his hands reaching down to adjust his shorts. "Hey," he said.

"Farah? Everything okay?"

"We're good," the boy said.

"Farah?"

Farah rolled onto her side, pulling down her dress. When she stood up, her eyes were moist and bright. "Very well, thank you."

"Jack's here," Julie said. "Outside."

Farah giggled, her eyes flicking over to the boy.

Was he a friend of Piper's kids? Julie needed to tell her this guy should not be trusted.

She took a step into the room. "I'm Julie, a friend of Piper's," she said, hoping the boy would leave.

"I'm Spencer."

Spencer? What was Spencer doing in a room on a bed with Farah? With her dress pushed up? Did Piper know about this?

He smiled: self-assured, debonair. "C'mon, Farah."

Farah skirted past Julie and followed him out the door, the hem of her white cotton dress swishing behind her. The yellow matelassé coverlet held the imprints of their bodies. Julie reached out to touch the coverlet. It was still warm.

"Mom," Jack called.

She forced herself to return to the hallway, where Jack waited outside the powder room door in his swimsuit, his face accusing. "Where were you? Where did you go?"

Julie stared at Spencer as he crossed the great room to the kitchen. He had to be eighteen, or almost. Farah was what, thirteen?

"I'm mad at you," Jack said.

"I'm so sorry. I'm back now." She guided Jack through the house to the party outside, shaking. Where was Mark? Had she seen what she thought she'd seen? She couldn't have. It was outrageous. But she had seen it. She knew it.

They passed the pool to the hot tub where Mark stood talking with another man. Beti was submerged in the tub, her head barely above water, along with eight teenagers. Julie hoped she wasn't boiling. Jack dipped in a toe and sat tentatively on the edge.

Julie tugged Mark aside, hissed the story into his ear.

"Are you sure?" he asked. "Could something else have been happening?"

"I'm positive. Nothing else was happening. What should we do?"

"Talk to Piper."

"And say what? You adopted a kid, and by the way your son is molesting her?"

"Ask if she's noticed anything."

"When? Now?"

"Tomorrow. When you're calmer."

Calmer. Tomorrow. She hoped she could wait that long, that nothing awful would happen before then.

From across the pool, Piper tinkled a bell for attention. "Josette has finished cooking the meal and setting up the buffet line. Everyone please move inside." Beti hopped out and wrapped herself in a towel. Jack ran up to Mark and Julie, completely dry.

"Let's pack up," Julie said. After what she'd seen, Julie knew she couldn't stay.

"We just got here," Jack pouted. "I'm hungry."

"We should feed him," Mark said.

Julie felt outnumbered. "Fine. Fifteen minutes."

In the kitchen, a few of the teenage girls sat on high stools. Julie heard one girl tell another her family was going to Haiti next summer on a mission trip. The second girl said her family was going to Kenya on a safari. Interspersed among the girls were the boys, legs spread and taking up space on the floor. Their knees bent as they moved to the music.

Farah stood, almost hypnotized, watching Josette spooning out food onto large platters and handing them to servers to place on the buffet line. Julie wondered if the girl remembered her Haitian mother in her kitchen. How strange would it feel to smell the same foods, eat the same flavors in California? A few feet away, Spencer leaned against the counter, talking to an athletic girl in a sarong and flip flops.

His sightline was directly on Farah, so focused he didn't notice Julie noticing him.

*

At just before two in the morning, Julie startled awake, already the third time she'd woken. Beside her, Mark slept, warm and solid. She couldn't erase it: the vision of Spencer on top of Farah, his red nylon running shorts, her white dress bunched up against the yellow coverlet, as vivid as a color photograph. Julie crept out of bed, tiptoed into the kitchen. A glass of warm milk, a slice of banana bread. That's what she needed. Waiting for the microwave, she picked up her phone. "Piper," she typed. The microwave binged. She slammed the phone down, unsure what to say or how to say it. She and Mark had agreed the conversation needed to happen immediately. She'd text Piper to invite her for a walk first thing in the morning.

She tossed and turned for hours, until the night finally passed. Mark set out for his usual run, and when he returned, promised to make Jack breakfast. Twenty minutes later, Julie pulled into an empty parking spot at the trailhead at the Cove, one down from where Piper waited beside her Volvo sedan, stretching her quads. Her silver hair glinted in the late morning sun. Piper smiled and waved as Julie fiddled with the radio knobs and slowly unbuckled her seatbelt.

She did not want to get out. She did not want to face Piper. Aside from Mark and Claire, Piper was the only person Julie talked to about adoption. Neither pretended everything was easy. Then Julie thought of Farah's eyes, the way they shone as she got up from the bed, hopeful and unguarded.

"Great party," she said, slamming shut her door.

"We stayed up way too late." Piper set a black baseball cap on her head and tucked in her hair.

"Score on the fried goat." Julie raised a palm for a high five.

"Not enough mouthwash in the world."

The women bent to tighten the laces on their shoes before setting off at a brisk pace, falling into a matching cadence. Their deep breaths disturbed the quiet, and the exertion filled Julie's nostrils with the acrid, oily smell of eucalyptus.

"I hear they eat grasshoppers," Piper said. "Not my taste, but vive la difference."

Julie kept her head down, nodding when appropriate. She was relieved Piper was going on and on. She wanted to stall for as long as possible.

"Josette's an amazing chef," Julie said.

"The girls were in heaven. Finally, food with flavor."

"Farah seemed really interested in Josette's cooking." Julie said, trying to find a way in to what she didn't want to say.

"Quite authentic, according to her." Piper dabbed a tissue under her dripping nose. "Whenever I walk here, the faucet opens."

Julie glanced ahead and behind, seeing no one else on the trail. "How's the adjustment for Spencer and Beckett? Suddenly having two girls in the house, I mean."

"Great. They love having little sisters."

"I'm just wondering. If, like, for Spencer, it's a challenge having a teenage girl around? Especially one who is so attractive."

"Spencer? No. Not at all. He has a girlfriend."

Julie trotted a few steps to keep up when Piper picked up the pace. "Let me ask another way. I mean, is it challenging to have an attractive girl like Farah living under the same roof, down the hall, as it were?"

Piper stopped. "No. Not challenging at all." She put her hands on her hips. "What are you asking? Spence'll be eighteen in three weeks. Farah's a kid. There's the normal brother-sister antics. When he's not at practice or doing homework, they sit on the couch and play games on his phone." She looked displeased by whatever Julie was implying.

"He has a girlfriend?"

"Girls throw themselves at him."

"But Farah's not a girl. She's quite developed."

"Stop talking in riddles." The sharpness in Piper's voice made Julie flinch. But Mark saw what she saw, too.

"I'm going to tell you something," Julie said. "Whatever you do with the information is up to you. I won't bring it up again, but you need to know. At the party. When I took Jack to get changed. I saw them together in a bedroom."

Piper stared at her, as if daring her to continue. She seemed suddenly large, and distant, a stranger. Julie wished she could say never mind, it was nothing, but it was Farah in that room, sweet Farah, who had held a bird, jumped on the trampoline with Jack, played a game to learn the alphabet. It wasn't nothing.

"They seemed close. Not brother and sister close."

Piper's eyes darted from side to side, as if she were evaluating thoughts as they raced by. Julie continued. "It felt like I was interrupting something."

"Like what?"

This was even harder than she'd imagined. Piper didn't want to hear any of this.

From below them on the path, two black Labs loped up, their heads low to the ground. Two women followed behind, tugging on leashes. They nodded a greeting and Julie waited until they rounded a curve before continuing.

"Something inappropriate." Julie lifted her shoulders in a gesture of helplessness. "Like something inappropriate. They were kind of wrestling." Without emotion, she described the scene: the two on the bed; her white dress; his red shorts.

Without a word, Piper turned toward the parking lot and started walking back to their cars. Julie followed. "Spencer's a lot stronger than Farah. A lot more mature," she said.

"They're almost the same age," Piper snapped.

"You said thirteen."

"Thirteen. Fifteen. Somewhere around there." Piper's hands swatted the air.

Suddenly, Julie was angry. How could Piper not see the danger right in front of them? "Listen. Slow down. He might be the first guy who's been nice to her. The first white guy for sure."

Piper kept walking. Julie said, "He shouldn't wrestle with her like that. Farah might be confused."

Piper stopped then, taking a wide stance, and closed her eyes, touching her index fingers to her thumbs. She began to chant and sway.

Julie looked away. Praying wasn't going to fix this. "You need to talk to him," Julie said.

The late morning sun grazed the tree line and the air felt chillier than it had the day before. Julie shivered. Charla T. often posted that parenthood wasn't for amateurs. Julie never asked if she meant every parent or only adoptive ones. No one could deny adoption added a layer of complexity.

Piper dropped her praying hands and opened her eyes. "He got into Stanford."

Julie crunched a sheet of eucalyptus bark under the heel of her shoe. *Who the hell cares where he was going to college?* "Talk to him, Piper. You need to."

*

Three days later, the recess bell rang as Julie clipped on her yard duty name badge and stepped onto the playground for her monthly Wednesday afternoon shift. The doors to the portables flew open and kids exploded out like they'd been shot from cannons. The single-minded energy with which they embraced their freedom from the task of learning usually made Julie laugh out loud. Not today.

Farah was easy to pick out. She ran straight to the knot of jump ropers. Dressed in her gray hoodie and black leggings, she wore giant, bright white tennis shoes that gleamed like polished catamarans. Maybe Julie was imagining it, but Farah seemed subdued. Had Piper spoken with her? Because she hadn't spoken to Julie. Not since Julie had confronted her on Sunday.

Because, frankly, Julie couldn't stand it anymore. Worrying about Farah was eating her alive. She'd role played the dialogue with Mark:

What kinds of games do you play with your brother? Do you spend time alone together? How does he treat you? When the right moment came, she'd pull Farah aside.

"Hey there. I got called to sub for Britney." Piper clutched a Peet's chai latte.

Julie felt nervous, found out. "Botox emergency?" she asked, lightly.

"Pilates crisis."

Across the playground, on the other side, Jack waited his turn for hopscotch, with Beti beside him.

"Check out Farah's tennies," Piper said.

"Where'd you get them?"

"Goodwill. Suddenly she's into thrift stores."

Piper pulled out a Chapstick with her free hand and swiped it across her lips. She wore a loose, mustard-colored top and not a speck of makeup, yet even with silver hair and wrinkles, somehow managed to look like a Nordic goddess. She shoved the Chapstick back in her pocket, shook her to-go cup, then tossed it into the recycling can behind them.

"He denied it," Piper said, her voice almost a whisper.

Julie hooked one arm around her friend's shoulder, stepping close. What could she say? Piper brushed away tears with a fist, took a deep breath, shook her head. "But I saw it. Coiled on the couch together, watching movies. Then later, in the hot tub."

Julie squeezed her friend closer. How desperately she had wanted to be wrong.

"The thing is," Piper said. "Farah doesn't realize what she's doing. Not consciously."

"Farah?" *Farah was the child in this,* Julie thought. Or the child-woman. How could she understand she was playing with fire? She couldn't.

Piper laughed bitterly. "Nick's worried because of Stanford. That's his world." Puffing out her chest, Piper imitated her husband. "If anyone finds out. What if she gets pregnant? We could be talking statutory rape." She looked at Julie with eyes slightly wild and spoke in her own voice, steady and low. "This shit simply cannot happen."

A long moment passed before Julie felt she could speak. "Can you keep them apart? Get Spencer into therapy?"

"A therapist would be required to report us to CPS. Guaranteed," Piper said. Once they learned of the potentially dangerous situation, Child Protective Services would stick Farah in foster care and pass her around until she aged out at eighteen. "Her vulnerability quotient would multiply times ten."

"When does Spencer leave?" Julie asked.

"August. But he never truly leaves." Piper drew out the final word, leaves. "He's our son."

And Farah's your daughter, Julie thought.

*

Julie dedicated the next two days to finding a solution for Piper. Huddled in her office with the door closed, she posted on Guate Parents and emailed Charla T. for advice. Farah needed more than five months to adjust to living in this world so different from the one in which she was raised. Who wouldn't? Even Julie had trouble adjusting to Redwood Glen and she'd grown up two hundred miles away in Fresno. Online she discovered respite care, residential therapy centers, boarding school. She found one therapist who specialized in adoption, booked solid for three months, but anyone could be helpful. Piper wasn't the first adoptive parent struggling, and she wouldn't be the last. Systems existed if she knew how to access them.

Julie sent Piper link after link, with zero reaction from her friend.

Julie was in bed Saturday morning when Piper texted her. "Can I see you today? Now?"

Julie was showered, dressed, and heating water to boil for tea when Piper's Volvo pulled into the driveway. The door was hardly open before Piper fell into her arms. "It's all right. Everything's all right," Julie said.

"It's not all right. It's not all right," Piper cried, pushing her away. She dug her fingers into her hair and yanked at the roots until she pulled out two long silver strands.

"Piper, Piper," Julie said, recalling Charla T.'s admonition not to escalate during crisis. Piper opened her palms and stared at the clump of silver hair. "I've officially lost my mind."

From the direction of Jack's room sounds drifted in. For once, Julie hoped he would sneak straight to the family room and turn on the TV.

She guided Piper, still crying, into the kitchen and over to the compost bin, where Piper deposited the hair. The kettle whistled, and Julie dropped tea bags into the pot and poured in the water. Steam rose and the air smelled of peppermint. *How bad was it?* Julie wondered. *How far did it go?* The important thing was to stay calm. As Piper's tea steeped, Julie poured herself a cup of coffee, and to give Piper more time to compose herself, opened the fridge for a splash of half and half. Piper's sobs subsided. Her breath hiccupped out in little gasps.

"What happened?" Julie asked.

"Farah snuck out. God knows why. It's not like we chain her. The cops brought her home."

"Where was she?"

"Down the hill at Jamba Juice. It wasn't even open. God forbid a black girl is seen walking downtown after dark."

"What did the cops say?"

"Took information. Brought her home. Told her to stay inside, it wasn't safe to be out."

Knock on wood, their neighborhoods were quite safe, perhaps safer to Farah than the inside of her house, Julie thought. She opened the lid to the teapot to check the color, poured out a cup and passed it to Piper.

Piper gripped the mug in both hands. "It spooked me, Julie."

"We'll take the girls for a weekend," Julie said.

She pulled out her phone and scrolled through her Places to find the ones she'd bookmarked. Photos of ranches and horses and blue skies dotted with white clouds filled the screen. "There are these residential centers. In states like Montana. I sent you links."

Piper put down her mug and glanced at the images for only a second before setting the phone on the table. "Last night when that policeman came, there was drama. Doorbell ringing, flashlight beaming. Beti running out of her room in her pajamas. Farah wailing and crying. And that's when I realized." Piper paused, her eyes suddenly clear and focused. "I don't love them. Not the way I love my own children."

Piper's words hit Julie like a fatal blow. A death kick. *My own children.* Julie felt flattened.

"I don't love Jack every minute of every day," Julie said finally. "I don't always love Mark, either, by the way. And here's a news flash: they don't always love me." Piper sat very still, listening, like a bird caught in a net who had given up hope.

"We decide to love," Julie said. "Love is an action, not a concept."

She strained her ears for sounds of Jack lurking and listening. All quiet. She walked to the table and pulled out a chair. "Here's what I figured out. We're the mothers they're allowed to hate. We're the mothers they can push and test and push and test to see how far they can go before we walk out. Except we don't. We're the mother who stays."

Piper nodded the tiniest amount, an acknowledgement.

"Our kids are traumatized. My son was signed away in a courtroom. Your daughters were separated from extended family. That may have been the least of what they endured. We do the best we can to try to help them heal."

Julie felt as if she were at the bottom of a tall building, trying to convince someone not to jump. Leaning forward, she rested her elbows on her thighs, as close to Piper as possible. "Monitor them. Set boundaries. Keep them apart. Farah needs your help. Your son does, too. You can't do this alone. Get therapy."

Piper's eyes were vacant. "It's like we live in a world that's upside down. We thought it was going to be one way, and it's the opposite."

That's exactly what it was like. Motherhood was not the fantasy they'd imagined. But here they were.

EIGHTEEN

BAY AREA, CALIFORNIA

JUNE 2009

Julie told the new babysitter not to bother trying to get Jack to sleep until they got home from the Gilberto Cruz opening, which should be around midnight.

"Bedtime is a suggestion," she said, leading the way to the dining room table. She pointed to a pile of clean laundry, and beside it, a gallon Ziploc filled with loose change. "After he irons and folds the clothes, he can roll the coins into these paper sleeves."

The babysitter, a child-development major at Marin Community College Julie found on a job board, raised her eyebrows at Jack. "I've never seen anyone actually use an iron. You can teach me."

Yes, Julie thought. *Jack would be fine.*

Organizing the Cruz exhibition had been the most satisfying experience in Julie's career. The sculpture garden was always magnificent, but with the addition of Gilberto's cardboard figures, it had been transformed into a space that felt complete, as if the trees and grass and permanent sculptures had been waiting for the figures to animate them. Julie almost couldn't imagine the space without the cardboard figures, although she'd have to. And that was the point. The sculptures forced the viewer to reflect on the way the addition of a single figure, a person, could change everything.

The searchlights in front of the Clay crisscrossed in the sky as Julie directed TV reporters toward Eames, who escorted them to the sculpture garden to interview Gilberto. The buzz on his debut was huge.

Three hundred invited guests were expected, with room for another two hundred crashers.

The last scheduled crew arrived, and Julie went inside to find Mark. He'd parked the car and they'd arranged to meet inside. The atrium was decorated in a Rio de Janeiro theme, with dancers in feathered headdresses moving through the space in a bossa nova rhythm as the singer on the bandstand crooned "Girl from Ipanema."

Dr. Conrad beamed from her station in the room's center, shaking hands. Gilberto Cruz was her discovery now, and Julie didn't care. Among the staff, in meetings, and in front of the board, Dr. Conrad credited Julie, which was what Julie cared about.

"Did you see who Mark is talking to?" Eames appeared beside Julie with two wine glasses filled with what Julie knew was sparkling water. She took the glass and looked to where he gestured.

Mark stood alone with a young woman— a striking, young woman in a royal blue mini-dress and thigh-high suede boots, a clever merge of sophisticated and edgy. On her best day, Julie never looked so good.

"Cassandra Forsythe," Eames said. "Oldest daughter of Edwin Forsythe, the engineer who invented a microchip used in virtually every handheld electronic device. The family's worth a gazillion."

"And her?" Julie was almost afraid to ask.

"Medical school," Eames said. "Wants to be a pathologist."

Mark leaned forward to listen to Cassandra, closely and intently. Cassandra tossed back long black hair over one shoulder before leaning in herself. Their foreheads nearly touched in a way that made them look like a couple. A pang of possessiveness seized Julie.

"Maybe he's asking for a big donation," Eames said.

"She probably wants a spot in his lab." Julie drained her glass and returned it to Eames. "I'll find out."

The music had segued to Gloria Estefan, and the dancers with feathered headdresses were samba-ing among the throng, inviting partygoers into a conga line. They hopped on, holding onto the shoulders of the person in front of them, and kicking out their feet from side to side. The entire room seemed to be dancing in unison, and Julie moved with the beat, shuffling across the floor to the corner where Mark stood with Cassandra.

"Hi, hi," she said, and Mark turned.

The conga line snaked alongside them and one of the dancers stuck out her hands to Mark and Cassandra. Laughing, they hopped on together, Cassandra first and Mark behind her, and, for a brief moment, as Mark adjusted his hands on her shoulders, they got tangled in her long hair. Julie slipped in behind Mark and grasped his shoulders. A large group patched themselves into the middle, and the line became unwieldy and bloated. Julie didn't let go of her husband. She moved forward and kicked sideways. She held on.

*

The next Friday, Piper texted Julie, inviting her to their town's annual "Kiss and Release" on Saturday morning. Kiss and Release was when five thousand chinook salmon fingerlings were released into a protected inlet in Richardson Bay near the Golden Gate Bridge to begin their journey to the Pacific Ocean. The fingerlings had been hatched from eggs in tanks by an Anglers Club. Julie had known about Kiss and Release for years, but they'd never gone.

"Hope to C U," Piper wrote.

"I sent her info about therapeutic boarding schools," Julie said to Mark as she told him Saturday's plan. "Everyone recommends them."

The release of the fingerlings was scheduled for 11:45 a.m., the peak of high tide. Mark dropped Julie and Jack off at the entrance before parking, while Julie paid admission. The bracelets the volunteers snapped around each of their wrists were pinky-orange, consistent with the salmon theme. Jack marveled at his band for a few seconds as though it were the highlight of the day, before spotting the giant red jumpy house near the barbeque grills and sprinting off.

Julie trailed behind him. White tents lined the pathways and volunteers handed out flyers on the perils of vaccination and the benefits of Ayurvedic healing. Craftspeople hawked handmade soap and silver jewelry. Moms and dads pushed strollers, kids walked dogs, and everyone seemed to be eating an ice cream cone.

Farah and Beti hopped up and down in the jumpy house like two pieces of popcorn, grinning ear to ear. Beti was color-coordinated with the salmon in head-to-toe pinky-orange. Farah was dressed in orange Capri pants and matching halter top that seemed to Julie to reveal an inch too much skin. Did Piper not see this child was growing up? Julie glanced around for Spencer.

Piper appeared, sliding her phone into her back pocket. "You're here. Nick's parking."

They hugged. "The Phantom Nick. He exists," Julie said. Nick had missed the pool party. A conference in Dallas.

On a raised platform, under the white tent closest to the jumpy, a three-piece band sawed out tunes on banjos and harmonica, while down in front, three or four couples danced a two-step— the men in vests and blue jeans and the women in colorful skirts that opened wide like parachutes with every whirl and dip.

"Cuteness, those two." Julie nudged Piper and gestured toward the jumpy, where Jack was now inside, holding hands with Beti as they soared through the air.

Piper's eyes teared up suddenly. She pulled out her sunglasses and pushed them up onto her head. "Jack's been such a good friend to her. I'm very grateful."

"Beti's the answer to Jack's prayers. Another kid who doesn't play soccer or T-ball."

The music stopped and a man's voice with a Southern accent came over the microphone. "Welcome Friends. To the Eighth Annual Kiss and Release." A cheer went up from the crowd. "In just a few minutes, we'll be setting those chinook salmon fingerlings on the road to a good life in the big wide bay and out to the ocean. In the meantime, grab a beer and some grub and swing your partner. Yee-ha, y'all."

Nick and Mark walked up together. They'd never met in person, but halfway to the jumpy house realized who the other was. Nick looked like a casting agent's profile of a preppy, successful businessman, an image of his sons grown up. He pumped Julie's hand. "You must be the lovely Julie." Where had she heard that accent? He sounded like a TV version of an old-money East Coast guy. He clamped Mark on the shoulder as if they were fast friends. "You're a lucky man, Mark." Everybody laughed while Julie blushed.

Nick ran a hand through his hair before tapping Julie's arm. His eyes twinkled boyishly. "First time at Kiss and Release, I hear."

Julie couldn't help smiling. There was something rakishly charming about Nick. "Complete novices," she said.

The Southern voice crackled over the loudspeaker again. "All righty, y'all. The boys from the Anglers Club gave the signal. Gather 'round and git yourself some fingerlings."

"Mark, shall we?" Nick trotted off to collect the kids with Mark behind him. The girls stopped bouncing and came to the jumpy house door. Jack bounced behind them, ricocheting against the net. Then all three bounded down the exit slide and barreled toward Julie and Piper like a stampede. Back several feet, Nick and Mark followed, Nick gesturing and talking while Mark was laughing harder than Julie had seen him laugh in years.

"Mom! Momma!" the children cried. "The fingerlings! Let's go!"

The crowd surged toward a flatbed "Anglers" truck parked underneath a white tent close to the waterfront. Two middle-aged men stood on the flatbed deck with a gigantic fish tank between them.

The parents funneled the kids to the white tent to get in line. When they got to the front, one of the anglers, in suspenders and with the name tag "Mike," handed each of them a child's beach pail filled with bay water, red for the girls and blue for the boy. Looking at the three of them, he asked, "Any y'all anglers?" They stared at him blankly. "You fish? No? Okay then."

He jerked his thumb toward his partner. "My buddy Rodney here's gonna drop a scoop of fingerlings into each of y'all's pails. Those are your baby fishies. Nobody else's. It's your responsibility to take those baby fish and dump 'em safely in the water. Then they can begin the migration home."

As the kids watched, rapt, Rodney opened the tank's lid. He dipped in a netted scoop the size of a flyswatter and moved his arm, making a show of trying to catch a few. Mike winked at the kids. "Rascally little critters."

In silence, each child handed up a pail to collect their fingerlings. When the fish were deposited safely inside each bucket, they bent their heads to inspect them. "I'm naming mine Wiggle Worm, Swifty, and Zoomer," Farah said. Jack grimaced. "I wanted to name mine Wiggle Worm, Swifty, and Zoomer."

"That's fine," Farah said. "I'll name mine Squirmy, Swimmy, and Fishy."

Mike hooked his thumbs under his suspenders. "Y'all from a camp or something?" he asked them.

"Us? These are our kids." Julie put an arm around Jack and Farah.

Piper stepped back from the kids, as if to give them more space. "Nick's started investigating the legalities," she said, when Julie stepped back beside her.

Mike rubbed his chin and said over the crowd to Julie, "One of my nieces got a girl from China. Little bitty thing. Sharp as a tack. Like you'd 'spect."

Julie didn't know if he said that because the girl was his niece, and thus related to Mike, or because of the stereotype that all Asians were smart.

"Good for her," she replied, and then to Piper, "Legalities about what?"

"Disruption," Piper said. "The laws are different in every state."

For a moment, Julie couldn't think. The last time they were together Piper was asking for solutions to the Spencer situation. Now she was disrupting the adoption?

"God bless you, ma'am." Mike put two fingers to his forehead, an informal salute. "All righty, y'all. Who's next?"

"We decided sooner is better than later," Piper said in a monotone. "Nick was disappointed at first, but eventually agreed."

"Beti, too?"

"We can't split them up. That would be brutal."

The loudspeaker called the time: 11:43 a.m., two minutes to release. Along with the other kids with buckets, Jack and Beti knelt on the rocky shore. Jack tried to pick up one of his fingerlings to kiss before release—Wiggle Worm, he said—but true to its name, the baby salmon escaped his grasp and flipped back into the pail. Beti couldn't hold any of her fingerlings long enough to kiss either.

"Where will they go?" Julie asked.

"Another family somewhere."

Julie's mind raced. This was horrible, the worst possible outcome. She had to stop it. "They've lost so much already. They'll be destroyed if you disrupt. You adopted them."

"And now we're un-adopting them," Piper said, and stepped up to peer into Farah's red pail. Nick came up behind them to peer in, too. He slipped in beside Farah, a centimeter too close, and when he bent to inspect the fingerlings, his left shoulder grazed her right side, so lightly you wouldn't notice unless you were looking. At first Farah didn't react. Then she pressed in toward him, subtle and slight, a butterfly landing on the petal of a flower.

Stop, Julie thought. *Just stop.*

A whistle blew and the kids cheered and yelled and turned over their buckets. The fingerlings were unaccustomed to the vastness of the bay, having been hatched as eggs in a tank and reared in pens. The water churned as they flopped and splashed before instinct took over and they swam straight into the deep, free.

The kids jumped up and down, arms over their heads, cheering.

Then the cheers of the kids turned to gasps. Overhead, the sky darkened, and a flock of seagulls appeared, so many, they seemed to blot out the sun. They must have smelled the fish, seen them, and been waiting, perched in every nook of every rock on the shore. The gulls numbered in the hundreds. They skimmed over the waves like a formation of fighter jets, hovered for a second, and dove down. Wiggle Worm, Swifty, Zoomer. Squirmy, Fishy, Swimmy.

A thousand defenseless fingerlings were caught up in beaks and swallowed whole.

"Oh my God," Julie said. She couldn't help it; she knew she was crying.

"Oh, never mind." Piper was beside her again. "That happens every year."

"I can't even talk to you," Julie said.

*

Nothing was going to stop Piper and Nick. Nothing ever did. They moved forward in their plan to move Farah and Beti. Placing them in the foster system was out of the question. Piper was going to re-home the girls herself, privately. Nick's lawyer handled the legal aspects, which seemed simple compared with what families went through to adopt. There was no state oversight. Piper and Nick simply would assign legal guardianship of the children to another adult. Piper joined two online groups of parents on the same mission and spent the next week conducting phone interviews.

She missed her next Wednesday yard duty, texting Julie she was too busy.

"What if we took the girls?" Julie wrote back. "Will discuss with Mark."

"Let me know," Piper said.

Julie couldn't let it go. She agonized over whether they should step up and take custody. Over and over, she weighed the pros and cons, decisive one minute, confused the next. She imagined two big sisters, going on picnics and hikes, playing cards and board games, jumping on the trampoline. Companions for Jack who would love and protect him. Unless they didn't. Every night after Jack was asleep, she crawled into bed and debated the subject with Mark.

"They need so much. They deserve so much. I don't know if I can give it to them."

"Raising Jack feels like enough," Mark agreed.

"He loves them. They're his only friends. What if we just took Beti? She's younger, easier."

"I'm thinking about three college tuitions," Mark said. "How will we swing that?"

"Loans. Scholarships. We go into debt. That's the least of our worries. The biggest concern is Jack. What if this screws him up?"

"We've hit a nice balance. A decent place. Our situation feels fragile, though. We might ruin it," Mark said.

"He's our first priority. And a second failure would shatter them."

Finally, after nights of going around and around, Mark said, "The fact that we can't decide is a decision."

Julie moaned, devastated. Mark was right.

She called Piper from her office the next morning. "I wish we could," she said. "We just don't know how it will turn out. The girls need a future that's utterly secure."

Piper brushed off Julie's apology. "It would be weird, anyway," she said. "Us being around. Them still here."

"Can Jack say good-bye? Can I? What's their last day at school?"

Piper cut the call short, saying she was scheduled to interview a family.

Twelve days later, after dinner, Piper texted that she and Nick had placed the girls with a mixed-race lesbian couple up north in Humboldt County. One of the mothers was a real estate agent, the other a psychiatric social worker. They had no other children. The women seemed ideal on paper, Piper said, and Julie hoped they were. There was nothing to be done. Piper was driving them up to Humboldt in the morning. She said it was best if Jack didn't say good-bye in person, but agreed to let Julie.

The next morning after drop-off, Julie drove to Piper's house, barely able to face what was ahead. She parked next to Piper's Volvo and flipped down the windshield mirror to inspect her eyes before stepping out onto the driveway. She couldn't make sense of how quickly the tide turned, how nothing she said or did seemed able to change it. There must have been a greater plan, with Piper and Nick the conduit to get the girls to the place they were meant to be. She needed to believe that.

Piper came out first, wearing gigantic sunglasses. She nodded to Julie, then moved quickly to unlock her car doors and open the trunk. Farah and Beti came through the doorway, each rolling a large duffel bag printed with pink Hawaiian flowers and monogrammed with their initials. Seeing those monogrammed duffels, with the trips they once must have promised, broke Julie's heart.

The girls stopped short when they saw Julie and she staggered forward, enfolding one in each arm. "You're such good kids," she whispered. "We're grateful we met you. We'll miss you."

They pulled apart and the girls nodded solemnly. Julie gave them the cards Jack had drawn and colored: One for each girl, showing them mid-jump on the trampoline, airborne, flying.

As Piper drove away, the girls turned around and waved through the back window until the car was a tiny dot Julie could no longer see. She'd call the museum to say she wasn't coming in. She was gutted.

When she picked up Jack from extended care, he dove into the car bursting with news. "Farah and Beti are gone for good. Everyone said they moved." Julie waited until they got home before she explained.

"Is that why I made them cards?" he wailed. "Why did they leave?"

"Sometimes situations change," she said. "It's nobody's fault."

Jack couldn't understand why Piper wasn't going to be the girls' mother or Nick their dad. "Did they do something bad? What did they do?"

He ran to his room for Ratón and rubbed the stuffie against his nose, his cheeks, the side of his neck. He rubbed his soft skin raw. He bawled inconsolably. In the end, Julie did something she'd vowed never to do to her son, which was lie. She told Jack the plan was always for the girls to live with Piper and Nick temporarily, until their permanent home got ready. She didn't know if he believed her.

After the girls left, Jack's orderliness reached the next level. He starched his shoelaces and slept on the floor in a sleeping bag so not to muss his ironed sheets. He brushed the fluff on the Goofy slippers they'd bought at Disneyland.

"Is this normal?" Julie asked, as she and Mark watched their son roll his t-shirts into four-inch burrito-like packets and insert them into his color-coded dresser drawers.

"Definitely doesn't take after me," Mark said, referring to his own habit of leaving clothes on the floor where he'd dropped them, inches from the hamper.

One Friday night Julie was cooking dinner and realized she hadn't heard Jack in a while. She walked down the hallway calling his name with curiosity and mild annoyance first, then an adrenaline rush that felt like a distress signal. "Jack? Jack? Where are you?"

She heard water running from the master bathroom and pushed open the door. Steam billowed out. A pungent stinging inflamed her nostrils. Jack knelt in front of the bathtub tipping a gallon jug of bleach into the stream of running water, his robe spotted white where the bleach had splashed.

"What are you doing?" She turned off the water.

"Mom!" He turned the water back on.

"Bleach is toxic. You'll burn yourself." She turned off the water again.

"There's mold under the edge." He pointed at a fleck of green mold, barely visible under the silicone caulking that surrounded the tub. Not a good sign that he noticed the microscopic particle, Julie thought, but not wanting to dismiss his concern, she said "You need an abrasive. The mold's underneath."

She reached under the sink cabinet for a canister of Comet. Jack shook out a pile of abrasive and began scrubbing. He scrubbed and scrubbed, putting his entire body into the effort. Finally, he held up the strip of silicone caulking, pocked and disintegrated. "There," he said, victoriously.

"Cleanest this bathroom has been in history. Thank you. But truly, Jack. You don't need to keep everything so very extra clean."

Jack dropped the strip of caulking into the trash can and dried the floor with the bath towel. He recapped the bottle of bleach, his brow beetled with worry. "I don't want to blow my chances with you guys."

Blow his chances? Just when Julie thought they were making progress. "Your chances can't ever be blown. Dad and I, we're not going anywhere. You're stuck with us forever." She gathered him into her arms.

Jack didn't look convinced. Julie was. This was her purpose as his mother: to help him know that he was loved. One step forward, five steps back.

*

In the next few months, the girls' names came up from time to time—"Remember when that bird got trapped in the tree?" Jack would ask. "Remember when those seagulls dive-bombed the fingerlings?"—and every time, they both got very quiet.

Julie didn't want to think she blamed Piper, but maybe she did. Then, one Saturday, as Jack sat on the floor putting together a puzzle and Julie scrolled through movie listings for ways to fill two hours in the afternoon, she realized something. If she blamed Piper, did she also blame Karla Inez? Karla Inez placed her son with another family. Although the situations were different, the outcome for the children was the same. Why, and however it happened, they still were living apart from their mothers.

NINETEEN

SAN LORENZO CHAL, GUATEMALA

NOVEMBER 2010

After Daniel and Tío Eldon died, Mamá believed she was cursed. So many sad things happened, there was no other way to explain. She began going to church, not only on Sunday, but every day. She prayed for God to wipe out her sin and make her clean.

Often, I went with her to take care of my little sister Isabel while Mamá did her penance.

To please God, penance must be difficult. There was only one way. Mamá kneeled at the altar rail to pray the five decades of the Rosary. Then she crawled backwards down the aisle to the back of the church. The floor was red tile and crawling so far was not easy. But Mamá did it.

Around the same time, the smuggler began knocking on our door asking for payment. Mamá knew who it was from his way of knocking, fast and loud. When she opened the door, she raised her fists like she was ready to hit him.

"Is Chelo alive or dead?" She was desperate to speak the name of her husband who abandoned us. The smuggler grabbed her wrists and pushed them down. "Give me my money."

I hid under the cot with Isabel and Yanira. We'd never heard her voice so loud.

In the first months after Papi left, he sent money through Western Union. He paid 5,000 quetzales on the debt. Then no other money came. Mamá owed the smuggler 10,000 quetzales more. He charged interest on the debts of poor people. If she didn't pay, he'd take our house and own it.

All this happened.

This is why, when I was fourteen, Mamá sent me to the town of San Pablo Sacatepéquez. We needed money to eat. The Peace Accord between the army and the guerrillas was signed, and *indígenas* like us moved to earn money. Someone in our church knew a family seeking a reliable girl who spoke Spanish, and my name was given. Padre Andrés taught us Spanish and I was a good student. San Pablo Sacatepéquez was many hours south of Chal, close to Guatemala's capital.

I was hired to work at Casa Alvarez. Casa Alvarez was grander than any house in Chal, bigger than the houses of Chal's richest citizens, almost as large as the church. I'd never seen anything like it. It was like a house of a queen or president. The outside walls were white, and the roof was made of red tiles. Ceramic pots that held orange flowers hung in the windows. The front door was wooden, with two doors painted green. Seven members of the Alvarez Hauer family lived there: the parents, Edgar and Monica; Monica's mother, Olga; and the children Rudy, Kevin, Blanca, and Kurt.

The Alvarez Hauer family was light-skinned, and the mother, Monica, had green eyes. These green eyes shone also in the faces of two of her children, the eldest boy, Rudy, and the girl, Blanca. For the first few days, I was shocked when I saw the green color. Then I discovered Monica's family name "Hauer" is German. Green eyes are common in Germany.

The parents, Edgar and Monica, slept in one room. Olga, the grandmother, by herself in another. And in two other rooms slept the four children, each with their own beds topped with cotton bed clothes and blankets made of wool. I also slept in a room by myself, with my own small bed. My bed was comfortable and soft, but at first, I couldn't sleep because I was used to the sounds of my family breathing.

My job at the house was to do everything. In the mornings I walked to the tortilla mill and returned before anyone else was awake to pat the tortillas. On Tuesday and Saturday, I walked to the market to shop for the food and carry it home. Every day in between, I cooked rice and beans and eggs and squash on a stove that lit by turning a knob. On Sundays, after early mass, I baked chicken with onion and tomatoes in a deep metal pot in an oven with a door that closed. Because the family was eight people who ate three meals—breakfast, a large lunch at midday, and soup in the evening—and because I was the only hired girl in the house, I washed many dishes.

When I wasn't cooking, I washed the clothes by hand in the outdoor sink. I hung them on a clothesline at the end of the courtyard that received the most sun. On the clothesline end of the courtyard was parked the family's car, which Edgar drove to his office in Guatemala City during the week. I fed the chickens and collected the eggs. I also swept the floors and changed the bed linens. I cleaned the oven and ironed the clothes.

Monica and Olga didn't wear embroidered blouses and woven skirts like we did, but modern dresses. The little girl, Blanca, dressed like one of the dollies that sat on a shelf in her bedroom, with ruffles and bows and bands for her hair and shiny black shoes that became scuffed if she wasn't careful. The dollies had green eyes like Blanca, and yellow hair, and Blanca was never allowed to play with them. Sometimes, when Blanca was out, I picked up one or another of the yellow-haired dollies and stared into her green eyes before putting her back.

The four children attended school while I worked. They came home with the most wonderful materials—pencils with gum erasers and pens that clicked open and closed, and notebooks of clean, smooth paper with lines. They also carried books—thick ones with many pages printed with many words. In Chal, only the teacher owned books, which we borrowed in the classroom. I have never wished for something I couldn't have, but seeing those books made me wish for them.

The four children studied the piano and practiced every afternoon on the black upright in the dining room before dinner. As I stirred pots in the kitchen, I heard them, Kurt and Blanca plunking out notes, and Kevin and Rudy banging out what they called scales, up the keys and back down again. Sometimes, the music pulled feelings out from deep inside me that I didn't know I had, and tears ran down my face, so many I was forced to put down my spoon and wipe my cheeks so the wetness wouldn't ruin the *sopa de pollo* or *hilachas* or whatever else I was cooking. Some passages made me remember Papi Chelo's smile when I learned something quickly or let me hear Daniel laughing. Music was as magic as any spell or prayer or miracle. It made me miss Chal and Mamá and my sisters. It made me remember when Tío Eldon shouted "Run." Sometimes when I listened, I tried to picture the mother and father I never knew. I let myself wonder how my life might be different if they had raised me.

For the first year after I moved to the Alvarez Hauer house, I was afraid to speak. First, I felt unworthy because my family was poor. And second, I worried my Spanish was not good because I spoke Ixil. When the family sat at table for meals, I served in silence, putting down dishes and picking them up, carrying them to the sink to wash. Any time someone asked me for more chicken or a spoon, I was afraid I might have to answer in Spanish. The family was not evil or unkind, but I was the hired girl and they were above me. I knew my place.

Eventually, I began to speak more, mostly to the youngest boy, Kurt, who reminded me of Daniel, and to Blanca, who liked to boss me around, asking me to brush her hair or trim her fingernails or pick up her clothes. I felt confident enough to answer the older boys, Kevin and Rudy, when they asked if their archery uniforms were spotless and ironed, their foils sharp.

It was then I understood there were two Guatemalas. One with large houses and food and contests for archery. The other Guatemala was for poor people who were hungry, with houses of mud and foils that were machetes meant for chopping and killing.

Still, I was able to wire-transfer money to Mamá every month and that made me content.

At the end of my second year, when I was sixteen, I began to shop for the food necessary to make the special dish *fiambre*, to be eaten on All Saints' Day. In Chal, we didn't eat *fiambre* on All Saints' Day, because we couldn't afford to buy meat— black and red chorizo, salami and ham. But *fiambre* was a tradition in Monica's family. I became skilled at making it. Monica said my *fiambre* tasted as good as Olga's. Monica was the one who taught me how, so I was glad she approved.

The *fiambre* had many ingredients and required two shopping trips to the market. The first trip I bought the vegetables, and the second trip the meats. I spent many hours in the kitchen chopping, slicing, mincing, and grilling. The vegetables were blanched in boiling water, and the meats cooked and chilled. Everything needed to be kept cold in the ice box before it was eaten. This was another reason we didn't eat *fiambre* in Chal. Even if we could afford the meats, we didn't have ice in boxes.

On the way home from the second trip, I walked through the plaza. San Pablo's stray dogs must have smelled the meat, because a pack of them surrounded me. They nipped and bit at my heels. I looked for a rock to toss. I didn't see one and started kicking at the dogs' snouts.

Then, out of nowhere, one rock sailed across the plaza, and then another. Each found their mark. The rocks hit two dogs. The dogs started yelping.

"*Señorita,*" a voice yelled. "Go."

I hurried through the plaza toward home. Only when I got to the next block did I turn to see who helped me. A cluster of young men were shooing apart the pack. One young man stood apart from the others, as though waiting for me to turn around. Like the other *muchachos*, he wasn't from San Pablo but the highlands. *Indígena*, like me. Half of his face was marked with a purple stain, a birthmark. He raised his hand in a wave and I turned away. The attention made me shy and nervous, but I couldn't help smiling.

Monica would not approve of me talking to a boy in a plaza.

I didn't tell her about him.

The next day around noon, Kevin and Rudy lifted Olga's wheelchair into the trunk of Edgar's large Mercedes Benz. The family was going to the cemetery for the All Saints' celebration. Kevin and I slid Olga onto the front seat with Edgar and Monica, and we squeezed in the back with Rudy, Blanca, and Kurt. Our destination was the cemetery, about half an hour by car from San Pablo. Monica's ancestors were buried in the cemetery, in the section for very rich families.

In a basket, Monica and I packed candles to guide the souls of the dead to move among us. We packed yellow marigolds to decorate the crypt. We also brought tamales and sweet corn cakes to eat while we visited with their spirits. On this day, the dead felt close to us. We remembered them by decorating their final resting place and sitting in their presence.

Other families already were gathered as we arrived. Everyone swept headstones and crypts and cleaned away old flowers and branches. As we walked toward the Hauer crypt, Monica hugged the matriarchs she recognized from many years of following the tradition while Edgar shook hands. Behind them, I pushed Olga in her wheelchair.

The mood in the cemetery was quiet yet lively. Strolling violin players stopped to play when requested, and a traveling band of musicians carried with them a portable marimba. Some people brought transistor radios, others their pet dogs on leather leashes. Many men drank from bottles of alcohol, and everyone ate tamales and sweet corn cakes.

The Hauer crypt was a small house made from marble. The stone was carved with horses and cattle to represent the family's ranching heritage. Inside were the tombs of Monica's ancestors, beginning from the days they arrived from Germany to grow coffee in Guatemala.

I secured the brake on Olga's wheelchair and asked if she was comfortable. She patted my hand to answer. Her kind gesture made me feel sad. It reminded me of my life before. The family I knew and the family I didn't know. My real family from the village of San Rolando, the village that burned down. I worried about my family because the army gave no one a proper burial. The spirits of the dead had no place to rest.

"I want to see the giant kites," Blanca said. She pulled on Monica's hand. "Please Mamá."

The giant kites have always been a tradition famous among the *indígenas* in Sumpango. Teams of men from different towns build them. They cut bamboo to make frames and cut up colored paper to paste into designs like mosaic. The kites are grand like the size of the municipal building, or small as the shell of a box turtle. The grand ones are made for telling stories. They show scenes of sadness like graveyards and widows praying and bodies fallen. They also show happy scenes like peacocks opening their feathers and the corn god blessing the land for a large harvest. Kites are used to communicate with our ancestors. They speak to us through kite strings we hold in our hands. Small kites are used in every cemetery in every village on All Saints' Day.

"We'll go to the soccer field later," Monica said. The soccer field was where they flew the kites.

"I want to go now," Blanca said. She turned swiftly toward Edgar to see if he heard. He never approved of the children talking back. He didn't seem to be listening, though. He was talking to the husband of the family from the crypt beside us.

"First, we must visit with our ancestors," Monica said. "And wait for Papa to be finished talking." Monica didn't say this, but she might not want to see kites of *indígenas*. Kites were not part of her Ladino family tradition.

"I'm hungry," Kurt said. Blanca joined in. "I'm hungry, too."

Monica snapped open her leather purse and pulled out a five quetzales note. She told me to buy a few ears of grilled corn to eat before we opened the basket of tamales and corn cakes. Grilled corn was special at fiestas.

"The blue kind," Kurt said. "Not yellow. With lime and salt."

I tucked the five quetzales into the neck of my *hüipil* and headed toward the soccer field with the kites, and the food cooking area.

The soccer field was filled with giant kites laid flat on the ground like colorful wheels, stretched in rows as far as I could see. The first showed the figure of the great Maya K'iché warrior Tecún Umán, who died in battle at the hand of the Spanish conquistador Pedro de Alvarado. His blood was said to have stained red the breast of our national bird, the quetzal. The second showed wrinkled faces of elders. On the third were pictured the great waterfalls of Semuc Champey.

I had never seen special kites like these. The teams who built the kites honored the history of *indígenas* with pictures.

The food area was on the opposite side of the field. As I walked past the kites, a man made a motion like sweeping a broom for me to get out of the way. One by one, men were pulling on ropes tied to the kites' bamboo frames to lift them from flat to a standing position. Around them, boys and young men watched. They shouted encouragement. To see the kites rise up was like watching a man be raised from the dead.

I was glad to be away from the cemetery. Among the gravestones and crypts, I felt the souls of my dead parents wandering. They weren't buried in boxes in the ground, and I wasn't sure how God knew where to find them. Even in the field among the kites, I felt uneasy, as though I were being followed by spirits.

The kite races didn't start until late afternoon, but already many people waited to see which kite flew fastest and highest. Around the field, families sat on metal bleachers stacked on top of one another like steps. Small boys ran up and down the benches, kite strings in their hands. Men stood at the bottom selling brimmed hats to keep out the sun.

The food area was on the other side of the bleachers. The seats backed up to a chain-link fence, so underneath was like a tunnel. I didn't go through the tunnel, but took the slower route through the crowd in front of the bleachers. At the other end of the bleachers, a pig cooked over black charcoal in a metal drum, skewered on a spit. A dark red apple crowded into the pig's mouth. The air smelled like burnt pig skin. Two round women tended the pig, one turning the spit and the other fanning the charcoal with a folded cloth. Behind them, girls patted out tortillas, their hands making a song.

My mouth watered and I could almost taste the pig and its smoky flesh, but my five quetzales were to buy roasted corn. I would never go against the wishes of Monica and buy something different. Kevin wanted blue, which was my favorite, too. I swallowed my desire for pig and approached the grills for roasting corn.

"Ten please," I said to the seller. The corn was steaming hot as I wrapped the ears in a plastic bag brought for that purpose.

Someone tapped on my right shoulder. I was so surprised, I almost dropped my corn. The boy with the purple stain over his face stood so close I could smell him. He smelled like something. Guaro liquor. I didn't expect to see him in Sumpango. I had seen him in San Pablo. He must have traveled far to watch the kite festival.

"*Buenas,*" he said.

"*Buenas,*" I answered. People behind me who wanted to buy corn nudged me aside.

"Are you going back? Let me help you," he said. He tried to take from me the bag of corn. "No, thank you," I said. What would I do if he took the corn from me? I couldn't return to Monica without the corn or the quetzales to buy it.

"You're from Chal." He must have known this because he recognized my *hüipil.* I looked at the boy sideways. He was shorter than Rudy, Kevin, and Edgar, but taller than I was. We both were from the highlands, although he didn't say from where, and I didn't ask. Somewhere familiar, I felt it. Somewhere like home. His birthmark didn't look so bad up close. I didn't mean to smile, but I did.

"You work in town, *qué?* I've seen you going in the house of white people. And later in the plaza, with the dogs." He spoke barely moving his mouth. His eyes looked glassy, and I wondered if he was drunk.

"Thank you for throwing the rocks."

"Dogs can be vicious. Especially in a pack." He reached again for the bag of corn, and I pulled back. "Don't you trust me?" he asked. "You should."

The announcer over a loudspeaker said the kite competition was beginning soon. Rows and rows of the large kites now stood up. In front of them, teams arranged themselves on the field to race the smaller ones. The day was perfect for kite flying, with enough wind to kick up yellow dirt from the soccer field. The boy and I watched the teams bring their smaller kites to the starting line, and the side of my body closest to him suddenly felt like it was on fire.

"I should go," I said.

"But they're starting." Somehow the boy got one of his legs behind me and one in front. The heat spread from my one side to my whole body. My insides felt damp.

"*La señora* might be worried," I said.

"*La señora*. Is she in charge of you?"

To feel him so close caused my stomach to turn over. Monica was in charge of me—Monica and Edgar both—but I wanted the boy to appreciate my independence. I lifted my shoulder to release his voice.

He entwined his arm through mine. It felt so natural I hardly noticed. I switched the corn to my other hand so not to disturb his leg with the bag bumping against it. He guided me to the tunnel under the metal benches. "This way. It's quicker."

My heart beat fast. We walked under the bleachers close together. Never had I stood so close to a boy before. Above us, people were cheering. The kite races had started. I knew I had to get back. But it felt good to have the boy's arm looped through mine. His skin was rough yet smooth and without hair. His knuckles were black with dirt. He smelled like liquor, but also like fields and air and sweat, like the people in Chal. I never smelled that in San Pablo. The people in San Pablo smelled like the squares of soap they cleaned with.

Our legs made steps the same size. We moved as if we were one body. When there was trash on the ground, the boy steered me around it. His consideration made me embarrassed. Usually I took care of everyone.

"You're very pretty," he said. "Has anyone ever told you that?"

"No."

"They should."

Heat rushed to my cheeks and I couldn't stop smiling.

The boy stopped in front of a small hole in the fence. "We can go through here. It leads straight to the cemetery. A short cut."

I looked down at the opening. The boy took the corn from my hand and passed it through the hole in the fence, setting it down on the other side. "You're not too big," he said.

I didn't want to be impolite and the boy was being kind. A part of me also wanted the boy to like me, because he felt familiar and like home. So I knelt to crawl through. My skirt caught a little on the fence, but then I was through. I stood up and straightened my skirt. I brushed the dirt from my bag of corn. The hole in the fence backed onto a clearing on the edge of a corn field. It was a place where people dumped trash. There were black plastic bags and muddy cartons and rotting chicken bones. In the middle of the trash was a large sandy anthill. Red ants marched up the sides carrying pieces of food twice their size.

The boy came through the fence behind me. "Lie down," he said.

"What?"

"Lie down."

"Why?" I didn't want to lie down in dirt. I didn't like this filthy place. I moved to go back through the fence, but when I did, he grabbed my arms and pushed my face toward the ground. My knees hit hard and he shoved my skirt up and yanked my underpants down. Dirt went in my mouth. He turned me over face up. Sharp rocks jabbed along my spine. His hands pressed on my shoulders while his knees grabbed around my hips.

I didn't know what to do. He felt like a big man on top of me. Not a boy. I was afraid. Bites from red ants stung on my bare legs and hips and on my neck and cheeks.

The boy lifted up from me a little to unzip his pants. Suddenly, I felt strong. I tried to push him off, and he pushed me back down. I pushed again and he pushed me back down harder. Something stiff shoved up inside me, and it burned and hurt, like a pole stuck all the way through me. I felt myself ripping open. The boy squeezed his knees tight. He grunted and collapsed onto my stomach. His body crushed me.

I lay there with wet slime inside me and dripping down the insides of my legs. I wished someone would come to help but didn't want anyone to see me. The boy sat up and laughed a mean laugh.

"You think you're too good for me. You're not. You're ugly and deformed. Nobody wants you."

He stood and zipped his pants. Ants were stuck to me, biting me. My legs, my arms, and every place that was private. I stayed still while the boy crawled back through the fence. Only when I was sure he was gone did I pull down my skirt and rush to brush off the ants from the roasted corn.

I picked up a black plastic bag from the trash pile and wiped the slime from between my legs. It was slick and wet and mixed with blood. I hid the black plastic bag under the pile of trash.

My body smelled different, like the boy.

I crawled back through the fence. I didn't want anyone to know. I was so ashamed. The bag of corn was steaming as I hurried under the bleachers. More slick dripped down my legs. I stopped to rub them against themselves and checked on the corn inside the bag. No ants had crawled in.

Monica took the bag of corn and gave one ear to everybody. She gave me mine last and I bit into it right away. I gnawed on the cob like an animal.

In one month, my blood stopped coming and I knew the boy planted a seed. I didn't tell anyone. Soon my belly became larger, yet I didn't want to eat. Not even tortillas tasted good. When I pushed Olga in her wheelchair, my breath came in short gasps. Olga was frail and thin, but to me she felt heavy. One evening, after dinner, as I stood at the sink washing dishes, Monica came into the kitchen and closed the door. Her mouth was drawn down in a frown. She only said my name, "Rosalba," and I began to cry.

"*Ay Dios,* please, Rosalba," she exclaimed, standing close to the door so no one else could enter. She waited as I gasped and sniffed.

"I'm sorry," I said. Monica's frown deepened and she leaned against the door with her arms folded.

"It's no secret you're in trouble. Can you tell me the name of the father?"

I buried my face in my hands. "I don't know," I said through tears. She lunged toward me and slapped me across the face.

"Tell me. Who is it? Tell me his name." She slapped me again.

"I don't know his name. It happened at the cemetery."

Monica put one finger under my chin and lifted it. "At the cemetery. When?"

"When I was buying corn. It was a boy. A stranger." Tears dripped onto my *hüipil* as I made this confession. I blamed myself for walking with him under the bleachers and believing he was kind. Many, many times as I cooked and cleaned and worked, I asked myself why I trusted him. Why I believed him when he said I was pretty. That was a mistake, but I couldn't go back. The problem was my fault. A baby was inside me.

"Please don't be angry," I begged.

Monica chewed on her thumbnail, plucking the sliced piece from her tongue and throwing it onto the floor. This shocked me because Monica never did anything impolite.

"You can't stay here," she said finally, as if she were thinking out loud. "It would set the wrong example for the children. You must return home to your family."

"I don't want to go back. Please let me stay."

I was ashamed to show Mamá my mistake. I was proud to be the responsible girl who stayed out of trouble. I liked earning money and wire-transferring it to Mamá's account. I liked speaking Spanish, serving food on nice plates. I liked living in a house with running water and a wood floor, under a roof that didn't leak. To return to life without electric lights, to spend my nights with an empty belly dreaming of food. I didn't want this, or to pick corn in the fields, either.

"The truth is, I'd hate to see you go" Monica said. "Of all the girls we've had, you're the best." She brushed her hands together, as if getting rid of something. "Give me a few days. We'll find a way."

TWENTY

REDWOOD GLEN, CALIFORNIA

AUGUST 2009

"Make a wish," Julie said, as Mark snapped the camera.

"X-Box," one of the blond-haired Jacks from school called out.

"Smart phone," Gunther shouted.

It was August 1, 2009, and at a small table inside the Snoopy Ice Rink's Warm Puppy Café, Jack drew in a breath to blow out seven candles on his tres leches birthday cake. The flames flickered, went dark, came to life again. "Trick candles!" the boys yelled. The three elbowed one another out of the way and blew. Success.

Claire palmed the camera from Mark and pointed it at him and Julie with a directive to say cheese. Julie nuzzled her head against Mark's chest, and he smoothed her hair.

"You guys look so young," Claire said. "What's your secret?"

"No sleep?" Julie said.

The boys wolfed down their cake and clomped behind Mark back onto the ice. A silver disco ball cast pink and purple light onto skaters young and old, novice and experienced, gliding backwards and forwards, straight and swerving. Strains of a brassy, pipe organ version of "Do the Hokey Pokey" blasted from truck-sized speakers. None of the boys had skated before, and they navigated the surface with turned-in knees and bent ankles, shredding a wake of slush that looked like snow.

Julie and Claire placed the left-over cake in a box and the gifts in a tote bag. "How's your friend who got rid of the girls from Cuba?" Claire asked.

"Haiti," Julie said.

"Cuba, Haiti. How is she?"

"Fine."

"Mark said they moved them to Humboldt."

Must the man blab everything to my sister? Julie thought. She went back to wiping up crumbs as Claire sighed.

"There are days I'd love to get rid of Gunther." Claire's voice lowered an octave as she narrowed her eyes. "But I would never. A real mother would never be so cruel."

Claire could flatter herself all she wanted, that she was an exemplary parent able to handle every situation and never make a mistake. At one time, Julie might have demonstrated the same hubris. Not anymore. "Plenty of foster and adopted kids come from 'real' mothers," she said. "Were those mothers cruel? Maybe, maybe not."

Claire threw back her head and guffawed. "Please. Spare me your platitudes. Tell me you would ever do the same thing."

Julie folded and refolded her crumb-filled napkin into a compact square. She'd posted about Piper on Guate Parents and dozens of her virtual friends weighed in. Everyone was sorry, but no one was shocked. Nobody judged Piper the way her sister did. Charla T. posted that an estimated twenty percent of all adoptions—international, domestic, kinship, foster—ended up failing. The statistic was sobering.

Julie tossed the napkin into the recycling bin. "We should get going."

Claire didn't move. "Tell me you would ever dump Jack."

The muscles in Julie's jaw clenched. She'd never be able to talk about Piper and the girls without feeling anguished, and defeated. Not now, possibly not ever. She picked up the box with the left-over cake and handed the gift bag to Claire.

"Here's the only thing I know," she said. "Everyone's doing the best they can."

The sisters crossed from the warmth of the restaurant to the polar chill of the rink to watch the boys in their final skating session. Hugging herself to conserve heat, Julie tracked Jack, round and round, her Guatemalan son, body heaving with effort, ankles so caved in she didn't know how he stayed upright. Her handsome, seven-year-old boy, pink and purple in the disco ball's refracted light, not giving up, trying.

Julie hugged herself tighter. As horrendous as the rate of failed adoptions was, seeing it stated had cheered her. Despite their challenges, her family was beating the odds.

*

August 14, 2009
Stewart's Tips for Attending Latin American Culture Camp:

Pack your finest Guate threads to Par-taaay at the Fiestas.
Stay in the Lodge. Everyone does.
Make friends. This is your tribe, people!
Have fun. All the cool kids go to Latin American Culture Camp!!!!
— Stewart, husband to Manny, dad to two Guate adorables, Eva and Nestor

Two weeks after Jack's birthday, the Cowans piled into the minivan to drive to Latin American Culture Camp, located on the south edge of Lake Tahoe. Camp got rave reviews on Guate Parents, and, after the Piper ordeal, the Cowans longed to connect in person with somebody, anybody, who walked in their shoes. Different cohorts cycled through for four-day weekends: African/Caribbean, Indian/Nepalese, Russian/Eastern European in July. Chinese, Korean, and Latin American in August.

The sun beat down like a heat lamp as they rolled into the parking lot at noon. As promised in the brochure photos, the main lodge was an enormous log cabin. A cold burst of air greeted them as they went inside. The room pulsed with the energy of a hundred black-haired, brown-skinned kids and their white parents—the kids running and shrieking, the parents at the check-in table asking questions of the organizers or greeting friends.

"Everyone here looks like me." Jack's face was filled with amazement. He dropped Julie's hand and merged into the pack of moving children.

"So far, so good," Mark said.

Julie picked up their packet of registration materials from the sign-in desk and checked for ID lanyards, schedules, and maps. She turned back to the anarchy of the room to look for Jack and was thrilled to see he'd fallen in with two—a boy and girl around his age. She waved to let him know all was well, and he ran over, pausing to say, "Those two kids are super nice. Their names are Eva and Nestor," before running back.

At lunch, Jack found Eva and Nestor in the buffet line. They weren't twins, they said when Julie asked, but close. They had two dads and lived in Oakland. Mark and one of the dads, Manny, shepherded the kids through the food line while Julie placed her tray on an empty table.

A short, balding, middle-aged man with a friendly, open face and spreading middle introduced himself as Stewart, Manny's husband. "I'm the guy who posts about camp on Guate Parents," he said. "I'm a little zealous." This was his family's third year at camp, and he wanted everyone to enjoy it as much as they did. He felt so familiar and his energy was so positive, Julie gave him a hug instead of a handshake.

"We're thirty minutes away, in Oakland," he said, pointing to her ID lanyard. "You need to join our group. Sit down. I'll tell you about it." Stewart's family belonged to a large group of adoptive families in the Bay Area who met monthly. He said he'd add Julie to the mailing list.

"Do you know anything about Jack's birth mom?" Stewart asked. "Tall or short, big-boned or petite?"

"She's petite," Julie said. "Young."

Stewart's eyes lit up. "We found the kids' birth mother last Christmas. They're bio sibs."

"You mean 'really' brother and sister." Julie made air quotes. She couldn't help it; she felt jealous. Meeting their birth mother meant Stewart was able to find her. The kids' paperwork was legitimate and legal, in other words.

Stewart reached for his phone on the table and scrolled through his photos. He explained his daughter, Eva, doted on every kind of animal. Dogs, cats, chickens, and especially birds. Their mother—her name was Claudia—raised chickens to sell to other families in her village. Before, they thought Eva liked creatures because they were cuddly and cute. Now, they figured she inherited this love from her mother. He passed Julie the phone. She enlarged the screen to see a Guatemalan woman in front of a ramshackle chicken coop, looking just like Eva, across the dining hall at the drink dispenser.

"Wow," Julie said.

Stewart said Claudia told him the father of Eva and Nestor worked at the garbage dump and was strong as an ox.

"We didn't meet him." Stewart made a chopping motion to indicate the subject was closed. The dad and Claudia weren't together anymore. Claudia had another daughter with a new man. She wanted Stewart and Manny to adopt her, too, but that was 2006, when adoptions were closed. The girl still lived with Claudia.

"Eva and Nestor are good with that?"

"They're kids. They deal."

Stewart said his family traveled to Guatemala every summer. If Julie was interested, he'd give her the name of a terrific travel agent.

Jack, Nestor, and Eva walked toward the table, balancing their trays and watching the liquid slosh in their glasses of chocolate milk. The kids jockeyed for seats, arguing over who got to sit where.

"What searcher did you use?" Julie asked. Stewart sang the praises of Xiomara and Zuneidy, X and Z, two names Julie had seen on the Guate Parents' list and not used. If only she'd done more research, hired X and Z instead of Candi. The outcome might have been different, although Kate said no. Falsified paperwork was falsified paperwork. One searcher or another made no difference.

As Stewart and Manny discussed the process with Mark, Julie glanced wistfully at Eva and Nestor. They had met their birth mother, knew her, recognized her traits in themselves. Over the course of their lifetimes, their lives would be different from Jack's because of that one simple fact.

"Finding Claudia is the most important thing we've ever done," Stewart was saying. "You guys should consider it."

Julie couldn't forget the moment she learned Jack's entire file was faked. The shock of the deception still hadn't worn off. "We might," she said, noncommittally.

The adults got out their information folders to peruse the weekend's agenda. "Sounds like an upbeat afternoon," Mark said sarcastically. "*Grieving the Losses of Adoption* and *Recovering from the Primal Wound: Mission Impossible?*"

He exaggerated a grumble as he closed the folder. "And I thought cancer cells were intense. Do we at least get points for showing up?"

Stewart winked. "We're the adoptive parents. We don't get credit for anything, except screwing up our kids' lives."

The kids had their own afternoon schedule of activities, tailored to them. Eva and Nestor said they wanted to go to art class first, then soccer, then cooking, then Spanish. Jack agreed. Stewart and Manny convinced the Cowans to join them at a presentation by adoptees talking about reunion with their birth mothers. They'd attended the presentation all three summers, and every year, it was the highlight.

"Soon enough," Stewart said in a stage whisper, "your guy'll be curious and asking questions. Be prepared."

They dropped off the kids at the art room and headed for the auditorium. Down in front, the stage was festooned with decorations representing Latin America: soccer jerseys, crepe paper flowers, and, tacked to the black curtain, a stuffed fabric likeness of Guatemala's national bird, the resplendent quetzal. Julie wondered if in a closet somewhere were stashed the remnants of the presentation for families with kids from Russia and China: samovar teapots and red silk table runners.

Stewart wasn't kidding when he said the presentation was popular. The auditorium was almost filled. They managed to find seats in the middle of a row near the front, and Julie filed in between Mark and Stewart.

"Déjà vu all over again," Mark said. "Remember our first adoption meeting? The tortillas they passed around?"

"We thought we knew everything. Talk about naïve," Julie said.

The moderator, an adoptive dad volunteer, stepped out from the wings and onto the edge of the stage. Like most of the people in the audience, he was middle-aged and white, dressed in cargo pants and hiking sandals with a neon-green FOREVER FAMILY t-shirt.

"Good afternoon and welcome," he said. "It's my great honor to introduce three voices of the adoptee spectrum. Sage from the U.S., Jenna from South Korea, and Milton from Guatemala. Why three voices? Because, ladies and gents, it's complicated."

Applause filled the room as the first speaker appeared. Sage Wheeler was a woman in her mid-forties, with a bleached white crew-cut and a crescent of shiny earrings in each ear. She strode into the circle of spotlight at center stage with the confidence of a TED talk pro.

Sage waited for the applause to die down before speaking into the standing microphone. "I was born in California in 1972. One year before Roe v. Wade, during the era we now refer to as the 'Baby Scoop.' Back then, pregnant women lacking husbands were called 'unwed mothers.' Their condition brought shame onto their families."

Sage's rounded, soothing tones recalled a late-night DJ. "My pain at being torn from my first mother has never left me. My separation from her feels like an amputation."

A subtle shift in the room occurred, as though a collective breath was being drawn in. A pall descended on Julie. Amputation? Is that what adoption felt like for Jack?

Sage continued. "My birth mother didn't sign a 'Consent for Contact,' because the people advising her didn't tell her to. For decades, the agency, with the blessing of the State of California, denied me access to my adoption file. My adoption file, with personal information about me, including the name of my birth mother and father, and my own name, given to me at birth by my first mother."

Directing her gaze over the heads of the audience to the back of the auditorium, she said, "If my life was a book, my biography started at Chapter Three. Where did I come from? Who looked like me?"

Sage's speech felt like an accusation directed at Julie. A child deserved answers, which she and Mark couldn't supply.

Beginning from the day she turned eighteen, Sage hounded the adoption placement agency, writing and calling, begging for information that belonged rightfully to her. The files are sealed tight, the agency said. No can do. They stonewalled her for eight years. Until one day, a sympathetic social worker excused herself from the office, and left Sage's sealed adoption file wide open on her desk.

"Annika." Sage paused, letting the three syllables land and resonate. "That was the name my mother gave me. She'd studied design in Amsterdam. The name translates as grace."

The private investigator Sage hired located her first mom in less than an hour. Her name was Clover Kendall. She was married with no other children and owned a thriving business as an interior designer. They arranged to meet at a restaurant in San Luis Obispo, the city where Clover Kendall worked, and the city where, as a graduate student, she'd been a professor's mistress, and had borne his child. San Luis Obispo also, coincidentally, was where Sage grew up, unaware her birth mother lived a few miles away.

A row of lights colored red, blue, yellow, and orange turned on over Sage's head, transforming the small stage into a fantastic rainbow.

"I stood in the parking lot of that restaurant and debated whether I should walk in. What if my mother didn't like me?"

Sage inclined her head for a long moment before looking up. "But she did like me. She loved me. Every single day of her life, she had thought about me. She hadn't forgotten. Not for one minute."

A surge of despair washed over Julie. Sage continued. "For the first time in my life, I understood who I was. The daughter of Clover Kendall, a brilliant designer. The progeny of her lover, Henry, a charismatic professor of architecture, madly attracted to Clover, but unwilling to leave his wife and their two children. At last, I had found my real parents. After twenty-six years, I knew who I was. I belonged."

The colorful rainbow faded, and a pin spot shone on Sage. She lifted her profile toward the focused beam of light, as if channeling a voice from heaven. "My name was Annika, and I was loved."

Julie wanted to shake the woman and her bleached white crew-cut. How could she view that cheating professor—her birth father—as some kind of hero? It made no sense. If Clover succumbed to societal pressure to relinquish Annika/Sage, that decision was on her.

Throughout the darkened auditorium, Julie saw the hands of adoptive parents raise to brush tears from their cheeks. Stewart pulled a handkerchief from his pocket and blew his nose.

"My adoptive mother was—how shall I say this? —less than over-joyed I found Clover. She was afraid she'd lose me. That I'd love my real mother more."

There it was. The punch to the gut. "My real mother."

Sage said more, but Julie couldn't hear it. It was as though her ears stopped functioning. She feared she was as shallow as Sage's adoptive mother, as desperate for her son's love, as clawing. Julie steeled herself for the next speaker.

Small and slight, Jenna was dressed in black. A red chiffon scarf around her neck provided the only slash of color. Her angled cheek-bones could have been hammered from copper.

Standing with the erect posture of a trained dancer, she pulled up her sleeve.

"You may not be able to see this in the back rows. But on my fore-arm is tattooed K1981-114. Translation: From Korea, born in 1981, the one hundred-fourteenth child abandoned to my orphanage that year."

She was a commodity, Jenna said. An export, a transaction. The one hundred-fourteenth transaction to be exact, one of thousands that year. South Korea was an industrialized democracy, but unmarried women with babies were shunned by society and parents. They were denied well-paying jobs. No man would marry them. Jenna's birth mother's choice was not a choice. Her child, if she kept it, would be ostracized at school. Which Jenna was, anyway, in the Ohio town where she grew up.

"Chink eyes, Jap, Ching Chong. None of the kids at school had heard of South Korea. I was Chinese to them. Vietnamese. Asian. Other."

Her parents, and by that Jenna meant her adoptive parents, cut her hair with a fringe of bangs and dressed her in frilly dresses. She was their reward for not having biological children. "They paraded me around like a trophy."

Julie cringed and felt Mark wince beside her.

After college, seeking to be among people who looked like her, Jenna moved back to South Korea, joining hundreds of adoptees who settled there. She'd graduated with a degree in finance and found work easily in an international bank. On the streets of Seoul, among other Koreans, she felt at home. She planned to apply for dual citizenship.

The pin spot shone down and highlighted the angles of Jenna's face. She leaned into the microphone and lowered her voice: "My deepest wish is to find my mother. My natural mother. I'd trade everything I own for that."

She'd consulted the police and taken ads in the newspaper. Dozens of women came forward, claiming maternity, but so far, they'd had no DNA match. One day it would happen. Jenna was confident.

She bowed gracefully and left the stage.

Julie felt emotionally thrashed. She didn't know if she could bear to listen to the third speaker, to absorb another story. Milton was the only Guatemalan panelist, though. She must stick it out.

Thunderous applause broke out as a young man with a mop of curly hair ambled over to center stage. He waved to the crowd like a practiced politician, pointing to a few individuals. "Greetings, salutations. Good to see you."

Raising the microphone a few inches, he lowered a hand to knee-height. "I've known most of you since I was this high. Yeah, my folks have brought me here that long."

The audience chuckled. Milton's voice turned serious. "Pat yourselves on the backs. It's important, your being here. Someday, your children might thank you for it. Not today, not tomorrow. But someday."

Milton said his mother left him in a basket under a bench in a bus station in Guatemala City, a location where she knew he would be found. That was the bad news. The good news was she also left a note containing her name and *cédula* number. Her real name and real *cédula* number.

"So, like, if she wanted me to be a secret, not sure why she left an easy trail. Anyway, we found her. My parents did." He peered into the audience, palm to his brow. "They're here somewhere. Hi, Mom. Hi, Dad. When I was seventeen years old."

A screen lowered at the back of the stage and the house lights dimmed further. "Enough about me. Just watch the movie."

Video began rolling: Milton standing in what appeared to be an outdoor courtyard of a hotel in Guatemala. A woman in a woven skirt and long braid approaching. Someone off-stage narrating, "The birth mother Deysi has arrived and is walking toward Milton. She's dressed according to her custom, in her local *traje*. Milton has spotted his mother. They see each other."

The camera frame jiggles slightly as the video operator widens the lens to capture the scene. A moment of hesitation as they study each other. Up and down, top to bottom. The camera pulls in tight. Their eyes disbelieving, as though viewing a ghost. A tentative greeting, *Is it true? Is that you?* A folding into arms, a collapsing together.

No one could deny they were blood related. It was the flip side of footage showing kids' arrival into the United States that she'd watched so many times, waiting for Jack. This was the going home. The relief, the elation, the closure.

Julie fortified herself against the rush of feelings welling up inside her. But over the inevitable dread she felt of losing him to his birth mother—superseding the dread—came a new feeling: a realization that she wanted this, desperately, for her son. She wanted Jack to meet his birth mother.

As the video ended and the house lights came up, the adoptive dad volunteer reappeared on stage, shaking Milton's hand. Sage and Jenna returned and the three settled into chairs at a panelists' table to answer questions. Audience members called out, "Do you blame your adoptive parents?" "Are you relieved adoptions from Guatemala stopped?"

"How old should the child be when you search?"

Sage leaned into the microphone: "Whatever age they are today."

Nodding, Jenna added, "Never too young."

It didn't matter how old Jack should be. They'd never find Karla Inez. Stewart was right. Someday soon, if not today or tomorrow, Jack would start asking questions. *Where is she? Why can't you find her? Did you even try?*

At last, the adoptive dad volunteer said time was up and thanked the panelists. "I'm so glad we found Claudia," Stewart said.

"Best thing we've ever done." Manny kissed his husband. He said they were dashing over to the lodge for cold drinks and promised to meet Mark and Julie at the next workshop, *Parenting the Transracial Tween*.

Julie rooted around under her seat, pretending to be looking for something she dropped. She needed to pull herself together. How was everyone in the room not crushed? How could they chat so casually? The rows around them emptied.

Julie followed Mark up the aisle and toward the lobby. People flowed past them on both sides, until the crowd became a haze of FOREVER FAMILY neon green. The phrase intended to unify them felt to Julie like a taunt.

She matched her steps with Mark's. "Every adoption story ends the same way. Reunion with the 'real' mother."

"It's like we're irrelevant."

"You can only be 'real' or 'good' if you've physically given birth. Or contributed the genetic material. What about our contribution? Doesn't that count?"

Mark stopped walking. "I wish I'd made you pregnant in medical school. We wouldn't have to go through any of this." He circled her with his arms protectively.

"But then we wouldn't have Jack," she said. "I wouldn't want our life without him. Jack is everything."

Mark murmured agreement against her hair, and they held each other.

"I wish we'd been able to find his birth mother," Julie said. "I wish we could give him that."

*

After dinner that evening, the campers and staff gathered in the main lodge for the weekend's first fiesta, and anyone who owned authentic *tipica* wore it: Woven shawls, hand-tooled leather sandals, embroidered *hüipiles*. Although Julie felt like a fraud when wearing one of the *hüipiles* she'd bought on eBay—"Gringa tries to pass as someone she's not"—Jack encouraged her to wear her Guatemalan finery. She gamely donned a *hüipil* with geometric designs from Santa Catarina Palopó, a village on the shore of one of Guatemala's most famous tourist destinations, Lake Atítlan, and threw a shawl around her shoulders. As soon as the sun set, the temperature at Tahoe dropped twenty degrees.

They filed into the lodge with Mark leading the way. The dance floor pulsated with little boys playing tag, little girls chasing the boys and screaming, and teenagers hanging onto each other and shuffling around in circles, or else keeping as far away from each other as physically possible. A few adventuresome parents attempted to execute the steps they learned in Latin dance class, but most sat in folding chairs on the sidelines, cheering their children while sipping margaritas and catching up with one another's lives.

Jack tugged on the hem of her *hüipil.* "Can I run around with Nestor and Eva?" He pointed to his friends and their dads near the drinks table, and Mark said he'd take him over.

"Margarita with salt?" he asked before leaving.

"A strong one."

Julie watched Mark and Jack vanish into the crowd before searching for a seat. She spied one a few yards away, next to a trio of attractive, long-haired teenage girls in leggings and camp t-shirts who appeared too self-sufficient to drape themselves on any of the teenage boys. Feeling awkward in her *hüipil,* she acknowledged the trio and slid onto the chair. The girls were of indigenous heritage, and to them, with her white skin and blonde hair, Julie was sure she looked ridiculous. Attempting to cover her blouse, she crossed her arms and pretended to listen to a song by Ricardo Arjona blasting over the loudspeakers. Between the lyrics, snippets of the teens' conversation reached her ears.

"Do you talk to them?" one said.

"Sometimes. Like at Christmas or my birthday."

"In Spanish?" said the third girl.

"Yeah. But like *Estoy bien, gracias.*"

"What do your parents say? Your parents here."

"They're fine with it. I mean, it was their idea. They arranged it."

The girls said nothing for a long time, and the sound of Ricardo Arjona filled the silence.

"I don't want to meet my birth mom," the third girl said.

"Ever?" asked the first girl. "Why not?"

"I don't know," said the third girl. "I just don't."

Julie dipped her head and stole a glance at the third girl. She was bright-eyed and exuded confidence, with a fissure above her lip characteristic of a repaired cleft lip and palate.

"I think you should," said the first girl.

"Why should I? I don't have to."

"No, you don't have to. I don't understand why you wouldn't want to," the first girl pressed.

"Because she gave me up," the girl said. "She gave me up."

Julie yearned to comfort the girl, to help her loosen whatever she had tamped down inside. But the girl's feelings seemed so deep and raw, they might need a lifetime of healing. There was pain and there was loss and there was love, side by side, all the time. None of it ever went away.

Julie stayed where she was, waiting for the return of Mark and Jack.

TWENTY-ONE

REDWOOD GLEN, CALIFORNIA

LATE AUGUST 2009

Friday afternoon, Jack flopped onto the couch in the family room. The new school year started Monday. He was enrolled at a day camp while Julie and Mark worked, and for the final Friday, the campers were shuttled en masse to the community pool where, Jack reported, he spent hours going up and down the giant water slide. Julie tucked a blanket around him and closed the blinds, removing his shoes and socks so he could take a short nap before dinner.

While Jack slept, she went into her bedroom to change from her black museum trousers to a pair of jeans. The jeans felt snug around her hips and she scowled as she sucked in her stomach to zip them. In the past three years, she'd eaten more ice cream and pizza than she had in the previous decades combined and had no time or energy to exercise. Whereas Mark never missed a run or swim and had just announced he was taking up cycling to train for a triathlon.

She turned to inspect her rear view in the wall mirror when her phone rang. Claire.

"Turn on CNN. A flood in Guatemala."

Julie hurried down the hall with her phone. In the dim light, Jack was curled under the blanket, his eyes closed. Julie aimed the remote at the television and clicked through to CNN. A shot of the studio interior flashed on; the words "Guatemala: Hundreds feared dead in tropical storm" crawled across the bottom. Julie sat on the ottoman and turned up the volume.

A newsman in a rain poncho and knit cap stood with a microphone, talking with one hand cupped against his ear. In the far background, the side of a mountain had been sheared off, leaving a gash like a scar. Trees were lifted out of the earth like toys and dropped down sideways, roots exposed to the sky. Adobe brick houses were splintered, their tin roofs ripped off and blown away in sections. Fences had been flattened.

The setting was too rural to be Guatemala City. The newsman called the area the Altiplano, Guatemala's northwest highlands. The major town was Nebaj. The mountains were the Cuchumatanes.

The news crawl identified the reporter as Tomás Rivera.

"Authorities are placing the number of fatalities at two hundred thirty-one, with many more missing," Rivera said. When howling winds threatened to drown out his voice, he pressed his mouth against the microphone and talked louder. Large sections of the Pan-American Highway were closed due to mud slides. Rescue teams continued to search for survivors. The tropical storm was the worst disaster to hit Guatemala since Hurricane Stan in 2005.

The coverage switched to a studio anchorwoman. She said the Altiplano had a long history of suffering, particularly during the country's civil war.

"Villagers live in conditions most would consider Stone Age. The women cook over wood fires on dirt floors, with no electricity or running water. Conditions are worse now." The anchorwoman paused. "We'll return after these messages."

Julie's phone rang. Claire again. "How do people live like that? Jack's mother isn't from there, is she?"

"Nowhere close. Other side of the country."

The CNN anchor returned with an update. The number of confirmed dead had climbed to three hundred twenty-seven. Entire villages had been wiped out by heavy rains and subsequent slides.

The camera showed Tomás Rivera again in his knit cap and poncho, reporting from a tight, enclosed area. Standing behind him was a group of women and children. Except for the narrow flood of light provided by the camera, the room was eerily dark. Rivera explained he was in the crypt of the church of San Lorenzo Chal with families who'd lost their homes. The adobe construction was unable to withstand the torrential rain and seventy-mile-an-hour winds. These lucky survivors escaped, but the little they owned was lost.

"Who is that?"

Julie turned to see Jack sitting up.

"People in Guatemala. A big storm."

"Why are they squeezed in that little room?"

"Their house fell down."

Back in the CNN studio, behind the anchor desk, a large weather map showed a swirling design over the shape labeled Guatemala. A few place names were noted. In the southern part of the country, Guatemala City and Antigua. Far north of that, in the Cuchumatanes Mountain range, Nebaj. And beside Nebaj, marked with a star to denote the epicenter of the storm damage, the village of San Lorenzo Chal.

Jack scooted close to Julie's ottoman and put an arm around her neck. "Are you crying? Why are you crying?"

"I'm sad because of the storm."

For all that culture camp emphasized connection to heritage and the importance of "going back," Julie never actively planned to return to Guatemala. With this flood, though, and seeing the harshness of people's lives, maybe she should reconsider, to try to help.

She untwined Jack's arm and pulled him gently to the dining room. She couldn't let him see how upset she was. She needed to shake it off and distract him. She hauled out a bin with colored pencils, glue sticks, scissors, and magazines, and told Jack to see what he could create.

She went to the kitchen to make dinner. Mark was working late, although she suspected workouts at the gym, especially when he came home with wet hair. She wished his motivation was contagious. Their weekends of long hikes together seemed like another lifetime. She cut up tomatoes for salsa and slid tacos in the oven to melt cheese.

She had just picked up her phone to call back Claire when it rang with a California number she didn't recognize.

It was Stewart from camp. "Did you hear about the flood?"

"Mind-boggling."

Stewart said folks from Guate Parents were organizing an aid trip. Charla T. had chartered a bus from Guatemala City to Nebaj. A couple of the Guate Parents were doctors and nurses. Several worked in construction, able to rebuild houses. They'd bring donations of clothing and shoes.

"Nestor and Eva are going. It's worth it to miss a few days of school," Stewart said, tempting her. "You in?"

She said she'd ask Mark.

*

Mark texted Julie telling her not to wait up for him. He'd run into another pathologist from medical school at the pool and they'd gone out for drinks. Hours later, the sound of the garage door opening woke her up, sleeping in Jack's bedroom. She unfolded herself stiffly and tiptoed to the kitchen, squinting at the light.

"There's tacos," she said, kissing him as he patted her distractedly on the bottom. He grabbed a container of leftover salad and a jar of dressing and set them on the counter. She opened a cabinet and handed him a bowl.

"Jack in bed?" he asked.

"I got him to draw before dinner. He sat at the dining room table for an hour."

She went to the dining room and came back with a picture Jack had made of the three of them. He'd drawn Julie very large, her skin peach, her short blonde hair standing straight up, a bejeweled crown on her head. Mark, also peach and half Julie's size, wore a white lab coat. Between them was Jack, very dark brown, larger than Mark, holding each of their hands.

"You're the queen, I see," Mark said.

She was, in her son's eyes, at least. And, even lacking a similar crown, Jack was her king. They were their own subset, a self-contained pair. She didn't know if that was good or bad.

She leaned against the counter and watched as Mark mixed the salad with dressing. "Not sure you heard," she said, and told him about the flood. As he made sounds of sympathy, she added that there was a group going to Guatemala to do relief work. They needed doctors. They'd stay in a small hotel in a village in the mountains. The cost was minimal. Flights and shuttles would be arranged. They only needed to show up.

Mark moved with his salad to the table, not answering. Frustrated, she took the drawing back to the dining room and set it down. Even without Mark, she and Jack could go. If they were going, though, she'd need to tie up loose ends at the museum. Now wasn't the best time, but no time was ever good. She returned to the kitchen and, watching Mark shovel salad into his mouth, waited for him to answer.

"It's not my idea of a vacation," he said finally.

"It'll be positive for Jack. To connect to his roots."

"You can't flush toilet paper or drink the water."

She didn't know how to respond. The fact was, she herself didn't think bringing her son to a disaster zone was the best way to reintroduce him to his birth culture, which was different from not being able to flush toilet paper or drink the water. Breathing intentionally, she chose to allow herself to remember better days. She thought of her first date with Mark, in his apartment at Davis, when they ate pizza by candlelight and he traced his thumb across her mouth. Julie had fallen in love that night. Mark's ability to genuinely listen back then had won her.

"Do you think we'll ever make love again?" she asked suddenly.

Mark gave her a long look. Then he stood up, shoved his dishes into the top tray of the dishwasher and said he was tired. He stalked off to the bedroom. Julie followed.

Mark unzipped his pants and left them on the floor where they dropped. He took off his shirt and threw it down at the bottom of his closet. Julie took her nightgown off from its hook in her closet and changed into it. She threw her clothes into the hamper and sat on the edge of the bed. On her dresser was a framed photo of the three of them at Jack's ice rink birthday party.

Mark sat beside her in his underwear. The muscles in his thigh were like iron. Beside him, her own thigh felt fleshy and squishy. On nights he swam, his body smelled strongly of chlorine. His odor was different now, not chlorine, something else, calming and sweet, like lavender. "I haven't been very happy lately," Mark said. "If you haven't noticed."

"Who said anything about being happy?"

He opened his mouth to respond, seemed to reconsider, and closed it. He scowled.

Julie shook his hand a little for emphasis. "It's not like I think about it. I do what needs to be done."

"Julie." He took his hand from hers, squeezed his palms together. "I've been seeing someone."

"Seeing someone? What does that mean?"

He stayed quiet.

"You mean seeing someone else? Dating someone? Sleeping with someone?"

He nodded.

It was as if the laws of gravity had been suspended and Julie was hurtling through space. Everything rushed past her, fast, fast. The universe was a blur of light. "Who?" she managed to whisper.

"Cassandra. Cassandra Forsythe."

"Cassandra Forsythe? The one with the boots at the opening? In the conga line?"

He nodded again. He couldn't look at her.

"How long?" she asked, though she knew. Before the girls were sent away. When she went to his lab. When he was working late. At culture camp. For months. "How can you do this to me? I love you, Mark. I love our life together." Her voice broke. "I'm not saying it was perfect. We could have gone into therapy. Why didn't you tell me you were unhappy?"

"What was the point?"

"We're married. We're a family. That's the point. I grew up in a broken home. You do not want that for our son."

"She's pregnant," Mark said, and a smile bloomed across his face. He thrust himself backwards and lay across the bed with his arms open. "We didn't think she could get pregnant. Her periods are irregular. She's a runner like me."

Julie stared at him, shocked, speechless. *We. We didn't think she could get pregnant.* How dare he? How dare he say this to her?

Mark sat up, groaning. "We're keeping it. I feel terrible saying this, but it's my chance to have a biological child. I want one."

Julie pounded the bed with both fists, suddenly furious. "So you'll make one," she said. "You'll make one with someone who can make one with you." She pounded the bed again, pummeled it.

Mark said nothing.

"What about Jack?" she said finally.

"This has nothing to do with Jack."

"This has everything to do with Jack. You selfish bastard. How can you not know that?"

"I'll still be his father. I'll always be his father."

"You'll be his father, but it won't be the same. It will never be the same. For him. For us. You need to know what you're walking away from."

"Or walking toward," he said.

Julie started shaking. She got up from the bed and strode to the closet to get as far away from him as possible. She was afraid of what she might say, what she might do. Throw something. Break something.

Smack the self-satisfied expression from his face. "Are you moving in with her?"

He nodded. "I'm sorry, Julie. I'm sorry."

"Go to hell, Mark. Go straight to hell."

TWENTY-TWO

REDWOOD GLEN, CALIFORNIA

AUGUST 2009

Monday morning, Julie woke up and looked at her clock: 8:10 a.m. She was alone in bed, wearing a pair of ratty sweats she'd put on the night before. She jumped up and hurried down the hall to Jack's room. "Apologies. I overslept. Get up and get dressed."

She dumped cereal and milk into a plastic container and grabbed a spoon and a dish towel. Jack ran down the hall, carrying his tennis shoes and backpack.

"Why didn't you wake me up?" Jack said. "I'll get a tardy slip the first day of school."

"I messed up. It won't happen again."

"Where's Dad? Why didn't he come home last night?"

"He had an emergency. He'll be home soon."

Jack climbed into the back seat of the minivan and Julie spread the dish towel over his lap. She drove to his school like a zombie, arriving with no idea how she got there. Car-line was empty, the last bell rung thirty minutes ago. "I love you," she called to Jack as he rushed to the front office to check in. She took out her phone and dialed.

"Eames? I won't be in today. I can't."

Julie filled him in, pausing to allow him to voice his outrage. "I don't know for how long. Just say I'm sick. Don't say my husband left me. Keep that under wraps for now."

She drove back to the house, parked in the driveway, and returned to her bedroom with the drawn shades. Still wearing the same ratty sweats, she lowered herself into bed.

For the next five days, Julie barely moved. She followed this routine: made Jack's breakfast and drove him to school, then turned around and drove straight home, where she crawled under the covers and didn't emerge until it was time to pick him up in late afternoon. She didn't eat. She didn't check email. She turned off her phone. She cried and slept and cried and slept until she needed to rally and collect Jack. The thing her son dreaded most—losing a parent—had come to pass and it took every ounce of her energy to distract him from the new reality. The effort of putting on a performance of normalcy was exhausting. She knew she should get them both into therapy, but that felt like too much. The research, the setting up of appointments, the trusting someone when the world felt like an untrustworthy place. The idea of it overwhelmed her. She felt lifeless and numb.

The Saturday after Mark left, Claire drove up alone from Fresno.

"Dad left," Jack said when he answered the doorbell in his pajamas. "Mom's in bed."

"Have you had breakfast?" Claire asked.

Jack shook his head.

Stepping into the kitchen, Claire surveyed the spotless kitchen. Every surface sparkled, from the front of the dishwasher to the hood over the stove. It looked like the kitchen of a home staged for selling. Claire opened the refrigerator door to find a half-filled carton of eggs and a stick of butter. A few pieces of raisin bread remained in a plastic bag in the bread drawer.

"Soft scramble with raisin toast?"

"Yes, please."

Claire scrambled eggs while bread toasted and set the dish in front of Jack. He ate hungrily.

"I'm going to check on your mom," said Claire, giving him a light squeeze on the shoulder.

Claire walked quietly down the hall, opened the door, and tiptoed into Julie's bedroom, closing the door behind her. The shades were drawn and the covers on the bed disheveled.

"Jules?" Claire said.

Julie sat up. "You came!"

"How could I not? After what that sleazebag did to you."

"How did you know?"

"You didn't answer my calls or texts. I called your office. I talked to Eames."

"Ah. Well."

"I can't believe he got her pregnant."

Julie ran a hand through her messy hair, resigned. "He was never really into it, the adoption. I mean, he loved Jack. Loves Jack. But I was the one driving the train."

"I, for one, will never forgive him," Claire said.

"I wish I had that luxury. But I need to forgive him, for Jack."

"You're a better woman than I," Claire said.

Julie smoothed the covers on her disheveled bed. Her marriage was over. She'd stayed in bed for five days and nothing changed. Mark was gone and he wasn't coming back. "You were too young to remember Dad," she said. "Our dad. He left when you were an infant. Who does that?"

"I always blamed myself. Like I must have done something wrong."

"You were his favorite," Julie said. "He adored you."

"You were mom's favorite. You were perfect. The talented one. The one who got out of Fresno."

"Look where it got me." Julie gestured to indicate the messy room. "Lord have mercy, we're a dysfunctional bunch." She patted the bed. "Sit. Stay a while."

Claire sat. "I'm so sorry this happened. And I'm sorry I haven't been a better sister." She leaned in to embrace her sister and Julie held on tightly.

"No, I'm sorry." Julie was suddenly blubbering. "Once I got married and started working, I didn't look back. Or I didn't look back enough. There was so little of everything to go around. We had to fight for it." She held on even tighter, swiping at tears with her fist. "And by the way, *you're* the perfect one. Perfect husband, perfect child, perfect life."

She pulled back and looked at Claire's belly, a little round bulge under her blouse. "Wait. Are you pregnant?"

Claire heaved out a sigh.

"You are," Julie said. "You are pregnant. See, what did I say? Perfect."

Claire laughed. She walked to the window and pulled up the shade. Julie shielded her eyes as the room brightened. Claire clipped her voice like a drill sergeant. "Listen, sister. We've got laundry to do, a room to clean, and a boy to raise to adulthood. Into the shower with you. This place smells like a gym."

TWENTY-THREE

ONE YEAR LATER

FALL 2010

Julie somehow missed the potential in Magnolia Bell. She'd visited Bell's studio and seen the large photographs of Magnolia's own body in assorted costumes—Buddhist monk, clown, Marie Antoinette—and the work felt derivative. The photographs depicted subjects Julie had seen before, handled in a more provocative way by other artists.

The art world disagreed. A curator from the Bilbray viewed Bell's work soon after Julie passed on it and gave the artist a solo exhibition. An art critic for the *New York Times* happened to be vacationing with her family in San Diego during opening week and popped in. The critic hailed the work as unexpected and fresh, and anointed Bell a rare new talent, and this on the front page of the Arts section on Sunday. Within hours, the value of Bell's work had quadrupled and an interview was scheduled for the cover of *ArtForum*.

"Ugh," Julie said to Eames, folding the *Times* and sliding it into a folder on the conference room table. "Her photographs left me cold. What am I missing?"

"I'm with you, Jules. Completely unoriginal."

It was Monday morning at the ideas meeting and out the window in the sculpture garden, a crew was rolling in crates for the upcoming Trina Gammage exhibition. Gammage's medium was light, and the crates were filled with bulbs, cords, and tracks for installation. The exhibition would be the Clay's first dedicated to an artist who worked exclusively in light, and Julie was exhilarated at the prospect of transforming the emerging gallery with Gammage's fluorescent tubes and multicolored theatrical gels.

The door flew open and Dr. Conrad strode in, followed by Doni with the silver tray. The tip of the director's nose was as red as her lipstick. The odor of lemon throat lozenges mingled with her usual rose perfume and cigarette smoke.

"This place," she said and began sneezing. She snapped her fingers toward Doni, who slid the director a cup of tea that smelled like fresh mint and ginger, instead of her usual coffee. Dr. Conrad blew her nose. Julie and Eames waited while she drank several sips.

"I've had a cold since I moved here." Dr. Conrad's voice was hoarse. "The air is so bloody damp. Everything mildews. Even my bath towels don't dry out."

"Have you been tested for allergies?" Eames asked.

"I'm not a person who has allergies," Dr. Conrad said, as though he'd accused her of spreading an untreatable foot fungus.

Julie reached for a scone. In the past year, she'd been so distracted by Mark moving in with Cassandra, meetings with her divorce attorney, and managing Jack's emotions and visitation schedule that she often forgot to eat. Her black trousers were swimming on her.

Dr. Conrad shook a finger at Julie as though she were a misbehaving child. "Magnolia Bell. I thought you were infallible."

Julie broke off a corner of her scone and chewed it, then picked up the entire pastry, broke it into parts, and shoved the pieces down. Nobody was infallible, including Julie, which didn't change her opinion that the Bell photographs were derivative. She wasn't going to argue either point with Dr. Conrad, however. Her goal was for Dr. Conrad to forget Julie's Magnolia Bell decision ever happened. Julie's sole mission was to oversee the installation of the Trina Gammage show and ensure it was as seamless as possible for the opening in two weeks.

That, and to hope Dr. Conrad and the board liked it.

"Orrin Clay will be in on Thursday," Dr. Conrad said. "The old man, not his son. He'd like to tour the Gammage."

"They're unloading the crates today," Julie said. "I'm not sure it can be installed by Thursday."

"We're the Clay Museum, emphasis on the word Clay," Dr. Conrad said. She blew her nose loudly. "We don't really have a choice, do we?"

Dr. Conrad sneezed again before announcing she was cutting the meeting short to go home and rest. Her cold made it impossible for her to focus. She suggested Julie use the extra hour to hurry the installation of the Gammage. Every minute counted.

Julie didn't have the option of working late. Even when she'd been married, she was forced to leave the office at five in order to make Jack's after-school extended care six p.m. pick-up. She reminded herself of this as she drove home after a hectic day of supervising the placing of moveable walls to hang the Gammage lights.

She wondered how Mark and Cassandra were managing. Their baby girl, Serafina, was nearly a year old. She was an ethereal child, a breathtaking blend of her parents, with Mark's blue eyes and Cassandra's black hair. Cassandra had graduated from medical school and was in a program to be a pathologist like Mark, working in a different lab with presumably the same demanding hours.

Their schedule was for them to figure out. Not Julie's problem.

The first month after Mark left, they had put their Redwood Glen bungalow on the market. It sold the first day, to young buyers who paid cash. The Cowans split the proceeds, which allowed Julie to buy a two-bedroom condo in San Francisco's Mission district, closer to the Clay and within walking distance of Jack's new elementary school. For the first time, Jack's classrooms were filled with kids and teachers who looked like him, and even spoke Spanish. Julie was ecstatic.

Mark lived in Cassandra's townhouse in Pacific Heights. Jack stayed with him and Cassandra on alternating weekends, and, on those two days, Julie missed her son terribly. She didn't allow herself to look back and imagine what might have been, but if she could have changed anything, she would have adopted a second child, a brother or sister for Jack. He liked being an older brother to Serafina. Julie had never counted on adoptions in Guatemala closing forever.

She couldn't think about it. She shifted her thoughts to what she had in the freezer to microwave for dinner as she picked up her son at extended care with seconds to spare.

After they ate, Julie set up Jack at the kitchen table with supplies to make a baking soda volcano—flour, baking soda, vinegar, water, and a soda bottle. She had an ulterior motive: Stewart had invited them on a heritage trip to Guatemala, land of many volcanoes, and she'd said yes. Or more accurately, Stewart had been inviting her for a year, since his post-hurricane service trip with Charla T., and had finally broken her down. She'd told him the whole story of hiring Candi and the failed search. She confessed her fear about going: that Jack's paperwork was falsified, and they might be stopped at the border.

"Lots of people find fake identification when they search," Stewart said. "It's not uncommon in Guatemala. Jack's a U.S. citizen. They can't strip him of that."

Stewart said that even if Jack couldn't meet his birth mother, he deserved to visit his birth country. He deserved to know where he came from. Besides, with social media and the internet, people were connecting in new ways. Stewart suggested genetic testing, where they might find cousins or siblings, in Guatemala or adopted to the United States. He suggested hiring a different searcher, who might have access to files Candi overlooked.

Julie reserved two spots on the heritage trip and booked their flights without telling Jack just yet. They were leaving in a month, over Thanksgiving. With the divorce final and life becoming a new normal, Mark agreed the timing was right.

While Julie stood overseeing the volcano production, Jack added drops of orange food coloring into the soda bottle's baking soda and vinegar concoction. Orange liquid belched out of the bottle's mouth and down the side of the flour volcano. "Did you see that, Mom?"

"You know where they have a lot of volcanoes? Like thirty of them? Guatemala."

Jack poured more baking soda and vinegar down the spout of the soda bottle, followed by a chaser of food coloring. "Watch. I'm making it red," he said. The liquid belched out again and Jack cackled. "You can do it with ketchup. I saw it on YouTube."

"Would you like to climb a real volcano? There's one you can climb in Guatemala and guess what? You can roast marshmallows over the vents. They're super-hot."

"Who else is going?"

"Eva and Nestor. You can also zipline and learn to make chocolate."

Jack darted to the sink for a sponge to wipe errant drops of vinegar and baking soda from the kitchen table. "Okay," he said.

*

Thursday morning, Julie met Orrin Clay at the door to his eponymous museum, noticing the gnarled hands that clung to the rail of his aluminum walker. Together, they crept through the atrium toward the emerging gallery, with Orrin Clay occasionally naming an artist whose piece they passed, once part of his personal collection: Ellsworth Kelly, Mark Rothko, Frank Stella.

The slow pace suited Julie. She was tired. She and the crew had worked until eleven the night before to finish the installation. She'd picked up Jack at extended care, bought hamburgers at the In-and-Out drive-through, and returned with him to supervise final touches.

Dr. Conrad was waiting for Orrin Clay and Julie at the gallery entrance. She air-kissed Orrin Clay on both cheeks and led him and Julie inside. The gallery's ambient light was dimmed so that only Gammage's bulbs shone. A series of white scrims formed temporary walls cast with subtle hues of blue, green, yellow, and red. Interspersed among the scrims were stately white columns that reached to the ceiling. On the floor were laid rectangles of Plexiglas, illuminated from below.

Orrin Clay clung to his walker. His gaze traveled around the gallery, from ceiling to floor from corner to corner. He turned to Julie.

"When will they put up the exhibition?" he asked.

"When? It's here now. This is it."

Dr. Conrad cleared her throat, displeased. Orrin Clay nodded slowly, a slight dribble leaking from the side of his mouth. "Very nice. Subtle."

"See the way the light changes," Julie said gently. "The atmosphere of the gallery changes with it."

Julie heard Orrin Clay's labored breathing. "Indeed it does. I feel the change."

"Standing in the light makes me a little more aware of how beautiful the world is," Julie said.

"It is beautiful, isn't it?" Clay lifted a hand from his walker and gave Julie a thumb's up before again clutching the aluminum railing.

"I want people to come here and experience that. To consider the world in a new way. There are endless possibilities."

Orrin Clay pushed his walker forward and moved deeper into the gallery space.

*

Julie sat at her desk on Tuesday morning when the announcement arrived in an email blast. Dr. Conrad had accepted a position as Director of the Chelsea Modern and was returning to New York. She was resigning her position at the Clay. Her start date at the Chelsea was January 1. She'd remain at the Clay until November 15, to ensure a smooth transition.

Julie pushed back her chair, incredulous. She read the announcement three times to make sure it was real. Dr. Conrad was leaving?

She stepped into the hallway to find Eames dancing in a circle, his head moving up and down in rhythm with his feet. Falling in behind him, she started her own little dance, feet pattering on the floor, head bobbing. Julie felt jubilant and free, as if she'd been unshackled from invisible chains. She grabbed Eames's hands and swung them back and forth.

She couldn't stop herself from squealing.

A minute later, Doni appeared. The director's assistant looked harried.

"There you are," Doni said to Julie. "Dr. Conrad wants to see you in her office, stat."

Julie excused herself from Eames and followed Doni through the office maze, imagining every possible scenario: Dr. Conrad hated the Gammage so much that her last act would be to de-install the show before it opened. Or her contempt for the emerging gallery ran so strong her last act would be to convince the board to phase it out. Or she'd lost so much confidence in Julie that her last act would be to fire her.

Or. Or. Julie literally could not stop wringing her hands.

She walked into the director's office to find Dr. Conrad behind the desk flanked by Orrin Clay in his wheelchair, and former Clay director Talbot Jones. The sight of her old boss took Julie aback, in a good way. She hadn't seen him in years.

"We won't mince words," Dr. Conrad said, and Julie held her breath.

"Under advisement from Mr. Clay and Talbot, the board has decided to name you acting director. Assuming you accept, you'll report directly to the board beginning Monday."

Julie hesitated, wanting to clarify what she'd been told. "I'd act as director until a permanent director is found."

Orrin Clay straightened up in his wheelchair. "There is no other director. You're it."

"What Mr. Clay means," Dr. Conrad interrupted, "is that the title of acting director is temporary. The board will interview several candidates before naming you Director. It's a formality."

Julie didn't believe what she was hearing. Talbot must have had something to do with this decision, as did Orrin Clay. She had no idea she had two such powerful allies.

"So," Dr. Conrad asked.

Julie took a deep breath. "I'd be honored. On one condition. I've signed up for a trip to Guatemala with my son." She explained their travel schedule and asked if she could start in her new role upon returning.

Orrin Clay leaned forward, clapping his gnarled hands. “Not a problem. We’ll wait.”

TWENTY-FOUR

TWO WEEKS LATER

SAN LORENZO CHAL, GUATEMALA

The tourist van filled with Guate Parents and their children chugged up the narrow winding road to Chal. They rolled past miles of detritus from the devastating flood the year before: branches peeled away from cypress trees and stacked into piles, and chunks of pulverized adobe pushed into heaps. A layer of mud still coated the roadway, as though entire sides of the Cuchumatanes Mountains had melted and dripped down. The distance between Antigua and Chal was around 185 miles, but the curving mountain roads made driving slow and treacherous. They'd left at dawn and eaten lunch in a roadside café an hour before.

The tires of the tourist van slipped and slid, spun and whined, and with each backward lurch, Jack pressed his Ratón against the window so the stuffed animal could see the plumes of muck spraying out from under the chassis.

"Think heavy," the driver instructed the group. The passengers in the middle seats scrambled onto the bench seat in the back to help the tires gain traction. Stewart called out, "What else can we do to help?"

"Only to pray," the driver answered.

The Guate Parents and their children thought heavy and their weight forced down the van's back axle, allowing the tires to gain traction and take hold. The group cheered as the van got underway, congratulating the driver as they returned to their seats. Buses filled with local residents zoomed past them, painted in oranges, yellows, and blues, and decorated with names: Wendy, Maria Angeles, Belén.

Higher and higher the van climbed, and the peaks of the mighty Cuchumatanes stretched across the horizon, an undulating slash of green with no visible endpoint. The children took in the scenery and fell silent, as if parts inside them were awakening and remembering, primal parts they didn't know they had. The parents got quiet, too, awed by the landscape and its effect on their children.

The driver said towns in Guatemala were labeled by size: pueblo, aldea, cantón, casería. Chal was a cantón or hamlet, with around seven hundred people. On the road approaching Chal, a little boy trudged through a deep gully carrying a net filled with chickens. Another boy plodded by hauling a pile of firewood, the weight supported by a strap across his forehead called a tumpline or *mecapal*. Jack stared at them—so like him and yet so unlike. A cluster of men moved toward them with a wooden box hoisted onto their shoulders, the unmistakable shape of a coffin, and the bus inched onto the muddy shoulder to allow them to pass.

Mothers with babies in slings across their backs passed by the windows, grasping the hands of toddlers, with three or four older children trailing behind. People died young in Guatemala. Life was capricious and severe. Here were these mothers and their children, these men carrying their dead. And here, too, were adopted children returning, brave after losing everything familiar to them in this place.

Julie sat beside Stewart who sat beside Manny. Jack sat in seats in front of them with Nestor and Eva. He missed his dad and hadn't wanted to come to Guatemala without him. But Julie prevailed, and Mark agreed their son would benefit from the trip.

During their first days in the capital and Antigua, the group had made chocolate from cacao beans at the Choco Museum and learned about traditional Mayan musical instruments at Finca Azotea. They'd ridden horses and zip-lined, wandered through art galleries and picked macadamia nuts. They'd shopped at the local market for ingredients to make *pepián* and spotted a resplendent quetzal during a return trip to the National Zoo. At every meal, they ate beans and rice and tortillas.

Now they were headed north to Chal, the small hamlet—cantón—near Nebaj, the epicenter of the country's thirty-six-year armed conflict.

Charla T., MSW, stood with a microphone beside the driver, reading from a script to give the group historical background. She was exactly as Julie had imagined her: square and strong and no nonsense.

"The leaders in this area ask that visitors not use the term 'civil war.' They prefer 'armed conflict,'" Charla T. said. "They want visitors to understand that during the violence, the army had guns, but the locals had no weapons. We're guests in Chal. Outsiders. We're here to listen and learn."

She reminded them of the itinerary. Drop off their luggage and get settled into guest rooms at Chal's one hotel. Assemble in the lobby. Two of the parents with teenagers would remain in the lobby with the kids to play cards and hang out, while the other parents toured the church and attended the Testimonial in the new community center. The Testimonial was a tradition in Guatemala, where a person stood up and told his or her life story. This particular Testimonial would be given by a woman who was a survivor of the conflict, a baby when the army attacked her village. The Testimonial was for parents only. The details of the conflict weren't appropriate for children.

The parents nodded, intrigued. A Testimonial was something they could witness only on a specially designed trip such as the one they were on. They felt good about that.

The next morning, the group would participate in a Mayan ceremony performed by a local shaman. In the afternoon, they'd visit a women-run weaving cooperative.

The town square was anchored by a whitewashed, mud-spattered church with dozens of people squatted on the steps. On another side of the square was a long, low building that looked official—the town hall—with half its red tiled roof missing. A choreographed team of men swung buckets of debris. The buckets moved hand to hand with a rhythm, until the phrase changed with the last man stopping to dump the bucketful onto a pile. A truck with a scoop could finish the job in a few hours, but the people of Chal didn't have a truck with a scoop.

The van pulled in front of Chal's hotel, brand new, with ten guest rooms. The oversized vehicle seemed to be a magnet: People appeared from everywhere to gawk as the group descended the steps and collected their luggage, passed down by the driver from the rack on the roof. With so many bags, the group looked like a royal entourage decamping.

After they checked in, young men hoisted the heavy bags onto their backs and showed the guests to their quarters. For the Cowans, the accommodations consisted of two single beds and a window with a crack in it. A shared toilet was installed at the end of the hallway with a shower rigged with an electric outlet in the showerhead.

Eager to begin, parents headed outside while the kids convened excitedly in the lobby. Charla T. raised a small U.S. flag and the group traipsed across the plaza.

Julie had never seen so many short people. She'd read the Guatemalan population had the highest percentage of stunted growth in the western hemisphere, second in the world only to Bangladesh, and she believed it.

Thirteen steps led to the church's front door, representing the thirteen months of the Maya's sacred year, one way conquering Spanish Catholics allowed the indigenous to retain an element of their cosmovision. Julie climbed the steps with the Guate Parents. Carved into the light-colored wood of the front doors were stylized birds, horses, and snakes. Julie stepped over the transom, pausing to let her eyes adjust.

The church was quiet and dark. Two columns of simple wooden pews flanked a center aisle. Down in front, a crucifix with a black Christ hung suspended from a beam over a simple wooden altar covered by a sacred, white cloth.

Scattered among the pews, mothers sat with babies and toddlers, the mothers with shawls over their heads; the kids dressed in what looked like donated clothes—washed out Gap sweatshirts and pilling acrylic sweaters. A few of the children turned to look at the Americans, and in their faces, Julie saw Jack's face, except gaunt and sunken. At home, she could pick out her son in any crowd. Here, too, he would stand out because of his solid body and thick hair.

The mothers reacted to their children turning to look, and, like mothers everywhere, gathered them close at the sight of strangers. Julie wasn't sure if she was permitted to sit in a pew and what she would do once she did. She'd feel like a pretender if she prayed.

On one side of the carved wooden door at the back of the church was a niche containing a large crucifix like the one over the altar, except surrounded by dozens of smaller crosses. "*Martires del Señor,*" the heading above the crosses said. "Martyrs of the Lord." Each cross was etched with a name, age, and dates of birth and death. Julie read the first few names. José Mario Mal Chapni, age 19; Martin Carrillo Chuj, age 16; Jacinto Brito Cobo, age 29; Juan Jorge Piox Oxlaj, age 32.

Stewart and Manny and the rest of the group pulled out cameras and began photographing the crosses.

"*Hablas inglés?*" A small, distinguished man in a red jacket and black felt hat appeared beside Julie. Before she answered, he held up a name tag—"*Estevan Laix, Guia*"—and began speaking.

"Excuse me as this area is well known for Guatemala's armed conflict, as you can demonstrate here. Behold. Each cross represents a soul departed."

Estevan raised a finger to the brim of his black felt hat.

"Before the conflict, we were joyful and calm. Our families lived in peace. When the violence came, there were many deaths. We had no food. We hid in the forest and ate leaves off trees. This is what they did to us."

"Most people don't know," Julie said. "Most Americans. They don't teach us."

"You have seen the candles? Come. The local Ixil people light them."

Julie nudged Stewart and Manny and the others to join her and Estevan. They followed the guide down the center aisle and stopped almost at the altar. He gestured toward the burning white candles affixed to the tile floor with melted wax. Scattered around the candles were modest offerings: a bouquet of wilted yellow marigolds, wrapped single Jawbreakers candy, two squares of Chiclets in a green box. Someone left each object believing her prayers would be answered, that amid the disaster of the flood, and, despite contrary evidence, some higher being paid attention and cared. The meagerness of the offerings and the faith they represented overwhelmed Julie.

A woman appeared from the side of the church and made a sign of the cross as she approached the altar. A shawl hid her head and face. Her feet were bare. She gathered her skirt underneath her knees and knelt, bending over to kiss the tile floor. She pressed her body back up, lifted her hands toward the crucifix, and began to chant in a language Julie didn't recognize, which must be Ixil. The music of her chanting reverberated through the church, with clicks and consonants and rounded *oo* sounds. The woman rocked from side to side on her knees and began crawling backwards. She crawled backwards past the candles and away from the altar.

The Americans stepped aside. The woman moved slowly, stopping every few feet to bend to kiss the floor.

"What is she doing?" Julie asked Estevan.

"The lady is sorrowful and asks for forgiveness."

"What did she do?"

"That's between her and God."

The woman proceeded, pausing to raise her hands to the heavens, pushing back one foot at a time. What could she have done? She wasn't even wearing shoes.

"Do you know her name?" Julie asked.

"Rosalba," Estevan said. "Rosalba Puzul Tuc."

Rosalba continued up the aisle, pausing to gather her skirt from under her knees, to raise up her hands toward the crucifix and chant her prayers. The humility of the act and desire for atonement touched Julie profoundly. She ached to drop to her own knees, to wash away her guilt at being so fortunate, for having everything. She had no one to turn to for forgiveness.

Rosalba finished her journey, pressing her palms against the floor to kiss it a final time before she stood, turned, stepped over the transom, and walked out of the church.

Stewart and Manny and the rest of the group watched her leave. Estevan made the sign of the cross and folded his hands. He said that Rosalba was the one giving her Testimonial in the town hall. An American missionary sister would translate.

Charla T. raised her flag to lead the way and the group filed out.

TWENTY-FIVE

SAN LORENZO CHAL, GUATEMALA

NOVEMBER 2010

"Three trucks carried the soldiers up the dark mountain road to San Rolando. They rolled past corn and bean fields, past grazing pastures for goats and sheep, past rows of adobe houses with thatched roofs."

Many times, I have heard these words, about the beginning of my life. Many times, I have asked God to have pity on me. And so, the end of my Testimonial.

As the days passed, I untucked my *hüipil* from my skirt to hide my growing belly. I prayed every day. I asked God to take away the baby. The baby I didn't ask for. The baby I didn't want.

There was a shack at the edge of San Pablo. Everyone knew about it. A witch lived there. A witch who used a wire or gave a potion. Those things were a sin. Which sin was worse? The sin done to me or the sin I might commit against a baby?

The door was closed. Around the dirt were empty bottles and candles burned to the bottom. In the air I felt souls floating. The souls of babies that were lost.

The door opened, and the witch poked out her head. She asked if I was in the right place. Her long hair was knotted and sloppy. Her face made me afraid, so I didn't stay. I turned and ran away. I didn't have the courage.

I stopped attending mass on Sunday, because I was ashamed.

Every night, I promised myself to call Mamá in the morning. I knew she would blame me. I had no one else. Every morning, I didn't call.

Then one morning, Monica asked me to go to the market to buy flowers. I brought my market basket and walked through the aisles of fruit and grains toward the area. The vendors watched me as I passed. They sat back on their heels, watching. When I was gone, they would talk about me. *Chismes*, we say. Gossip. They knew a baby was inside.

I reached the flower area and asked for a bouquet of yellow roses. Those were Monica's favorite. The flower seller reached into her blouse for her change purse. She gave me the flowers and Monica's change.

A warm hand pressed on my arm unexpectedly. I drew back like it was a scorpion.

"Forgive me for startling you," a *señora* said.

She was light-skinned like Monica. She wore the same gold hoop earrings. Her hair was pulled back in a low bun. Because her skin was pale, her eyes looked very brown. They were outlined in black.

She stared at my *hüipil*, untucked and bulging. She said she'd noticed my condition.

My condition. I looked to see if anyone else heard what she said. The flower seller turned her head away, so I knew the answer was yes.

The *señora* pointed toward tables close by, in the eating area. She said for us to sit down and be comfortable. She said "Please. Allow me to buy you a Pepsi-Cola."

A *señora* with gold hoop earrings had never asked me to sit down. Or offered to buy me a Pepsi-Cola. Never, never.

When the *muchacha* came, the *señora* said, "Two Pepsi-Colas. For my friend Rosalba and me."

She knew my name. But I hadn't told her. My friend Rosalba, she said.

Her name was Mayra. She introduced herself.

The *muchacha* returned with two bottles of Pepsi-Cola and two glasses. Mayra poured each of the bottles into a separate glass. She pushed one glass over to me.

I must tell you this meeting was the first time I drank Pepsi-Cola from a glass. Monica sometimes had me serve Pepsi-Cola during a party. She never gave me any. Sometimes I drank a small amount at the market. I drank it from a plastic bag.

The bubbles from that glass of Pepsi-Cola fizzed and jumped and tickled my nose. Mayra handed me a straw to drink from.

"Imagine a life where you can drink Pepsi-Cola every day. At every meal. That is life in los Estados."

I stirred my straw in my glass and took a long sip. It tasted very sweet.

"Your baby could have that life," Mayra said.

My baby could drink Pepsi-Cola? I was confused.

Mayra said if my baby lived in los Estados, she'd go to school. She'd have opportunities I could only dream of. A horse to ride. Books to read. Her own room. Chicken for dinner if she wanted it.

Finally, I had to speak up. How was this possible? The baby would live in Guatemala.

For now, Mayra said. The baby will live in Guatemala for now. But she could live in los Estados. With a mother who was rich and white. Who would give her everything.

I still didn't understand.

Mayra set her arms on the table. She asked if I was listening. Rich white people in los Estados paid money for babies from Guatemala, she said.

Rich white people paid money for babies that were brown? The thought was unbelievable.

The Americans didn't care that the skin was brown. They just wanted a baby.

"*Mira,* Rosalba. You have nothing to offer a baby. No husband. No money, and soon, no job." Mayra said this as if she knew it was true.

I tried to understand what she was saying. The direct meaning.

"I give the baby to someone else. And then someone else is the mother."

"Exactly. The baby goes to university and learns to speak English and drive a car."

I wouldn't have to commit a sin. It was the opposite of sin. A blessing. Papi Chelo said everyone in los Estados wore shoes. Everybody was rich. The baby would have a life in los Estados filled with opportunity.

Mayra placed a pink fingernail to her mouth. Shhhh. Money was involved. *Poquito, poquito.* Not a lot. She pinched her fingers to show the amount. Enough to help Mamá with her expenses.

The offer from Mayra felt like something alive at the table with us. As real as the bottle of Pepsi-Cola.

I asked what I had to do.

"Sign a paper. Easy." She held up a make-believe pen and signed. She laughed a carefree laugh.

She called me *amiga*. She told me to think about it. Think about the life I could give a baby, and the life she was offering. A life fit for a *princesa*. She said, "You live in Casa Alvarez, *sí?*"

I lived there, *claro*. And she knew.

Mayra said she'd come by in a week or two. To talk again.

I'd heard about bad people stealing babies to cut out their insides. Mayra didn't look like a bad person. She looked like she was good.

One more thing she needed. She asked me for my *cédula*.

Everyone's records were burned, I told her. From the army. During the violence, in San Rolando. I never had a *cédula*.

I tried to smile. I wanted to do everything right, the way she asked.

Mayra took a long drink of her Pepsi-Cola. A small burp came up and she swallowed it down.

"We can fix that," she said.

My first thought every morning was that the baby was inside me. The baby kept growing. I couldn't do anything about it. One day, the banging of the door knocker filled Casa Alvarez. Before I could get there, Monica herself had opened it.

"Mayracita," she said.

"Monica. *Bellisima.*" The voices of the two ladies mingled in the parlor as I made my way down the stairs. I held the wooden railing. My belly was as big as I was. I shuffled into the parlor and they both turned.

They were friends from before Mayra approached me. Now I understood.

"Have you made your decision?" Mayra asked. She and Monica stared at me, their two faces pale as moonlight.

I decided in that moment. My answer was yes.

The two women grabbed each other's hands like little girls excited to play a game. Quickly they dropped them. Mayra said they wouldn't tell Mamá.

Monica agreed. Mamá would never see it.

"We won't tell anyone in your village," Mayra said.

"Because if one person knows." Monica and Mayra blinked at each other. Like they knew how news in the villages spread. I wanted to ask Mayra about the money, but I didn't know how. I coughed a little. They didn't notice.

Monica asked me to serve the tea, so I walked myself and my belly into the kitchen to heat the water. Now that I had made my decision, I wanted the baby out. I wanted it finished.

I drew the water to fill the kettle and lit the match. I leaned against the wall to wait. The voices of the women came through the wall.

"How do you stand it?" Mayra said. "Those eyes. They're so cold. So distant."

"She's *indígena*. They're all like that."

"Don't I know it. It's sad, really. What they've been through. With so many slaughtered, losing their land."

Monica cleared her throat. She didn't believe in the suffering of others.

Mayra said almost every girl they got was *indígena*. Close to one hundred percent.

"Can you imagine giving away your baby?" Monica said. "Your own blood."

"Never. But they do it. We don't have enough cribs to keep up."

They didn't understand because their lives were good. Their lives were easy. They didn't crawl under a fence and have a boy push them down. They didn't know what shame was in a village.

I watched the flame under the kettle. I waited for the whistle. The ladies were quiet. Then Mayra said it was one less child for a poor mother to raise. One less mouth for Guatemala to feed.

Monica made an agreeing sound. She said she bet the baby would be pretty. Those thick eyebrows. That lovely face.

Lovely face. That was me she was talking about.

Mayra said she hoped it was a girl. Americans like girls.

When my time was close, Monica drove me to Mayra's house in Guatemala City. The baby needed to be born in a hospital, with doctors and nurses and real medicine. Monica dropped me off at Mayra's on a Tuesday morning. Hardly any cars were out. I had only been to the capital twice, when cars and buses jammed the streets.

I hardly recognized Mayra when she answered the door. The pencil around her eyes was missing. Without it, her face seemed smudged. Monica carried in my belongings. She said for Mayra to call when it was finished. Monica would come to collect me. Mayra led me into a room with four beds. She pointed to the empty one and said it was mine.

Sleeping girls filled the other three beds. Later, when they woke up, they told me their stories. One was twelve and the father was her older brother. One was fifteen, and the father was her mother's new husband. One was sixteen, and the father was her boyfriend, who would use the money to go to los Estados. She had given another baby to Mayra, her first one.

Mayra made us breakfast of orange juice and eggs, which I ate because they no longer made me queasy, and tortillas folded over white cheese. When she went out to meet with other girls having babies, she left dishes in the sink and said not to clean them. The three girls and I couldn't believe she didn't ask us to clean the dishes. Or that she served us, either.

No one had done that for us before. Especially someone in a big house.

We spent the rest of the day resting in the parlor on couches. Each of us was covered with our own wool blanket. We watched telenovelas. Mayra returned carrying a bucket of fried chicken and four paper bags of French fries from a restaurant. After we ate, she collected the chicken bones and gave each of us a vitamin pill. She said we should nap.

After our naps, she fed us dinner. Pieces of meat and green beans with bread and butter instead of tortillas. And then small cups of chocolate custard topped with fresh cream.

We couldn't believe we spent a day like this. Eating and napping and watching telenovelas. Mayra said this was life for *princesas*.

One by one the girls left and never came back. Finally, it was my turn. It happened in the morning after a night when two new girls arrived. I tried to get out of bed and had to sit back down. Water was everywhere, and the baby was coming. Mayra came with a wheelchair she kept by the back door and wheeled me out to the car. I tried not to grunt, tried not to feel anything. I cursed the boy who did this to me, cursed his stained face. If only he had never seen me, if only I had never spoken to him, or climbed through that fence.

I wasn't thinking of the future, of what the baby someday would think of me, of how she might miss me. I was thinking only that I wanted this baby out. I wanted this baby to go away and not make problems.

I was thinking of myself.

The baby was born. It was a boy. Not a girl like we expected. A beautiful, handsome boy. More handsome than my sister's baby, as handsome as my brother Daniel. With ten little fingers and ten little toes. Ears like edges of shells in the riverbank. He was crying loudly.

He's hungry, someone said, and I latched him on and watched him suck. His eyes closed, calm in a second. His weight on me felt solid. It felt right. He was of me and from me. My son, I thought. My son, my son.

I stared and stared at him to memorize every detail of his birth. His powerful pushing through me like an animal trying to escape. His head between my legs, his black hair wet, his body bloody. His face wrinkled like an old man.

His tiny mouth opening and closing opening and closing like a bird's beak.

Never had I seen anything so perfect as that small body, those fingers clutching. My son, I wanted to shout. My son, my son.

Nobody brought me to the healing water the way we did in Chal. We performed no ceremony over the cord. It was cut and removed and put where I didn't see. Somebody told me to drink from a cup of warm liquid and I did. It tasted like our corn drink, atole, like Chal. I fell asleep.

I woke to bright sunlight. The room was bright white. Everything was white—the ceiling, the walls, the floor. My body felt sore and hollow and without weight. I sat up and shook out the blanket and searched around myself. Where was he? No one was there to answer. My arms were empty. My milk had dried where he nursed so I knew I hadn't imagined him sucking.

Footsteps passed in the hallway and I called out. Again, I asked for my son. Again, nobody answered. It was as if his birth and the moments after never happened, as if my son died or never was born. I fell back on the pillow, and felt wetness from my tears, and pulled the blanket under my chin.

Why hadn't I told Mamá? Why hadn't I asked my sisters to help me? They could have boiled the water and squeezed my hands and caught him. They would have known what to do. One of them would have kept him and raised him as her own. The way Mamá raised me.

I hated the boy for planting the seed. When my son was growing inside me, I thought of him as a bad thing the boy put there. But when he came into the world and I heard him take his first breath, I thought only that this small perfect being was alive. I needed to protect him.

There was nothing else, no other thought except that.

I didn't know his birth would change me. That in those final hours and moments I would become his mother. I didn't think I would care, but I did.

Excuse me. I apologize for this.

And so.

Mayra stood in the doorway with her face stiff like a wooden mask. Her eyes were rimmed with the black.

A woman wearing a white cap held a clipboard and pen. "Mother's name?"

Mayra spoke before I could. "Karla Inez Garcia Flores."

Clipboard spoke again. "And baby?"

"Juan Rolando." Mayra said his name without looking at me. I had asked if I could name him for the village where I was born, and for my father who died there.

"Same last names?" the white cap asked.

Mayra said yes. I waited until the white cap left.

I was so relieved they were talking about him because that meant he wasn't dead. I asked Mayra where she took him, and she shushed me. She reached into a large bag over her shoulder and took out a pile of papers. She passed me the papers and said they got me a new name.

I was now Karla Inez Garcia Flores.

"Where is he?" I asked again.

"Where he needs to be."

She clicked open a pen and stood against the bed. She forced the pen on me. My hand shook as I took it. I stared at the papers and read the words, Consent to Give the Baby in Adoption. I asked her to repeat my new name. I'd already forgotten.

She grabbed a second piece of paper from her large bag and tore the pen from my hand. She wrote in rounded script, Karla Inez Garcia Flores, and pushed the second paper toward me.

"This."

Carefully, I copied the letters onto the line near the X. It felt strange to write a name that wasn't my own. Mayra leaned over me, breathing. When I finished, she took the paper and slid it back into her bag. In a few weeks, she said, they'd bring me back to the capital for the DNA test and photo. I'd see my baby then.

I asked about the money. Mayra said the money came later, after every paper was signed.

I spent one more night in the hospital. At every hour, I woke, listening for footsteps that might stop and bring me my son. I moved my hand under the sheets and around the blankets in case someone left him there. No one stopped in my doorway with him in a bundle, saying it was a mistake.

My bed stayed empty.

The next morning Mayra returned. Milk flooded into my *chiches* and wet my blouse. I crossed my arms, embarrassed. I asked who was feeding him. She said he was receiving excellent care.

We walked to her car parked outside the hospital, me slowly because of soreness and pain. I slid into the front seat and tried to find a comfortable spot. Mayra started the car and drove through the streets of Guatemala City to return me to San Pablo.

Outside the window were the dirty streets and poor people begging and children standing at stoplights selling Chiclets, and I was glad. I was glad because the city was foul and dirty and dangerous. My son was leaving for a new life in los Estados. A girl tapped on my window when we stopped, and Mayra pressed hard on the gas pedal and drove off. We passed out of downtown to the roundabout that led to the road to San Pablo.

She turned the steering wheel and signaled to turn left and right. She didn't care that my *chiches* leaked or that my body missed my son. For her, the deal was done, and already he belonged to someone else.

Mayra dropped me off at Casa Alvarez with a promise to call when the DNA test was ready. I walked through the front door a different person, older and more alone. I hated everyone inside. They should have insisted I call Mamá. They should have let me keep my position in the house. Instead, they abandoned me like a street dog.

Monica avoided me. This was hard to do because I worked in the kitchen and the courtyard and with taking care of Olga. My presence was everywhere. If I moved upstairs, she moved downstairs, and when we passed, her footsteps hurried in the opposite direction. Her husband Edgar behaved the same as Monica when he was home. As if to breathe the same air was to be infected with poison. They kept the children away, too. I was invisible, even more than before.

My guilt was torture. What I did was unnatural, to give away my baby to someone else. Men often left their wives for another woman. They often abandoned children. They crossed borders to other countries to get far away. Women never did.

Mayra had said I was unselfish to give Juan Rolando a better life. I wanted to believe that. Only God could forgive me. I returned to church. After mass on Sunday, I waited until everyone was gone except for the widows in black mantillas who moaned in the pews. They also mourned lost loved ones. I started at the front of the church and crawled backwards on my knees. I asked God to take away my sin, to wash my soul clean.

I prayed someday my son would understand why I did what I did, even if I didn't understand myself.

I begged God to let my son forgive me for separating him from me, his mother.

A few weeks later, Mayra knocked on the front door to take me to an office in Guatemala City. She and Monica spoke before she led me outside to the curb. She opened the car door for me. Before we had driven one block, she prepared me for the interview ahead.

"They'll ask for your name, and you say Karla Inez Garcia Flores. Like you've said it a million times before. They'll ask if you're sure. You say 'yes.'"

I'd practiced already, many times. Karla Inez Garcia Flores. It was a simple name, not like Rosalba Puzul Tuc.

"You're twenty-two years old and live in Escuintla. Your job is to pick coffee. You've worked on Finca Adelina for seven years."

She turned to me suddenly. "Where do you live, Karla?"

"Escuintla?"

"You must say it with conviction." Mayra lifted her hands off the steering wheel as though presenting a gift. "Escuintla. Escuintla. Your address there?"

I raced through the lines she had taught me. The right one appeared. "The barrio. The barrio in Escuintla."

"Excellent. And how long have you lived there?"

I stared straight ahead. I needed to keep the facts straight. "All my life. For seven years, I have picked coffee. Since I finished school."

"Are you able to read, Karla? Is this your signature? You gave your permission?" Mayra's arm reached across the seat. She pretended to ripple a paper under my nose.

"I can read. This is my signature."

Hot tears filled my eyes. The last words choked in my throat. I hated seeing proof I gave permission.

They were going to sweep the inside of my mouth with a ball of cotton. It would be quick and wouldn't hurt. If it did hurt, I was to say nothing. Not a word. I was to let them sweep their cotton.

I swallowed, showing I understood. Mayra pointed to a pile of clothes near my feet—a zippered jacket with a hood and a pair of denim pants. She told me to change in the back seat. To look like a Karla Inez.

I had never worn a jacket with a hood or pants before and was embarrassed to look like a boy. Mayra was right. I had become Karla Inez.

The office was in the basement, down a flight of narrow stairs. The lights in the ceiling hummed like swarming bugs. Many women walked in different circles bouncing babies up and down to keep them from crying. Mayra whispered to me that the women were the foster mothers hired to mind the little ones.

The foster mothers wore tight shirts and black pants and pointed leather shoes. The babies' mothers were *indígena* like me, some wearing traditional clothes, some not. Most of the blankets were pink. I searched only the faces in blue blankets for Juan Rolando. My heart jumped when I spotted him. His head was up, looking around the room as though a guest at one of Monica's parties. He was bigger than I remembered.

Mayra kept me close beside her until a man called my name to go to a chair in the front of the room. The foster mother who carried Juan Rolando brought him, too. I couldn't help myself, I reached for him, and he turned his head. Pulled away and ducked his head down, no longer the guest at a party. He was a baby faced with a stranger.

"He doesn't know you," the foster mother said, also drawing back while she covered my son's head protectively. The boy I gave birth to, the baby I gave life. He didn't know me? He was from my own body, my own blood. I prayed for strength.

"Karla Inez Garcia Flores," a man said. He showed me the chair where to sit. His hand was covered in a blue glove. He held a white stick with a top of cotton.

I sat in the chair as the foster mother walked in circles, bouncing Juan Rolando up and down. She didn't know anything about babies. Bouncing like that could damage his head and neck.

"Open," the man said. His blue glove pushed into my mouth with the stick, pressing against my tongue. I coughed and swallowed, but the glove forced the stick against the inside of my cheek. It rubbed the stick back and forth, back and forth against the inside of my cheek, hard, tearing my skin. My eyes watered and I gagged, almost as if a rope was tied to hang me.

"That's enough," the man said, and his blue glove let up from my tongue and the stick pulled away and moved backward across my teeth and out of my mouth. My jaws ached from staying open and my lips burned where they tore to make so much space for his hand.

The man put the white stick into a plastic bag and picked up a camera. The foster mother circled back with Juan Rolando and placed him in my lap.

Don't move, the man said, pointing the camera at me, and I didn't. I never wanted to move again. I wanted to sit with Juan Rolando forever, and never let him go.

My arms held Juan Rolando and we faced the camera together.

The light flashed, and I closed my eyes and said my prayer. I asked God to let my son forgive me for separating us from each other.

Excuse me again. I apologize for my tears.

Life continued after I gave away my baby. The dark sky turned bright in the morning as the sun rose, and at night, the sun sank down and disappeared and the sky became dark again. Leaves appeared on the trees and fell off. Flowers poked up their heads and blossomed. In Chal, they would plant corn, and weed it carefully, and pray for a good harvest. Mamá would meet a new man and have more babies, and Marta's husband would stop drinking and they'd move into their own house. Yanira and Isabel tended the corn field and helped Mamá and Marta with their babies.

I blamed Monica for my decision to give up Juan Rolando. She introduced Mayra to me. She sent Mayra to the market to find me. Mayra's gold hoop earrings and pink nail polish were intended to convince me, and they did.

At the same time, I blamed myself. I was who signed the papers and agreed. I was the one who opened my mouth for them to swab my cheek for the DNA test. I was the one who took the money to give to Mamá, who kissed Juan Rolando a final time and breathed a silent prayer. I was the one who let him go.

I left Monica and her family at Casa Alvarez soon after. San Pablo had given me good food and a bed. Once that had been enough, but no longer. I gathered my belongings in a plastic bag and boarded a bus to Chal. I never spoke to Monica again.

I moved in with Mamá and helped her and Marta raise their children as if they were my own. I never married or had other children. I never wanted to.

Not a day goes by that I don't think of Juan Rolando, ten or a hundred or a thousand times. I have never given up hope that someday we will be reunited.

I will recognize him the way a mother recognizes her child. By his flesh and his smell, the rhythm of his beating heart, equal to mine. If he lets me, I will gather him close in my arms to study his face and let him study mine. I will memorize the shape of his hands and his eyes. The softness of his hair, the size of his ears. Every detail. The sound of his voice. The sound of his breathing.

I admit to wanting to find myself in him. Together, we can compare the ways we are the same, and always will be.

I pray my decision was the right one. That I gave my son a better life.

I know someday he will find me, in this life or in heaven.

TWENTY-SIX

CODA

Her drooping eye. That distinctive drooping eye. The eye is what convinced Julie, made her sure. How many women in Guatemala had an eye like that? How many women used a *cédula* for Karla Inez? In the seats around Julie in the community center, the audience of adoptive parents rose to its feet, clapping loudly, supportively. At the podium, Rosalba shrugged modestly, as if embarrassed by the attention.

Julie sat glued to her seat. If she approached Rosalba; if she said *I recognize the name Karla Inez. I know a boy who was named Juan Rolando.*

Jack was with the other kids and chaperones, far away, thank God.

What if Rosalba claimed he'd been kidnapped? What if she screamed?

But what if Rosalba walked out the door and Julie never saw her again?

Julie felt apart from her physical body, able to watch herself watch Rosalba. In her own face, Julie saw shame. She saw terror. And she saw something else: love for her son.

Julie pried herself from her seat and inched her way toward the front of the room. She was close to Rosalba now. Close enough to see Jack's skin in Rosalba's skin, Jack's eyes in Rosalba's good eye. Julie felt a prick of pain at their undeniable sameness. The fact of it. She was the one who was different.

A few parents had gathered around Rosalba, and Julie waited until the others finished. She reached out a hand to introduce herself. "May I speak with you in private?" she asked. "It's about Juan Rolando. Our son."

Acknowledgments

Thank you to Kevin Atticks, Lauren Battista, and Katherine Kiklis at Apprentice House Press, for giving a home to this manuscript and seeing it through during the days of Covid-19.

Thank you to everyone in my adoption circle—real and virtual—who ever shared a story with me. You broadened my understanding of what I feel is life's most complicated relationship. Thank you to my children's birth families for welcoming us with love and acceptance.

I'm grateful to Susan Hurst, Wende S. DuFlon, and Gretchen B. Wright, who are as obsessed with Guatemalan history as I am. I'm also grateful to Jeffrey C. DuFlon, for sharing stories from his Antigua childhood; to Kallie Kull, for relaying her experiences in the Peace Corps; and to everyone in Guatemala who answered my endless questions and revealed deep memories.

Thank you to Bethany Nelson, Diana Gaston, and Penny Taylor, who gave me insight into the curatorial brain and artist's mind, and to all my colleagues from the museum world. Permission to use the beautiful painting on the cover, *Nahualá*, was generously granted by artist Hugo González Ayala and La Antigua Galería de Arte.

Early readers believed in this novel and helped me hone it. A thousand thanks to Virginia Bellis Brandabur, Vicky Mlyniec, Mark Jacobson, Vivian Lee, Ellen Sussman, Marya Wintroub, Lisa Troland, Nina Vincent, and Lisa Scheffer. Thanks, too, to Stephen Skartvedt, Carol Burbank, Marie Lappin, Susan Milikien, Tiara Inserto, Eve Lynn, Lorrie Goldin, Gale Lipsyte, Molly Delaney, and Avvy Mar. I appreciate helpful suggestions by Cynthia M. Guerra and Rosanna Pérez.

Jessie Glenn, Emily Keough, Bryn Kristi, and Deborah Jayne at Mindbuck Media were generous with marketing savvy, as was my dear friend since high school, Sharon McCarthy, who brainstormed with me to find the book's title. I'm grateful to Joanne Hartman and Mary C. Hill for their copyediting skills, and to Janine Kovac and Tarja Parsinnen of Moxie Road for their publishing acumen.

A bow of gratitude to mentors, teachers, and fellow students at my Antioch MFA program, especially Sarah Van Arsdale, Victoria Patterson, Alma Luz Villanueva, and Steve Heller, who helped me cross the finish line. A shout-out to workshop leaders and groups at the Community of Writers at Squaw Valley, Sirenland, Bread Loaf, and Write by the Lake; and to my many generous buddies from Write On Mamas, including Dorothy O'Donnell and Marianne Lonsdale. Joyce Maynard has encouraged my work since our first meeting. My gratitude has no end.

I'm deeply grateful to my non-writer friends, past and present: the ones in carpool line and at school, on the playground and walking path, on volunteer duty and at church, as well as those from the old neighborhoods in New York, New Jersey, and Delaware.

I'm blessed with the best sisters and brother a person could ask for: Patrice O'Dwyer, Adrienne Phillips, Deanna O'Dwyer-Swensen, and Robert O'Dwyer, and their families; as well as the Berger, Euhus, and extended O'Dwyer clan. Family means everything.

My children, Olivia and Mateo, are my reasons for living. My beloved husband, Tim Berger, saw who I could be. Words aren't enough.

Many, many people helped me during the seven years I spent researching and writing this book. I'm grateful to every one of them.

About the Author

Jessica O'Dwyer is the adoptive mother to two teens born in Guatemala and author of *Mamalita: An Adoption Memoir*. Her essays have been published in the *New York Times*, *San Francisco Chronicle*, *Marin Independent Journal*, and elsewhere. A former teacher of jazz dance and high school English, Jessica has also worked as a legal proofreader, magazine staffer, and art museum publicist. She earned an MFA in fiction writing from Antioch Los Angeles.

Jessica grew up at the Jersey shore, the daughter of a high school shop teacher and Radio City Music Hall Rockette. She lives in California with her husband, son, and daughter. This is her first novel.

Note to the Reader

Mother Mother is a work of fiction with some basis in fact.

United Fruit Company (now Chiquita Brands International) was a corporation that forever changed the political and economic landscape of Guatemala. Jacobo Arbenz was the democratically elected president of Guatemala, deposed in a coup and exiled in 1954. A series of brutal dictators followed, including General Efraín Ríos Montt. The country was engulfed in a thirty-six-year armed conflict ("civil war") that led to the slaughter of 200,000 people, mostly indigenous farmers and their families, and the destruction of more than 600 villages. Peace Accords were signed in 1996.

The resulting social upheaval was a contributing factor to the growth of international adoption from the 1980s to the mid-2000s. In the months before adoption closed permanently in December 2007, one percent of all children born in Guatemala were adopted to the United States.

Hopeful adoptive parents did flock to hotels like the Marriott (now Barceló) in Guatemala City, filling restaurants and splashing in swimming pools. Online forums like Guate Parents (not its real name) were and are lifelines for many adoptive parents, providing support and community. Heritage and culture camps were and are places where families meet to share experiences and learn—from psychologists and sociologists, from adults who are adopted, and from one another.

Reuniting with birth mothers does occur with frequency among families who have adopted from Guatemala. Each family, each person, must make a decision right for them. My recommendation is to hire a professional searcher who is trusted in the adoption community. We've reunited with both our children's birth mothers and visit every summer during a month-long trip to Guatemala. We're one of hundreds of adoptive families who visit the country: to study Spanish, to connect with blood relatives, and to explore Guatemala's fascinating and beautiful historic sites. Meeting up with families like ours is a highlight of our year.

Adoption is multi-faceted and complex. To capture that complexity, I created the parts of the book that are fiction. Redwood Glen, San Lorenzo Chal, and San Pablo are not actual towns. The entire cast of characters is invented. I imagined a chorus of voices from multiple points of view: the adoptive mother, the birth or first mother, the person who is adopted, the adoption facilitator, and extended family of these individuals.

Mother Mother is not the first novel to explore adoption as a theme. *Mother Mother* is simply my attempt at conveying truths I believe after nearly two decades of lived experience as an adoptive mother. Other writers will come forward to express their own truths, to grapple with this subject in their own way.

I encourage these stories. I welcome them.

Apprentice House is the country's only campus-based, student-staffed book publishing company. Directed by professors and industry professionals, it is a nonprofit activity of the Communication Department at Loyola University Maryland.

Using state-of-the-art technology and an experiential learning model of education, Apprentice House publishes books in untraditional ways.This dual responsibility as publishers and educators creates an unprecedented collaborative environment among faculty and students, while teaching tomorrow's editors, designers, and marketers.

Outside of class, progress on book projects is carried forth by the AH Book Publishing Club, a co-curricular campus organization supported by Loyola University Maryland's Office of Student Activities.

Eclectic and provocative, Apprentice House titles intend to entertain as well as spark dialogue on a variety of topics. Financial contributions to sustain the press's work are welcomed. Contributions are tax deductible to the fullest extent allowed by the IRS.

To learn more about Apprentice House books or to obtain submission guidelines, please visit www.apprenticehouse.com.

Apprentice House
Communication Department
Loyola University Maryland
4501 N. Charles Street
Baltimore, MD 21210
Ph: 410-617-5265
info@apprenticehouse.com
www.apprenticehouse.com